PR.
Nevermoor: The Tr

GW00726181

Exciting, charming and wonderfully imagined, it's the sort of delightful, grand adventure destined to be many a reader's favourite book.

— Trenton Lee Stewart, *New York Times* bestselling author of The Mysterious Benedict Society series and *The Secret Keepers*

Will hook readers aged 10 and up with intricate, imaginative detail and its sheer energy . . . a compulsively readable romp that fans of 'Harry Potter', Terry Pratchett or Studio Ghibli will gobble up.

— *Books+Publishing*

Exciting, mysterious, marvellous and magical . . . quite simply one of the best children's books I've read in years.

— Robin Stevens, author of *Murder Most Unladylike*

Readers, like Morrigan herself, will feel at home in this evocative novel where magic and confidence go hand in hand. An excellent and exciting work.

— *School Library Journal*

Readers will feel as though Harry Potter is meeting Alice in Wonderland.

— *Kirkus*

Fearsome and funny and original, it's requisite reading for fantasy lovers of all ages.

— Libby Hathorn, CBCA Award-winning author of *Thunderwith*

It's a fast-paced read that is sometimes funny and sometimes scary, but always completely magical.

— *Readings*

Townsend's intensely cinematic writing, quirky humour and superior world-building conjure a genuinely fresh take on magical fantasy.

— *The Bookseller*

Unexpected, exciting and funny. Like *Alice in Wonderland*, Harry Potter and *Doctor Who* swirled up together. I loved Morrigan Crow, and I want to check in at the Hotel Deucalion.

— Judith Rossell, ABIA Award-winning author of *Withering-by-Sea*

Nevermoor is brimming over with imagination and fun . . . A wonderfully assured debut from a young Australian author, *Nevermoor* sparkles with zest, wit and inventiveness.

— Kate Forsyth, author of The Impossible Quest series

It really is brilliant, with an engaging plot, plenty of twists, memorable characters and a marvellous sense of humour. Pick it up and the hours disappear, just like magic.

— *Daily Telegraph*

An extraordinary story full of magics great and small, from the Hotel Deucalion to the Magnificat . . . Townsend has created a book of wunders. In Morrigan Crow I've found a heroine I'm willing to step boldly after, and follow her wherever her adventure takes her next.

— Kiran Millwood Hargrave, author of *The Girl of Ink and Stars*

Wundersmith

The Calling of
Morrigan Crow

The second book in the Nevermoor series

Jessica Townsend

LOTHIAN
Children's Books

A Lothian Children's Book
Published in Australia and New Zealand in 2018
by Hachette Australia
(an imprint of Hachette Australia Pty Limited)
Level 17, 207 Kent Street, Sydney NSW 2000
www.hachettechildrens.com.au

10 9 8 7 6 5 4 3 2 1

A catalogue record for this
book is available from the
National Library of Australia

978 0 7344 1822 7 (paperback)
978 0 7344 1900 2 (hardback)

Cover design by Christabella Designs
Author photograph courtesy Emma Nayler
Paperback cover illustration by Jim Madsen
Hardback cover images courtesy Shutterstock
Hardback endpaper illustration © Beatriz Castro 2017
Reading notes © Robyn Sheahan-Bright 2018
Text design by Bookhouse, Sydney
Digital production by Bookhouse, Sydney
Printed and bound in China by Asia Pacific Offset Ltd.

This book is dedicated, with love and thanks,
to the women who got me to the other side of it:

Mostly Gemma and Helen,
but also Fumie Takino's squad of
Japanese cheerleading grannies.

CHAPTER ONE

The Angel Israfel

Spring's Eve,
Winter of One

Morrigan Crow leapt from the Brolly Rail, teeth chattering, hands frozen around the end of her oilskin umbrella. The wind had whipped her hair into a state of extreme disarray. She tried her best to smooth it down while hurrying to catch up with her patron, who was already yards ahead, pelting along the noisy, swarming high street of the Bohemian district.

'Wait!' she called out to him, pushing her way through a knot of women wearing satin gowns and lush velvet cloaks. 'Jupiter, slow down.'

Jupiter North turned back, but didn't stop moving. 'Can't slow down, Mog. It's not in my repertoire. Catch up.'

1

And he was gone again, running headlong through the mess of pedestrians and rickshaws and horse-drawn carriages and motorised coaches.

Morrigan hurried after him and walked into a sickly-sweet-smelling cloud of sapphire-blue smoke, puffed right at her face by a woman holding a thin, gold cigarillo in her blue-stained fingertips.

'Ugh, *foul*.' Morrigan coughed and waved the smoke away. For a moment, she lost sight of Jupiter through the haze, but then she spotted the top of his bright copper head, bobbing up and down in the crowd, and sprinted to catch up with him.

'A child!' she heard the blue-fingered woman exclaim in her wake. 'Darling, look – a child, here in Bohemia. How frightful!'

'It's a performance piece, darling.'

'Oh, indeed. How novel!'

Morrigan wished she could take a moment to stop and look around. She'd never seen this part of Nevermoor before. If she wasn't so worried about losing Jupiter in the crowd, she'd have been excited to see the broad streets lined with theatres and playhouses and music halls, the colourful jumble of bright lights and neon signs. People, dressed in their finest, piled out of carriages on every corner and were ushered inside grand theatre doors. Street hawkers shouted and sang, beckoning customers into rowdy pubs. There were restaurants so overflowing with diners that their tables spilled out onto the pavement, every seat occupied, even on this frosty Spring's Eve, the last day of winter.

Morrigan at last made it to where Jupiter stood waiting for her outside the most crowded – and most beautiful – building on the street. A shimmering establishment of white marble and gold, Morrigan thought it looked a bit like a cathedral and a bit like a wedding cake. A brightly lit marquee across the top read:

NEW DELPHIAN MUSIC HALL PRESENTS
GIGI GRAND
and the
GUTTERBORN FIVE

'Are we . . . going in?' Morrigan puffed. A stitch bloomed painfully in her ribs.

'What, this place?' Jupiter cast a scornful look up at the New Delphian. 'Heavens, no. Wouldn't be caught dead.'

With a furtive glance over his shoulder, he ushered her down an alleyway behind the New Delphian, leaving the crowd behind. It was so narrow they had to walk in single file, stepping over piles of unidentifiable rubbish and bricks that had crumbled loose from the walls. There were no lights down here. It had a strong smell of something dreadful that got stronger the farther down they went. Like bad eggs or dead unnimals, or maybe both.

Morrigan covered her mouth and nose. The smell was so noxious she had to fight the urge to vomit. She wanted more than anything to turn round and go back, but Jupiter kept marching behind her, nudging her along.

'Stop,' he said, when they were near the end of the alley. 'Is this . . . ? No. Wait, is it . . . ?'

She turned to see him inspecting a section of the wall that looked exactly like every other section. He gently pressed the grouting between the bricks with his fingertips, leaned in to sniff it, and then gave the wall a tentative lick.

Morrigan gave him a look of horror. 'Ugh, *stop that*. What are you *doing*?'

Jupiter said nothing at first. He stared at the wall for a moment, frowned, and then looked up at the narrow patch of starry sky between the buildings. 'Hmm. Thought so. Can you feel that?'

'Feel what?'

He took her hand and pressed it to the wall. 'Close your eyes.'

Morrigan did so, feeling ridiculous. Sometimes it was hard to tell when Jupiter was being silly or serious and she suspected, on this occasion, he was playing some stupid joke on her. It was her birthday, after all, and although he'd promised her no surprises, it would be just like him to pull an elaborate, embarrassing stunt that ended in a room full of people singing *Happy Birthday*. She was about to voice her suspicions, when—

4

'Oh!' There was a very subtle, fuzzy tingle in her fingertips. A faint humming in her ears. '*Oh.*'

Jupiter took hold of her wrist and pulled it back, ever so slightly, from the wall. Morrigan felt resistance, as if the bricks were magnetised and didn't want to let her go.

'What is that?' she asked.

'A little bit tricksy,' Jupiter murmured. 'Follow me.' Leaning back, he placed one foot on the brickwork, and then the other, then – casually defying the law of gravity – proceeded to walk skywards up the wall, hunched over to avoid hitting his head on the other side of the alley.

Morrigan stared at him in silence for a moment, and then gave herself a little shake. She was a Nevermoorian now, after all. A permanent resident of the Hotel Deucalion and a Wundrous Society member to boot. She *really* ought to stop being so surprised whenever things took a slightly odd turn.

She took a deep breath (nearly retching again at the horrible smell) and copied Jupiter's actions exactly. Once both her feet were planted on the wall, the world pitched out of kilter and then righted itself again, so that she felt perfectly at ease. The dreadful smell instantly disappeared and was replaced with fresh, crisp night air. Suddenly, walking up an alley wall with the starry sky stretching out in front of her seemed the most natural thing in the world. Morrigan laughed.

When they emerged from the vertical alley, the world lurched right-side-up once again.

They were not – as Morrigan had expected – on a rooftop, but in yet another alleyway. This one was noisy and bustling, and bathed in a sickly green light. She and Jupiter joined the end of a long queue of excited people, held back by a velvet rope. The mood was contagious; Morrigan felt a little thrill of anticipation and stood on tiptoes to see what they were queueing for. At the front, plastered to a worn pale blue door, was a messily handwritten sign:

OLD DELPHIAN MUSIC HALL

STAGE DOOR

TONIGHT: The Angel Israfel

'Who's the Angel Israfel?' Morrigan asked.

Jupiter didn't answer. He twitched his head for Morrigan to follow him, then sauntered right up to the front of the queue, where a bored-looking woman was checking names off a list. She was dressed all in black, from her heavy boots to the pair of woolly earmuffs hanging around her neck. (Morrigan approved.)

'Queue's back there,' she said, without looking up. 'No photos. And he won't be signing nothing till the show's over.'

'I'm afraid I can't wait that long,' said Jupiter. 'Mind if I sneak in now?'

The woman sighed and gave him a blank, perfunctory glance, chewing a wad of gum with her mouth half open. 'Name?'

'Jupiter North.'

'You ain't on the list.'

'No. I mean, yes. I know. I was hoping you might remedy that for me,' he said, smiling through his ginger beard. He gave the little golden *W* pin on his lapel a subtle tap.

Morrigan cringed. She knew that members of the elite Wundrous Society were admired in Nevermoor, and often received special treatment that ordinary citizens could only dream of, but she'd never seen Jupiter try to use his 'pin privilege' in such a blatant fashion before. Did he do it very often, she wondered.

The woman was – understandably, Morrigan thought – unimpressed. She scowled at the little golden *W*, before flicking her thickly glitter-lined eyes up to Jupiter's hopeful face. 'You ain't on the list, though.'

'He'll want to see me,' said Jupiter.

Her top lip curled, revealing a mouth full of diamond-encrusted teeth. 'Prove it.'

Jupiter tilted his head to the side and raised one eyebrow, and the woman mirrored his expression impatiently. Finally, with a sigh, Jupiter reached inside his overcoat and pulled out a single black feather, shot through with flecks of gold, and twirled it – once, twice – between his fingers.

The woman's eyes widened slightly. Her mouth fell open, and Morrigan could see the wad of bright blue bubble gum wedged between her teeth. With an apprehensive glance at the queue growing behind Jupiter, the woman pushed open the faded blue door and jerked her head, motioning the two of them inside. 'Hurry up, then. Five minutes to curtain.'

⌐▬▬▬

It was dark backstage at the Old Delphian. There was a hushed, expectant air as black-clothed stage hands moved about quietly and efficiently.

'What was that feather?' Morrigan asked in a whisper.

'More persuasive than a pin, apparently,' murmured Jupiter, sounding a bit put out. He handed Morrigan one of two pairs of earmuffs he'd pilfered from a box marked *CREW*. 'Here, put these on. He's about to sing.'

'Who, you mean the Angel Is . . . er, thingy?' she asked.

'Israfel, yes.' He ran a hand through his copper hair, which Morrigan recognised as a sign that he was nervous.

'But I want to hear it.'

'Oh no, you don't. Trust me.' From where they stood, Jupiter looked through the curtain out into the audience beyond, and Morrigan took a quick peek too. 'You never want to hear one of his kind sing, Mog.'

'Why not?'

8

'Because it will be the sweetest sound you'll ever hear,' he said. 'It will trigger something in your brain that will bring you a perfect and unbroken peace, the best you could ever hope to feel. It will remind you that you are an entirely whole human being, flawless and complete, and that you already have all you will ever want or need. Loneliness and sadness will be a distant memory. Your heart will fill up, and you'll feel the world could never disappoint you again.'

'Sounds dreadful,' Morrigan said in a flat voice.

'It *is* dreadful,' Jupiter insisted, his face sombre, 'because it's transient. Because Israfel can't keep singing forever. And when he stops, eventually that feeling of perfect happiness will fade away. And you'll be left here in the real world, with all its hardness and imperfection and muck. It will be so unbearable, and you will be so empty, it'll feel as if your life has stopped. As if you are trapped in a bubble, while the rest of the world carries on living imperfectly around you. You see those people out there?' He drew the curtain back very slightly, and they looked again into the audience.

The sea of faces, lit by the glow of the empty orchestra pit, all shared the same expression – eager but somehow vacant. Wanting. *Wanting.* 'They're not patrons of the fine arts,' Jupiter continued. 'They're not here because they appreciate a masterful performance.' He looked down at Morrigan and whispered, 'Junkies, Mog. Every last one of them. Here for their next hit.'

9

Morrigan peered out at those hungry faces and felt a coldness creep upon her.

A woman's voice pierced the atmosphere. The audience was silenced.

'Ladies and gentlemen! I present to you, on the evening of his one hundredth triumphant, transcendent performance here at the Old Delph . . . the one and only, the celestial, the *divine* . . .' The amplified voice dropped to a dramatic whisper. 'Please show some love for the Angel Israfel.'

The hush instantly splintered, the music hall erupting into joyful noise as people applauded, whooped and whistled. Jupiter elbowed Morrigan hard in the side and she snapped her earmuffs tightly into place. They blocked out every scrap of noise, so all she could hear was the blood rushing in her ears. Morrigan knew they weren't here to see a show. They had a much more important job to do, but even so . . . it was a bit annoying, really.

The darkness of the hall was replaced with a pure golden glow. She blinked into the glare. Above the crowd, high up towards the ceiling, in the centre of the opulent space, a spotlight illuminated a man of such strange, otherworldly beauty that Morrigan actually gasped.

The Angel Israfel floated in midair, held aloft by a pair of powerful, sinewy wings – feathers black as night, veined with iridescent, glittering gold. They protruded from between his shoulderblades, beating slowly and rhythmically. He must have had a wingspan of at least three metres. His body too was strong and muscular, but lithe, and his cool black skin was veined in tiny rivers of gold as if he had been broken apart like a vase and repaired with precious metals.

He looked down at the audience and his gaze was at once benevolent and coolly curious. All around, people stared up at Israfel, weeping and shaking, clutching themselves tight for comfort. Several audience members had fainted right there on the floor of the music hall. Morrigan couldn't help but think this was all a bit much. He hadn't even opened his mouth to sing yet.

Then he did.

And the audience stopped moving.

And they looked as if they might never start back up again.

A still, abiding peace descended like snow.

Morrigan could have stayed there, huddled at the side of the stage, watching this strange, silent spectacle all night . . . but Jupiter got bored after a few minutes. (*Typical,* Morrigan thought.)

In the dim and smoky backstage depths, Jupiter found Israfel's dressing room and he and Morrigan let themselves in to wait for him. Only when the heavy steel door was fully closed did Jupiter indicate it was safe to remove their earmuffs.

Morrigan gazed around the dressing room, wrinkling her nose. It was overflowing with detritus. Empty cans and bottles littered every surface, along with half-eaten boxes of chocolates and dozens of vases filled with flowers in various stages of death. Clothes were piled up on the floor, the sofa, the dressing table, the chair, and there was a musty smell of unwashed fabric. The Angel Israfel was a slob.

Morrigan gave a snort of puzzled laughter. 'You sure this is the right room?'

'Mmm. Unfortunately.'

Jupiter made a space on the sofa for Morrigan to sit, delicately removing items of rubbish and placing them in the bin . . . then he got carried away and spent the next forty minutes tidying, wiping down surfaces and making the room as habitable as he possibly could. He didn't ask Morrigan to help, and Morrigan didn't offer. She wasn't touching this health-and-safety hazard with a ten-foot pole.

'Listen, Mog,' he said as he worked. 'How are you? You okay? Feeling happy? Feeling . . . calm?'

Morrigan frowned. She'd felt perfectly calm until he'd asked her whether she was feeling calm. Nobody ever asked anybody if they were feeling calm unless they thought the person had a reason *not* to feel calm. 'Why?' She narrowed her eyes. 'What's wrong?'

'Nothing's wrong!' he replied, but his voice had gone a bit squeaky and defensive. 'Nothing at all. It's just . . .

when you meet someone like Israfel, it's important to be in a good mood.'

'Why?'

'Because people like Israfel . . . absorb other people's emotions. It's, uh, it's very bad manners to visit one if you're feeling particularly sad or angry, because you're bound to put them in a dreadful mood and ruin their day. And, frankly, we can't afford for Israfel to be in a mood. This is too important. So, er . . . how are you?'

Morrigan plastered a very large smile on her face and gave him two thumbs up.

'Right,' he said slowly, looking a little disconcerted. 'Okay. Better than nothing.'

A voice, sounding over the backstage PA system, announced there would be an intermission of twenty minutes, and moments later the dressing-room door was flung open.

In strode the star of the show, sweat-soaked, his wings tucked behind his back. He made a beeline for a trolley filled with rattling glass bottles of spirits in varying shades of brown and poured himself a small glass of something amber-coloured. Then another. He was halfway through the second when he finally seemed to clock that he had company.

He stared at Jupiter and downed the last of his drink.

'Picked up a stray, have we, dear?' he finally asked, inclining his head towards Morrigan. Even his speaking voice was deep and melodic. Hearing it made Morrigan feel a strange little twinge of something, like nostalgia or homesickness or longing, right at the back of her throat. She swallowed thickly.

Jupiter smirked. 'Morrigan Crow, meet the Angel Israfel. None sing so wildly well.'

'Pleased to—' began Morrigan.

'Pleasure's mine,' Israfel cut across her and waved vaguely around his dressing room. 'I wasn't expecting guests this evening. I've not got much in I'm afraid, but . . .' he indicated the trolley. 'Help yourselves.'

'We haven't come to be fed and watered, old friend,' said Jupiter. 'I have a favour to ask. It's rather urgent.'

Israfel flopped onto an armchair, swung his legs over the side and stared sulkily at the glass in his hands. His wings twitched and rearranged themselves, draped over the back of the chair like a voluminous feathery cape. They were sleek and smooth, with soft downy bits underneath. Morrigan only just managed to stop herself reaching out and stroking them. *Might be weird,* she thought.

'I should have known this wasn't a social call,' said Israfel. 'It's not as if you ever visit any more, *old friend*. You haven't been round since Summer of Eleven. You do realise you missed my triumphant opening night?'

'I'm sorry about that. Did you get the flowers I sent?'

'No. I don't know. Probably.' He shrugged petulantly. 'I get a lot of flowers.'

Morrigan felt sure that Israfel was trying to make Jupiter feel bad, but she couldn't help feeling bad herself. She'd never met Israfel in her life and yet she couldn't bear the thought that he was unhappy. She felt a strange urge to give him a biscuit. Or a puppy. Something.

Jupiter pulled a tattered scroll of paper and a pen from his coat pocket and silently held it out to his friend. Israfel ignored it. 'I know you got my letter,' said Jupiter.

Israfel swirled the glass in his hands and said nothing.

'Will you do it?' Jupiter asked simply, his hand still outstretched. 'Please?'

Israfel shrugged. 'Why should I?'

'I can't think of a decent reason,' admitted Jupiter, 'but I hope you'll do it anyway.'

The angel was watching Morrigan now, his face closed and wary. 'Only one thing I can think of that might draw the great Jupiter North into patronage.' He took a sip of his drink and shifted his gaze back to Jupiter. 'Please feel free to tell me I'm wrong.'

Morrigan looked to her patron as well. The three of them sat in a still, uncomfortable silence that Israfel seemed to take as some sort of confirmation.

'*Wundersmith*,' he hissed under his breath. He sighed deeply, ran a hand over his face wearily and snatched the scroll from Jupiter's hand, ignoring the pen. 'You are my dearest friend and the biggest fool I've ever known. So yes, of course I'll sign your stupid safeguard pact. Pointless though it is. A *Wundersmith,* honestly. How ridiculous.'

Morrigan shifted in her seat, feeling awkward and a bit resentful. It was galling to be called *ridiculous* by someone whose dressing room was this much of a cesspit. She sniffed, trying to look haughty and unbothered.

Jupiter frowned. 'Izzy. You can't know how grateful I am. But this is highly confidential, you realise. It stays between—'

'I know how to keep a secret,' Israfel snapped, reaching back and, with a wince, plucking a single black feather from one of his wings. He dipped it into a pot of ink on the dressing table and scrawled a messy signature at the bottom of the page, handing it back to Jupiter with a dark look and tossing the feather aside. It fluttered prettily to the floor, its golden flecks catching the light. Morrigan wanted to pick it up and take it home like a treasure, but she thought that might be a *bit* like stealing his clothes. 'I really thought you might have come sooner than this, you know. I suppose you've heard about Cassiel?'

Jupiter was blowing on the ink, trying to dry it quickly, and didn't look up. 'What about him?'

'He's gone.'

He stopped blowing. His eyes met Israfel's. 'Gone?' he echoed.

'Disappeared.'

Jupiter shook his head. 'Impossible.'

'That's what I said. And yet.'

'But he's . . .' began Jupiter. 'He can't just . . .'

Israfel's face was sombre. Morrigan thought he looked a bit afraid. 'And yet,' he said again.

After a silent moment, Jupiter stood and grabbed his coat, motioning for Morrigan to do the same. 'I'll look into it.'

'Will you?' Israfel looked sceptical.

'I promise.'

Down the alley wall they went, out into the garish Bohemian high street lit up as bright as day, and through the crowd towards the Brolly Rail platform – but at a much more civilised pace than before. Jupiter held a hand firmly on Morrigan's shoulder, as if he'd just now remembered they were in a strange and swarming part of town and he really ought to keep her close.

'Who's Cassiel?' asked Morrigan as they waited on the Brolly Rail platform.

'One of Israfel's lot.'

'Cook used to tell stories about angels,' said Morrigan, recalling her family home, Crow Manor. 'The Angel of Death, the Angel of Mercy, the Angel of Ruined Dinners . . .'

'This isn't the same thing,' said Jupiter.

Morrigan was confused. 'They're not really angelkind?'

'I think that's probably stretching the imagination a bit, but they are celestial beings, of a sort.'

'Celestial beings . . . what does that mean?'

'Oh, you know. Sky-dwellers. Fancy flying types. Them wot have wings and use 'em. Cassiel is an important figure in celestial circles. If he's really missing . . . well, I suspect Israfel is mistaken, anyway. Or exaggerating – he likes a bit of drama, old Izzy. Here it comes. Ready to jump?'

At the exact right moment, Morrigan and Jupiter hooked their umbrellas on to the steel loops of the passing Brolly Rail frame and held on for dear life as they sped through the maze of Nevermoor boroughs. Brolly Rail cables ran all over the city in unfathomable patterns, criss-crossing low through high streets and back alleys, then soaring high above roofs and treetops. It seemed stupidly dangerous to Morrigan, whizzing all over the place with nothing but your own grip on your umbrella to stop you from falling and splattering all over the ground. But as terrifying as it was, it was also exhilarating, seeing all those people and buildings fly past as the wind whipped at your face. It was one of her very favourite things about living in Nevermoor.

'Listen, I have to tell you something,' said Jupiter, when they'd finally pulled the levers to release their umbrellas and leapt from the speeding Brolly Rail, landing in their own neighbourhood. 'I haven't been totally honest with you. About . . . about your birthday.'

18

Morrigan's eyes narrowed. 'Oh?' she said coolly.

'Don't be cross.' He chewed on the side of his mouth, looking guilty. 'It's just that . . . well, Frank got wind that it was today and you know what he's like. Any excuse for a party.'

'Jupiter . . .'

'And . . . and everyone at the Deucalion loves you!' His voice pitched several notes higher than normal in unprecedented levels of wheedling. 'I can't deprive them of a reason to celebrate the birth of their very *favourite* Morrigan Crow, can I?'

'*Jupiter!*'

'I know, I know,' he said, holding his hands up in surrender. 'You said you didn't want a fuss. Don't worry, all right? Frank promised to keep it low-key. Just the staff, you, me and Jack. You'll blow out some candles, they'll sing *Happy Birthday* –' Morrigan groaned; just the thought of it sent a pink-hot flush of embarrassment creeping up her neck and all the way to the tips of her ears. '– we'll eat some cake, job done. It'll all be over for another year.'

Morrigan glared at him. 'Low-key? You promise?'

'I swear to you.' Jupiter held a hand over his heart, solemnly. 'I told Frank to rein himself in, then rein himself in some more, and keep reining it in until he got to what he thought was woefully understated, and then rein it in about ten times more than that.'

'Yeah, but did he listen?'

19

Her patron scoffed, looking highly offended. 'Listen, I know I'm Mr Cool-Guy Laidback Relaxington and all that –' Morrigan raised a politely incredulous eyebrow, '– but I think you'll find my employees *do* respect me. Frank knows who the boss is, Mog. He knows who signs his pay cheque. Trust me. If I tell him to go low-key, he's going to go—'

Jupiter cut off, his mouth open, as they turned the corner onto Humdinger Avenue, a street dominated by the huge, glamorous façade of the Hotel Deucalion, where Morrigan lived with her patron . . . and which Frank the vampire dwarf, party-planner extraordinaire, had evidently dressed for the occasion.

The Deucalion was draped with millions of flamingo-pink fairy lights that lit up the whole night and could probably, Morrigan thought, be seen from outer space.

'Completely over the top?' she finished for Jupiter, who had been rendered speechless.

Gathered on the Deucalion's front steps were not just the staff, but what seemed like every guest currently staying at the Deucalion and a few ring-ins besides. Their faces shone with excitement and they surrounded a lavish nine-tiered, pink-iced birthday cake that Morrigan thought looked more appropriate for a royal wedding than a twelfth birthday. A brass band was positioned by the fountain and on Frank's signal they launched into a rousing celebratory march, just as Morrigan and Jupiter arrived. Topping the scene off was a huge marquee sign running the entire length of the rooftop. Its enormous flashing letters read:

MORRIGAN IS TWELVE

'HAPPY BIRTHDAY!' shouted the mob of staff and guests.

Frank pointed to Jupiter's teenage nephew, Jack, who lit a cluster of fireworks that went whizzing and whistling into the air, showering the scene with trails of stardust.

Dame Chanda Kali, the famous soprano and Dame Commander of the Order of Woodland Whisperers, launched into a very theatrical version of the birthday song (which immediately attracted three robins, a badger and a family of squirrels to worship adoringly at her feet).

Charlie, the Deucalion's fleet manager and chauffeur, had groomed and bridled one of his ponies, ready to carry the birthday girl inside.

Kedgeree the concierge and Martha the maid held armfuls of presents, beaming brightly.

And Fenestra, the giant Magnificat and head of house-keeping, used the commotion as a cover to discreetly swipe a huge paw full of pink icing.

Jupiter shot Morrigan an anxious sideways glance. 'Shall I, er . . . shall I have a quiet word to our Roof-Raiser-in-Chief?'

Morrigan shook her head, trying – and failing – to control a smile that was twitching at the corners of her mouth. She felt a warm, sunshiny glow right in the centre of her chest, as if a cat had curled up there and was purring contentedly. She'd never had a birthday party before.

Frank was all right, really.

Later that night, deliriously sugared up on birthday cake and exhausted by the never-ending well-wishes of a hundred party guests, Morrigan crawled into the cocoon-like nest of fleecy blankets her bed had turned into that night (it obviously knew what an awfully long day she'd had). She fell asleep almost the moment her head touched the pillow.

Then, what felt like half a second later, she was awake.

She was awake, and not in her bed.

She was awake, and not in her bed, and not alone.

CHAPTER TWO

Sisters and Brothers

Spring of Two

Shoulder to shoulder beneath a starry, cloudless sky, the nine newest members of the Wundrous Society stood outside its gates, sleep-rumpled and cold.

Morrigan might have felt alarmed at having awoken in the middle of the night in the chilly streets of Nevermoor wearing only her pyjamas, but two things kept her worry in check:

Firstly, that the gates of Wunsoc had been transformed into an enormous, unseasonably botanical welcome sign – a rainbow-coloured floral tapestry of roses, peonies, daisies, hydrangeas and twisting green vines that read, thrillingly:

Come in and
join us.

Secondly, that the boy standing to her right – ganglylimbed, curly-headed, one corner of his mouth smeared with the remnants of a bedtime chocolate – was her best friend in the whole world. Hawthorne Swift rubbed his eyes and grinned at her blearily.

'Oh,' he said, as unruffled as ever. He craned his neck around to look at the seven other children lined up on either side of them. They too were shivering and pyjama-clad, and looked grumpy and alarmed to varying degrees. 'One of those weird Wunsoc things, is it?'

'Must be.'

'I was having the best dream,' he croaked. 'I was flying over a jungle on the back of a dragon and I fell off and tumbled down into the trees . . . and then I got adopted by a gang of monkeys. They made me their king.'

Morrigan snorted. 'Sounds about right.'

My friend is here, she thought happily. Everything was going to be okay.

'What're we meant to do?' asked the girl standing on Morrigan's left. Brawny, square-shouldered, pink-faced and at least a head taller than Morrigan, she had a thick Highland accent and tangled red hair that hung halfway down her back. This, Morrigan remembered, was Thaddea Macleod. The girl who'd fought a full-grown adult troll in her Show Trial and won.

Morrigan couldn't answer her question. Partly because she didn't know, but mostly because she was reliving in her mind the moment Thaddea had swiped Elder Wong's chair out from underneath him and used it to kneecap the troll with a sickening *crack*. Terrifying, Morrigan thought – but also, to be fair, quite resourceful.

'Just a guess,' Hawthorne said, through a wide-mouthed yawn, 'but I think we're meant to go in and join them.'

And as he said it, the gates began to slowly open with a great groaning *creeeeaaaak*. Behind the floral welcome and the high brick walls, the grounds of Wunsoc sloped gently up to Proudfoot House, its every window lit like a beacon calling them onwards.

The air changed as the nine successful candidates – chosen from hundreds of hopeful children to become the new scholars of Unit 919 of the Wundrous Society – stepped inside the gates.

For the first time ever, the strange 'Wunsoc weather' phenomenon didn't take Morrigan by surprise. Outside the gates in the streets of Old Town, it was a cool, brisk night. Inside the climate bubble of Wunsoc, where everything was a bit *more*, the grass was covered in a thick layer of frost. The air smelled like snow – crisp and clean and bitingly cold. It turned their breath to clouds of mist. Morrigan shivered, as did the others, rubbing their arms and hopping on the spot for warmth. The gates groaned closed behind them, and silence fell.

They had all seen Wunsoc last year, of course. Their first challenge – the Book Trial – had taken place inside Proudfoot House itself. Morrigan remembered sitting with hundreds of other children in an enormous room filled with rows of desks. A little blank booklet had asked her questions, which she'd had to answer truthfully, otherwise the booklet would burst into flames. Almost half the children who'd been in that room with her had watched their answers go up in smoke and were instantly disqualified.

Wunsoc looked different now, and not just because it was night-time. The drive was still lined with bare, black-trunked trees – fossilised remains of the now-extinct fireblossom genus. But tonight, perched in their branches like silent, overgrown birds, hundreds of Wundrous Society members – young and old, older and ancient – gazed down at the new arrivals. Just as in the Black Parade last Hallowmas, they were dressed in formal black cloaks, faces lit only by the candles they held.

The effect should have been frightening, but somehow Morrigan wasn't afraid. She was already in the Society, after all. The hard part was over.

There was something almost comforting about the presence of these black-cloaked strangers staring down at her from the trees. They weren't unfriendly, just . . . still.

As Unit 919 instinctively began to make its way up the sloping drive towards the hulking, red-brick building of Proudfoot House, the black-cloaked Society members broke into a quiet, murmuring chant that Morrigan recognised. It had been delivered to her at the Hotel Deucalion days earlier, written in small, careful handwriting and sealed in an ivory envelope with instructions to memorise and then burn the words:

Sisters and brothers, loyal for life,
Tethered for always, true as a knife.
Nine above others, nine above blood,
Bonded forever through fire and flood.
Brothers and sisters, faithful and true,
Ever together, the special and few.

It was an oath. A promise that each new Society member had to make to their unit – their eight new brothers and sisters. In joining the Society, Morrigan knew she was gaining not just an elite education and a world of opportunities, but also the thing she had craved above all else: a proper family.

The chant followed Unit 919 all the way up the long drive, and so did their fellow Society members. They jumped down from the trees and crowded in behind the new recruits, forming a sort of guard of honour, repeating the words of the Wunsoc oath over and over.

Their welcome to Wunsoc grew and gained momentum as Unit 919 marched further up the drive. A band of musicians scrambled down from a tree on their right and struck up a triumphant melody. A pair of teenagers on either side of the path conjured a rainbow for them to walk beneath like a misty, ethereal archway. When at last they reached Proudfoot House, a huge elephant at the foot of the steps trumpeted their arrival like a town crier.

And there waiting on the wide marble steps, stood nine men and women – one with a bright ginger head – watching the arrival of their candidates with pride and delight.

Jupiter looked like the sun itself was shining out of his face as Morrigan ran up the steps to greet him. He opened his mouth to speak but closed it again, his blue eyes welling up ever so slightly. Morrigan was surprised, and rather touched, by the unexpected display of emotion. She showed her appreciation by reaching out to punch him in the arm.

'Pathetic,' she whispered. Jupiter laughed, wiping his eyes.

Beside Jupiter stood Hawthorne's patron, young Nancy Dawson, her cheeks dimpling as she grinned down at her own candidate. 'All right, troublemaker?'

'All right, Nan,' Hawthorne replied, grinning.

An older patron on Nan's other side shushed them, frowning disapprovingly.

'Oh, shush yourself, Hester,' Nan said good-naturedly, turning back to make a funny face at Hawthorne and Morrigan.

Further down the line of patrons, Morrigan spotted a man she'd be happy to have never seen again: Baz Charlton.

Baz had spent the previous year trying to thwart Morrigan's chances in the trials and get her thrown out of Nevermoor, all while helping his own candidates to cheat.

Baz's candidate, the mesmerist Cadence Blackburn, stood with her arms folded across her chest. She tossed her long, braided black hair over her shoulder with a flick of her head, looking so perfectly at ease in this bizarre situation that she could almost have been *bored*. Morrigan was somehow both impressed and annoyed by that.

Jupiter leaned down to whisper in her ear. 'Look around, Mog. This is what you've worked for. Enjoy it.'

Behind them, the Wunsoc crowd pressed in close together. They'd stopped chanting now and were chatting happily among themselves, grinning up at the newest Society members and enjoying the celebration.

A sudden, unearthly cry rent the air and everyone looked up. A pair of dragons and their riders flew above Proudfoot House, spelling out nine names in fire and smoke across the sky:

ARCHAN
ANAH
CADENCE
FRANCIS
HAWTHORNE
LAMBETH

MAHIR
MORRIGAN
THADDEA

Since surviving her so-called curse and escaping to the secret city of Nevermoor exactly one year ago today, Morrigan had experienced some odd things. Seeing her own name spelled out in dragon fire was only the latest in a series of firsts, but she had to admit it was one of the better ones so far. Gasps of delight from the other members of Unit 919 told her she wasn't alone in her astonishment. In fact, only Hawthorne (who had, after all, been riding dragons since he could walk) seemed politely unfazed.

When the last name had turned to wisps of smoke in the sky, the riders steered their dragons away from Proudfoot House and the patrons led their scholars inside. The crowd of Wunsoc members behind them erupted into cheers and applause, waving them into the house as if they were genuine celebrities. Morrigan couldn't help but laugh at Hawthorne, who was waving so enthusiastically back at them he had to be pulled inside by Nan, just before the huge front doors swung shut, completely extinguishing the noise outside.

In the sudden quiet of Proudfoot House's vast, brightly lit entrance hall, a frail voice called from the back of the room.

'Welcome, Unit 919, to the first day of the rest of your lives.'

There stood the three esteemed members of the Wunsoc's High Council of Elders – Elder Gregoria Quinn, a woman whose fragile appearance Morrigan knew to be extremely deceptive; Elder Helix Wong – a serious, grey-bearded man covered in tattoos; and Elder Alioth Saga – who was, in fact, a large talking bull.

Compared to the welcome they'd received outside Proudfoot House, the inauguration ceremony itself was brief and unexciting. The Elders said a few words of welcome. Each patron took a black cloak and draped it around the shoulders of their candidate, then fastened a little golden *W* pin to the collar.

The scholars of Unit 919 recited the oath they had memorised, pledging lifelong loyalty to each other. They spoke in strong, clear voices. Nobody fluffed their lines. It was, Morrigan knew, the most important part of the ceremony.

Then it was over. That was that.

Almost.

'Patrons,' said Elder Quinn at the end of the ceremony, 'I'd like you to remain for a few minutes, if you please. There is an important matter we must discuss. Scholars, please wait on the steps outside Proudfoot House for your patrons.'

Morrigan wondered if this was a normal part of the ceremony; a few curious glances between the patrons suggested it probably wasn't. She tried to catch Jupiter's eye as she followed her unit outside, but he didn't look at her. His jaw was clenched.

Outside Proudfoot House, the grounds were chilly, empty and silent. Not a single person remained, not a scrap of evidence to suggest the uproarious welcome they'd received just minutes ago was anything more than a collective hallucination.

The silence stretched out between them. Except for Morrigan and Hawthorne, none of these children really knew each other. A few slightly embarrassed glances were exchanged, and there was some awkward giggling from Anah Kahlo – a plump, pretty girl with blonde ringlets who, as Morrigan vividly recalled, had sliced open her patron's abdomen during the Show Trial, removed her appendix and stitched her back up . . . all while blindfolded.

Hawthorne was, predictably, the first to speak up.

'You know that thing you did at the Show Trial,' he began, giving Archan Tate a quizzical look, 'that thing where you went around the audience and pickpocketed everyone's stuff while we all thought you were just playing the violin?'

'Um . . . yes?' Archan was a sweet-faced, almost angelic-looking boy who seemed entirely too innocent to be such a talented thief. He looked uncertainly at Hawthorne. 'Sorry about that. Did I steal something of yours? Did you get it back after? I tried to make sure I gave everything back to the right people. It's just, my patron thought it would be—'

'Absolutely brilliant,' Hawthorne interrupted, eyes wide with awe. 'It was *absolutely brilliant*. We were blown away, hey, Morrigan?'

Morrigan grinned, remembering Hawthorne's sheer delight at the Show Trial when he'd realised Archan had pilfered his own dragonriding gloves right out of his pocket, without him noticing a thing. She'd been impressed, but Hawthorne had been positively *thrilled* by Archan's knack.

'It was amazing,' Morrigan agreed. 'How did you learn that?'

Archan flushed pink all the way to tips of his ears. He smiled shyly at Morrigan. 'Oh! Um, thanks. I suppose I just sort of . . . picked it up.' He gave a modest little shrug.

'Brilliant,' said Hawthorne again. 'Maybe you can teach me a bit. Archan, isn't it?'

'Just Arch.' He shook Hawthorne's offered hand. 'Only my grandma calls me—'

At that moment, the doors of Proudfoot House flew open with a loud *bang*, and Baz Charlton swept dramatically out onto the marble steps, beckoning his candidate.

'You – what's yer name – Blinkwell. Let's go. We're leaving.'

Cadence Blackburn looked horrified. 'Wh-what? Why?'

'Did I say you could ask questions?' he said in his sneering, slurred voice. 'I *said*, we're *leaving*.'

But Cadence didn't move. The other patrons hurried from the house after Baz, their faces by turns fearful and furious. Every one of them was staring at Morrigan.

She felt ripples of dread radiate through her, as if her body was a pond into which someone had just dropped a very large, very heavy stone. In that instant, she knew exactly why the Elders had kept the patrons behind. She knew exactly what – exactly *who* – they'd been discussing.

Hester, the older woman who had shushed Nan earlier, marched straight over to Morrigan. Her pale face was hawkish and severe, her greying auburn hair pulled back tight against her skull. She stared down at Morrigan for several seconds, looking angry and confused.

'How do you know?' she barked, directing the question over her shoulder at Jupiter. 'Who told you?'

'Nobody told me.' Jupiter, who had sauntered out of Proudfoot House after them, leaned casually against a pillar. He gestured to Morrigan. 'I can see it. Plain as day.'

'What do you mean *see* it? I can't see anything.' Hester grabbed Morrigan's chin forcefully, twisting her face left and right as she peered into her eyes.

Jupiter's demeanour changed in an instant. He rushed forward, shouting, 'Oi!' but Morrigan didn't need him to intervene; without thinking, she slapped the woman's hand away. Hester gasped, leaning back as if burned. Morrigan glanced at Jupiter, wondering if she'd overstepped the mark, but he gave her a grimly satisfied nod.

Anah's patron, a young woman called Sumati Mishra,

gave a weary sigh. 'You *know* what North's knack is, Hester. He's a Witness. He sees things.'

'He could be lying,' said Hester.

Though Jupiter himself seemed untouched by the accusation, Morrigan felt herself bristle on his behalf.

Nan Dawson was equally indignant. 'Don't be a fool, Hester,' she said. 'Captain North is no liar. If he says Morrigan's a Wundersmith—'

As soon as Nan uttered the word, it felt like all the oxygen had been sucked from the air around them. *Wundersmith.* Like the striking of a gong, the word reverberated, bouncing off the red-brick building.

'—then she's a . . . Wundersmith,' Nan finished.

Wundersmith. Wundersmith. Wundersmith.

The patrons seemed to flinch in unison. The other children's faces snapped to Morrigan, wide-eyed and thunderstruck. Cadence's eyes narrowed to slits. Morrigan had the familiar, desolate sensation of standing on a shoreline and watching her fondest dreams float out to sea, unable to haul them back.

These were supposed to be her brothers and sisters. Loyal for life. But with a single word, they were looking at her as if she was their enemy.

'I-I'm . . .' Morrigan's throat tightened. She wanted to say something, to offer explanations or reassurances, but the truth was . . . she had none. She'd known for weeks what she was. The only other living Wundersmith, Ezra Squall, the evillest man who ever lived, had dropped the news on her like a bomb. And although Jupiter had tried his best to clean up the mess afterwards, to explain to her what it meant, Morrigan still had no idea what it was to be a Wundersmith, and that frightened her.

Jupiter had insisted that 'Wundersmith' wasn't a bad word. That it hadn't always meant something evil. He'd told her that Wundersmiths used to be honoured and celebrated – that they used their mysterious powers to protect people, even to grant wishes.

But Morrigan didn't know a single person in Nevermoor who agreed with him. And, having met the terrifying Ezra Squall herself, she found it hard to believe that Wundersmiths had *ever* been good.

Squall commanded the Hunt of Smoke and Shadow, his own ghoulish, fiery-eyed army of hunters, horses and hounds, who he'd mercilessly set upon Morrigan in the hope of bringing her to him. She had seen him bend iron with a flick of the wrist, create fire with a whisper, destroy her family home with a click of his fingers and rebuild it in an instant. She had seen past his mild and ordinary façade to the shadow of his true face – dark hollow eyes, blackened mouth and sharp, bared teeth.

And worst of all, Ezra Squall, Nevermoor's greatest enemy, had wanted Morrigan for his apprentice. Squall, who had built an army of monsters and tried to conquer Nevermoor. Who had massacred the brave people who stood up to him and had been in exile from the Free State ever since. Jupiter's reassurances couldn't erase the fact that the Wundersmith had seen something of himself in Morrigan.

What could she possibly say to dispel the fears of her unit, when she could barely contain her own?

Once again, only Hawthorne seemed unbothered. He already knew Morrigan was a Wundersmith. When she'd broken the news, his only concern was whether it meant she'd be exiled from the Free State, like Ezra Squall. Hawthorne had never believed for a *second* that his best friend was dangerous. Morrigan wished she had even an ounce of his certainty. Even in the depths of her stomach-gnawing worry, she felt a small surge of relief – not for the first time – that this strange, unflappable boy had decided to befriend her.

'And if Jupiter says she ain't dangerous, she ain't dangerous,' declared Nan, breaking the weighty silence. She gave Morrigan a small, encouraging smile. It made Morrigan feel a tiny bit braver, even if she couldn't make herself smile in return.

Elder Quinn had emerged from Proudfoot House with Elders Wong and Saga at her side, watching the scene with quiet resignation.

A very young patron wearing thick spectacles and blue bows in her hair stood beside Mahir Ibrahim. She placed her trembling hands on his shoulders and pulled him closer – though she didn't look particularly capable of protecting him, or anyone – and cleared her throat. 'Excuse me, Elder Quinn, but how can this little girl be a Wundersmith? There are no more Wundersmiths. Or at least, there's only one – the exiled Ezra Squall. Everybody knows that.'

'Correction, Miss Mulryan,' said Elder Quinn. 'There *was* only one. Now, it seems, there are two.'

'But isn't anyone worried about what this could *mean?*' demanded Hester. 'North, we know what Wundersmiths are capable of. Ezra Squall showed us that.'

Jupiter pursed his lips and squeezed the bridge of his nose. Morrigan could tell he was taking a moment to muster some patience. 'Squall didn't do the things he did *because* he was a Wundersmith, Hester. He happened to be a Wundersmith *and* a psychopath. Unfortunate combination, but . . . there you have it.'

'And how's he know that, eh?' said Baz Charlton, appealing to the Elders. 'We all know what Wundersmiths do: they control Wunder. Look at this little black-eyed beast – anyone can see she's a wrong'un. What's to stop her using Wunder to control *us?*' He looked at Morrigan with undisguised hatred. Morrigan clenched her teeth; the feeling was entirely mutual.

'Or worse,' Hester added, 'to destroy us?'

'For goodness' sake.' Jupiter ruffled his great ginger mane, exasperated. 'She's a *child!*'

Hester scoffed. 'For now.'

'But why must she be in the Society?' asked Miss Mulryan
in a timid, tremulous voice. Her face had turned three shades
whiter than milk, and her small, thin fingers dug tightly into
Mahir's shoulders, as if she was worried Morrigan might
whisk her candidate away in some dastardly, Wundersmith-
like fashion. Mahir himself was stony-faced, frowning so
deeply his eyebrows knitted into one. He was nearly as tall
as his patron, and together they made Morrigan think of
a mouse trying to protect a wolf. 'Why risk pl-placing her
among . . . among other children?'

Morrigan felt her face grow hot. They were speaking about
her as if she was a disease.

It was all beginning to feel a little too familiar.

For the first eleven years of her life, Morrigan had believed
she was cursed. That everything bad that ever happened –
in her family, in her town, in almost the whole Wintersea
Republic, where she'd grown up – was her fault. She'd learned,
at the end of last year, that this wasn't really true. But the
feeling of being cursed was one she could recall keenly, and
she had no desire to go through it again. She had an impulse
to run down the long drive and straight through the flower-
covered gates, but then she felt Jupiter's warm, steadying
hand on her shoulder.

'Oh, you'd rather she was somewhere *out there*, would you?' asked Elder Saga pointedly, stamping his hooves. 'On her own? Doing heaven knows what?'

'Yes,' insisted Hester. 'And so, I am certain, would every other patron and candidate here.'

'Then they may leave,' said Elder Quinn in a cool, measured voice. Hester and the other patrons looked taken aback. Elder Quinn inclined her head. 'If they wish to. These are not, after all, ordinary circumstances. I understand the gravity of this matter, and I understand your concerns. However, my fellow Elders and I have discussed this at great length, and we will not be removing Miss Crow from Unit 919. That is our final word.'

Baz Charlton hissed under his breath, shaking his head. 'Unbelievable.'

'Believe it,' snapped Elder Quinn, and Baz shrank down against the collar of his cloak.

Hester seemed to think Elder Quinn was bluffing. 'With all due respect,' she said through gritted teeth, 'I highly doubt the Society wishes to lose *eight* talented new members only to gain *one* dangerous entity. I'm certain you'll change your minds after you've watched these eight brilliant children walk out those gates. Come along, Francis.' She started down the steps towards the tree-lined drive.

'Aunt Hester,' said Francis, a quiet plea in his voice, 'I want to stay. Please. My father would want me to—'

40

'My brother would *never* want you to risk your life!' said Hester, spinning back wildly to face them. 'He would never want you anywhere near a-a *Wundersmith*.'

Elder Quinn cleared her throat. 'Patrons, this is not a decision you can make for your scholars. Children, if any of you wishes to leave Unit 919 – to leave the Wundrous Society – you may come forward now and hand over your pins. There will be no judgement and no repercussions. We shall wish you well and speed you on your way.'

She stood with her hand out. There was silence, but for early-morning birdsong somewhere in the distance. The air itself seemed frozen, clouding with the white, frosty breaths of the patrons and their candidates. All except Morrigan, who was barely breathing at all.

Anah's shaking fingers crept up to her pin, and she bit her lip. Francis looked guiltily at his aunt, but Cadence didn't even glance in Baz's direction. She didn't even blink.

Nobody handed over their pin. The thought was, of course, pure madness. After all they'd been through in the trials last year, to imagine that any one of them might surrender that little golden *W* and all that it promised? Unthinkable.

'Well, then,' said Elder Quinn, letting her hand drop, 'if you are certain. But let me be clear, scholars – *and* patrons.' She shot a piercing look at Hester and Baz, who both looked deeply resentful. 'The nature of Miss Crow's unusual –' she paused, seeming to catch herself before calling it a 'knack',

'– *situation*, will remain absolutely confidential until the High Council of Elders sees fit to share it with the rest of the Society, as we cannot risk it being discovered outside Wunsoc. To share the truth would be to cause mass panic. That means that with a very few necessary exceptions – the Scholar Mistresses, for example, and the conductor of Unit 919 – the fact that we have a Wundersmith among us must remain a secret known only to those of you now present. Our teaching staff will be instructed not to ask questions or discuss the matter of Miss Crow's knack, and the Mistresses will deal with any nosy scholars as they see fit.'

She turned to the nine children, who seemed somehow to have shrunk, their triumphant evening blighted by the dreadful news.

Her voice was like steel. 'You are a unit now. You are responsible for each other. You are accountable to each other. Therefore, if anyone – *anyone at all* – is found to have broken our trust . . .' Elder Quinn paused, her face grave. She looked at each one of them in turn, until finally her gaze landed on Morrigan. '. . . then all nine of you will face expulsion from Wunsoc. For life.'

CHAPTER THREE

The Not-Tattoo and the Not-Door

When she woke the next morning, Morrigan could almost have convinced herself the midnight trip to Wunsoc had been a strange and wonderful and horrible dream. If it wasn't for the golden tattoo.

'It's not a *tattoo*,' Jupiter insisted, pouring two glasses of juice while Morrigan lashed chaotic swirls of honey and sprinkles of cinnamon across a plate of toasted crumpets (a little burned from where she'd held them too close to the fire, but still edible). After the events of the night before, they'd both woken much too late for breakfast in the dining room and Jupiter had instead called for a tray to be sent to his study. The pair of them sat on either side of his desk, a miscellany of food spread between them ranging from the respectfully breakfast-like (smoked trout and scrambled eggs) to the unabashedly not (tomato soup and artichoke hearts – Jupiter had a craving). 'Do you really think I'd let them give you a tattoo?'

Morrigan took a very large bite of her crumpet so that she didn't have to answer. Truthfully, she never *quite* knew what Jupiter would and wouldn't allow.

Her pointed silence wasn't lost on him. He looked aghast. 'Mog! Don't be ridiculous. Tattoos *hurt*. Does it hurt?'

Morrigan shook her head as she swallowed. 'No,' she said, licking honey off her right index finger so she could examine the new addition to her fingerprint: a golden *W*, identical in style to her Wunsoc pin but much smaller, slightly raised on her skin and faintly shimmering in the light. 'It doesn't hurt at all. It just feels a bit . . . like it's . . . there.'

She didn't know how else to describe the mark, which she'd mysteriously woken up with that morning. It didn't burn or sting or tickle or any other sensation she could precisely pinpoint. It wasn't a thing that had been inflicted by some external force – not a scar, exactly, or a wound. It was more like it had pressed its way from the inside of her skin to the outside. Before she'd seen it with her own eyes, before she'd even fully awoken, Morrigan had simply known it was there. 'It's weird, isn't it?'

Jupiter was examining his own index finger with an expression of mild surprise. He'd told Morrigan that just like her mark, his own had shown up the morning after his

Wunsoc inauguration – many, many, many years ago. He looked as if he hadn't properly considered it in a very long time. 'Mm. I suppose. Useful, though.'

'What for?'

'All sorts.' He shrugged and returned his attention to the breakfast spread, carefully choosing his next morsel.

'Such as?'

'Gets you into places. Helps other Society members recognise you.'

'But we've got our *W* pins for that.'

'No.' He settled at last on a piece of half-burnt toast, and reached for the jam. 'That's different.'

Morrigan narrowed her eyes. 'How?'

He was doing his annoying Jupiter thing, drip-feeding information like a special form of torture. It could be because he didn't really want to tell her, or it could be because their current conversation was the least important train of thought out of the dozen that were probably steaming through his head. It was always hard to tell the difference with Jupiter.

'The pin is for Unwuns.'

'Unwuns?'

'Mmm.' He chewed and swallowed a mouthful of toast, dusting stray crumbs off his shirtfront. 'Other people, you know. Non-Society members. The pin is how people outside the ranks of Wunsoc tell who we are. The imprint is different.' He held up his finger, wiggling it, and the *W* mark reflected the light from the fireplace, seeming to almost glow. 'The imprint is for us.'

Something occurred to Morrigan and she was suddenly annoyed. 'How come you never showed me before?'

'No point, Mog. You can't see anyone else's imprint until you have your own. Like I said, it's for *us*. It's how we recognise each other. A sort of . . . family emblem. You'll start to notice them all over the place now, you'll see.'

A family emblem. Those words tugged gently at Morrigan's heart. She prized her golden *W* pin above all her other possessions (except, perhaps, her brolly), but it was still just that . . . a possession. An object that could easily be broken or lost. The imprint felt different; it was a part of her. And it proved that she was a part of something important, something bigger than just herself. A family.

Sisters and brothers, loyal for life.

But was that what she had? She'd thought so, right up until one word had been uttered – *Wundersmith* – and the illusion had shattered into a million pieces.

'Hey.' Jupiter tapped on the butter dish with his knife to get her attention. She looked up. 'You have just as much right to be in the Society as they do, Mog,' he said, as if he'd read her mind. He leaned in, dropping his voice to a whisper. 'More, really. Don't forget who finished the Show Trial in the number one spot on the leaderboard.' He paused for a moment, then added, 'It was you. In case you actually did forget.'

Morrigan hadn't forgotten. But what did their positions on the leaderboard matter now? What did any of last year matter, if her unit didn't trust her? If they were *afraid* of her?

'Give it time.' Once again, Jupiter seemed to know exactly what she was thinking. That was the unfair advantage of being a Witness – he saw the world in ways she could never fathom. Her hidden feelings and secret truths were his for the taking, as plain as the scowl on her face. It was somehow both comforting and really, *really* aggravating. 'They'll come around. They just need to get to know you, that's all. Then they'll see the same charming Morrigan Crow I know.'

Morrigan was about to ask who this charming Morrigan Crow was and if she'd like to trade places, when there was a knock at the door. Sprightly old Kedgeree Burns popped his snowy head inside the study. 'Message came back for you, sir. From the Celes—'

'Thank you, Kedge,' Jupiter interrupted. He jumped up to take the note, and the concierge left, with a wink at Morrigan and a smart little click of his heels, shutting the door behind him.

The note was sealed with silver wax. Jupiter crossed the room and leaned on the mantelpiece, hunching down to read by the light of the fire. A few silent moments passed, and Morrigan stared into the fireplace.

He's right, she thought. She was a full and proper member of the Wundrous Society now. She had fought hard in the trials, just like the others in her unit.

Not in the last one, you didn't, said a little voice in her head. It was true that in the Show Trial – the fourth and final test in which each candidate had to display their special 'knack' – Morrigan had done nothing but stand in the middle of the Trollosseum, confused, as Jupiter had shared his unique sight with each of the Elders in turn, showing them what he'd known all year long – what he'd kept from them, and from Morrigan herself. That she was a Wundersmith. That the mysterious magical energy source they called Wunder – a source that powered the world in ways Morrigan couldn't fathom – was gathering to her constantly, like moths gather to a flame, waiting patiently for her to come into her (still stubbornly nonexistent) powers.

The Elders had instantly awarded Morrigan a place in the Wundrous Society, to the outrage and disgust of many other candidates and their patrons, each of whom had done *much* more for their Show Trial performance than simply stand dumbly in the Trollosseum while the Elders stared at them, silent and awestruck.

Morrigan cleared her throat and sat up straight. 'So.' Her voice, at least, was resolute. 'When do I start?'

'Hmm?'

'At Wunsoc. When do I go back? When do my classes start?'

'Oh,' said Jupiter, still frowning at the note in his hand. 'Not sure. Soon, I expect.'

Morrigan's excitement faltered. Did he really not know? Was this typical Wundrous Society mystery, she wondered, or typical Jupiter North vagueness? She felt a bit of worry creep in.

'Monday?' she asked.

'Um, yeah. Maybe.'

'Could you . . . find out?' Morrigan asked, trying to keep the impatience from her voice.

'Hmm?'

She sighed. 'I said, could you—'

'I've got to go, Mog,' said Jupiter suddenly. He turned from the fire, shoving the note into a trouser pocket, and snatched his coat from where it lay across the back of an armchair. 'Sorry. Important errand. Finish your breakfast. I'll see you later.'

The door swung shut in Jupiter's wake. Morrigan threw a piece of toast at it.

⌐■━

The imprint wasn't the only thing that had shown up overnight.

'It doesn't even have a doorknob.' Martha sat next to Morrigan on the end of her bed later that afternoon, staring at the brand-new, glossy black, ornate wooden door that had appeared in the opposite wall. 'So it can't really be a door, can it?'

'I suppose not,' said Morrigan.

It wasn't unusual for her bedroom to change and grow and shrink, to add new features one night and take them away the next. It was very temperamental, as bedrooms go. But it had never built a second door before.

Morrigan wouldn't have minded having a second door, except for two things. One: it had grown right next to the fireplace, which threw off the symmetry of the room (a small detail, but one she found surprisingly vexing). And two: she couldn't open it, and therefore it was entirely without function. Morrigan was *much* too practical a person to ever want a purely decorative door in her bedroom. And yet . . . it was quite unlike the room to transform into something she wouldn't like.

She frowned. Was her bedroom mad at her for some reason? Or could it be unwell? Maybe it had the architectural equivalent of a head cold. Maybe this door was her bedroom's version of a great big snotty sneeze.

'Still,' said Martha with a shrug, 'it's not the weirdest thing this room's ever done, is it?' She cast a look at the octopus-shaped armchair in the corner, which gave a sinister flick of its tentacles. The maid shuddered. 'I do wish you'd get rid of that thing. It's a nightmare to dust.'

Jupiter hadn't returned by the time Morrigan went to bed. A note from the League of Explorers arrived on Sunday morning, advising the Deucalion staff that he'd been 'unavoidably delayed on an interrealm task' – a typically unhelpful message in both volume and detail, though Morrigan strongly suspected it had to do with the missing angel. She was disappointed, but unsurprised. The downside of having a famous, much-admired patron was that she had to share him with the League of Explorers, the Wundrous Society, the Federation of Nevermoorian Hoteliers, the Nevermoor Transport Authority and every other organisation or individual that wanted a bit of his time and attention.

Jupiter did, at least, follow up the League's note with one of his own, addressed to Morrigan.

> *Mog,*
>
> *Won't be back before your first day. I'm really sorry.*
>
> *Forgot something important: UNDER NO CIRCUMSTANCES are you to travel anywhere outside of Wunsoc by yourself. I mean it. I'm trusting you.*
>
> *Good luck! You will be great.*
> *Remember, you belong there.*
> *—J.N.*

By that afternoon, Morrigan was feeling antsy and irritable, wondering when her classes were going to start and where she had to go. She didn't want to miss her first day and give her unit even more reason to dislike her. She'd even asked Kedgeree to send someone to Hawthorne's house with a message – but Hawthorne had sent her note back with his response written on the reverse: simply, 'Dunno.' She'd rolled her eyes at that, wondering if he'd even *thought* to ask Nan. She doubted it, somehow.

So Morrigan sought advice from the only other person she could think of who might be able to help.

'My darling – *la la la LA!* – you do *fret* so.' Dame Chanda Kali was preparing for an intimate concert she was to give that evening in the Music Salon, by simultaneously performing vocal warm-ups and hunting for the perfect costume. The floor of her enormous, ballroom-sized wardrobe was scattered with jewel-coloured gowns of silk and satin and sequins that she'd tried on and abandoned, sad casualties of the soprano's reckless multitasking. 'I wouldn't worry about these things, Miss Morrigan, I really wouldn't. You know what the Wundrous Society is like.' She raised her index finger and wiggled it at Morrigan conspiratorially; her *W* imprint gleamed in the light. Besides Jupiter, Dame Chanda was the only other resident of the Hotel Deucalion who was a member of the Society. Even Jack, despite sharing Jupiter's talent as a Witness, had never tried out for Wunsoc – instead, he attended a very posh boarding school called the Graysmark School for Bright Young Men, where he played cello in the school orchestra, wore a top hat and bow tie to school every day, and rarely came home, even at weekends.

'No, I don't,' said Morrigan, with thinly-veiled frustration. She did *not* know what the Society was like. Unlike everyone else in Nevermoor, she'd grown up outside the Free State. She'd never even *heard* of the famous, all-pervading Wundrous Society until a year ago.

'Of course you *do-re-mi-fa-so-la-TI*,' sang Dame Chanda, turning from side to side as she examined herself in a gilt-framed mirror. Her impressive voice bounced around the high ceilings and gave Morrigan a satisfying shiver of gooseflesh, all up and down her arms. A tiny mouse poked its head out of a gap in the floorboards, looking lovesick, and Dame Chanda shooed it away. 'The Society is demanding. Intrusive. Utterly without consideration for anyone's time or privacy.' She turned and fixed Morrigan with a pointed look. 'In short, my angel: when they want you, you will know about it. They'll go straight to the source. *Mi-mi-mi-mi-MI!*'

'You?'

Dame Chanda looked confused for a moment, then laughed. 'No, Miss Morrigan. *You.* They'll fetch you when you're needed. Never fear, sweet girl. You'll be deep in the twisting labyrinth of Wunsoc before you know it. Then you'll be itching to get out. Believe me – I try to limit my visits to mandatory events and special occasions *only*.'

'Why?'

'Oh, you know,' she said breezily, gathering up another armful of hanging gowns and dumping them unceremoniously on a chaise longue. 'If I start showing my face around the hallowed halls too often, people will think they can rope me into their ridiculous exploits. As if I don't have enough demands on my time.' Morrigan knew of precisely seven demands on Dame Chanda's time: her famous and well-attended concerts in the Hotel Deucalion's Music Salon every Sunday night, and the six handsome and charming suitors with whom she spent the rest of her evenings. Fellow de Friday, as Jupiter had secretly christened him, had attended Morrigan's birthday party and given her a massive bouquet of pink and purple roses (undoubtedly to impress the opera singer, but Morrigan appreciated the gesture nonetheless). 'And I simply couldn't *bear* to run into Murgatroyd.'

'Who's Murgatroyd?' asked Morrigan.

'Murgatroyd, of Dearborn and Murgatroyd. The Scholar Mistresses.' Dame Chanda shuddered. 'Two horrid peas in a frightful pod. Well, perhaps that's unfair . . . poor Dearborn's not so bad. Murgatroyd's the one to avoid, if you can.' She threw a look of sympathy at Morrigan's reflection in the mirror behind her. 'Although I'm very sorry to tell you, darling, that you probably can't.'

Dame Chanda was right. When they wanted Morrigan, she knew about it.

It was early on Monday morning – much, *much* earlier than she would have liked – when she was woken by three knocks on the door.

Not her bedroom door.

The new door. The not-really-a-door. The *mystery* door.

The one that didn't open.

CHAPTER FOUR

Hometrain

Morrigan sat up in bed and stared at the door. Her heart thumped in the quiet. A minute or two passed, and she'd nearly convinced herself that it had just been her imagination, when—

Knock, knock, knock.

Morrigan held her breath. She wanted to ignore the knocking. She wanted to burrow deep into her blankets and put her pillow over her head until whoever – whatever – it was, went away.

But that's not *what a Wundrous Society member would do,* she told herself firmly.

Making up her mind, she threw off her blankets and stomped loudly to the door, hoping that the person (or thing) on the other side would hear her booming footsteps and think she was much bigger and scarier than she really was. She leaned in, breathing hard, with the idea of pressing her ear to the door . . . but then stopped. Close up, she saw something she hadn't noticed before – a small golden circle, right in the centre of the black wood. A circle the size of a fingertip.

It began to glow – a diffused golden light, emanating from the metal itself. Gently at first, then a little brighter, until finally the glow crept into the centre . . . illuminating a tiny metallic *W*.

Ah, thought Morrigan. She pressed the *W* imprint on her right index finger to the glowing circle. It was warm to the touch.

The door swung open so quickly, so easily, that she jumped back with a gasp, expecting somebody to pounce at her.

Nobody was there.

She blinked into a small, brightly lit room that was something between a hallway, a utility room and a walk-in wardrobe. The dark panelled walls were lined with hanging spaces for clothes and glass-fronted display cupboards, all empty.

Had this always been here, Morrigan wondered. Was it part of the Deucalion, or had the mystery door delivered her somewhere else altogether?

Across from the door she'd just entered was another, identical to the first. Morrigan ran to it and pressed her finger to the golden ring, but nothing happened. With a dull thud of disappointment, she realised it was both cold and unlit.

'What now?' she whispered, turning around to examine the empty room.

Her eyes landed on the answer. The room wasn't *entirely* empty. On the back of the first door hung a single outfit: boots, socks, trousers, belt, shirt, jumper and coat. All black, except for the shirt, which was grey. All smart, new, freshly pressed . . . and in Morrigan's size.

'Ah-HA.'

In less than a minute, she was ready – shirt buttoned, boots laced, pyjamas abandoned on the floor – and the circled *W* on the second door immediately began to glow. Morrigan grinned, reaching out to press it.

The door swung out onto a small Wunderground station. It was neat and tidy – despite the residual smoke, and slight air of neglect – and unadorned but for a gleaming brass clock hanging from the ceiling and a wooden bench at the end of the platform. Morrigan felt her ears pop as she stepped across the threshold. The atmosphere had changed; there was a dense chill in the air here, and a subtle scent of something like engine oil.

That answered her question, then. She wasn't in the Hotel Deucalion any more. No matter how changeable the Deucalion was, no matter how many octopus armchairs and swinging hammocks and talon-footed bathtubs it could conjure up, it definitely *wasn't* underground, and it definitely *didn't* have a train station, sitting empty, next to Morrigan's bedroom on the fourth floor.

Well . . . *almost* empty.

A girl with thick braided hair sat alone, shoulders hunched, legs hanging over the edge of the platform. Morrigan's door closed behind her with a loud click, and the girl turned at the noise.

'Hello,' said Morrigan, a little stiffly.

'About time.' Cadence Blackburn was glowering now, but Morrigan was certain she'd seen her expression change from worry to relief just a second ago. Perhaps because she'd realised she wasn't alone; that another member of her unit had shown up after all.

'How long have you been here, Cadence?'

Not for the first time, Cadence looked surprised to be remembered. She'd told Morrigan after the Show Trial that nobody apart from Morrigan ever remembered her – that was the downside of being a mesmerist.

But Morrigan had never had a problem remembering her. In fact, she found Cadence extremely memorable. She'd memorably stolen Morrigan's coveted ticket to the Elders' Dinner during the Chase Trial. She'd memorably pushed her into a pond on Hallowmas night. Then she'd memorably – amazingly, *bafflingly* – saved her from being kicked out of Nevermoor. It was safe to say Morrigan had *very* mixed feelings about Cadence.

'A while,' said Cadence. 'The door locked behind me.'

Morrigan turned back to see that the golden ring on her own door had stopped glowing. Did that mean the way back was blocked to her now? That made her feel a little uneasy. She tried pressing her finger to it.

Nothing happened. It was cool and dim.

'Mine's that one,' said Cadence, pointing to a forest green door, three along from the black one. There were eight doors besides Morrigan's own; eight different styles and colours, leading to eight different homes, she supposed. 'It showed up in our living room overnight. Mum wasn't happy. I had to stop her from calling the Stink.'

'Mine arrived right in my bedroom.'

Cadence gave a disinterested grunt. Silence stretched between them.

The platform was tiny – certainly not long enough for any regular Wunderground train to stop at. Yet the sign hanging above the platform read *STATION 919*.

'Is this . . . wait. No. Do we get our own station?' asked Morrigan, her mouth falling open in disbelief. 'Our own *private* Wunderground station?'

'Seems that way.' There was a slight note of wonder in Cadence's normally gruff voice that she couldn't disguise. Jupiter had joked about Wundrous Society members getting reserved seats on the Wunderground, but their own private station – no matter how tiny – was infinitely cooler than even

60

that. Cadence stood up and dusted off her black trousers. She fixed Morrigan with a searching look. 'So . . . is it true, then? Are you really a Wundersmith?'

Morrigan nodded.

Cadence looked as if she didn't quite believe her. 'How do you know?'

'Just do.' She didn't want to tell Cadence the truth. That Ezra Squall himself had told her. That she'd had an actual conversation with Nevermoor's most hated man. 'Jupiter can see it.'

Cadence raised an eyebrow and Morrigan watched her warily. She had the cagey, irritable look of someone who might be about to say something cutting, but you couldn't be sure with Cadence. It was becoming clear that 'cagey and irritable' might just be her default expression. Morrigan could sympathise.

'That makes us both Dangerous Entities. Two in one unit, that's brave of them.' Cadence laughed, a little bitterly. 'Did they make you have a safeguard?'

'Yes,' said Morrigan. The safeguard pact had been a strict condition of her entry to the Society. Nine upstanding, influential citizens of Nevermoor who all agreed to vouch for Morrigan's trustworthiness and . . . well, she didn't really know what else they had to do. It was one of those strange Wundrous Society traditions Morrigan didn't fully understand, but the important thing was that if Jupiter hadn't been able to convince the Angel Israfel to become the final signatory to Morrigan's safeguard pact before the inauguration, she wouldn't be a member of 919 right now.

'Me too,' said Cadence. 'Three signatories. You?'

'Nine.'

Cadence let out a long, low whistle.

They were both quiet for a moment, then the silence was suddenly broken by three of the other doors flying open at once. Anah Kahlo, Francis Fitzwilliam and Mahir Ibrahim appeared looking equally dazed and intrigued, adjusting their unfamiliar uniforms. Within moments, they were joined by Thaddea, Archan, Lambeth and—

'How good are these BOOTS?' Hawthorne stomped dramatically onto the platform. He grinned at Morrigan and put his hands on his hips, pushing out his chest. 'How cool are these clothes? I can see why you like wearing black. I feel like a SUPERHERO. Don't you feel like a superhero?'

'Not very,' admitted Morrigan.

'They should give us capes! Don't you reckon? Should we ask if they can give us capes?'

'Let's not.'

'Is this a Wunderground station? It looks like one.' His attention darted all over the place, quick as a dog spotting squirrels in the park. 'It's a bit grubby, isn't it? I don't mind, though. Mum says dirt's good for the immune system. Where are we? Station 919? I haven't heard of any – oh! OH! No way. Morrigan, I think this might be—'

'Yep,' she cut in. 'Our own—'

'Our own STATION?'

'Yep!'

'No WAY.'

Morrigan grinned. She found she was gladder than usual of Hawthorne's boundless enthusiasm for the world around him. It provided a distraction from the silent, mistrustful stares of the other unit members. Anah had pressed herself against the wall, as far away from Morrigan as it was possible to be in such a small space. Given that the first time the two of them met, Morrigan had been defending Anah against a bully, she had to admit she found this behaviour a little insulting. Nonetheless, she tried to keep her expression neutral, lest Anah think she was putting a hex on her or something.

Hawthorne jumped high, reaching up to touch the platform sign hanging above them. It swung back and forth, creaking loudly. 'When do you reckon the train—'

'Now,' said a matter-of-fact voice from the corner of the platform. They all turned around. Lambeth was sitting on the floor, cross-legged and straight-backed, gazing into the dark mouth of the tunnel. She was small and serious-looking, with a tawny complexion and long, black hair as smooth as silk.

The rest of the unit exchanged glances, waiting for her to elaborate.

Morrigan cleared her throat. 'Sorry, what . . .'

Lambeth turned back to look at the rest of the unit, holding one finger up in the air as if telling them to wait for it. Seconds later, the ground began to rumble beneath their feet. A whistle sounded from somewhere inside the tunnel and the answer to Hawthorne's question chugged into view.

'Spooky,' said Hawthorne.

'You mean *creepy*,' said Thaddea, casting a sidelong look at Lambeth, who looked just as regal and tranquil sitting on the floor of the station as a queen sitting on a throne.

It wasn't a train, exactly, but a single carriage. It looked odd on its own, like a head that had lost its body. It was a bit dented and battered-looking, but clean and shiny as a brass half-kred coin, sending cheerful little puffs of white steam into the air as it slowed to a halt. On its side was a large black *W*, and underneath that the number '919', which looked freshly painted.

The train whistle sounded again, the doors opened and a young woman stepped out onto the platform, holding a crumpled piece of paper. Coltishly long-legged and tall, she didn't hunch the way some tall people hunched, so that others wouldn't be intimidated by them. She stood like a ballet dancer, Morrigan thought – shoulders back, feet slightly turned out.

'Lambeth Amara, short-range oracle,' the woman called out, consulting her paper. 'Cadence Blackburn, mesmerist. Morrigan Crow, Wundersmith. Francis Fitzwilliam, gastronomist. Mahir Ibrahim, linguist. Anah Kahlo, healer. Thaddea Macleod, fighter. Hawthorne Swift, dragonrider. Archan Tate, pickpocket.' She looked happily around at the nine faces staring back at her. She hadn't flinched or grimaced when she'd said the word 'Wundersmith'. She hadn't even blinked. Morrigan liked her already. 'What a mix. All here?'

The members of Unit 919 looked around at each other and nodded vaguely.

'All aboard, then.' She beckoned them over, beaming, and disappeared inside the carriage door. Hawthorne followed eagerly, and Morrigan and the others lined up behind him.

'Whoa,' said Hawthorne as they stepped inside.

'Cool,' breathed Mahir.

'Brilliant,' said Thaddea.

Quite, thought Morrigan.

It looked just as if somebody had taken an old Wunderground train carriage, gutted it, and turned it into a long cosy sitting room. Big lumpy cushions and squashy armchairs, an assortment of coffee tables and lamps and an old, worn-out sofa were configured neatly around the space. There was a small wood-burning stove with a copper kettle in the corner, a crate full of kindling, and a pile of crocheted blankets in a rainbow of colours. A single wooden desk, painted red with stickers all over it, sat at the very front of the carriage. The walls were covered with posters spouting inspirational sayings like *BE THE VERY BEST YOU CAN BE* and *THERE'S NO 'I' IN TEAMWORK,* and a corkboard tacked with colourful notices and picture cards. The space was cramped, but comfy. Chaotic, but clean. It was wonderful.

'Decorated it myself. What do you think?' The young woman watched them breathlessly, with the air of someone bestowing a carefully chosen Christmas gift on a loved one. She was practically bouncing on her toes. 'You should have seen it before, it was *well* spare. I feel sorry for the last unit who had this carriage. Nine boring desks, nine hard chairs. No couch! No beanbags! No fire – and it's *freezing* in here during winter, believe me. Not even a biscuit jar! Can you believe that?' She pointed to a large polar-bear-shaped ceramic jar sitting on the red desk. 'I hereby promise that that jar will always be full of biscuits. None of your rubbishy ones, either – I'm talking your proper chocolate biscuits. Your pink iced rings. Your custard creams and so on. One thing you all should know about me: I've got very high biscuit standards.'

She took the jar and passed it around, smiling as they nibbled quietly, and looking utterly thrilled that she'd been able to meet this most fundamental of needs.

'Sit down, sit down.' The children all sat, settling in among the hodgepodge of furniture. Morrigan took one of the huge floor cushions, and Hawthorne the one next to hers. The woman made herself comfortable in a plush velvet armchair. In her oversized pink jumper, green chequered leggings and yellow sneakers, she looked like a melted box of crayons – in stark contrast to the black-clad Unit 919, who could have passed for mourners at a funeral. A curly, bulb-shaped cloud of black hair was tied back from her face with a yellow-gold scarf.

'I'm Miss Cheery. Marina Cheery. Your conductor.' Morrigan glanced at the others, wondering if she was supposed to know what a conductor was. Hawthorne caught her eye and shrugged. 'Bit of a stupid name, Miss Cheery, but I promise I'll do my best to live up to it. I'm *supposed* to make you call me Conductor Cheery, but if you ask me that sounds even stupider. So, let's just agree on Miss Cheery, all right?'

Unit 919 nodded, mouths full of biscuit.

Miss Cheery watched the unit with a proud, energised expression, like they were the nine most important people in the world. Her eyes were bright and kind, her skin the deepest, warmest brown, and she had perhaps the nicest smile Morrigan had ever seen on any face. Ever.

'Welcome to Hometrain,' she said, throwing her arms out around her. 'For your next five years as junior scholars, this comfy little carriage will be your transport, your refuge and your base camp. We'll start and end each school day right here, all of us together. I'll pick you up at Station 919 every morning, Monday to Friday, and then I'll drop you back here at the end of the day. Easy-peasy. We call it a Hometrain because that's what it's for, you see? Bringing you home. But that's also how I want you to think of this place.' She looked seriously at them. 'As your second home. A place where you can feel safe and happy. Where everyone's got your back, and no question is a dumb question, and nobody's going to judge you. So. With that in mind – any questions?'

Francis stuck his hand up in the air. 'What's your knack?'

'Glad you asked, Francis,' she said, smiling. 'I'm a tightrope walker. Graduate of the School of Mundane Arts and proud of it.'

Bingo, thought Morrigan. Not a dancer, but close enough. No wonder she had such excellent posture.

'What's the School of Mundane Arts?' asked Mahir.

'Ah! What an excellent question.' Miss Cheery jumped up out of her chair and crossed the carriage to where a large black-and-white poster was hanging. It showed three concentric circles like a target sign – a grey outer ring, a white middle ring, and a black circle in the centre. 'The Wundrous Society is split into two streams of expertise: the Mundane and the Arcane.' Miss Cheery pointed to the grey outer circle. 'This big circle here represents the Mundane – yours truly included. This is the largest Wundrous Society sector, engaging in public-facing arts, acts and services, comprising knacks based predominantly in the medicinal, sporting, performing, creative, engineering and political disciplines. First line of attack in managing the popular and financial support crucial for the Wundrous Society to continue its vital work.'

Morrigan frowned at those words. What exactly *was* the Wundrous Society's vital work? Nobody had ever told her . . . and, she realised with a small amount of embarrassment, she'd never really thought to ask.

Miss Cheery continued, reciting the words as if she'd had to memorise them for a test. 'Mostly, we Mundanes charm the public and bring in the money. Think of your favourite musician, your favourite athlete, the best circus you ever saw, the cleverest politician you've heard on the news, the city's most brilliant architects and engineers – they're probably from the Wundrous Society, which means they're probably graduates of the School of Mundane Arts. We do amazing things in the world to keep popular opinion firmly on the Wundrous Society's side.' She grinned. 'Our motto inside Wunsoc is *"Just Try Getting On Without Us"*.'

She pointed to the white middle circle. 'This bit represents the Arcane. Barely a third as many members as the Mundane, but just as important and – *some* people would say – twice as powerful. Engaging in private-facing arts, acts and services, comprising knacks based predominantly in the magical, supernatural and esoteric disciplines – your witches, your oracles, your psychic mediums, your sorcerers and so on. They're usually the first line of defence in protecting the

Society, the city and the Free State from forces that wish to harm. Their motto is *"If Not For Us, You'd All Be Speaking Zombie".'*

'What's the black circle for?' asked Cadence, pointing to the centre of the chart.

'Oh . . .' Miss Cheery stared at the poster and shrugged, as if she'd never really thought about it. 'That's just meant to represent the Society as a whole.'

'When do we find out which school we're in?' asked Thaddea, sitting up as straight as possible in her beanbag. She cracked her knuckles, looking keen to start *protecting the Free State from forces that wish to harm.*

'Unbutton your coats,' Miss Cheery instructed, 'and pull out your shirtsleeves.'

They did so, and Morrigan noticed for the first time that while most of them were wearing grey shirts, the same as hers . . . two among them were wearing white.

'Ah, there you go,' said Miss Cheery. 'So my fellow grey-sleeves are Anah, Arch, Mahir, Hawthorne, Morrigan, Thaddea and Francis. And our Arcane whitesleeves are Lambeth and uh . . . um –' she looked down at her piece of paper, running her finger down the list of names, '– Cadence! Right. That makes sense. Cadence is a mesmerist, you see, and—'

'Who's Cadence?' asked Francis.

Miss Cheery nodded to where Cadence sat glaring stormily at them. The entire unit – except for Morrigan – turned to her with looks of surprise, as if they'd only just noticed she was sitting there. (They *had* only just noticed she was sitting there.)

'Hmm,' said Miss Cheery, writing herself a little note. 'Yes. We're going to have to do something about that. Anyway, Cadence is a mesmerist, and Lambeth is a radar – which is a very specific type of oracle – more short-term forecasts than long-range prophecies. Those are two rare knacks, even in the Arcane arts. We're lucky to have you in our unit, girls.'

Cadence looked slightly mollified by this. Lambeth was reading the posters on the walls and whispering under her breath and didn't seem remotely interested in the conversation. She gave a small, quick smile as though someone had said something funny, then frowned, and then brightened again. Morrigan watched her closely. If Lambeth was a radar, she was obviously tuned to an entirely different frequency to everyone else.

The rest of the unit was split between those stealing surreptitious glances at Morrigan, and those who were outright staring at her. She knew what they were thinking, because she was thinking precisely the same thing.

Why was she in the School of Mundane Arts, when Cadence and Lambeth were in the Arcane? What was so mundane about being a *Wundersmith*?

'Are you any good, Miss?' asked Thaddea, licking chocolate off her fingers and changing the subject altogether. 'On the tightrope?'

That was a rude question, thought Morrigan . . . and not a very clever one, since Miss Cheery was *obviously* good enough to get into the Wundrous Society. She suspected Thaddea was only asking because she was annoyed that *she* wasn't in the School of Arcane Arts. Morrigan doubted she'd enjoyed the phrase, 'just as important and twice as powerful'.

'Pretty good, yeah,' Miss Cheery said with a shrug. 'I've never been a conductor before, though, so I expect I'll be lousy at that, at least to begin with. Go easy on me while I learn the ropes, all right?'

With those words, she smiled directly at Morrigan, and Morrigan couldn't help smiling in return. She already liked Miss Cheery. Feeling braver, she put her hand up. 'Miss, what exactly is a conductor?'

'Oh yeah.' She slapped herself gently on the forehead, laughing. 'Only forgot the most important bit, didn't I? Every new unit in the Wundrous Society has a conductor, who stays with them for their junior scholar years. My job is to get you where you need to be. I obviously mean that in a practical, day-to-day way – I will physically transport you to and from Wunsoc, as the conductor of this Hometrain.

'But in a broader sense, I'm here to help you get *where you need to be* by the end of your junior years, a sort of . . .

guide, I suppose. Here to help you navigate your Wunsoc education. If there's anything you need for your classes, any special equipment or kit or anything, I'll make sure you have it. I've already put in a big order to the Commissariat this week.' She checked off an imaginary list on her fingers. 'Boxing gloves, fireproof armour, a full set of kitchen knives, a sensory deprivation tank . . . you're an interesting lot, aren't you?'

Laughter rippled gently through the unit. Morrigan looked at Hawthorne and grinned. This was really it; it was *really* happening. The first day of the rest of their lives. She couldn't wait to start.

'I'll be working with each of you,' Miss Cheery continued, 'and your patrons, and the Scholar Mistresses, to make sure you have a schedule of classes designed to maximise your potential as Wundrous Society members – and as well-rounded human beings and citizens of the Free State. To help you perfect your knacks, but also to polish the many other gifts you bring to the world. Including – no, *especially* – your good hearts and brave spirits. And I hope more than anything that we can all be friends. It seems the most sensible option, since you're stuck with me for the next five years,' she finished, beaming.

If anyone else had talked about her 'good heart' and 'brave spirit' with a look of such glowing approval, Morrigan might have made gagging noises. But there was something about

Miss Cheery that made her want to simply sit quietly and listen closely to every word she said.

'Right then,' said the conductor, clapping twice. 'Time to get you where you're going. It's orientation time, and you've got a VIP tour with Paximus Luck, you lucky ducks!'

'No WAY,' said Hawthorne, his face lighting up like this had just turned into the best day of his life. 'Paximus Luck? For real?'

'For real,' said Miss Cheery, grinning.

'The real, *actual* Paximus Luck? Plucky?' Mahir clarified. 'The famous master illusionist slash stealth prankster slash vigilante street artist?'

'The very same.'

Mahir and Hawthorne exchanged awestruck grins.

Morrigan had no idea who Paximus Luck was. *Must be a Nevermoor thing,* she thought.

'But I thought his identity was a secret?' said Cadence.

'Yeah, well he's a lot less fussy about that than you'd imagine,' said Miss Cheery. 'At least inside Wunsoc. Pax gives the tour to new scholars every single year, he's been doing it for decades.' The conductor jumped up from her seat and ran to the front of the carriage, where she took command of a series of levers and buttons. The engine gave a great groan and thrummed into life. 'You just wait. He always does an epic first-day trick for the newest unit. Last year he made a herd of woolly mammoths stampede out the front doors of Proudfoot House and then disappear into the forest, like ghosts. Just an illusion of course, but still – it was cool.'

'Wow,' breathed Arch.

'Right, let's get going or you'll be late for the best day of your life,' Miss Cheery called back over her shoulder. 'Any more questions?'

Hawthorne stuck his hand straight up in the air.

'Miss, can we get capes?'

CHAPTER FIVE

Dearborn and Murgatroyd

'Proudfoot Station. Oldest Wunderground station in Nevermoor,' announced Miss Cheery. 'Most people don't even know it's right here on Wunsoc campus, in the middle of the Whinging Woods.'

Hometrain 919 emerged from the Wunderground tunnel into the bustling, buzzing brightness of the loveliest train station Morrigan had ever seen. She counted six platforms, connected by picturesque red-brick footbridges covered in climbing ivy, just like the vines that crept up the walls of Proudfoot House. There were polished wooden benches and small glass-walled waiting rooms. The station was surrounded by thick green forest and the trees curved protectively over the top of it, forming a natural domed canopy. It was still early – the sky was a cool dawn blue – but what little light there was filtered through the foliage in dappled pools. Gas lamps hanging on the platforms were just beginning to extinguish, one by one.

Despite the early hour, three more Hometrains (the numbers 918, 917 and 916 painted on their sides), a full-length steam engine and a knot of small brass train carriages were already parked at various platforms.

Miss Cheery pulled up to Platform 1, which was teeming with Wuns, young and old, and opened the carriage door to let Unit 919 out. The platform walls were covered with sign-up sheets for all sorts of clubs, groups, bands and societies-within-the-Society. Morrigan didn't like the sound of the Goal-Setting and Achieving Club for Highly Ambitious Youth, which met on Monday, Tuesday, Wednesday and Thursday evenings, and all day Sunday. But she thought she could probably get on board with Introverts Utterly Anonymous, which promised no meetings or gatherings of any sort, ever.

There was an air of agitated excitement at the station. People clustered together, talking in whispers. Morrigan heard snatches of passing conversation.

'. . . nobody knows, the Elders aren't saying anything . . .'

'. . . one of his tricks, maybe?'

'. . . never done this before . . .'

Miss Cheery frowned, looking a little disconcerted at the scene.

'Is something wrong, Miss?' asked Morrigan.

'Not really, but it's usually a bit more festive on the first day back after break. And Paximus Luck is usually here waiting for—'

'All right, Marina?' A young man was leaning out the door of Hometrain 917, calling to Miss Cheery. He jumped down onto the platform and jogged over. 'Heard you'd been made a conductor. Congratulations.'

'Cheers, Toby,' she said distractedly. 'What's going on? Where's Plucky?'

Toby looked grim. 'Nobody knows. He disappeared overnight.'

Miss Cheery made a face. 'But that's impossible.' Morrigan was struck by a sudden memory of Jupiter's nearly identical conversation with his friend Israfel on Spring's Eve, about Cassiel, the angel who had gone missing. 'Plucky wouldn't disappear the night before an orientation tour. He's never missed one, not in twenty-five years.'

Another disappearance.

A vague and nameless dread began to coil in Morrigan's stomach like a snake. It was a feeling she was familiar with. The feeling that something, somewhere, had gone terribly wrong, and that she might be to blame.

Stop that, Morrigan told herself fiercely, and she shook her head as if to shake the awful thought right out of it. *This is nothing to do with you. You. Are. Not. Cursed.*

She wished she could get a note to Jupiter.

Miss Cheery slumped, looking hopelessly around the station. 'Who's taking the tour, then?'

'Er . . .' Toby had the air of someone about to deliver truly dreadful news.

Miss Cheery led Unit 919 out of the station and pointed up a wide, tree-covered path that took a straight line all the way to Proudfoot House, looking dignified in the distance. 'Stay on the path, yeah? And, whatever you do, do *not* stray into the Whinging Woods.'

'Are they dangerous, Miss?' asked Francis, peering nervously through the undergrowth.

'No, just annoying.' Miss Cheery leaned in, as if she didn't want the trees to overhear. 'Once they start moaning, they never shut up, so don't show any sympathy. Now, listen up, you lot. It seems that, er, one of the Scholar Mistresses will be giving your tour. Ms Dearborn or Mrs Murgatroyd will meet you on the steps of Proudfoot House, so –' she paused, sighing heavily, ' just . . . just behave yourselves, keep your heads down and muddle through, all right?'

With those inspiring final words, the conductor waved them off from the station and Unit 919 began the short, now slightly frightening walk to Proudfoot House.

Morrigan thought she heard a low, resentful muttering somewhere in the trees far off to her left ('. . . traipsing through here with their great clodhoppers this early in the morning, no respect . . .'), but following Miss Cheery's advice, ignored it. She and Hawthorne fell to the back of the group, talking quietly.

'I can't *believe* it,' grumbled Hawthorne. 'We nearly got to meet Paximus Luck, and he goes and disappears! Of all the rotten luck. Unless – oh!' Something dawned on his face. 'Ohhhh. Wait. Do you think this is just part of the prank?'

'Maybe,' said Morrigan doubtfully. 'Bit of a lame prank.'

'Nan told me all about the Scholar Mistresses,' Hawthorne continued. 'She said Murgatroyd's a proper menace.'

(There was a rustle of leaves to their right, a pitiful moan. A creaky, muffled voice from the trees: 'Oof, are my branches ever aching today . . .')

'That's what Dame Chanda said too,' Morrigan said a little louder, trying to drown out the Whinging Woods. 'Sort of.'

'Nan said if I'm going to make trouble—'

Morrigan snorted. '*If?*'

'—then I'd better hope it's Dearborn who finds out, not Murgatroyd. She said it's best to make yourself as unnotice-able as possible when it comes to Murgatroyd. I told her – Nan, firstly I'm insulted that you would assume I'm going to make trouble.' He grinned sideways at Morrigan, who snorted again. 'And secondly, I'll obviously just have to make sure neither of them find out, won't I?'

The sky was lightening when the Wundrous Society's newest scholars emerged from the woodland path. As they climbed the sloping, frost-covered hill towards Proudfoot House, a line of pale gold on the horizon turned to pink, blossoming in the sky like a gigantic flower and illuminating the red-brick façade.

A woman stood on the steps of Proudfoot House, waiting to welcome them. Or not *welcome them,* exactly, Morrigan saw as they came nearer. More . . . *stare at them in chilly silence.*

She was still and statuesque, dressed in typical Wundrous Society black, but for the grey shirtfront tucked beneath her cloak. Her hair was so blonde it was almost silver, piled on top of her head in an old-fashioned topknot that made her seem much older than her young and unworn face suggested, Morrigan thought. She had the unblemished, moon-like complexion of someone who took excellent care of herself and probably spent an awful lot of time indoors. Her eyes were ice-blue; her cheekbones sharp as knives. These things combined could have made her beautiful. Instead, the overall effect was of a glacier in human form: cold, hard, unassailable. She looked down at them from the top step of Proudfoot House as if they were insects she was planning to squash beneath her elegant black shoes.

This must be Murgatroyd, Morrigan thought. Remembering the advice Nan had given Hawthorne, she tried to shrink back and make herself unnoticeable.

'Good morning, Unit 919,' said the woman. Her voice made Morrigan think of a sheet of glass: perfectly smooth all along its surface, with a sharp edge concealed at the end. 'I am Dulcinea Dearborn.'

Morrigan swallowed a small sound of surprise.

'I am the Scholar Mistress for the School of Mundane Arts,' she continued. 'Yet, despite the infinite responsibilities and workload that come with such a title – and thanks to the untimely disappearance of one irresponsible buffoon – the Elders, in their wisdom, have appointed me as your tour guide today. I console myself with the knowledge that you'll enjoy it even less than I will.

'You may call me Ms Dearborn, or Scholar Mistress. You may not call me Mrs Dearborn, or Miss Dearborn, or Professor Dearborn, or Mother, or Mama, or Mummy, or any other derivative thereof. I am not your parent. I am not your nursemaid. I have no time for childish problems. Should any arise, you will either take them up with your unit conductor, or squash them deep down in the pit of your soul where they shall no longer bother you. Have I made myself clear?'

Unit 919 nodded mutely as one. After the warm, joyful welcome from Miss Cheery and the cosiness of Hometrain, meeting Ms Dearborn felt like being doused in ice water. Morrigan couldn't help but wonder which poor, deluded scholar had ever accidentally called this arctic shelf of a woman 'Mummy'.

'The thing you must remember above all else, scholars, is this: You. Are. Not. Important. It is the same every year: the newest unit of scholars is inducted to our ranks, the latest nine in a long and unbroken line of the Free State's most Wundrously Wundrous individuals. You come with the baggage of a lifetime of specialness, of having been the most talented, the cleverest, the most adored and admired in your humdrum little families, schools and communities.'

Morrigan tried not to scoff. She deeply, vehemently, wholeheartedly – but, of course, silently – disagreed with this assertion.

'And when you arrive on my doorstep,' Dearborn continued, 'you expect the same treatment. You expect to be coddled and cooed over. Lauded and loved. You want all the busy, important grown-ups who walk the grounds of Wunsoc to stop in their tracks and admire you. To exclaim, "Oh! It's our newest batch of little Wunders! Aren't they all so very marvellous?"' She paused, looking at each one of them in turn, giving a sickly-sweet smile that warped into a sneer. 'Well, you can forget that. Remember: YOU. ARE. NOT. IMPORTANT. Not in these hallowed halls. Nobody's going to hold your little handies or wipe your little nosies. Everybody at Wunsoc has a job to get on with – every junior and senior scholar, every graduate, every teacher, every patron, every Elder and every Master. That includes you. Your job is to be respectful of your betters, to do as you're told and to constantly improve yourselves, ready for the day when – if you are lucky – you might be called on to make yourselves useful. Understand?'

Morrigan didn't. She wasn't sure what Ms Dearborn meant by 'make yourselves useful'. But in that moment, she would rather put her hand into a tank full of flesh-eating piranhas than ask for an explanation, so she murmured along with the rest of them, 'Yes, Scholar Mistress.'

'Very convincing.' And with that, Dearborn turned on her heel and headed straight for the grand entrance of Proudfoot House, evidently expecting them to follow. 'Our academic schedule follows the calendar year and is broken into two terms, the first beginning in spring and the second in autumn. During the summer holidays you are expected . . .'

They trooped up the steps as the lecture droned on, and Hawthorne leaned over to Morrigan. 'Lovely speech,' he whispered in her ear. 'I feel all warm and fuzzy inside.'

⸻

Their first lesson was to discover that deep beneath the five bright, elegant storeys of Proudfoot House, the true halls of Wunsoc were dark and labyrinthine, and never-ending.

'There are nine subterranean levels,' said Ms Dearborn, leading them from the entrance hall down a long, echoing hallway. Her voice was brittle and business-like, her shiny black court shoes loud against the wooden floorboards.

Morrigan, Hawthorne and the rest of the unit had to walk twice as fast as usual just to keep up with her.

'Level Sub-One is dedicated primarily to dining, sleeping and recreational facilities for academic staff and visiting adult Society members. Off-limits to you. On Sub-Two you will find the dining hall for junior and senior scholars, the Commissariat and boarding rooms for senior scholars, who may live on campus if they wish.'

A whirlwind tour of Sub-Two gave Morrigan a passing impression of daily life at Wunsoc. The scholars' dining hall was a busy circular space with a comfortable, lived-in air, filled with a random collection of tables and chairs. At one end, small café-style wrought-iron tables jostled for space with chipped, paint-specked rectangular slabs of wood and mismatched stools, while at the other well-worn armchairs were dotted around an enormous hearth.

A few of the tables were occupied by senior scholars eating breakfast, reading the morning papers and talking over shared pots of tea. Morrigan almost had to hold Hawthorne back when he caught a whiff of bacon.

'I haven't even had breakfast yet! Can you *imagine*?' he whispered to her, scandalised. 'Went through the stupid door before I thought of it, didn't I?'

'Mmm.' Morrigan wasn't really listening. She thought she could sense an urgency in the senior scholars' murmured chatter, and wondered if they were discussing the disappearance of Paximus Luck. Ms Dearborn led them through the dining room and out the other side to a bank of large brass spheres hanging from a rail, then whirled round to face them.

'Our internal railpod network travels in all directions across all subterranean levels,' she said in a bored, almost mechanical voice. 'These pods will take you anywhere in Wunsoc, so long as you have permission to be there, as well as to selected Wunderground stations outside the campus. Junior scholars are only to travel off-campus with explicit permission from a Scholar Mistress or their patron. Your imprint knows where you're allowed to go. Strict maximum of one dozen passengers per pod.

'Levels Sub-Three, Sub-Four and Sub-Five comprise educational facilities for the School of Mundane Arts. Levels Sub-Six, Sub-Seven and Sub-Eight are dedicated to the School of Arcane Arts. Sub-Nine is out of bounds to all scholars.

'The seven of you who fall under my dominion as Mundane Scholar Mistress will obviously have no need to venture beyond Sub-Five, and therefore your permissions will extend no further than that. Miss Blackburn and Miss Amara – you will both be taking classes in the School of Arcane Arts. Mrs Murgatroyd, the Arcane Scholar Mistress, will be along later this morning to take you there.'

Once she'd ushered them all inside a single, spherical brass pod, Ms Dearborn pressed her *W* imprint to its glowing counterpart on the wall, then pulled a series of levers in a complex pattern that Morrigan tried – and failed – to memorise. They sank several levels down at a gut-churning, ear-popping speed. Then – to everyone's surprise but Ms Dearborn's – the pod was wrenched forward, sharply to the left, backwards and then left again . . . then up, up, up in a lurching zig-zag motion, the lights above the door flashing in a chaotic pattern all the while.

At last the pod came to an abrupt halt and the nine members of Unit 919 all smashed into the wall. Ms Dearborn was tall enough to steady herself by holding on to one of the looped leather handles hanging down from the ceiling, and she didn't seem bothered that none of the children could reach them.

'Sub-Three. School of Mundane Arts.' The pod door opened and she led them down a long, empty corridor with a polished wooden floor. Morrigan felt dizzy and nauseated, but she tried to keep up.

'This level is dedicated entirely to what we call the Practicalities,' continued Ms Dearborn. 'Medicine, cartography, meteorology, astronomy, gastronomy, engineering, unnimal husbandry and so on. Those everyday, earthbound interests most vital to keeping the world running. Also on Sub-Three you'll find the laboratories, the observatory, the Map Room, lecture theatres one through nine, the zoological facilities, the test kitchens and, of course, the hospital.'

The Scholar Mistress took them into a darkened lecture theatre where a professor called Dr Bramble was giving a talk on the 'Ethical Responsibilities of the Modern Unnimologist' to some visiting Society members from around the Seven Pockets. Beside her on the stage was what looked, at first, like a huge pile of dirty white rags in a basket, but turned out to be—

'A Magnificat!' said Morrigan, nudging Hawthorne's side. Ms Dearborn instantly turned to glare at her, and Morrigan pressed her lips together, staring determinedly at the stage below until she felt the Scholar Mistress's gaze shift away.

'It isn't *enough* to believe one is acting in the best interest of a species,' Dr Bramble was saying to her audience. She reached out to give the creature an affectionate scratch under its chin. 'One must consider the *individual*.'

'It's not as big as Fen,' Hawthorne whispered from the side of his mouth.

'I think it's a baby,' replied Morrigan, as the cat bared its fangs at the audience in a manner that was half threatening, half adorable. 'Oh, *look*!'

But Ms Dearborn whisked them on, and down to the next floor.

'Humanities,' she announced when they reached Sub-Four. 'Comprising philosophy, diplomacy, languages, history, literature, music, art and theatre.'

She led them through dozens of classrooms, studios, art galleries, music rooms and theatres on Sub-Four before they made their way down to Sub-Five, home to what Dearborn referred to as the Extremities – the third and final branch of the School of Mundane Arts.

Whereas the previous floors had the calm, formal atmosphere of a museum or university – all broad corridors, high ceilings and polished wood floors – Sub-Five had the unpredictable, slightly chaotic air of a place where anything could happen.

Dearborn showed them an entire wing dedicated to learning the craft of espionage. (they caught five minutes of a workshop titled 'Faking Your Own Death'), a noisy martial arts dojo (where, on the first morning of term, several scholars already had broken bones) and – to Hawthorne's delight – the enormous, cavern-like dragon stables and arena where he would be spending much of his time.

Morrigan was just thinking that Sub-Five felt a bit like the Hotel Deucalion, when an older boy came running towards them from the other end of the hall.

'Scholar Mistress!' shrieked the boy as he ran to catch up with Ms Dearborn and the group, his long, braided hair flying behind him, eyes bright and wild. 'Scholar Mistress, please may I talk to you?'

'Not now, Whitaker.'

'*Please*, Ms Dearborn,' said the boy, leaning over, hands on waist, trying to catch his breath. 'Please, you've got to talk to Murgatroyd. She said she's going to shave my head tomorrow because my unit failed our last Civic Duty exam. But it's not my fault, she—'

'Entirely your own problem.'

'But she said –' the boy whimpered, '– she said she's sharpening her razor blade tonight.'

'I don't doubt it.'

'*Please*, couldn't you talk to her or—'

'Don't be absurd. Of course I can't talk to her,' hissed Ms Dearborn. She closed her eyes and cracked her neck to the side. Morrigan winced at the sound. The older boy flinched away, drawing in a sharp breath. 'You are a whitesleeve, Whitaker. A student in the School of Arcane Arts. *Must* I remind you that I am not your Scholar Mistress? It's up to Mrs Murgatroyd to discipline her students as she sees fit. Now, get to class before you make it worse for yourself. She'll be here any minute.'

The boy backed away from the Scholar Mistress looking sick, before turning and running back the way he came. Morrigan swallowed as she watched him leave. Was the notorious Murgatroyd *really* going to shave his head? Was that *allowed*? She glanced around – the rest of Unit 919 looked equally distressed.

And tired too. Having woken at dawn, walked what felt like hundreds of miles through the maze-like subterranean campus, and eaten only two biscuits *all day*, Morrigan thought she might simply collapse where she stood and be unable to get up again. Just when she'd decided she *must* ask when the tour would be over (or when they'd at least be fed), Ms Dearborn brought them back to a bank of railpods.

'Blackburn and Amara,' said Ms Dearborn. Cadence returned Ms Dearborn's unflinching gaze, but Lambeth was looking up at the ceiling, frowning. Morrigan wasn't even certain she knew she was being addressed. 'Mrs Murgatroyd, the Arcane Scholar Mistress, will be along shortly to continue your tour of levels Sub-Six through Sub-Eight.'

Part of Morrigan felt envious that Cadence and Lambeth would see parts of Wunsoc that were forbidden to her and the others . . . but another, much more insistent part of her hoped this meant the tour was nearly over for her and her fellow greysleeves.

'Once Mrs Murgatroyd arrives,' continued Dearborn, 'the rest of you will make your own way back through the subterranean levels and outside to the steps of Proudfoot House, where your conductor will be waiting to escort you home. I trust you can manage to find your way back to the ground floor from here.'

No chance, thought Morrigan. She turned to Hawthorne, who looked equally alarmed. Were they supposed to have memorised what she did in the railpod with all those levers?

'How come they get to go home already, when we have to stay?' asked Cadence.

'Oh, *poor* you,' snapped Thaddea, rolling her eyes in disgust. 'Must be *so* hard, having such a special-snowflake talent that you get to see three whole floors the rest of us are banned from. I'm positively *aching* with sympath—'

'Oh dear,' Lambeth murmured, still gazing up at the ceiling. She held up a finger, just like she'd done at the station. It was hard to tell if she was demanding silence or testing the direction of the wind. 'Here she comes.'

'Can somebody *please* make her stop that?' muttered Mahir. 'She's creeping me out.'

'Quiet.' The Scholar Mistress's voice hadn't lost its bite, but Morrigan thought she suddenly seemed nervous. She was pulling at the cuff on her left sleeve in a tense, agitated way. Morrigan wondered if she too was afraid of the infamous Mrs Murgatroyd. She was not at all comforted by this thought.

'While we're waiting, let's go over some housekeeping,' continued Ms Dearborn. 'You are responsible for ensuring you have the correct clothing and educational items for your lessons.' She paused here, closing her eyes momentarily and cracking her neck to the side. Morrigan winced. 'Should you require something, be it rosin for your instrument, or a set of scrubs, or a machete –' she eyeballed Archan, Anah and Thaddea by turns, '– then you must either ask your conductor to arrange it, or make a formal written request yourself, using the forms provided at the . . . at the Commissariat.'

Here Dearborn paused once again, and something strange happened. Squeezing her eyes tight as if to block out a bright light, she hunched her shoulders up high and rolled them back slowly, twisting her neck like an eel underwater. Morrigan heard the woman's spine crack all the way down, a series of tiny *pops* in quick succession, and she cringed; the sound of it made her skin crawl.

She glanced around at the others. Their faces mirrored her own rapidly deepening horror. What was *wrong* with the Scholar Mistress?

'If your failure to do so . . . results in . . . your exclusion from lessons,' Dearborn continued, eyes still closed, her chin jutting out from her neck at a strange and unnatural angle, 'then it is entirely –' she made a funny, gurgling noise in the back of her throat, such an awful sound that Morrigan jumped backwards in fright, '– entirely your own lookout, and you'll find . . . there isn't a soul in this campus who will . . . sympathise . . . with your plight.' The glass-slick voice was all but gone. She spoke in a frightening, guttural rasp that had an awful singsong musicality about it. It sounded . . . *wrong*. 'Correct, Mrs Murgatroyd?'

Dearborn opened her eyes.

Morrigan gasped. The rest of her unit had turned in the other direction, confused, expecting to see Mrs Murgatroyd the Arcane Scholar Mistress approaching. Morrigan alone had noticed what they'd all missed.

Dearborn was . . . different. On their own, the changes were subtle: a sloping curve to her shoulders, a deepening of the hollow in her cheeks. Her ice-blue eyes had lightened to a dead, murky, pale grey, the colour of a flat winter sky, and sunk further into her skull. The topknot on her head was no longer a shining silver-blonde, but *white* – stark and stripped of colour. Her lips – purpling and cracked – peeled back in an unpleasant leer, revealing a mouthful of sharp brownish teeth.

Morrigan fixed her wide eyes firmly on this new face, watching the ghastly transformation unfold. Her creeping, confused horror turned to understanding.

'Just so, Ms Dearborn,' rasped the woman, answering her own question.

So *this* was Murgatroyd.

The students of the Mundane Arts began to edge their way out and, not for the first time that day, Morrigan was very glad to be a greysleeve.

CHAPTER SIX

Missteps, Blunders, Fiascos, Monstrosities and Devastations

'Dragonriding ALL MORNING!' shouted Hawthorne the next day, throwing a fist in the air. 'YES!'

They were pulling into Proudfoot Station, but Miss Cheery had to wait for the two trains in front to drop off their scholars and clear out from the platform before she could move into place and open the doors of Hometrain 919.

'I'm glad you're excited,' Miss Cheery said to Hawthorne. The members of Unit 919 had spent the trip to Wunsoc passing their timetables around, excitedly comparing the many interesting workshops, lectures and classes they'd be attending that week. Morrigan was particularly looking forward to her lesson on Thursday morning, the curiously titled *Opening a Dialogue with the Dead.* 'But don't wear yourself out too much in the arena. Notice you've got a three-hour class in Dragontongue after lunch?' She tapped a finger on his timetable. 'You wanna be fresh for that; it's a tricky language.'

Hawthorne's fist dropped from the air. He looked down at his timetable, nose scrunching up. 'Why would I need to learn Dragontongue?'

Miss Cheery widened her eyes at him. 'I *know*. Nevermoor's most promising junior dragonrider, trying to communicate with the ancient reptiles who take his life in their talons every day? What a mad idea.' She snorted. 'Hawthorne, don't you reckon it might be *useful* to talk to a dragon?'

'But . . . I *do* talk to them,' said Hawthorne. 'I've been riding since I was three. If you don't believe I can make a dragon take orders, come and watch me—'

'Oh, I know you can,' said Miss Cheery. 'I saw your trial. But all that time you've been learning how to make a dragon understand *you*, have you ever tried to understand a dragon in return?'

Hawthorne looked at her as if she'd sprouted antlers.

'Dragontongue's an *amazing* language,' she continued. 'I learned some myself when I was a junior scholar. And look – Mahir will be taking the class with you. That'll be fun!'

Hawthorne leaned over Mahir's shoulder to see.

'But he only has to do one hour!' Hawthorne protested.

'Well . . . I thought it might be decent to give you a head start, that's all. Our Mr Ibrahim already knows a bit of Dragontongue – don't you, Mahir?'

'*H'chath shka-lev*,' said Mahir, bowing his head seriously.

Miss Cheery looked impressed. '*Machar lo'k dachva-lev*,' she replied, bowing in return.

'What does that mean?' Hawthorne grumbled, eyeing the pair of them with suspicion and, Morrigan suspected, a little jealousy.

'It's a Draconian greeting,' Miss Cheery replied, and when Hawthorne looked even more confused, she added, 'Draconian's just another name for Dragontongue. *H'chath shka-lev* means *long may you burn*.'

Hawthorne made a face, and so did Morrigan. *Long may you burn* sounded more like a threat than a greeting.

'And the polite response is *Machar lo'k dachva-lev*, meaning *I burn brighter knowing you*,' continued Miss Cheery. 'To dragons it's like . . . you're wishing someone good health, and they're thanking you for your friendship in return.'

Thaddea was scouring her classes, looking increasingly annoyed. 'Miss, how come I don't have any cool dragon stuff in my timetable? It's not fair. I love dragons.'

The conductor took a seat on the couch next to Thaddea, leaning in to look over her shoulder. 'Well, you do have other cool stuff.'

'Like what?'

'Look – roller derby on Friday afternoon, with Linda.'

Thaddea looked doubtful. 'What's so cool about Linda?'

'She plays roller derby, for starters. And bass guitar. And she's a centaur, that's pretty cool. Oh, and look – you and Morrigan have a workshop in Magnificat Care with Dr Bramble on Tues— oh. No.' She frowned and took out a pen to draw a line through the class. 'Sorry, I need to update this. Poor old Dr Bramble's Magnificub has gone missing. She's distraught.'

'Missing?' said Morrigan, looking up from her own timetable.

'Mmm. She swears it was stolen, but I'm pretty sure it did a runner . . . I mean, Magnificats as a species are known for their independent streak. The poor thing was probably sick of being cooped up.' Miss Cheery nudged Thaddea, who was looking sulky. 'Don't worry, I'll find you something else just as interesting. I promise.'

Morrigan frowned. This was the third disappearance she'd heard about that week. Cassiel, Paximus Luck, and now the Magnificub.

'Miss,' Francis piped up. 'What's this class – *Recognising Mesmerism*?'

'I've got that one too,' said Anah. 'Wednesday morning.'

Morrigan checked; she had the same class.

'So do I,' said Thaddea.

'And me,' added Mahir. 'Eight o'clock.'

'Ah,' said the conductor. 'Yeah. The Elders think this'll be a useful skill for all of you to learn, since you have a mesmerist in your unit.'

Cadence's head shot up. She scowled and gave a little huff of indignation, but Miss Cheery ignored this, her expression calm and neutral.

Hawthorne looked bewildered. 'We've got a what?'

'A mesmerist.'

'Huh.' He frowned. 'Do we?'

'Yup,' said Miss Cheery, as patiently as ever but with the *tiniest* hint of a sigh. 'Cadence Blackburn is a mesmerist. She's sitting right next to you.'

Hawthorne turned to Cadence and gave a little start of surprise. 'Oh. Blimey.'

'Yeah, exactly,' said Miss Cheery. 'A course in recognising mesmerism is required for all of you, to help you remember your new friend, and so that you know what to look for when Cadence is putting her excellent knack to use.'

'But Miss,' said Cadence, looking appalled, 'how am I supposed to mesmerise them if—'

'That's just the point, Cadence,' said Miss Cheery gently. 'You're not *supposed* to use your knack against your unit. Sisters and brothers, remember? Loyal for life?'

'I said I'd be *loyal*, I didn't say I'd never mesmerise anyone! How come they all get to use their knacks just as they like but I can't?'

'That's not true. Arch isn't allowed to pickpocket any of you. Francis isn't allowed to make you sob into your soup. You've all sworn an oath.'

Cadence gave her a calculating look. 'Since I've sworn an oath then why do you have to teach them how to recognise mesmerism? If you trust Arch not to pickpocket anyone, why don't you trust that I won't mesmerise them?'

Miss Cheery glanced down, looking as if she thought Cadence had a point. She pressed her lips together for a moment. 'I understand your frustration, Cadence. No, really – I do. But mesmerism and pickpocketing are two very different knacks, with very different potential for consequences. Some of the patrons thought—'

'That I couldn't be trusted,' Cadence finished for her, eyes blazing. 'That I'm a mesmerist, so that makes me a criminal. Typical.'

Morrigan thought back to the Show Trial, when a film of Cadence's various mesmerist exploits had, in fact, shown her vandalising public property and handcuffing a police officer with the officer's own handcuffs. She raised an eyebrow at Hawthorne, but didn't say anything.

'Nobody thinks you're a criminal, Cadence. I promise. They're just being extra cautious.'

But Cadence didn't look at all placated. Morrigan thought she'd been off with them all morning. Earlier at Station 919, Morrigan and her fellow greysleeves had all been desperate to know what was on Sub-Six, Sub-Seven and Sub-Eight, but when Morrigan asked, Cadence refused to even acknowledge the question. That said, Lambeth had done the same when Thaddea questioned her, so perhaps they'd been instructed not to say anything.

As soon as the Hometrain doors opened Cadence stormed off, over the footbridge and out of the station. The other scholars lingered on the platform, seeming to forget about Cadence again, chatting amiably with one another, still comparing timetables.

'What have you got this morning?' Hawthorne asked Morrigan.

'*Mindfulness and Meditation*,' Morrigan read aloud, 'on Sub-Four. Then *Stealth, Evasion and Concealment* on Sub-Five after lunch.'

'I've got that this afternoon, too,' said Hawthorne. 'Look – *Stealth, Evasion and Concealment*. I'm not sure I need that class, though. I mean, who do you know that's stealthier than me?'

Morrigan tilted her head. 'Shall I list them?'

'CONDUCTOR CHEERY!'

A cutting cry heralded the arrival of Ms Dearborn. The Scholar Mistress was stalking towards their carriage, clutching a piece of paper tightly in her fist. Hawthorne, Morrigan and a few of the other scholars stopped in their tracks. There was something about Dearborn's voice that made it impossible not to.

Miss Cheery stuck her head out of the carriage door. 'Scholar Mistress.' She smiled uncertainly. 'Morning. How can I help?'

Dearborn scowled at her, a deep frown knotting her forehead. 'We need to discuss *this*.' She tossed the piece of paper at Miss Cheery, who scrambled to catch it.

'Morrigan's timetable,' she observed. Morrigan froze at the mention of her name. 'Is there something wrong with it?'

'Quite a few things, yes.' Dearborn snatched the timetable back from Miss Cheery with a sneer. 'Almost all of them, in fact. *Mindfulness and Meditation* with Cadel Clary? No.' She took out a pen and drew a line through the class with a theatrical swipe. '*Self-Defence Through Unarmed Combat?* I think not.' Swipe. '*Treasure Diving for Beginners? Stealth, Evasion and Concealment?* No and no. What *exactly* are you trying to turn this girl into?' she hissed. 'A weapon of mass destruction?'

Morrigan frowned. She'd thought all *her* classes sounded relatively tame, compared to some of the other scholars' timetables. On Anah's she'd spotted a master class called *How to Stop a Human Heart (Temporarily)*, and Cadence would be taking several rather alarmingly titled workshops that included *Identifying Arsenic, The Art of Interrogation, Amateur Surveillance Techniques* and *Bomb-Defusing Basics.*

'What's wrong with *Mindfulness and Meditation?*' Miss Cheery asked.

'The girl is a Wun—' Dearborn caught herself, looking over her shoulder before continuing in a whisper, 'The girl is a Wundersmith, Miss Cheery. Is that what we want, a *mindful* Wundersmith who could use her very *mindful* mind to *mindfully* send us all to an early grave?'

Morrigan almost laughed out loud at the idea that she could meditate the Scholar Mistress to death. Hawthorne had less self-control and had to cough to cover up his snort.

Miss Cheery didn't seem to find it so funny. Morrigan saw a stormy expression flash across her face, but the conductor took a moment to compose herself before speaking. 'What classes would *you* like Morrigan to take, Scholar Mistress?'

'I've amended the timetable,' Dearborn said shortly, handing her a second piece of paper. 'See that you implement the changes immediately.' She turned to go and was nearly at the footbridge when Miss Cheery called out.

'Scholar Mistress – I think you've made a mistake. This timetable only has one class on it.'

Dearborn stared back at her. 'I don't make mistakes, Miss Cheery. Good day.'

As soon as the Scholar Mistress marched away, Morrigan and Hawthorne hurried back aboard Hometrain, peeking over Miss Cheery's shoulder to see what had caused her look of dismay.

'*History of Heinous Wundrous Acts* with Professor Hemingway Q. Onstald.' Morrigan was confused, and sorely disappointed. 'Is that . . . is that it? Just that one class? Every day?'

'Apparently,' said Miss Cheery in a voice tight with controlled emotion. 'I've never heard of it before, so it must be a new class they created just for you. How very . . . exciting!'

But Morrigan wasn't fooled.

Miss Cheery gave her an anxious smile. 'Better go on now, or you'll be late.'

Hemingway Q. Onstald was more human than tortoise, but he was still a *lot* tortoise.

Morrigan knew that in Wunimal circles, the professor would be considered a Wunimal Minor – meaning that he had more humanoid characteristics than unnimal (unlike the almost entirely bullish Elder Saga, an obvious Wunimal Major). Living at the Hotel Deucalion had given her a solid education in Wunimal etiquette. They often hosted Wunimal guests, and both Jupiter and Kedgeree had made sure Morrigan understood the difference between Wunimals and unnimals. Wunimals were sentient, self-aware, intelligent creatures capable of complexities such as language, invention and artistic expression, just like humans. Unnimals were not.

Morrigan had also learned the proper way to address them – that a Wunimal bear, for instance, was not referred to as a bear (which would be highly insulting), but a *bearwun*. To confuse a bear with a bearwun was an *enormous* and near unforgivable faux pas. Morrigan knew this because she had accidentally done so and it had taken mountains of apologies, charm and complimentary picnic baskets for Jupiter and Kedgeree to appease their valued bearwun guest. (Her 'bearwun, get one free' joke didn't go down very well either.)

Fenestra, on the other hand, was technically neither Wunimal nor unnimal. Morrigan had asked her about it, and Fen had replied scathingly, 'Would you ask a human if they were a Wunimal? Would you ask a centaur if they were an unnimal? No. I'm a Magnificat. End of.' Fen had accepted Morrigan's bewildered apology, but only *after* replacing the feathers in her pillow with a collection of hair pulled from every shower drain in the hotel.

It was hard to ignore the enormous domed carapace on Onstald's back, or his leathery greenish-grey skin, or the fact that at the end of his trousers there were round, scaly, soft-padded tortoise feet where one might expect a smart pair of brogues to be.

The rest of him, though, was quite ordinary. His head was mostly skin, with a few strands of white hair poking up here and there, and his tiny, pale green, pink-rimmed eyes squinted as if he desperately needed glasses. He wore formal black academic robes over an old-fashioned suit, complete with plaid bowtie and a mismatched waistcoat bearing stains down the front.

His classroom in the Humanities Department on Sub-Four was just the sort of place you'd expect a part-man, part-tortoise to spend his days teaching (if, Morrigan thought, she'd ever taken the time to consider such a thing before now). There were rows of wooden desks, of course, with straight-backed chairs, and the walls were lined with bookshelves filled to bursting with serious-looking clothbound volumes. But beneath it all, where there ought to have been floorboards, there was instead cool, grassy ground, and one corner of the room was taken up entirely by a pond.

Professor Onstald was perched on a stool by the blackboard when Morrigan entered his classroom. He peered at her over his nose and indicated a desk in the front row, heaving long, slow, deep breaths that rattled in his chest. Morrigan sat, and waited.

'You,' he finally said, ponderously, pausing for breath before continuing, 'you are the girl the Elders say is . . . a Wundersmith.'

He didn't have any teeth at all and his wrinkled, gummy lips seemed to collapse into his mouth like a sinkhole. Tiny bits of spittle gathered in the corners of his mouth. Morrigan wrinkled her nose, trying not to imagine the spit flying off and hitting her in the face.

'Yes,' she said, leaning back as a precaution. 'That's me.'

She was surprised at the question. She'd thought only the Scholar Mistresses and Miss Cheery were supposed to know about her . . . little problem.

He frowned down at her. 'Yes . . . *professor.*'

'Yes, professor.'

'Hmm.' He nodded, gazing into the middle distance.

For some time after that, he said nothing. Morrigan started to wonder if he'd forgotten where he was. She was just about to clear her throat when he took a great wheezing breath and looked back at her. 'And do you . . . understand . . . what that means?'

'Not really,' Morrigan admitted, then added hastily, 'professor.'

'You have heard of . . . the last living . . . Wundersmith, I . . . presume?'

'Ezra Squall?'

Professor Onstald nodded, a tiny little bobbing nod that went on and on for some time, almost like he'd lost control of his head and was waiting for it to stop. 'What do you . . . know of . . . him?'

Morrigan sighed quietly. 'I know that he's the evillest man who ever lived and everyone hates him.'

'Correct,' said Professor Onstald in a heavy voice. His eyes drooped a little; Morrigan thought he might fall asleep. There was also the possibility that *she* might fall asleep. 'That is correct. And do you know . . . why . . . he was the . . . evillest—'

'Because he was a man who became a monster,' Morrigan interrupted. She didn't wish to be rude, but she also couldn't bear to wait for him any longer. 'A man who made monsters of his own.' She was quoting what Kedgeree had told her about Ezra Squall the year before, and she tried to make her voice dispassionate, but couldn't quite manage it.

The truth was, no matter what Jupiter said, no matter how much he insisted that being a Wundersmith didn't mean being evil, Morrigan found it hard to shake the thought that somewhere, deep down, she was just like Ezra Squall. Hadn't Squall told her as much? Hadn't he looked into her eyes, and smiled, and been pleased? *I see you, Morrigan Crow. There is black ice at the heart of you.*

'And because of the Courage Square Massacre,' Morrigan added as an afterthought. 'When he killed the people who tried to stop him taking over Nevermoor.'

Professor Onstald nodded again, drawing another rattling breath. 'That is . . . correct. But . . . that is not . . . all.'

The professor stood up from his stool painfully slowly, and Morrigan winced as she heard his bones groan and creak. He shuffled inch by inch across the dusty classroom and, approximately ten years later, arrived at the bookshelves on the far wall. He lifted from the shelves such an enormous tome that it looked like it might fall to the ground and take the old tortoisewun with it. Morrigan leapt up from her chair to help him, and together they carried it to a desk and dropped it down with a great *oof*, a cloud of dust puffing out from its pages.

The professor wiped away a thick coat of dust from the cover with the sleeve of his academic robe. Morrigan squinted at the old-fashioned writing.

MISSTEPS,

BLUNDERS,

FIASCOS,

MONSTROSITIES

AND DEVASTATIONS:

AN ABRIDGED HISTORY OF THE

WUNDROUS ACT SPECTRUM

By Hemingway Q. Onstald

'An abridged history,' Morrigan read aloud. 'What does that mean?'

'It means . . . edited. Abbreviated. Shortened. The full . . . history . . . would undoubtedly fill several dozen . . . more volumes.'

Morrigan raised her eyebrows at this, silently thanking her lucky stars that he had only bothered to write an abridged version.

'I have been . . . instructed . . . to oversee your thorough . . . education . . . in the history of your . . . predecessors.' Onstald paused here, coughing from all the dust, and it turned into such a dreadful fit that for a moment Morrigan was afraid she might have to report to the Scholar Mistress that her teacher had died ten minutes into their first lesson. Eventually, however, he got his lungs under control and continued. 'So that you have a full and . . . unflinching grasp . . . of the dangers and . . . disasters . . . Wundersmiths present to . . . us all.'

Morrigan's heart sank. *This* was what she'd be learning? All about the many terrible things Ezra Squall had done?

How tedious.

She already knew he was a monster. Why did she need a book about his many evil exploits?

Professor Onstald tapped the cover of the colossal book with his fingertips. 'You will . . . read . . . chapters one to . . . three . . . for the rest of . . . your lesson.' He checked his fob watch. 'You have . . . three . . . hours.'

While he tottered – slowly, slowly – from the room, Morrigan stared miserably at the cover of *An Abridged History of the Wundrous Act Spectrum* for some time before at last, with a sigh, she opened it.

CHAPTER ONE

Chronicling the misdeeds of the First-Line Wundersmith, Brilliance Amadeo, her predecessor the Wundersmith Deng Li, his predecessor the Wundersmith Christobel Fallon-Dunham, her predecessor the . . .

'Who are these people?' Morrigan called out to Professor Onstald just as he reached the door.

'Hmm?'

Jupiter had told her that there were other Wundersmiths. But she'd never really thought about any of them as actual people. It was quite enough to worry about one known Wundersmith. 'It's just . . . well, where's Brilliance Amadeo now? Is she still—'

'She's dead.'

A dull weight dropped into Morrigan's stomach.

'Your kind are . . . all . . . dead,' continued Professor Onstald. 'And if they're . . . not –' he blinked his watery eyes at her and took a long, rasping breath, '– they should be.'

Morrigan hadn't thought she could feel worse about being a Wundersmith, but she was wrong. Professor Onstald's book read on like a laundry list of everything that 'her kind' had done wrong for the past several hundred years. It wasn't *just* that Squall himself was evil. It wasn't *just* that a Wundersmith's powers were threatening by their very nature. Not according to Professor Onstald.

His book painted a most unflattering picture of a succession of selfish, destructive and power-mad people whose pleasure-seeking lifestyles were propped up by the royal family and the government, and funded by taxing the poor. For centuries, Wundersmiths had lived on the coin of ordinary Nevermoorians and repaid them, according to Onstald's book, with miseries and injustices both great and small.

At their best, Wundersmiths were self-indulgent eccentrics, abusing their positions of privilege by creating Wundrous vanity projects that inconvenienced many and benefited few. Like Decima Kokoro, who'd demanded public funds and resources to create a Wundrous skyscraper made entirely of water – an expensive and hazardous folly that resulted in several people drowning before it was shut down. Or Odbuoy Jemmity, who'd demolished an entire block of houses in a poverty-stricken borough to build an adventure park, which upon completion he named after himself and never allowed anyone inside.

At their worst, they were dangerous despots who used their powers to tyrannise others, and to keep themselves in positions of wealth and prestige. Despots like Ezra Squall, of course, but also like Gracious Goldberry a hundred years before him, who'd called for the imprisonment of Wunimals both Major and Minor before eventually being assassinated by a scorpionwun. Or like Frey Henriksson, who'd started the Great Fire of Nevermoor six hundred years ago that had wiped out half the city and killed thousands.

Jupiter had it wrong, Morrigan now realised. An unpleasant, heavy feeling was settling in the space behind her ribs. How had he got it all *so wrong?*

Wundersmiths really were horrible. Every last one of them.

After three miserable hours, Onstald returned, tottering back to his desk at a snail's pace. Morrigan was already finished reading her assigned chapters and had spent the last twenty minutes staring at the front of the classroom. Brooding.

'Tell me . . . what . . . you have learned.'

Morrigan summarised what she remembered of the three chapters in a dull, despondent voice. The centuries of Wundersmith cruelty and carelessness. The many wrongs that had never been righted. When she finished, she sighed deeply and stared down at her hands.

Professor Onstald was silent for a long time. When he finally spoke, it was in a voice so tired – so ancient and grim – that he could have been rising from the dead.

'And why do you . . . think . . . I have chosen . . . to teach you this?'

Morrigan looked up. She thought about it for a minute. 'So that I know the dangers of being a Wundersmith?' Professor Onstald said nothing. Something clicked in Morrigan's head. 'So that I can avoid them! So that I don't make the same mistakes as all those other . . .'

But she trailed off, catching the shrewd, cold look in Onstald's beady eyes. He shuffled off his chair and began walking slowly towards her. 'You think that I . . . expect . . . better . . . from you?'

Morrigan was confused. Better than being one of the worst people in the realm? Surely. 'Well—'

'Better from you . . . *more* from you . . . than these –' he leaned over her desk and tapped the cover of *An Abridged History of the Wundrous Act Spectrum*, '– these *monsters*?' he rasped.

'Well – well, *yes*,' said Morrigan. 'I mean . . . don't you? Surely you don't *want* me to be like—'

'You are like them . . . already,' said Professor Onstald, his voice rising. His heaving breaths became faster and more laboured. Little flecks of spittle flew from his withered mouth. 'You are a . . . monster . . . already. My duty is not . . . to save you . . . from yourself. It is to show you . . . that you are . . . beyond saving. All of your . . . kind . . . are beyond . . .'

But Morrigan didn't hear the rest. She leapt from her seat and fled the classroom, a furious sort of unhappiness building inside her. She ran through the tangled corridors without a clue where she was going but finally, somehow, she made it out of Proudfoot House, down the woodland path and back to Proudfoot Station.

She slumped onto a wooden bench and, through a haze of tears, looked up at the clock. Hometrain wouldn't be there for hours.

Fine, she thought. *No Hometrain.*

It didn't matter. She had two legs and a heartbeat.

Moments later, Morrigan was bolting down the tree-lined drive, through the gates and straight for the Brolly Rail platform, umbrella in hand. Jupiter's note popped into her mind, like a little prickling of her conscience. *UNDER NO CIRCUMSTANCES are you to travel anywhere outside of Wunsoc by yourself. I mean it. I'm trusting you.*

He could mean it all he wanted, Morrigan thought bitterly as she launched herself at the approaching rail, catching her brolly handle on a loop. She didn't care any more. She just wanted to go *home*.

Of course, it wasn't until Morrigan was halfway to the Deucalion – adrenaline and recklessness fading, common sense returning from its brief holiday – that she realised what a dreadful idea this was. If she showed up at home now, hours before she was due, she'd face a barrage of questions from Fenestra, Kedgeree and Martha. They would surely tell Jupiter what she'd done, and he'd never trust her again.

In a slight state of panic, Morrigan jumped off at the very next stop – The Docks – and took a deep breath. She wasn't going to return to Wunsoc now. She couldn't bear it. There was only one thing to do: she'd just have to kill time until she could stroll into the Deucalion lobby at a less suspicious hour.

It was cold down here on the River Juro, and the place smelled strongly of fish. But it was nice, in a way, to roam by herself among the boats and listen to the companionable sounds of fishing crews hauling in their nets and blaring music on the wireless. A group of noisy children, much younger than she was, were boiling mud crabs in a metal drum full of river water and taking turns to stoke the fire around its base.

The closer Morrigan got to the Juro's muddy edge, the colder she felt. But the squawking of seagulls and the lapping of water was soothing, and she soon felt her tearful upset simmer down to the slightly more manageable feeling of bitter, seething resentment.

Everything was rubbish.

She kicked a pebble along the shore as she walked. 'Onstald is rubbish, Wundersmith history is rubbish, Wundersmiths are rubbish. Dearborn is rubbish. The Wundrous Society is rubbish.'

Miss Cheery's all right, said the sensible part of her brain. *And Hometrain.*

'Oh, do shut up,' she told it.

Occupied with her sulking, Morrigan failed to notice she'd walked much farther than she meant to. The air was cooler and, looking back, she was struck by how much higher the water had risen up the riverbank. She turned to go but was stopped suddenly by a noise that didn't belong.

Crrrreeeeeeak. Click-clack. Click-clack.

She didn't want to look. There were some things in Nevermoor you really didn't want to see, Morrigan knew that better than anyone. But she couldn't help herself.

Crrrrrreeeeeeeeak. Click-clack. Click-click-click-click.

And turning her head slowly to the side, she witnessed perhaps the strangest, most grotesque thing she had ever seen. Rising from the muddy banks of the River Juro was a figure made of bones – not a skeleton, exactly, as that suggested some sense of order and anatomy.

There was no order to this . . . this person? This creature? It was barely a caricature of a human being. Even stranger, it was growing – *drawing together* – before Morrigan's eyes, out of what was presumably the bones and debris of many Ages buried in the sludge.

The most frightening thing of all was the way that it was looking at Morrigan.

There were no eyes in its skull, and yet she was certain. It was *looking at her.*

As if it wanted something from her. Perhaps her bones.

Morrigan didn't wait to find out. Heart racing, she ran and ran, squelching all the way back along the shore – the water lapping closer to her ankles now – up the concrete steps and across the docks, panting as she made a beeline for the Brolly Rail platform.

'You wanna be careful, miss,' a gruff fisherman called to her from the deck of his boat. He cast a nervous glance back the way she'd come. 'You get some dangerous sorts hanging round here. Off home with you now, that's the way.'

Morrigan was disinclined to argue. She should never have come. Jupiter told her not to leave Wunsoc on her own for a reason. He'd trusted her, and she'd broken the rules and been repaid for her stupidity with the fright of her life. She could *never* tell her patron about this.

If she was lucky, Morrigan thought, she could make it back to Proudfoot Station in time to catch Hometrain, and nobody need ever know she'd left. She reached out for a passing Brolly Rail loop and was carried off at high speed, shivering uncontrollably all the long and dismal ride back to Wunsoc.

CHAPTER SEVEN

A Pinkie Promise

When Morrigan entered the Deucalion's lobby through the glossy black double doors from the service entrance on Friday evening, she was cold, tired, wet, miserable and *starving*.

It had been the worst ending to the worst week of her life.

A week of increasingly wretched lessons with Professor Onstald, every single day. A week of watching her unit compare timetables to see where their classes overlapped and differed, of watching them puzzle out exactly where in the nine subterranean floors of Proudfoot House their next *fascinating* lesson would take them.

A week of listening to Thaddea sing the praises of her wrestling coach, a bearwun called Brutilus Brown who'd won twenty-seven consecutive Interpocket Wrestling Championships. Of hearing the hilarious exploits of Arch's lessons in theoretic larceny, including a heist masterclass with Henrik von Heider, the greatest art thief in history. A week of bearing up under a barrage of excitement from her unit about their classes in zombie dialects and surveillance techniques and river-surfing and hot-air ballooning and the care of venomous snakes and dozens of other skills that Morrigan wanted *so desperately* to be learning too.

But the worst thing of all was how jealous she felt of her own best friend.

Hawthorne had been just as appalled as Morrigan about her one disappointing subject. It felt wrong and uncharitable to have any ill-feeling towards him, when she knew it wasn't his fault.

On Wednesday afternoon, he'd invited her to watch his dragonriding lesson on Sub-Five, thinking it might cheer her up. But it had the opposite effect. Watching her friend zoom around the underground arena on dragonback with a look of pure joy on his face, a look that said he was doing what he was made for, that he was exactly where he ought to be . . .

Morrigan knew she ought to be happy for Hawthorne, and she *was*, really. But her envy was a beast. A hungry wolf she couldn't control. And it had been howling, deep in her heart, all week long.

Then, to top off the worst week ever, in Professor Onstald's class that day he had made her write a three-thousand-word essay titled 'The Immediate Impact and Aftermath of Jemmity

Park, a Fiasco by the Wundersmith Odbuoy Jemmity', and wouldn't let her leave the classroom until she'd finished the whole thing. Naturally it had taken hours, so she'd missed lunch, and then Hometrain.

Morrigan had waited at the platform a long time for Miss Cheery to return, her panic growing as the station emptied out, as the sun went down and the Whinging Woods grew worryingly dark. She knew she'd be breaking Jupiter's trust twice in one week, but Morrigan couldn't just stand around on her own, waiting for things to get even creepier. When it started to rain, she finally gave up on Miss Cheery and made her own way home via the Brolly Rail and the Wunderground.

She just had to hope that nobody at the Deucalion would tell Jupiter. Perhaps, by the time he'd got back, they'd have forgotten all about it. At least that was one good thing about him being gone all the time.

A note had arrived on Monday from the League of Explorers to say he'd be away 'indefinitely'. (Just 'indefinitely'! No further explanation required, apparently.) So it had also been a week of coming home every night and hoping against hope that her patron would be there for her to talk to . . . only to be disappointed each time she ran to the concierge desk and Kedgeree shook his head apologetically.

All the long, rain-soaked journey home, she had dreamed of her favourite dishes from the Hotel Deucalion kitchen: steaming bowlfuls of chicken dumpling soup, gooey baked cheese and crusty bread still warm from the oven, spiced rice pudding with honey-fried pears, blueberry buttermilk pancakes stacked a foot high and smothered with syrup . . . and *scones!* What she wouldn't give for a single, perfect Deucalion scone.

Stomach rumbling, face stormy, Morrigan pushed through the black doors of the hotel into the vibrant foyer with its black-and-white checkerboard marble floor, potted trees, luxurious furniture upholstered in pink velvet . . . and of course her favourite thing: the enormous, iridescent black chandelier in the shape of a bird. As always, its outstretched wings moved slowly, gently up and down in a slow-motion flight to nowhere.

'Miss Morrigan, you're home!' Martha's voice cut across the lobby. The maid enveloped her in a warm hug, and Kedgeree rushed out from behind his desk, clapping his hands as if Morrigan were a hero returned from the war. She sighed, relieved there was still a place in the world where nobody thought she was evil. (Not yet, at least.)

'There you are, lass! Your conductor just left a minute ago. She said she went back to Proudfoot House to fetch you and couldn't find you anywhere. The poor wee thing's in a terrible state.'

Martha gasped. 'Oh, Kedgeree, quick – send someone after her, tell her Morrigan's safe.'

'Right you are, Martha.' Kedgeree ran across the lobby himself, straight out the front door into the rain.

'There she is!' said Charlie the chauffeur, jumping down the last of the spiral steps and bouncing over to them excitedly. 'I told them you were clever enough to make your own way home, but they wouldn't listen. Bet you're glad it's the weekend, aren't you? Frank's hosting a staircase mattress-sliding race tonight. You're just in time to register, shall I put your name down?'

'Definitely,' said Morrigan with a grin. A mattress-sliding race was the best thing she'd heard all day. Her terrible first week at Wunsoc began fading to memory. She was *home*.

'Your little hands are frozen stiff!' Martha cried, fussing as she removed Morrigan's black coat. 'Oh, and you're soaked to the skin, poor dear! I'll draw you a nice hot bath. Would you like green mossflower bubbles that tingle your skin? Or – ooh! I've got champagne bubbles that play classical music.'

'Now wait a moment, Martha,' said Kedgeree, as he returned from running after Miss Cheery. He brushed the rain off his smart pink jacket. 'She can't—'

'They're non-alcoholic,' she assured him.

'It's not that. The girl's wanted elsewhere.' He handed Morrigan a folded slip of paper which read:

Meet me in my study right away.
–J.N.

'He's home?' Morrigan asked. Relief and happiness surged through her, quickly chased by the lingering memory of Jupiter's irritating, inconvenient absence during the worst week of her life. He was *definitely* going to hear about it.

'Just got in ten minutes ago,' said Kedgeree. 'Looked about as miserable as you do. Seems you've both had a rough week.'

She chewed on her lip, suddenly worried. 'Did, er . . . did he speak to Miss Cheery too, or . . . ?'

'No, and thank goodness you arrived when you did; I was worried for a moment I'd have to tell him you were a missing person! He might have thrown me from the rooftop.'

Morrigan exhaled her relief in a low *whooooosh*. Relaxing a little, she peered down the hall that led to the kitchens. 'Right. Okay. I'll just grab—'

Kedgeree handed her a second note.

I have food.
–J.N.

'You're here!' Morrigan and Jupiter shouted simultaneously as the study door flew open. They laughed and hugged briefly before Morrigan made a beeline for the little table by the fire. It held a delectable tray laid out with tea, milk and sugar cubes, butter and thickly cut bread, fat pork sausages with fried onions and horseradish, a slab of chocolate broken into shards and, most heavenly of all—

'Scones!' groaned Morrigan, dropping into a leather armchair and breathing them in – warm, golden-brown, perfectly baked. They were surrounded by little dishes of clotted cream, comb honey, lemon curd and two different types of jam. Morrigan could have composed a ballad about the miracle of this tea tray, if she wasn't immediately occupied with its demolition.

Fenestra was laid out on the rug in front of the hearth, snoring softly and taking up half the room. Jupiter's study was one of her favourite spots to nap, although she also seemed to favour the long table in the staff dining room and the roof of the range cooker in the kitchens. Morrigan kicked off her boots and stuck out her cold, damp-sock-covered feet to dry by the fire. She felt a strong temptation, just for a moment, to rest them on Fen's soft, furry back. But almost as if the Magnificat could read minds, one large amber eye opened to glare at her.

'Don't even think about it,' Fen grumbled. Then she stretched, clawed at the rug, and rolled over into sleep once more, the tip of her pink tongue sticking out between her teeth.

'So?' Jupiter said as he took the second armchair. 'How was your first week?'

'Horrible,' Morrigan replied, liberally slathering one half of a scone with blackberry jam, which dripped oozily down the side of her hand. She licked it off, too hungry for minding manners. 'Really horrible. Where have you been?'

'I'm so sorry, Mog. I was leading an expedition.' He sighed and rubbed both hands over his face. He did look sorry. And tired. 'A *failed* expedition. It wasn't meant to take so long, but . . . well, I'm sorry.'

'What sort of expedition?'

'The top-secret sort.'

Morrigan scowled, but her mouth was too full of scone to properly voice her disapproval.

'I wish I'd been here for your horrible week,' Jupiter said, and even though she knew he was changing the subject, she allowed it.

'Why didn't you tell me *how* horrible it would be?' she demanded.

'Very remiss of me,' he agreed, pouring her tea. 'What sort of horrible are we talking about? Just so I'm clear.'

'Vehworfkime,' Morrigan said through another delicious mouthful, and then, swallowing, repeated, 'the worst kind. No – all different kinds.'

'I'm listening.'

If she was going to tell him about her frightening encounter down at the docks, now was the time. But . . . there were just so many other things she wanted to say. And she was so happy to have him home, it didn't seem right to spoil things by breaking the news that she'd betrayed his trust.

'Let's see,' Morrigan continued, shaking off her residual guilt, 'there's the kind of horrible where everyone else in my unit is having an amazing time and learning amazing things and I'm *not*. There's the kind of horrible where the Scholar Mistress won't approve any of the classes my conductor planned for me. My *one* teacher in my *one* class is the *most* boring person alive, and he's *mean,* and he—'

'Wait – what did you just say?' Jupiter looked suddenly serious and alert. He froze, his teacup halfway to his mouth.

Morrigan sighed. 'I know I shouldn't call a teacher boring, but *honestly* Jupiter, if you'd met him—'

'No, not that – the thing about the Scholar Mistress,' he said, frowning deeply. 'She hasn't approved your timetable?'

'No. It's because she hates me and she thinks Miss Cheery's trying to turn me into a weapon of mass destruction.' She rolled her eyes, wrapping a pork sausage in a slice of bread and smearing it with peppery horseradish. 'The only class I'm allowed to do is *History of Heinous Wundrous Acts* with Professor Onstald, and all he does is make me read from this stupid book he wrote about how Wundersmiths are all evil, and then he gives loads of homework and it's always *more reading,* and I'm so—'

'What book?' asked Jupiter.

Morrigan tried to remember the full title. She took a bite of her sausage-in-bread, and the horseradish was so hot it made her eyes water, giving her time to think while she

recovered. '*Missteps, Blunders . . .* um, *Fiascos . . .* Somethings
*. . . and Devastations: An Abridged History of the Wundrous
Act Spectrum.* Oh! Monstrosities.'

'Hmm.' Jupiter made a face. 'Not a very cheerful title.'

'Remember last year, when you said . . .' She faltered,
suddenly unsure. 'You said that Wundersmiths used to be
good. That they were wish-granters and . . .'

'Mm?'

'Well, I was just wondering.' Morrigan wasn't sure how
to put it delicately, so she didn't bother. 'Are you sure you're
right about that?'

Jupiter smiled. 'Quite sure.'

'Are you, though?' she pressed. 'Because I'm already twelve
chapters in, and so far they're all terrible.'

He watched her for a moment. 'Tell me about the other
Wundersmiths in old Onstald's book.'

Morrigan looked up at the ceiling, reaching back into
her memory.

'Well, there was Mathilde Lachance,' she began, counting
on her fingers. 'And Rastaban Tarazed. Gracious Goldberry.
Decima Kokoro—'

'That name sounds familiar,' Jupiter said. 'Tell me about
Kokoro.'

'Well . . . she liked to build things, but they all went
wrong. She actually sounds a bit stupid, to be honest.' Jupiter
raised an eyebrow, but said nothing. 'What? She does! There

was this whole chapter about how she tried to make a building out of water – I mean, *water,* really! – and of course it was classified a Fiasco—'

'You two are a fiasco,' said Fenestra, stretching out and scratching behind her ear with one huge, tufty paw. 'Can't you see I'm trying to sleep?'

'Yes, I can see you've been sleeping here quite a lot.' Jupiter threw her a resentful look. 'The floor's got more cat fur than rug.'

'Have you any idea how much Magnificat fur is worth?' Fen drawled, rubbing her head against the floor to dislodge a few more strands. 'Sell it to the aristocracy; you'll make a fortune.'

'It's only valuable if it's still attached to your skin, Fenestra. I doubt you'd enjoy the removal process. Besides, it's Magnificub fur those people want, you're much too old and matted.' Fenestra opened one sleepy eye and hissed at him. Jupiter grinned, but then his face fell. 'Oh. Speaking of which, have you heard anything?'

Fenestra sighed. 'Not yet. We've put the word out. Looked in all the usual places, shaken up the usual suspects. Hopefully he's just a very clever cub who's found himself a good hiding place.'

Morrigan sat up straight. 'Are you talking about Dr Bramble's missing Magnificub? Do you think he could have been stolen for his *fur*? That's horrible.'

'Probably just ran away,' said Fen, rolling sleepily onto her back. 'And good on him, frankly. Bramble sounds like a drip.'

'Miss Cheery said Dr Bramble was distraught when he disappeared.' Morrigan remembered the affection she'd seen between them, that day in the lecture theatre. 'She seemed to really care about him, she had him in a nice basket and every—'

'A *nice basket?*' Fen shot her a look of disdain. 'A Magnificat is not a *housecat.*'

Morrigan said nothing, but looked pointedly from Fenestra, to the rug, to the fireplace. For not-a-housecat, Fen sure knew how to make herself comfortable.

Jupiter swished his teacup and took a sip, staring into the fireplace. 'The streets of Nevermoor are no place for a cub, though, Fen.'

'You think I don't know that?' Fen snapped. 'My lot have got a handle on it, all right? We'll find him. End of.'

'Your lot?' asked Morrigan. 'Who's your lot?'

The Magnificat glared at her and rolled over, effectively ending the conversation. Morrigan stared at her enormous backside, wondering if she would ever fathom the surprising depths of Fenestra's world. She was still reeling from last year's discovery that Fen was a former Free State Ultimate Cage Fighting champion.

Giving up on Fen, she turned to Jupiter instead. 'Someone else disappeared too. Paximus Luck. Did you know?'

'Mmm.' He had a cagey look about him, and Morrigan knew instantly there was something he couldn't – or didn't want to – say.

'Oh! Is that where you've been?' She bounced up and down on her armchair. 'It is, isn't it? You've been looking for Paximus Luck!'

He seemed to think about his answer for a long time. 'No. I've been looking for Cassiel. I only heard about Pax from the Elders today.'

'So they want you to help investigate?'

'I can't talk about it, Mog. That would be breaking the Elders' trust.'

'But are they connected, do you think?' she pressed.

'Not sure. I doubt it, to be honest.' He cleared his throat. 'Anyway, go on – Kokoro's building made of water. I'm fascinated.'

'Oh, *that*.' Morrigan made a face.

'Who classified it a Fiasco?'

'Um, the Committee for the Classification of Wundrous Acts,' she said with a sigh. 'They were the people who decided if a Wundersmith had done something bad, like a Misstep or a Blunder, or something terrible, like a Fiasco or a Monstrosity, or the worst thing they could do, which was a Devastation. And Cascade Towers was a Fiasco bordering on a Monstrosity, because anybody who tried to walk through the front doors got washed away or completely soaked and they couldn't keep anything *inside* the building of course, because it was too damp. So . . . yeah.' Morrigan finished with a shrug. 'Kokoro was a bit of an idiot, really.'

'But not evil?' said Jupiter.

Morrigan considered this as she buttered the second half of her scone. 'Maybe not evil. But definitely stupid.'

'Who else?' he asked, leaning over on one elbow and hiding a smile behind his hand.

'Odbuoy Jemmity built an adventure park.'

He nodded encouragingly. 'Go on.'

'But that was *definitely* a Fiasco,' said Morrigan, rolling her eyes. 'On the opening day there was this crowd of people and reporters all waiting to get inside, and they could see the rollercoasters and waterslides through the gates, and everybody was getting excited. But Jemmity never showed up, and the gates never opened, and nobody ever got to go inside.'

Morrigan hated to agree with Professor Onstald, but truthfully, she was outraged at the very thought of it. An adventure park you could never go inside! Granted, she hadn't visited an adventure park herself, but she could certainly *imagine* how much fun it might contain. How frustrating it would be to see all those marvellous rides and attractions, and never be able to enjoy them. 'So Jemmity was clearly also a bit stupid and selfish and – what?'

Jupiter's jaw was clenched, a sure sign that he was trying not to say something he *really* wanted to say. 'I just . . .' he began, then paused to take a breath. 'Look, I don't have any proof to show you. But I suspect Professor Onstald might be giving you a rather –' he took a moment to search for the word, '– *lopsided* version of Wundersmith history. I shall have to speak with the Scholar Mistress about it . . . and about the rest of your timetable,' he finished in a low, irritable mutter.

'But Professor Onstald *literally* wrote the book on Wundersmith history – his name is on the cover! Who could know more about Wundersmiths than he does? Have you met any?'

Jupiter rubbed the back of his neck. 'Well, no, but Wundersmith history goes back hundreds of years – thousands. They can't all have been bad, can they? Not in all that time.'

Morrigan slumped back in her chair, her brow knotted in frustration. 'So, you're just guessing, then.'

'Look.' Jupiter sighed and ran a hand through his long ginger hair, roughing it up a little. 'There have been some dodgy Wundersmiths, Mog, I grant you that. Ezra Squall chiefly among them. A lot of Wundersmith history has been lost, and what remains of lost history – the stuff people remember longest – is usually the worst of it. There are things we just can't know for sure. I know Professor Onstald's one of the few people alive who remembers what it was like to live in the time of Wundersmiths, and I certainly don't wish to impugn his teaching methods – he *is* a respected member of the Society – but I don't believe he has the full story. I can't believe it's that black and white.'

'But you can't be sure.'

'Neither can Onstald, Mog! He wasn't there for all of it.' There was a note of desperation in Jupiter's voice now. He sounded just like a man who knew he was losing his audience. 'The city of Nevermoor was *created* by Wundersmiths through the Ages. I refuse to believe they were all wicked or useless. Nevermoor's still standing, after all. It's still the greatest city in the Unnamed Realm. In all the generations of Wundersmiths who built it from the ground up, there *must* have been some good.'

Morrigan felt her heart sink to the floor. *Must have been.* She brooded for a minute over the uncertainty of those words, listening to the fire crackling in the hearth and the soft rumble of Fen's snoring. She could feel Jupiter watching her over the rim of his teacup.

'So,' she said finally, 'when you said last year that Wundersmiths were good once . . . that they were revered and . . . and all that other stuff you said –' she shook her head, looking down at the floor, '– you really had no idea.'

'Mog, listen to me. I *know* that Wundersmiths can be good.' He leaned forward and fixed her with a serious, searching look. 'I know it because I know you. You are a Wundersmith. And you are good. I don't need any more proof than that.'

Morrigan sipped her tea, and wished that she felt the same way.

Cᵇᵗ◄━

The next morning, Jupiter was gone again.

'Who needed him this time, Kedge?' she asked the concierge, who'd delivered Jupiter the message that had sent him running off again.

'Oh, some hoity-toity little upstart from the League of Explorers,' said Kedgeree. 'They won't leave him alone at the moment. Oi – hands off the desk, Miss, I've just polished that.'

'Sorry.' Morrigan stopped drawing frowny-faces with her finger on the shiny marble concierge desk, sighed, and slumped away.

She supposed it would be selfish to complain if he was helping to search for missing people, but even so, she couldn't help feeling put out. He'd only just got back, after all, and she hadn't had a chance to tell him all she'd meant to. They hadn't talked about the mystery door or Station 919 or lovely Miss Cheery. She'd wanted to ask Jupiter if he had been in the School of Mundane or Arcane Arts (her guess was Arcane), and why he thought *she'd* been put in the Mundane school, and what *exactly* was so mundane about being a Wundersmith.

Morrigan slid into a pink velvet loveseat in the busy lobby, cutting a dramatic figure as she gazed up at the blackbird chandelier. Her view was suddenly interrupted by an enormous furry face, with tufty whiskers and a pair of glowering amber eyes.

'Fen!' she cried, clutching her chest and sitting bolt upright. 'Don't *do* that, you nearly scared me to death.'

'Good,' said the gigantic grey cat with a scowl. 'If you die of fright, perhaps I won't have to play the role of lowly messenger on the whims of our eccentric proprietor any more. As if I don't have better things to do.'

Morrigan shook her head. 'What are you talking—'

'He wanted me to pass on a message,' Fen growled. 'He says he's going to find proof. He says he doesn't need it, but he knows you do. So he's going to find it, no matter how long it takes.'

Fen paused for a moment, as if reluctant to deliver the next part.

Finally, with a deep sigh and a hearty roll of her eyes, she added, 'He *pinkie promises*. Blech, revolting.'

Fen skulked away, presumably to wash out her mouth, and Morrigan lay back against the cushions. Above her the chandelier beat its silent wings, steadfast on its flight path, radiating light across the floor. Her heart lifted, just a little.

CHAPTER EIGHT

The Living Map

'That patron of yours is a bit good, isn't he?'

Miss Cheery was grinning from ear to ear when Morrigan boarded Hometrain on Monday morning. She held up a timetable, waving it gleefully.

Morrigan took it, then sat on an old couch next to Hawthorne. In addition to her dreaded lessons with Professor Onstald every day that week, she also had a new class on Monday, Wednesday and Friday afternoons.

'"*Decoding Nevermoor: How to Successfully Navigate the Free State's Most Dangerous and Ridiculous City*",' she read aloud.

Hawthorne peered over her shoulder. 'I've got that one too! *Decoding Nevermoor* with Henry Mildmay, in the Map Room, Sub-Three, Practicalities Department. Excellent.'

'So have I,' said Anah from across the carriage. She sounded rather less pleased about it than Hawthorne. There was a rustling of timetables as the others went to compare their lessons.

'Yes, you'll all be decoding Nevermoor together.' Miss Cheery clapped her hands with delight. 'This morning Ms Dearborn told me she's decided that ALL NINE of you need to learn how to get around the city if you're going to be "useful human beings".' Her eyes flicked briefly upwards. 'So, you get to have a class together as a unit, at last! Isn't it marvellous?'

Apparently it was not marvellous, judging by the faces around her. Francis and Mahir were gazing determinedly at the floor, while Thaddea looked openly appalled.

Anah – who always took the furthest seat from Morrigan on their brief trips to and from Station 919 – seemed positively terrified at the thought of spending any more time in a confined space with the dreaded Wundersmith.

But nothing was going to dampen Morrigan's spirits. She finally had a lesson that wasn't about how evil Wundersmiths were, and it was with Hawthorne. It was a start.

When they arrived at Proudfoot Station, Morrigan made sure she was the last to leave Hometrain.

'Thank you,' she said to Miss Cheery, indicating her timetable. '*Really.*'

The conductor winked at her. 'Thank the bearded wonder. I don't know what Captain North said to convince the Scholar Mistress, but it was all down to him, I'm sure of it.'

c▬▬-

As the most under-scheduled member of Unit 919, Morrigan was the first to make it to the Map Room for their lesson that afternoon. When she pushed open the heavy polished wooden doors into a huge, circular room with a domed ceiling, her heart gave a little leap. It was aptly named – every single surface in the room was a map. The dome itself was painted like the night sky, a dark blue chart of the heavens with each twinkling constellation marked and named: *Althaf the Dancer, Gurita Minor, Craig, Goyathlay the Wakeful* . . .

Along the curving walls, Morrigan trailed her fingertips over the bumpy topography of the Highlands, on to the tiny, bristly trees of the Zeev Forest, and through the gently lapping waves of the Black Cliffs coastline. She snatched her hand back at the unexpected texture – the oceans on the map were *wet*. Morrigan pressed a finger to her lips; the water was salty.

But these were all just warm-up acts, compared with the main event. The centre of the enormous room was dominated by an irregular-shaped structure covered in what looked like little dolls' houses, and surrounded by a raised walkway made of glass. Morrigan climbed up three steps and leaned against the railing that separated her from what she realised, with a gasp, was the most extraordinary map she'd ever seen.

It was Nevermoor. The entire city of Nevermoor, laid before her in precise miniature. There were tiny winding streets lined with perfectly built shops and houses, pockets of greenery dotting the landscape here and there, and the mighty River Juro snaking through the centre of the city.

Morrigan leaned over the glass rail; the tiny people on the streets were *moving!* Hyper-realistic and barely an inch tall, they were riding their bicycles in the parks, carrying their shopping bags down Grand Boulevard, hailing the Brolly Rail. Flocks of tiny seagulls gathered at the docks, and little boats sailed down the Juro. A large black cloud hovered over the southern end of the city, drizzling rain onto the streets below, and Morrigan saw the tiny map-people pulling out their umbrellas and hurrying to find cover.

It was a perfect representation of Nevermoor in microscopic, *moving* detail. Not just a model town or a dollhouse village . . . a living, breathing, three-dimensional city.

'How does it look out there? Still raining?'

Morrigan jumped. She turned to see a bright-eyed, pink-cheeked young man rushing into the Map Room, his shirt half untucked. He abandoned his satchel on the floor and ran up the steps to the walkway, where he leaned over the glass rail beside Morrigan, gazing eagerly down at the miniature city. His golden-brown fringe flopped down in his eyes, and he brushed it back.

'Beautiful, isn't it?' he said. 'Have you ever seen anything like it?'

'Never,' Morrigan admitted.

'Henry,' said the young man, holding out a hand to shake Morrigan's. 'Mr Mildmay, I suppose. Gosh, doesn't that sound odd. Perhaps I'll just go with "Mildmay". That's better, isn't it? More relaxed. Oh – it's my first class,' he explained, noticing Morrigan's look of polite confusion. 'I'm new. Just graduated as a senior scholar last year. Go easy on me, won't you?'

Morrigan smiled. 'It's my first class too. Well – second.'

'Smashing, we can muddle through together.' Morrigan liked the way that Mildmay's hearty, friendly tone took the edge off his terribly posh accent. 'You're . . . Miss Crow, yes?'

'Yes,' said Morrigan cautiously. She wondered if he knew what she was. If he did, he didn't show it.

'Smashing,' he said again. 'I've memorised all your names and faces already. Anyone else joining us?' He consulted a piece of paper. 'Says here I'm meant to have your whole unit for this class. They haven't gone AWOL already I hope?' He gave her a lopsided, knowing grin. 'Perhaps awful old Murgatroyd's scared them off.'

Morrigan didn't know what to say. She'd never met a teacher quite so . . . unteacherly.

The doors swung open again, and Thaddea stalked into the Map Room, closely followed by Anah, running to keep up.

'Just let me look at it, Thaddea,' she said, fussing around the taller girl's face with a damp cloth. 'It looks dreadful. You don't want to get an infection, do you?'

'For the millionth time,' said the red-headed girl through gritted teeth, 'I'm FINE. Stop your bleating.'

'You're being ridiculous,' huffed Anah, shaking her head of ringlets. 'And you're BLEEDING! I bet Miss Cheery would tell you—'

'Nobody asked you,' Thaddea snapped. She was, indeed, bleeding from what looked like a fairly serious gash in her forehead.

'Good afternoon, scholars,' said Mildmay, frowning deeply. Morrigan could tell he was trying to look stern, and that it didn't come naturally to him. 'What's all this about?'

'Nothing, sir,' echoed Thaddea, looking him squarely in the face, her chin jutting defiantly upwards.

Mildmay pressed his mouth into a line as if he was trying not to smile at Thaddea's bullish expression, and cleared his throat. 'Right-o, then. Where are the others?'

Morrigan was surprised. Was he just going to ignore the gash on Thaddea's forehead? Anah was right, it *did* look serious – there was now a thick rivulet of blood dripping down the side of Thaddea's face.

'Lambeth is in a sensory deprivation hydro-meditation chamber,' said Anah, looking up to the ceiling as if reciting from a list emblazoned on her memory. She hadn't so much as glanced in Morrigan's direction, and was giving her a wide berth. 'Francis is in the kitchen garden, learning to identify rare herbs. Hawthorne is at a firefighting demonstration. Arch is in the teaching hospital, having the fingers on his left hand broken and reset for maximum dexterity. Mahir is—'

The doors opened again and Hawthorne strode into the room talking loudly. He was followed first by a grinning Mahir and then Francis, Cadence and finally Lambeth, who trailed in several steps behind them looking peacefully dazed, as if she'd only stumbled on the Map Room by accident.

'Ah, excellent,' said the teacher, clapping his hands together. 'We're all here, more or less.' Morrigan frowned, counting the unit. They were most certainly not *all here*. Arch – and his broken fingers – were still missing. Once again it seemed Mildmay cared not a fig.

She was beginning to see that Ms Dearborn had meant exactly what she'd said about grown-ups in the Wundrous Society. *Nobody's going to hold your little handies or wipe your little nosies.* Yet they were quite happy to *break* their little handies, apparently.

'Everyone up here on the walkway, quickly now,' said Mr Mildmay. 'I want you to look down and tell me what you see.'

'It's Nevermoor! I can see my house,' said Hawthorne immediately as he took the spot beside Morrigan at the glass rail. He squinted hard at the map, leaning so far over that Morrigan had to grab the back of his shirt to stop him tumbling head-first onto the tiny people below. 'Wait – I can see my MUM! Look, Morrigan, that's her curly head – that's her purple jumper with the rainbow on the front. She was wearing that this morning! Is this—'

'A live, almost one hundred per cent realistic depiction of Nevermoor and its inhabitants,' said Mildmay. 'Well, *nearly* live. There's a few seconds' delay in some boroughs. I mean it's really old, this map, it's bound to have a glitch or two. Now let's delve a little deeper, class. Look closely. See what's really there.'

The scholars of Unit 919 exchanged confused looks, but tried to concentrate on the miniature city sprawling before them.

'A labyrinth, professor?' said Francis, looking bug-eyed at the tangle of streets and alleyways.

'Absolutely!' agreed Mildmay. 'Well done, Mr Fitzwilliam. Although, please – just call me plain old Mildmay. I'm not a professor – you'll find very few of us here at Wunsoc are. Nobody can sit still long enough to get the proper qualifications. There are a few patient souls among us, of course – Professor Kempsey, and Professor Dresser (though she prefers to go by "Molly", for obvious reasons), and Professor Onstald. The rest of us are just enthusiastic amateur educators who are willing to share our expertise. I myself am a member of the Geographical Oddities Squadron,' he said proudly, and blew his fringe out of his eyes. 'When I heard that the Elders were looking for someone to teach you how to get around this bizarre and beautiful city, I jumped at the chance to show off what I know. So, what else? Fire away. No wrong answers. Miss Amara, are you still with us?'

Lambeth was looking in the wrong direction, at the glittering constellations above.

'Hello?!' Thaddea shouted, waving a hand in front of her face. Lambeth flinched. She recovered quickly to turn a haughty, disapproving glare on Thaddea, who quailed slightly and lowered her voice. 'We're meant to be looking down there, not at the ceiling.' She pointed at the three-dimensional map of Nevermoor.

Lambeth frowned silently at the map for several moments.

'Well?' prompted Mildmay. 'Any thoughts?'

'Yes.' Her eyes skittered across the streets and boroughs before landing on Begonia Hills, then pointed at a busy intersection. 'Motor accident.'

Mildmay blinked. 'No, I meant thoughts about—'

He was interrupted by a screeching of tiny wheels and a honking of angry horns, signalling that two vehicles had just ploughed into each other. A pair of tiny drivers jumped out to bellow and shake their little fists, bringing the traffic to a standstill. Lambeth returned to watching the stars, which seemed a lot less stressful.

'Oh,' said Mildmay. 'Right. Well. Anyone else?'

'A game – no, a puzzle,' said Anah. She looked at the teacher hopefully, clearly eager to please. 'For us to figure out.'

'Wonderful!' he enthused, aiming an electric smile in Anah's direction. Anah glowed right back at him. 'I certainly hope you'll *try* to figure it out, Miss Kahlo, but as nobody has ever been able to do so in Nevermoor's entire history, I hope you'll forgive me if I don't hold my breath. Though undoubtedly you shall tackle the task with your trademark surgical precision.' Anah giggled at this, blushing. 'What can the rest of you see?'

'Streets, buildings, squares, temples,' said Thaddea, sounding a little bored, or perhaps woozy.

'A bustling metropolis!' shouted Mahir.

'A bustling mess,' muttered Cadence.

'Good. Now, let me tell you what *I* see when I look at Nevermoor,' said Mildmay. He looked down at the tiny, teeming city with a rapture that lit his eyes from the inside. 'I see a monster. A beautiful, terrible monster that feeds us all with stories and history and *life*, and demands to be fed in return. A monster that, over the Ages, has grown fat on the unwitting, the gullible, the vulnerable . . . has chewed them up and swallowed them down, never to be seen again.' He tore his eyes away from the map and turned to face them, holding up one finger. '*But* . . . it's a monster that can be tamed, if you are willing to learn its behaviours, its weaknesses and perils. I have dedicated my life to taming this monstrous city, and I love her with every fibre of my being. If you wish to survive and thrive in Nevermoor, you must do the same.'

Morrigan wondered if it really was possible to *tame* a city so wild and . . . well, ridiculous. She doubted it.

Mildmay slapped both hands on the rail. 'But we'll start small.' He gestured to a table at the end of the walkway, on which sat two small wooden bowls filled with slips of paper. 'I want you all to begin by taking one piece of paper from each bowl. The first location will be your starting point, the second your endpoint,' continued Mildmay. Crossing to the other end of the viewing platform, he tugged on a chain and a blackboard came rolling down, bearing two separate lists of Nevermoorian landmarks. 'I want you to plot the simplest route from A to B, and write a detailed set of directions. But here's the catch: see these two lists?' He pointed at the board. 'The first is a list of landmarks you *must* include on your route. The second – landmarks you must avoid. And remember, this is an above-ground journey: no cheating by taking the Wunderground.' He grinned at them. 'Sounds straightforward, but you might find it trickier than you'd expect. You have one hour. Go!'

Morrigan's first slip read, 'Tumbledown Road, Bittern & Bustard' and the second, 'Grouse Street, Southey-Upon-Juro'.

It was more than tricky – it was maddening, and involved a lot of running back and forth on the glass walkway and footbridges. Every time Morrigan thought she had her path set, she'd notice that some part of it meandered straight past Dredmalis Prison or the Royal Nevermoor Playhouse or some other forbidden landmark from the second list, and she'd have to backtrack and find another way round.

There were constant groans, frustrated sighs and even a few muttered curse words from Unit 919. By the end of the hour, a few of them had almost given up altogether.

'It's impossible,' grumbled Thaddea, moving away from the map of Nevermoor to slump against the curved wall. She made a noise of disgust and pulled away, realising too late that she'd leaned against a part of the wall showing the Albertine Ocean in the Fourth Pocket, and it had soaked through the back of her jumper. 'Nevermoor is ridiculous.'

Morrigan, however, was enjoying herself for perhaps the first time since coming to Wunsoc. While some of the other scholars were easily discouraged when their route was dead-ended, she found it strangely satisfying to puzzle out an alternative path.

'Time's up!' called out Mildmay when the hour was over. 'Well done, everyone. We'll discuss your work in detail during our next class. Miss Crow, please stay behind.' He didn't look up from the papers he'd just collected. Hawthorne hovered near the door for a moment. 'You may go, Mr Swift,' the teacher added.

Morrigan slowly approached Mildmay's desk. 'Sir?'

'Don't worry, you're not in trouble,' he said. 'Quite the opposite. I wanted to tell you how impressed I am. You did terrific work today.' He held up her set of directions, shaking his head in amazement. 'This is *perfect*.'

Morrigan smiled, feeling her face grow warm. 'Thank you.'

'Did you enjoy the lesson?'

'Yes!' she said with sincere enthusiasm. 'I've never done anything like it before.'

'Oh, I'm glad somebody did.' He brushed his floppy fringe back out of his eyes, looking relieved. 'You have an unusually good knowledge of Nevermoor. It's a strange place, but your grasp of it seems very intuitive. You obviously grew up here, yes?'

Morrigan hesitated. 'I . . . um, not exactly . . .'

Last year, when horrid Inspector Flintlock of the Nevermoor City Police Force had been (rightly) convinced that she was smuggled in from the Republic, and the threat of deportation had hung over her head, Jupiter had advised her to keep quiet about where she'd come from.

But that was last year. Morrigan hadn't been a member of the Wundrous Society last year, and she didn't have the protection of the little *W* badge that now gleamed on her collar. Now that she was a fully-fledged member of Nevermoor's most prestigious group, was it all right to be honest about the fact that she grew up in Jackalfax, deep in the heart of the Wintersea Republic, among the enemies of the Free State? That she hadn't even *known* about this place until she'd met Jupiter? The Seven Pockets of the Free State kept strict border laws and even stricter secrecy, and her patron had risked everything to smuggle her in. Would she be putting him at risk if she told the truth now?

Morrigan didn't know. She made a mental note to ask Jupiter's advice.

'Not exactly?' prompted Mildmay.

'I grew up outside of Nevermoor,' Morrigan admitted, and left it at that. 'I moved here to take the Wundrous Society trials, last year.'

He looked deeply impressed. 'Goodness. You've only been here a year? And yet you and Nevermoor seem to go hand in glove. It's almost like this place was made just for you.'

Morrigan beamed with her whole face, feeling a glow emanating from somewhere deep inside. That was *exactly* how she felt about Nevermoor! Like it *belonged to her.* She was thrilled – almost to an embarrassing degree – to hear this from somebody else, somebody entirely objective.

'If you'd like to visit the Living Map outside of our lessons, you're more than welcome,' offered Mildmay. 'I do. Always have done, even when I was a scholar.' He gazed out over the miniature Nevermoor with obvious affection. 'I was pretty lonely at your age. The other members of my unit thought cartography was a pretty boring knack. Lots of whitesleeves in my unit, see – we've got a couple of sorcerers, and Tilda Green's a fire oracle, and Susan Keeley can speak to water—'

Morrigan's eyebrows shot upwards. '*Speak to water?*'

'—and they didn't really think I belonged with them. Sometimes I would come here and sit for hours, watching all the tiny trains carrying the tiny people to their tiny houses. Watching the lights come on all over the city as night fell.' He grinned sheepishly. 'Pathetic, I know. But I thought it was fun.'

'I don't think my unit likes me much either,' Morrigan admitted. She felt surprised at herself. She hadn't planned to say anything of the sort, but it just . . . came out. 'I mean, except Hawthorne.'

'Why, do you have a boring knack too?' Mildmay asked ruefully, then his face immediately turned red. 'I-I mean . . . I apologise. I wasn't prying. I know we're not supposed to ask you. I was only joking.'

In that moment Morrigan wanted very much to throw caution to the wind and tell Mildmay she was a Wundersmith. She thought perhaps – just perhaps – *he* wouldn't look at her with fear or hatred.

But Elder Quinn's warning rang in her head. *If anyone* – anyone at all – *is found to have broken our trust . . . then all nine of you will face expulsion from Wunsoc. For life.*

Anyone at all. Even Morrigan herself.

She couldn't risk it.

'Yes,' she said simply. 'It's very boring.'

He smiled at her. 'Well, sometimes the boring knacks turn out to be the most useful ones. My unit won't be laughing when I join the League of Explorers.'

Morrigan perked up. 'My patron's in the League of Explorers!'

'Jupiter North, I know,' he said, nodding with enthusiasm. 'He's a real inspiration. I'm going to run interrealm expeditions one day too. I'm going to be a captain in the League. Just like North.'

'You are?'

'Don't you realise, Miss Crow?' He chuckled, his face lighting up with possibility. 'We're in the Wundrous Society. We can be anything we want to be!'

The sound of a gong being struck reverberated in the Map Room, so loud she and Mildmay both covered their ears. An officious voice sounded from horn-shaped brass speakers mounted in the corners of the ceiling.

'*Ahem. Elders, Wuns and Scholars, a moment of your time please. A member of our teaching staff, Paximus Luck, has now been missing for almost a week. Students in Mr Luck's popular* Stealth, Evasion and Concealment *class have, most unfortunately, continued attending lessons, believing his mysterious absence to be merely . . . ahem . . . "part of the syllabus".'* Morrigan thought she could almost hear the woman rolling her eyes. '*This is* not *the case. We are currently investigating*

Mr Luck's disappearance, and anyone with relevant information should speak to the High Council of Elders immediately. In the meantime, we ask that any scholars continuing to attend Mr Luck's classes despite his evident absence . . . stop doing that. Good day.'

The announcement ended with a mechanical squeal that made Morrigan and Mildmay both wince.

'Strange,' she said, wondering vaguely how Jupiter's investigation was going. 'All these disappearances. Paximus and Dr Bramble's Magnificub and—'

Mildmay chuckled. 'That's Paximus Luck for you, though, isn't it?'

'What do you mean? Has he done this before?'

'Well yes, I mean . . . that's his knack, you know,' he said. 'Disappearing. Reappearing. Trust me, this is just some elaborate stunt to prove his cleverness. He'll be back in no time, expecting applause.'

Morrigan frowned. She sometimes felt that her true knack had nothing to do with being a Wundersmith. That it was, in fact, her remarkable ability to assume the worst. It came, of course, from a lifetime of believing she was cursed, and it seemed to be stitched into the very fabric of her being, even now. Telling her not to worry about bad things happening around her was like telling Hawthorne not to get excited about dragons, or Jupiter not to be ginger.

As she left the Map Room, Morrigan thought about the last time a pattern of strange, unwelcome things started happening in Nevermoor, and the man who was behind them.

Last year, there had been reports of disturbances on the Gossamer – the invisible, intangible web of energy that tied together everything in the whole realm, living and dead. Ezra Squall had been locked out of Nevermoor for more than a hundred years – kept at bay by police, military forces and sorcery of all kinds, and more than anything, by the powerful magic of Nevermoor itself. But he'd found a way to visit undetected, by using the Gossamer Line, a highly dangerous, top-secret mode of travel that allowed him to leave his body behind in the Republic, while he wandered – free and incorporeal – all over the city from which he was exiled.

It was impossible to stop him from using the Gossamer Line, because it didn't *technically* exist. At least, not in the physical realm.

With a shudder, Morrigan wondered where Squall was now, and what he was doing, and if – *when* – he would visit her on the Gossamer again.

CHAPTER NINE

The Charlton Five

'*Neheran dunas flor.*'

Arch frowned in concentration, letting beef stew dribble from his spoon back into his dish. 'Nehelans doonaz—'

'*Neherrrrrran,*' Mahir corrected him, rolling his Rs. '*Neheran dunas flor.*'

'*Neherrrran dunas florrrr,*' repeated Morrigan. She tried to copy Mahir's fluid pronunciation but sounded a bit like she was gargling mud instead. The rest of the unit were also rolling their Rs around their table in the dining hall, with varying success. Morrigan thought Thaddea's attempt sounded the closest. '*Neherrran dunas florrrr.*'

'Good.' Mahir gave Morrigan a little nod as he reached for a bread roll. 'Well, not good, but better than Arch.' They all laughed at that, even Arch himself.

It had taken weeks, but Unit 919 had gradually begun to thaw towards Morrigan. Or at least, they'd stopped greeting her on the platform each morning with looks of profoundest dread. Anah no longer squeaked in fright every time Morrigan sat near her on Hometrain. Francis had asked her to taste-test a batch of his strawberry tarts for quality control – a task she took to with great enthusiasm. One bite brought on the specific sensation of bittersweet late-summer nostalgia . . . which sent Francis straight back to the test kitchen, as he'd *actually* been aiming for the carefree abandon of a mid-summer music festival.

Even bad-tempered Thaddea had offered once to kick an older boy in the shins when he'd loudly called Morrigan 'The Knackless One' on the steps outside Proudfoot House. She strongly suspected Thaddea would enjoy any excuse to kick someone in the shins, but nonetheless . . . Morrigan was beginning to feel that she might indeed have, if not eight brothers and sisters, at least eight friends.

When she'd expressed a passing interest in learning Serendese, Mahir had insisted on teaching them all a few key phrases over lunch.

'*Neheran dunas flor!*' Hawthorne called out to an older scholar passing by with a wave of his hand. The girl merely looked perplexed.

'Nice,' said Mahir, smirking. 'You said that perfectly.'

Hawthorne looked pleased with himself as he took a big mouthful of milk. 'Whassit mean?'

Mahir grinned, glancing conspiratorially at Morrigan. 'You have a bum for a face.'

Hawthorne snorted milk and it dribbled down his chin, as the others erupted into laughter. 'Serious?'

Mahir shrugged. 'It's my favourite romance language.'

This defrosting of unit relations made life at Wunsoc infinitely more bearable for Morrigan, even though Ms Dearborn had continued to reject every single one of Miss Cheery's suggested additions to her class timetable. At least Morrigan still had *Decoding Nevermoor* to look forward to on Mondays, Wednesdays and Fridays – especially since, as it turned out, she was excellent at it. Almost every lesson, Mildmay had cause to proclaim her genius. Morrigan strongly suspected that the eye-rolling of most of her unit had turned from openly mocking to sort of . . . begrudgingly respectful? Maybe that was her imagination, but they *did* often ask for her help in class, which gave her a feeling she'd never really had before. At last she'd found something she was good at, something that made her special – and it had nothing to do with being cursed, and nothing to do with being a Wundersmith.

All in all, things were going better than Morrigan could have hoped.

Until the morning that the note arrived.

'We should take it to the Elders.'

'Can't you read? It clearly says—'

'I KNOW what it says, but I still think we should—'

'We are NOT telling the Elders.'

'Who died and made you the king of this unit?'

Morrigan had emerged from her mystery door onto Station 919 to find the rest of her unit gathered in a tight scrum, peering down at a piece of paper – except Lambeth, who stood a little apart as usual.

'Oh, I'm glad you've finally remembered we're a UNIT, Thaddea.' That was Hawthorne's voice. He snatched the note from Mahir's hand. 'If you think for a second I'm going to let any of you—'

'What's going on?' asked Morrigan.

As one, their eight faces turned to her, expressions ranging from forehead-wrinkled worry to blazing anger. Hawthorne merely looked grim, and he stepped forward to silently hand her the note.

Morrigan read.

We know the terrible truth about Unit 919.
We have a list of demands.
If you want your secret to stay a secret,
you'll await our instructions.

Don't tell a soul.
If you do, we'll know.
And we'll tell the whole Society.

'The terrible truth about . . . ?' She turned from one distressed face to the next. Lambeth looked particularly agitated, and Morrigan wondered if it was because of the note, or if she was tuning into something bad about to happen. 'What does that—'

'It's *obvious* isn't it?' snapped Thaddea. 'It's talking about you. The truth about *you* being a *Wundersmith*. We're being blackmailed, because of *you*.'

'Shut up, Thaddea,' growled Hawthorne.

'Who sent it?' asked Morrigan. 'Where did you find it?'

'It was sitting here on the platform,' he told her. 'Anah found it.'

Anah was trembling. 'Thaddea's right. We ought to tell the Elders,' she said. 'Or Miss Cheery! She'll know what to do.'

'But who could have left this on *our* platform?' said Morrigan, frowning. 'I thought only our Hometrain could come here.'

'Who cares how it got here?' said Francis. He paced the platform, his light brown skin sporting a faintly sweaty sheen. 'How did they find out about you? If the rest of the Society finds out, we'll be expelled, remember? My aunt will *kill* me if I get expelled. My whole *family* is in the Society. Both sides! Four generations on Dad's side, seven on Mum's.'

'Calm down, Francis,' said Hawthorne.

'You don't understand! My great-grandmother was Elder Omowunmi Akinfenwa! Fitzwilliams and Akinfenwas practically *worship* the Wundrous Society. I can't get kicked out.'

Thaddea shook her head. 'We won't get kicked out if someone *else* tells everyone. It's not our problem, Francis. I say whoever they are, they can fill their boots. Let them tell. Maybe they'll get found out, then *they'll* be the ones who are expelled.'

'Yeah but *we're* the only ones who are supposed to know,' Mahir pointed out. 'If it gets leaked, we could still get the blame.'

Morrigan stared at the wall across the train tracks. She wasn't thinking about getting expelled. She was thinking about how it would feel to have the whole Society know she was a Wundersmith. Right now, people were curious about her, and perhaps a bit suspicious. But if they knew the truth . . . it would be just like being cursed again. Everyone hating her. Everyone fearing her. It would be as if she'd never left Jackalfax at all.

An old, familiar panic unfurled in the pit of her stomach, like a bear waking from hibernation. Heat rose in her chest.

Thaddea snatched the note back from Hawthorne. 'This note *proves* it's not our fault, though! I'm taking it to the Elders. I don't care what you— OW!'

In a flash, the note burned up in her hand, and the ashes fluttered to the ground.

'How – how did they do that?' Thaddea put her burned fingers in her mouth. Her eyes darted around the station, looking for whoever had magically sent the letter up in flames. No one was there.

Morrigan swallowed. She could almost taste the ash, right at the back of her throat.

'Well . . . that solves that problem,' Hawthorne said uneasily.

Thaddea scowled. 'We can still—'

'We are NOT throwing Morrigan under the bus.'

'Yeah you have to say that, you're her *friend*.'

Hawthorne made a strangled noise of outrage. 'We're ALL supposed to be friends! We're supposed to be a unit. Sisters and brothers, remember? We're supposed to be a FAMILY.'

'I never asked to have a WUNDERSMITH in my family!' snarled Thaddea.

'Stop,' said a calm, low voice from somewhere near the back of the group. They all turned to Cadence in surprise. Once again, it was as if they hadn't known she was there. 'We're not telling the Elders. We're going to keep this to ourselves for now. Wait and see what happens.'

'Stop mesmering us!' Thaddea protested, a slight note of panic in her voice.

Cadence scoffed. 'I'm not *mesmerising* you, you moron, I'm telling you what to do – there's a difference. If I wanted to mesmerise you, you wouldn't even know it. Those stupid classes obviously haven't taught you anything.' A distant rumbling sounded. The platform began to vibrate ever so slightly and a light from the tunnel announced the arrival of their Hometrain. 'We don't even know what these people want yet. Let's just wait for the next note. Then we'll decide what to do. Agreed?'

One by the one, the scholars all nodded – even Thaddea, who looked as if that simple act of concession was torture.

The train screeched to a halt and Miss Cheery stuck her head out, beckoning them inside. Morrigan hung back.

'Um,' she said to Cadence, suddenly feeling awkward, 'thanks for that.'

Cadence shrugged. 'Don't thank me yet. I'm just waiting to see what the next note says.'

When the others departed Proudfoot Station for their first lessons, Morrigan lingered a while, watching the morning trains come and go across the platforms. She puzzled over the note. Who could possibly know she was a Wundersmith? Had someone from 919 betrayed her already? Or one of their *patrons*? Morrigan thought immediately of Baz Charlton, and Francis's Aunt Hester, who had so vehemently opposed Morrigan's admission to the Society. Could one of them have let it slip, or . . . or could they have *written the note?*

Surely not, Morrigan thought. Surely even odious Baz Charlton wasn't that stupid. Would either of them risk being exiled from Wunsoc, just so they could get a bunch of junior scholars to give in to whatever was on their list of demands? Baz and Hester didn't want to *blackmail* her – they wanted her *gone*.

Morrigan took a deep breath and left the station, starting down the woodland path to Proudfoot House. With an hour to kill before her dreaded *Heinous History* lesson (Professor Onstald always needed much longer to get to his classroom than the other teachers), perhaps she could spend the extra time on Sub-Three, studying the Living Map. The idea gave her a cheerful boost, and she walked a little faster.

'Oi. You! Knackless! Come back here!'

Morrigan's good mood evaporated as she paused and turned around. There was a small knot of older scholars following her along the path. Three boys, two girls. 'Sorry, were you talking to me?'

'*Were you talking to me?*' mimicked one of the girls. She was tall with long, stringy hair on which someone had done an appalling green dye job. Her head looked like it was covered in moss. She caught up to where Morrigan was, her friends close behind. 'Yes, halfwit. Do you see anyone else here without a knack?'

'I have a knack,' Morrigan said. 'It's just—'

'Classified, yeah,' said one of the boys, coming to stand over Morrigan. He *must* be a fourth or fifth year, she thought – he was so big and broad-shouldered he could have blocked out the sun. 'We know. Our conductor said we're not allowed to ask about it. So we're not asking. You're going to tell us.'

Morrigan looked at him blankly. 'But I can't tell you. It's *classified*. That means—'

'We know what it means,' said the green-haired girl. 'We also know you're an illegal. Smuggled in from the Republic.'

Morrigan steeled herself. 'No I'm not, I'm from—'

'You should know, nobody likes liars around here,' spat the girl, 'and nobody likes secrets. Not among scholars. We're meant to stick together, aren't we? So you'd best show us your knack. Now. Or would you like to see mine first?' Her mouth split into a malicious grin. She took five spiky steel throwing stars from her pockets, holding them between her fingers like little silvery claws.

'Um, no, thank you,' Morrigan said, swallowing as she turned around, walking faster towards Proudfoot House.

The other girl – short, pinch-faced and, unlike her four greysleeve companions, wearing a shirt of Arcane white – jumped in front to block her way, laughing. 'Go on, Heloise.'

Morrigan felt herself lifted into the air by her arms and pinned against a tree trunk at the edge of the path, the broad-shouldered boy on one side and the surprisingly strong Arcane girl on the other. She struggled against them, trying to pull herself free, to no avail.

'Let go of me!' she demanded.

'Or what? Are you gonna call for your conductor to come and save you?' Heloise made an exaggerated pout. 'Go on then, if you're such a baby, go and call—'

'MISS CHEERY!' shouted Morrigan, who was not *at all* above calling for her conductor, no matter what they thought of her. 'HELP—'

But a sweaty hand clamped tight over her mouth, muffling her cry. Heloise lifted one hand in the air, balancing the sharp point of a star precariously on her forefinger, showing off. 'You might want to stay still for this.'

Her friends laughed. Morrigan squeezed her eyes tightly shut. She heard – and felt – a small *whoosh* of air and a dull *thud* as the first star found its mark right next to her head.

She cracked open one eye and saw a gleam of silver barely an inch to her left, and Heloise lining up her next shot. Morrigan's breath came in short, sharp gasps. Her heart was racing.

'My Alfie here reckons you're a shapeshifter,' said Heloise, looking up adoringly at the boy with the enormous shoulders. 'But I don't. Alice Frankenreiter in 915 is a shapeshifter, and they never kept that a secret.' *Whoosh, thud.* Morrigan flinched as the second star landed terrifyingly close to her right ear. 'But maybe he's right. Only one way to find out.' *Whoosh, thud.* Star number three pinned the sleeve of Morrigan's coat to the tree trunk. 'Go on then. Shift if you're shifty.'

'She ain't a shifter,' said the second boy, a weedy thing with the beginnings of a fluffy moustache loitering sadly on his top lip. 'She's a witch, innit.'

'Don't be stupid,' said Heloise, throwing her fourth star up in the air and catching it by the tip. 'You've got two witches in *your* unit, you numbskull. Are their knacks classified?'

'Oh,' said the boy, looking crestfallen. 'Nah.'

'Shut up, Carl,' said Alfie the bruiser. 'Heloise, hurry up and throw, will you, I've got to get to—' *Whoosh, thud.* 'Oi! Watch your aim, that one nearly hit *me*.'

'I meant it to, sweetie,' said Heloise with a saccharine smile. She ran a finger along the edge of her fifth and final star, snarling at Morrigan, 'Come *on*. This is boring. *Do* something. Show us your knack.' *Whoosh—*

No thud.

Eyes shut tight, Morrigan felt a rush of blood to her head, and a rush of something more urgent than blood, something *angry*. It felt like the tide going out all at once, like she was being emptied and then suddenly, in a searing flash of heat somewhere in the back of her skull, filled back up again all the way to the top. She was a dam overflowing. About to burst.

She opened her eyes.

Five steel throwing stars in the air. Five scholars frozen.

Morrigan could feel her own fear and fury pooling in the air around her, beading like condensation on a glass, heavy with the weight of the terrible thing that was about to happen.

Each scholar reached out with one stiff arm, as if unable to stop themselves, their movements jerky and unnatural, like puppets on a string. Each hand plucked a star from the air, and turned it on its owner. Each gleaming silvery spike drew closer, irresistibly closer, to a face contorted in horror and confusion.

'No,' whispered Morrigan, unable to move. 'NO! Put them down. Stop it! STOP.'

Five bodies were drawn up in the air as if sucked into a vacuum, then dropped simultaneously to the woodland path. Limp as ragdolls. Throwing stars clattering harmlessly to the ground beside them.

'Morrigan!' came a shout from somewhere near the station. Miss Cheery was racing down the track, followed closely by two other conductors, who went straight to help Horrible Heloise and her friends up from the ground.

'What happened here?' demanded one of the other conductors. He was glaring right at Morrigan, clearly expecting an answer from her. But Morrigan had no words. She shook her head, her mouth hanging open.

'Are you all right?' Miss Cheery asked her quietly.

'Is *she* all right?' said the man. 'She's not the one sprawled on the ground, Marina!'

'Oi, wait a second,' said Miss Cheery indignantly. 'Don't you go blaming my scholar for this when you don't have a clue what's happened. What are those things doing all over the place, Toby? It's *your* scholar who's the star-thrower, isn't it? And anyone with a weapon-based knack is only meant to use their weapons inside a classroom.'

Toby glared at Miss Cheery and reluctantly said, 'Heloise, why are your stars out?'

Heloise didn't say anything. She still looked shaken.

'Come on, Morrigan.' The conductor took her arm and turned away. 'Hometrain.'

Morrigan stumbled alongside her in a daze, trying not to look back at the scene of what felt very much like a crime.

'What happened?' Miss Cheery whispered, her eyes widened in distress.

'They pinned me to a tree and tried to make me tell them my knack by throwing stars at my head!' Morrigan's voice had reached a pitch that surely only dogs could hear, but Miss Cheery was following her every word, biting down hard on her lip. 'And then . . . and then, I don't know what happened. I felt this weird rush of . . . *something.*'

She described in a frantic whisper the way that each of the older scholars had grabbed one of the sharp little weapons as if compelled by some unseen force and turned it on themselves. 'But I wasn't trying to . . . I didn't do it deliberately, Miss, I *swear,*' she finished, gulping air into her lungs at last, as they finally stepped inside the carriage. Her hands were shaking.

'I know you didn't.' Her voice was unwavering, but Morrigan could tell that she was worried too.

'How do you know?' She felt her breath catch in her throat. 'You only met me a few weeks ago.' Her mind flicked to Jupiter, the person who knew her best. She felt a pang of sadness when she remembered that he was away again, and wouldn't be there to talk to when she got home. Miss Cheery was nice, but it wasn't the same.

'I know a good sort when I see one,' said the conductor, smiling.

Morrigan didn't return her smile. In that moment, she wanted to confess everything – about the note left on their platform, and how it had burned up in Thaddea's hand, how her chest had seared and she'd tasted ash at the back of her throat. About the rush of fury she'd felt just before Heloise's stars had turned on their owner. The thrill of power that coursed through her in that moment, that sent agreeable little jolts of aftershock through her even now.

She couldn't. The words wouldn't come.

Morrigan swallowed, looking down at her shoes. Was she really a good sort, she wondered. *Maybe you didn't do it deliberately . . . but some part of you enjoyed it.*

But wasn't that normal? Wouldn't *anyone* feel that way, if they'd just been attacked and had pointy objects thrown at their head?

Or was it just her corrupt Wundersmith nature coming through?

'And I know a bad sort,' continued Miss Cheery. 'The Charlton Five – they're bad sorts.'

Morrigan glanced up. 'The what?'

The conductor rolled her eyes. 'That's what they call themselves. They're all Baz Charlton's lot. He's been collecting candidates for Ages, and he seems to get at least one in every unit. Toby's got two of them in his.'

The Charlton Five. Now it made sense – what had Heloise said to her? *You're an illegal. Smuggled in from the Republic.* Baz must have told them. He wasn't just mad about the fact that Morrigan was a Wundersmith; he was still fuming that she'd made it into the untouchable safety of the Wundrous Society at all. Especially since he believed she'd taken the rightful place of one of his other candidates in the trials.

'Five of them in the junior school alone . . . well,' Miss Cheery continued thoughtfully, 'six now, I suppose. With Cadence. Ugh, I hope they don't get into her ear. They're a nasty little gang. Sometimes it seems like they're more loyal to each other than their own units. I must remember to warn Cadence to keep away. And you – you steer clear of them too, okay?'

Morrigan nodded. She had no desire to encounter Heloise, her gang *or* her throwing stars ever again.

Of course, she couldn't speak for Cadence. Nobody could speak for Cadence. Cadence was entirely her own person: strange, impenetrable, unpredictable.

And if the mesmerist wanted to turn the Charlton Five into the Charlton Six, Morrigan didn't like Miss Cheery's chances of talking her out of it.

CHAPTER TEN

Demands and Dragons

Summer of Two

By the time the early warmth of summer had arrived in Nevermoor, inside the walls of the Wundrous Society they were already enjoying long days of blazing sunshine and still, baking heat.

Unit 919 had settled into the strange, somewhat choppy rhythm of life at Wunsoc. No longer awed by the depth and breadth of Proudfoot House, they navigated its subterranean halls with increasing confidence. They were also learning to navigate the changeable nature of the dual-sided Scholar Mistresses, and the unpredictability of their weekly timetables. Aside from Morrigan, of course, whose timetable remained predictably sparse.

Morrigan's schedule ought to have given her plenty of time to spend outside, enjoying the glorious Wunsoc weather, but in reality, she was busy looking over her shoulder and trying to avoid another encounter with the Charlton Five. Hawthorne had been incensed when he found out about the star-throwing. He'd marched into Hometrain the next morning with a ten-item revenge list that Morrigan and Miss Cheery only *just* managed to talk him out of (although Morrigan was rather tempted to let him carry on with item number six: toilet papering Heloise's Hometrain).

She'd decided against sharing the incident with Jupiter, whose trips away had become shorter but more frequent. Each time he came home, barely a day or two would pass before another message arrived from the Wundrous Society or the League of Explorers, and occasionally even other organisations Morrigan hadn't heard of, like the Celestial Observation Group. Then he'd be off again, following another lead on Cassiel or Paximus Luck or the Magnificub. He was still insisting the disappearances were unrelated, but Morrigan thought he sounded less and less certain. He seemed increasingly dejected every time he came home from a dead-ended investigation, which made Morrigan hesitant to pile on with her own worries about school bullies and mysterious blackmail notes.

And then the first demand arrived.

'What's this?' Thaddea asked one afternoon, after Miss Cheery had dropped them all back at Station 919. She was staring at her door, which had a piece of folded blue paper stuck to it.

Morrigan paused at her own door with a sigh. She'd spent a long and miserable day in Onstald's grassy, humid classroom, researching and writing an essay titled 'Wundersmith Blunders of the Avian Age and Their Effects on Air Travel'. All she wanted in the world was to walk through that black door and collapse onto her bed.

Thaddea's face dropped as she read the note. 'No. No way.' She gave a ferocious shake of her head. 'NO. WAY.'

Cadence snatched the note, and Morrigan and the others crowded around to read it over her shoulder.

Thaddea Millicent Macleod.

*You have a fight scheduled in tomorrow
afternoon's Combat Club
against an unknown opponent.
You will throw the fight.
If you do not deliberately lose, we will reveal the
secret of Unit 919.*

*Remember:
Tell no one.
Or we will tell everyone.*

'I've never lost a fight in my life,' Thaddea said, folding her arms across her chest. 'And I'm not going to start now.'

'Even if it means getting us all kicked out of the Society?' snapped Cadence.

Thaddea was silent.

Morrigan read through the note again. Why would someone want Thaddea to – *oh,* she thought suddenly. *Oh!* 'Thaddea, who will you be fighting?'

'Why do you care?'

'*Because,*' she said, trying to keep the impatience out of her voice, 'if we know who it is, we might be able to figure out who wrote this! Maybe the person you're supposed to fight is the one who—'

'It's random,' Thaddea interrupted flatly. 'Opponents are picked out of a hat just before you step in the ring. It could be anyone, in any unit, from any combat class.' Her face was growing stormier by the second. 'Whoever it is, they don't want someone else to win. They just want *me* to lose. But I'm not doing it.'

'I can't get expelled,' said Francis. He looked like he might cry. 'Thaddea, please. I just can't. My aunt will—'

'Oh, my aunt, my aunt,' said Thaddea in a mocking voice. 'Be quiet about your aunt for once. What about my dad? He'd probably die of shame if he knew I'd deliberately lost a fight. This is a matter of principle! Macleods don't throw fights.'

Hawthorne scowled. 'What about the principle of being loyal to your—'

'Oh, *shut up,* Swift.'

'ENOUGH,' shouted Cadence. 'We'll put it to a vote. All in favour of ignoring the notes and allowing whoever this is to let the cat out of the bag?'

Thaddea stuck her hand in the air, staring bullishly at Cadence. Anah followed suit, as did Mahir. Arch's hand crept into the air too, but he at least had the decency to look embarrassed about it.

'All *opposed* to the betrayal of our fellow unit member and flagrant display of contempt for the morals and principles that make up the very foundation of this Society?' said Hawthorne, glaring at Thaddea as he shoved his hand in the air.

Cadence, Francis and Lambeth raised their hands too, although Morrigan wasn't sure Lambeth was really paying attention to the conversation.

'*Morrigan*,' Hawthorne said in a fierce whisper, looking at her significantly.

'Oh! Right.'

Morrigan raised her hand.

Thaddea kicked the wall.

'All right, Swift, now pull back! Easy now . . . he wants to go into a dive, but don't let him. Pull back, check his balance. Remember you're in charge. Stay aloft. Stay aloft. There now – good. Chin up, head back. Your head, Swift, not the dragon's. A bit sharper on that left shoulder dip next time, please.'

Hawthorne's Tuesday morning dragonriding coach was a rather battered-looking man called Fingers Magee who had, during his forty years of professional dragonriding, lost five of his fingers (two on one hand, three on the other).

In the absence of anything better to do, Morrigan had been spending much of her spare time – and she had an awful lot of it – in the dragonriding arena on Sub-Five, watching Hawthorne's training sessions.

It was odd. On one hand, it gave Morrigan a genuine thrill to see her friend so in his element. Dragonriding brought out a side of Hawthorne she rarely got to see, and the transformation was extraordinary. Gone was the excitable rascal with the short attention span. In his place was a serious, capable boy who was focused on the task at hand, attentive to his coach and committed to improving his skillset.

And the dragons themselves were just . . . something else. Morrigan felt privileged just to be in the same space as these ancient reptiles – creatures so exquisitely beautiful, and at the same time so frighteningly powerful and intelligent, that it felt like being in the presence of true magic.

But on the other hand, being here was a mild form of self-inflicted torture.

This was what she had expected the Society to be like. Just like the rest of Unit 919, Hawthorne's class schedule was exciting and robust. Today he had training in the arena followed by an afternoon orienteering lesson in the Whinging Woods. Tomorrow – *Wrangling Hostile Creatures* in the morning, and a lecture called *Achieving Immortality: Is It Possible?* after lunch.

She was *trying* to bring the howling wolf of her envy to heel, she really was.

Today, the wolf was quiet. But only because Morrigan couldn't stop thinking about what had happened at the station the day before.

She gazed up into the cavernous arena ceiling. Her eyes tracked Hawthorne and the dragon as they performed a tight loop-the-loop (to a shout of approval from Fingers Magee), but she wasn't really seeing them. She was seeing Thaddea's twisted scowl. Francis's tearful horror at the threat of expulsion. The timid, guilty way that Arch raised his hand, voting to let Morrigan's secret be exposed.

She'd been so close. *So close.* She wondered if whoever was sending these stupid notes realised how fully they had torpedoed her burgeoning hopes for a happy life at Wunsoc. Perhaps whoever was blackmailing them hated her so much they'd constructed this perfect way to split her unit in half.

But who was it? And how had they discovered her so-called knack? Morrigan had been turning those two questions over in her mind all morning.

'All right, now bring him down slow,' Fingers called up to Hawthorne. 'I want a soft landing, none of your kangaroo-hop nonsense. That's the way. Easy now.'

Today Hawthorne was riding a Dappled Lanternscale, a mid-sized dragon (roughly the size of two elephants) whose scaly turquoise skin shimmered and rippled like lantern light on water. When he brought it smoothly to the ground, the impact through the dragon's muscular hind legs sent gentle, luminous waves skittering across its body.

During his break, while another rider took to the arena, Hawthorne climbed into the stands two steps at a time and flopped down in the seat next to Morrigan. He was sweaty, red-faced and exhausted – but the satisfying kind of exhaustion that comes from having worked hard at something you love.

'That flip thing you did at the end,' she said, handing him his water flask. 'That was brilliant. How'd you not fall out of the saddle?'

'Thanks!' He flicked his curly brown hair out of his face. 'It's just about engaging the right leg muscles and hoping the dragon doesn't do anything stupid. He's a good one, though. Reliable.'

'What's his name again?'

Hawthorne rolled his eyes as he took a swig of water. 'Depends who you ask. His official, tournament-registered name is *Glides Through the Air Like a Hot Knife Through Lard,* but I call him Paul.'

'Mmm,' Morrigan said distractedly.

'You thinking about those notes?' Hawthorne propped his feet up on the back of the chair in front and started to untie his leather shin guards. 'Who do you reckon is sending them?'

'Well . . . I've been wondering. What if it's that Heloise and her gang? The Charlton Five?'

Hawthorne frowned. 'Yeah. She seems the type. But how could she know you're a –' he looked around to make sure nobody was sitting nearby, then whispered, '– *Wundersmith*. Do you think Baz told them?'

'I don't know,' she said truthfully. They sat in silence while Hawthorne fiddled with the strap on his wrist guard. A strange, squirming guilt bubbled away inside Morrigan like poison. 'Thaddea will never forgive me.'

'Forgive you?' sputtered Hawthorne. 'For what? It's not your fault!'

'It's my secret she's protecting.'

'No, it's *our* secret,' he insisted. 'Whoever is sending the notes is threatening all of us – we're in it together.'

Fingers called Hawthorne's name and he began gathering his discarded gear. 'Listen,' he said quietly. 'What's the point in worrying about this when we have no way of knowing who it is? Let's just wait and see what the next note says.'

But as Morrigan watched him descend the steps to the arena, she was struck by a fresh determination. She couldn't simply wait around for the next note, wondering if this demand would be the one to make her entire unit turn against her.

There *was* a way of figuring this out, there had to be. She was going to find it.

And she knew exactly where to start.

C·—

In the biggest dojo on Sub-Five, Thaddea had already entered the ring. Combat Club was a weekly event in which all the different combat disciplines at Wunsoc came together for a series of one-on-one challenges. It was a chaotic, absurdly unfair, all-ages free-for-all in which a barefoot kickboxer might find herself fighting a swordsmith in chainmail, and it was – inexplicably – Thaddea's favourite thing in the world. She liked to recap her matches to the rest of her unit each week, in violent and unflinching detail. Despite being the youngest fighter, she was Combat Club's undefeated champion.

Until today.

'Right. Who's taking on Macleod?' shouted a burly, muscular woman with wiry grey curls, holding up a hat in the air. She pulled out a name and chuckled as she read it. 'Will Gaudy! Up you come, lad. Good grief, this'll be quick,' she added in a low mutter, and the audience responded with groans and jeers of laughter. Brutilus Brown covered his face with one paw.

Will Gaudy was a mouthy boy from Unit 916 who liked to tell nonsense stories in which he starred as the biggest, baddest and toughest hero in town – usually beating up whole gangs of bullies without breaking a sweat. Everyone knew they were nonsense, because Gaudy didn't have any real fighting prowess. His knack wasn't even anything to do with combat; he was a talented composer, but insisted on taking combat classes so that he could tell people outside the Society that he was really a boxer. Morrigan knew Thaddea couldn't stand him.

Thaddea's face fell as she watched him enter the ring. Of all the fighters in the dojo, to record her first ever loss against Will Gaudy, the mouthy shrimp . . . This was going to be humiliating in the extreme. If Will won this fight, he would never, ever, *ever* let her hear the end of it.

Was this rigged, Morrigan wondered. Had their black-mailers *planned* for Will's name to be drawn from the hat somehow? The only way she could see this being true was if the blackmailer was the burly woman drawing out the names, and somehow Morrigan doubted it.

It surely wasn't Will himself – who, despite his bravado, was looking positively queasy at the thought of fighting Thaddea.

Morrigan almost couldn't bear to watch. Part of her wondered if Thaddea was going to change her mind and refuse to throw the fight. Part of her thought she ought to.

But she didn't. In the first round – in the first *minute* – Thaddea allowed herself to be overwhelmed by Will's ridiculous footwork and weak, ineffectual jabs. She didn't even try to make it believable. The first time Will's fist connected with her face (because she basically served it up to him on a platter), she hit the floor and was out for the count.

The audience couldn't believe it. Morrigan could scarcely believe it herself, and she'd been expecting it.

But she had to shake off her shock, because *this* was the moment she'd come for. If the blackmailers wanted Thaddea to lose this fight, surely they'd be here to watch it. She scoured the crowd, examining each and every face in the room, looking for someone to betray some hint of . . . *something.*

But there wasn't a single flicker of smugness or satisfaction to be seen. Everyone present wore an expression of deepest shock at Will's impossible victory. If the blackmailers were here, they were the world's greatest actors.

While Will basked in a shower of cheers and applause, Thaddea jumped down from the ring and trudged straight past Morrigan.

'Thaddea!' she called out. 'Wait, I'm—'

'Leave me alone,' Thaddea barked over her shoulder.

'I just want to say—'

'Just *don't.*'

Morrigan watched her go, feeling worse than ever.

The second demand arrived that Friday afternoon at Station 919, stuck to Francis's glossy blue door. He opened the note with a slightly trembling hand. His eyes narrowed as he read.

'They want . . . *cake*.'

'Cake?' repeated Hawthorne.

'That's what it says.'

Morrigan screwed up her face in confusion. 'Just . . . cake?'

'JUST cake?' Francis looked up from the note in his hand to glare at her. 'No, not JUST cake. READ it.'

Francis John Fitzwilliam.

You will bake and decorate a Grand Caledonian Coronation Crest and place it on Platform 919 by six o'clock tomorrow morning, and then return to your home immediately.
If you do not follow these instructions exactly, we will reveal the secret of Unit 919.

Remember:
Tell no one.
Or we will tell everyone.

'What's a –' Morrigan read from the note, '– Grand Caledonian Coronation Crest?'

'Only the most complicated and difficult cake I can think of,' huffed Francis. 'Three tiers, each a different flavour and density, decorated with hundreds of sugar flowers painted in gold leaf, caramel spirals all over and a lacework sugar crown on the top.'

Hawthorne's eyes widened. 'Can you make extra?'

'This is going to take me all night!' Francis snatched the note back from Morrigan, ignoring Hawthorne. 'And I have four hours of knife skills tomorrow morning. I can't do that on no sleep! I'll lose a finger!'

'Tomorrow's Saturday,' said Hawthorne.

'I *know* tomorrow's Saturday.' Francis glared at him. 'Aunt Hester says my knife skills aren't up to scratch so she's making me take extra weekend lessons.'

Hawthorne gasped. Morrigan had never seen him so affronted as he was by the idea of doing extra schoolwork on the weekends. He seemed to have temporarily lost the capacity for speech.

'This is ridiculous,' she said, indicating the note. 'Why would they want you to make them a *cake?*'

Francis looked wounded. 'Why *wouldn't* someone want me to make them a cake? Have you *tasted* my cake?'

'It is *very* good, Francis,' Hawthorne agreed. 'If I were blackmailing you, I'd definitely get you to make me a cake. And some of those pastries with the custard inside that you did that time. And one of those—'

'Shush, Hawthorne,' said Morrigan. 'I just mean . . . these demands are . . . well, they're *silly*.' She glanced at the black door that led to her bedroom. She'd been looking forward to an evening spent in the Music Salon (Frank had booked a new act who could whistle show tunes through his nostrils), but she knew the guilt of knowing Francis was up baking all night just to safeguard her secret would gnaw away at her insides. She sighed. 'Look. I'll come and help, okay? I'll be your assistant. You don't have to do it on your own. Or – oh, you could come to the kitchen at the Hotel Deucalion! I bet our chef could whip up a . . . a Grand Crusty Caledonia thing.'

This was, apparently, the wrong thing to say. 'I do NOT need help from some second-rate hotel fry cook!'

And with that he was gone, slamming the blue door shut in Morrigan's face.

She shook her head in disbelief. 'Fry cook? Chef Honeycutt's been awarded THREE Royal Lightwing Spatulas.' She waved goodbye to Hawthorne and went through her black door, still muttering to herself. '*Fry cook.*'

She sighed with relief as she swung open the door into her favourite room in the whole world. Her bed seemed to be celebrating the fact that it was at last Friday, and had turned into a giant bird's nest full of soft woven fabrics in a dozen shades of green, with three huge egg-shaped pillows in the centre. Morrigan held out her arms like a bird and fell backwards into its cosy depths, landing with an appreciative *oof*.

She lay there, staring at her ceiling, which had recently become an expanse of dark blue night sky, filled with friendly twinkling stars. It reminded her of the ceiling in Wunsoc's Map Room, and she hoped it would stay that way.

She couldn't stop thinking about Thaddea. About the look on her face when she'd left the dojo, and the miserable silence she'd kept in the days since. Morrigan felt dreadful for her. She'd been so proud of her Combat Club record, so rightfully proud. And to lose to Will Gaudy, of all people. Morrigan was astonished and heartened that Thaddea had kept her word, and sacrificed something so important to her, all for the good of the unit.

It was this last thought that galvanised Morrigan's will. So, the fight had been a bust. She still didn't know who the blackmailers were. But she wasn't going to give up. If Thaddea was willing to lose to Will Gaudy, and if Francis could stay up all night long baking the world's most ridiculous cake, then *she* could find out who was behind all this.

It wasn't like she had anything better to do.

CHAPTER ELEVEN

The Stealth

'He's worried about something.'

'About what?'

'I think . . . money.'

Jack and Morrigan stood by the rail of the spiral staircase, leaning over to observe the spectacle that was Saturday night in the Deucalion lobby. The whole, enormous room had become a lagoon for the evening, and was filled not with its usual gilded velvet furniture and potted trees, but small gondolas and canoes. The vessels carried raucous, glamorous partygoers, all dressed in nautical attire as Frank's invitation had instructed. The costumes were elaborate; so far Morrigan had spotted seven mermaids, four mermen, bands of sailors and pirates, a starfish, an oyster and a violently purple, fully-sequined octopus.

'How can you tell?' Morrigan asked.

Jack squinted both eyes. His eye patch was pulled to the side (another rare occasion), resting against his temple. 'His fingers are green. Green fingers mean he's itching to get hold of some money, or he just lost some.'

Morrigan peered down at the man Jack was studying – a handsome, over-confident man in a tailored admiral's uniform. Standing at the head of a gondola, his eyes glided over the lobby as if he owned the place and all the people in it. 'He looks rich,' she said. 'Look at the jewels around his wife's neck.'

'Rich people worry about money too. Sometimes more than poor people. And that's not his wife, it's his mistress.'

Morrigan gasped, equally scandalised and delighted. This was her new favourite game.

Lately, weekends at the Deucalion were even more lively than usual. Frank was locked in battle with a pair of rival party planners at a new establishment that had opened nearby, the Hotel Aurianna. Every Saturday night he threw some lavishly themed party or dance or masked ball, sometimes closing off entire wings, sometimes taking the celebration to the rooftop so that it could be seen and heard for miles around. Then every Sunday morning, he would pace the lobby, waiting for the delivery of the *Nevermoor Sentinel*, the *Morning Post*, and the *Looking Glass*. When the papers arrived, he would turn immediately to the society pages, and the lobby would ring either with booming, triumphant laughter, or howls of rage, depending on which hotel had garnered the most column inches that week. Frank won more often than not (his parties were legendary, and well-attended by celebrities, the aristocracy and occasionally even royalty), but his infrequent failures were dreaded by everyone at the Deucalion. They were usually followed by several days of dramatic moping, then a renewed frenzy to make the following Saturday's revelries 'the best we've ever had!'.

All of this made Saturday nights at the Deucalion an excellent opportunity for people-watching, and Jack's increasing confidence in his abilities as a Witness made people-watching *much* more fun.

Fenestra – who hated water – was *furious* with Frank over his theme for the evening, and had already threatened to a) call the Stink, b) fill Frank's bedroom with garlic bulbs and c) burn down the hotel. She had of course done none of those things, but *was* hanging threateningly from the black chandelier, hissing and baring her claws at any guests who dared float close enough.

'What about them?' Morrigan pointed at a group of young women dressed as bright tropical fish, their dresses an array of fringe and feathers and beadwork, all terribly modern, and *fabulously* improper. They rowed rather haphazardly around the lobby, drinking pink champagne by the bottle and pestering Wilbur the pianist – stationed with his baby grand on a small sandy island – to play something 'more upbeat'.

Jack looked at them a minute, frowning in concentration. 'That loud one dressed as a clownfish would much rather be at home. Or somewhere else, anyway. There's a . . . it's like a thread, or something. Silver thread. Keeps trying to pull her right out the front door.'

Jupiter's nephew had shown up that afternoon after his cello lesson for a weekend at home. Morrigan was surprised by how much his arrival had improved her day, after what had been a lousy beginning.

Intending to catch the blackmailers red-handed on Station 919 and see who came to take Francis's cake, she'd woken that morning to an alarm set for five minutes to six, quietly pushed open the mystery door and crept through her walk-through Wunsoc wardrobe . . . only to find the whole plan scuppered, because her station door wouldn't budge. There was something blocking it from the other side – the black-mailers were irritatingly clever. When the door finally opened, it was too late: the cake was gone, and there was no trace of anybody on the platform.

Morrigan had knocked on Francis's door to ask how he'd managed with the cake and if he'd seen anything in the station that might give them some clue about their blackmailers. But he'd merely glowered at her – covered in flour, icing and sticky caramel – and slammed the door shut in her face yet again.

Her day had gone further downhill when she'd found that Jupiter was still away, *and* the lobby was completely off-limits all day long while Frank set up for the party that evening.

All in all, Morrigan had been so pleased to see Jack that she'd thus far resisted the urge to mock his posh uniform from the Graysmark School for Bright Young Men, and felt deeply virtuous in her restraint.

'What about her?' She pointed at a woman in a hammer-head shark hat.

'Furious that her younger brother just inherited the family fortune.'

Morrigan looked at him in surprise. 'That's specific.'

'Well . . . I think that's right. She's complicated. Green fingers – that's money problems. Black cross over her heart, that's a recent bereavement. She has a second, smaller shadow – problem with a younger sibling, I'm guessing a brother. And her whole body is glowing a deep wine red; that's the colour of well-nourished anger. She's sad, but she's *livid.*'

Morrigan watched the woman, and fancied she could see a bit of sadness in her, even though she was throwing back Green Lagoon cocktails and flirting with the pretty blonde starfish sharing her canoe.

'What about him?' Morrigan asked, nodding towards a baboonwun gentleman in full pirate regalia carrying a large, brightly coloured parrot on his shoulder.

Jack snorted. 'Desperate for someone to ask about his bird. Annoyed nobody seems interested.'

'You know, you could make a fortune doing this! We could tell people you're clairvoyant. I'll take twenty per cent.'

Jack rolled his eyes, smirking. Morrigan knew he didn't like to take his patch off very often. She and Jack had never discussed it, but Jupiter told her that it had taken him years and years of training as a Witness to be able to 'make sense of the madness', as he called it – to learn to understand the layers and threads, to sift out the important things and ignore the rest – and that Jack wasn't quite there yet. He'd said that for now, Jack's eye patch acted as a sort of filter, disrupting his vision so that he didn't have to see all those things, all the time. So that his strange talent wouldn't drive him to insanity.

'What about you?' Jack said unexpectedly, turning to face her. He held one hand up to shade his eyes as if against a bright light, squinting to see past the glowing Wunder Morrigan knew must be gathering to her even now. She felt her face grow warm. Jack was looking at her the way Jupiter sometimes did, as if he knew something she didn't. As if he perhaps knew lots of things she didn't. It was annoying enough when Jupiter did it, but when Jack did it, she wanted to poke him right in the eye.

She scowled. 'What about me?'

'Black cloud,' Jack said, nodding at her left shoulder. 'Following you around. Problems at school?'

Morrigan hesitated, then said, 'Something like that.'

'What's going on?'

Where to even start, she wondered. Could she tell him about the blackmail? Jack already knew she was a Wundersmith, so it wasn't as if she'd be breaking her promise to the Elders.

Morrigan took a deep breath and, throwing caution to the wind, told him everything: about the three notes they'd received so far, and the vote her unit took, and how at least half of them resented her. Once she got going, she found she couldn't stop. She told him about Professor Onstald, and *An Abridged History of the Wundrous Act Spectrum*, and about Heloise and the Charlton Five. She told him that Jupiter had been on endless top-secret missions, which she suspected were something to do with the missing people. She spoke in a circular ramble, and Jack listened quietly without asking questions, and once she'd said every single thing that was on her mind, Morrigan felt . . . lighter, somehow.

'Is the cloud gone?' she asked finally, trying to look over her left shoulder, though she knew she couldn't see it whether it was there or not.

Jack shrugged. 'It's smaller.'

'Good.'

He nodded, and didn't pry any further. That was one good thing about Jack; he hated people asking him nosy questions, so he didn't tend to ask any himself.

'Speaking of blackmail,' he said, reaching into a concealed inner coat pocket, 'I've been meaning to give you this.' He handed her a folded paper square. It was a dark silvery-black, as thin as a dried leaf, but soft and supple. 'If you ever need me – a proper emergency, I mean, not just some nonsense – if you're in trouble and you need help, write down an address, or a landmark, on the paper. Somewhere I can come and find you. Then say my full name – John Arjuna Korrapati – three times, and burn the paper. It's bonded to me, so no matter where you are, it'll show up in my hand.'

Morrigan raised an eyebrow. She wasn't certain she believed him. 'How does that work?'

'I have absolutely no idea. It's a system my mate Tommy invented so he could cheat on tests, although why he needs to cheat on tests when he's clever enough to invent stuff like this, I'll never know.' Jack shrugged. 'His mum's a witch, she must have helped him. Anyway, it's called the Black Mail. We used to use it to send messages to other dormitories after lights out, until we started running out of blackpapers. Tommy's not allowed to make any more of them because he was caught cheating and got himself suspended, the idiot. I've only got a few of my blackpapers left, but with Jupiter away so much, and everything that's . . . well. I think it's best if you can reach me, that's all,' he finished, looking awkward.

'Okay.' Morrigan pocketed the paper, smiling. 'Um, thanks.'

'Proper emergencies only,' Jack said again, turning back to lean over the stairs.

'I know, I know.' She propped her elbows up on the rail, scanning the lobby for their next subject. 'What about . . . him?'

The man she'd pointed to had just entered and was making his way across the lobby, leaping from rowboat to canoe to gondola as if they were stepping stones in a pond. Guests called out to him in greeting, applauding and shrieking with laughter when he nearly overturned a vessel. His own face remained sombre. He ran a hand through his waves of ginger hair.

'Jupiter!' Morrigan called out to him. He looked up and spotted her and Jack on the staircase, smiling grimly as he gave them a small wave. He held up two fingers and mouthed the words, 'Two minutes.' Then, finally making it to the half-submerged concierge desk, he sat on top of it and began sifting through the large stack of messages Kedgeree handed to him.

Jack's eyes darted over the space around his uncle. 'He's searching for something. That's why he keeps going on all these expeditions. Whatever it is, he can't find it anywhere.'

'What does that look like?'

'Like a grey fog, all around his head,' murmured Jack. 'And dim, flickering lights just out of his reach.'

They didn't notice that Fenestra had abandoned her hostile chandelier-swinging until her enormous shadow suddenly darkened their view, and her low, scathing voice came from behind them. 'What are *they* doing here?'

Morrigan jumped, clutching her chest as she looked up into the Magnificat's menacing glare. 'Can't you wear a bell or something?' she asked, her heart racing. 'What are *who* doing here?'

'The Stink,' said Fen, pointing one paw towards a small group of black-coated men and women who had commandeered a rowboat and were steering it determinedly towards the concierge desk.

Morrigan blinked in surprise. 'Fen! You didn't *actually* call the police on Frank, did you? What a rotten thing to—'

'Do I look like a grass to you?' growled Fen. 'Course I didn't call them. Snitches get stitches.'

'Then why are they—'

'That's not the Stink,' said Jack in a hushed voice. He looked awestruck. 'That's the *Stealth*.'

'The what?' asked Morrigan.

'The Wundrous Society Investigation Department,' said Jack. 'Secret police. They hardly ever show themselves like this, they're usually a bit more . . . you know. *Stealthy*.'

'How do you know it's them?'

'Look at their uniforms: black leather coats, shiny lace-up boots – and see their top pockets?'

Morrigan squinted down at the nearest officer and saw a small golden eye embroidered on his right chest pocket, with a *W* inside the iris.

'Definitely the Stealth. They came here for Uncle Jove once before,' continued Jack, 'a few years ago, when they needed his help on a crime scene investigation. But that was . . . that was for a *murder*,' he said in a whisper. 'Some famous sorcerer. Turned out he was killed by his apprentice, and Jupiter helped them figure it out. The Stealth only get involved in the really serious crimes, and only if they involve Wundrous Society members.'

'They're investigating the disappearances,' said Morrigan.

Jack shook his head, squinting at the black-coated squadron. 'They're definitely searching for something, or someone, but this thing isn't weeks old. It's fresh. They've got that same fog around them as Jupiter, but theirs is thick and . . . I don't know how to describe it, but it's sort of *glittery* – like a thunderstorm. It's new.'

They watched the conversation happening below. Jupiter ran a hand through his wilting hair, looking agitated and deeply tired. Morrigan pushed away from the bannister. 'Let's go down and find out— *ow!*' she squealed, halted suddenly by a single large claw digging into her shoulder. 'Fen!'

'If that *is* the Stealth, you're not going anywhere near them,' the Magnificat growled. 'When Jupiter wants you to know what's going on, he'll tell you. Now, off you go – it must be past your bedtime.'

'I don't have a bedtime,' said Morrigan, frowning.

'Now you do.'

'You can't—'

'Just did.'

'But—'

'BED.'

Morrigan turned back to look at Jupiter, hoping to catch his eye, but he was already on his way out again, heading for the front doors in the little rowboat surrounded by Stealth.

He hadn't even bothered to take off his coat.

CHAPTER TWELVE

Devilish Court

Nobody knew anything about another disappearance. Not Kedgeree or Fenestra or Dame Chanda – Morrigan had spent all of Sunday pestering them in turn. Not Miss Cheery, who'd seemed genuinely surprised (and a little worried) in Hometrain on Monday to hear the Stealth had been to Morrigan's home. Not Professor Onstald, who'd called her 'insolent', 'impertinent' and 'improper' during their morning lesson for daring to ask questions about the inner workings of the Wundrous Society law enforcement system.

Onstald had spent the rest of the class giving Morrigan a long, wheezy lecture about nosiness and propriety . . . which was at least preferable to copying down yet another passage from *An Abridged History of the Wundrous Act Spectrum.*

Her class that afternoon with Mildmay was much more interesting.

'Swindleroads. Tricksy Lanes. Shadowstreets. Ghostly Hours,' he read from a list he'd written on the blackboard. 'Who can tell me what these are?'

Blank faces stared back at him.

'Nobody?' Mildmay looked surprised. 'Lucky you.'

'What are they, sir?' asked Mahir.

'Swindleroads are an old-fashioned tool of scoundrels and highwaymen. A straightforward bit of geographical trickery in which one walks down one end of a laneway and comes out the other end in a different location, sometimes miles away, where a band of blackguards would be waiting to rob you. Most Swindleroads have been blocked off or signposted now, but back in the Age of Thieves, there was a whole plague of them all over the Free State.

'Tricksy Lanes, on the other hand, are a uniquely Nevermoorian bit of nonsense.' He made himself comfortable and started swinging his legs off the edge of the desk. Morrigan had noticed Mildmay did this whenever he got on to a topic that really interested him. 'Awfully inconvenient and occasionally quite frightening, but *mostly* harmless, if you know what you're doing. "Tricksy Lane" is sort of a catch-all term for the little alleys or walkways in Nevermoor that transform in some way, once you're inside them.'

'What do you mean, transform?' Morrigan asked.

'Well, sometimes it means you walk halfway down and then suddenly find yourself facing back the direction you came without ever having turned yourself around. Or perhaps the further you walk down the lane, the closer the alley walls become around you, until you must either turn back the way you came, or risk being squashed to death.'

'Blech,' said Arch, shuddering.

'Yes, I don't recommend it. I once came across a Tricksy Lane that had less gravity the further down you went. I kept floating up into the air, until finally I had to grab on to the wall and drag myself back to where I'd started.'

'Oh!' Morrigan had suddenly remembered her excursion with Jupiter on Spring's Eve. 'I think I've seen one!'

She told Mildmay about the strange little alley on their way to see the Angel Israfel at the Old Delphian Music Hall (omitting, of course, the reason they were visiting him).

'Bohemia, you said?' asked Mildmay. 'Blimey, I'm not sure I was aware of that one. Excellent, Miss Crow! Yes, there are Tricksy Lanes dotted all over the city. Most of them have been mapped, and – like the Swindleroads – are either blocked off or carefully marked with warning signs so you know what you're getting into. But some of them, unfortunately, have a terrible habit of wandering – they'll disappear from one spot and reappear somewhere else entirely. So in truth, the official Tricksy Lane map provided by the Nevermoor Council is sometimes a bit useless. Naturally, I prefer the

Living Map. It's not perfect, but it's pretty good at updating itself.' He picked up a stack of folded maps from the desk beside him and handed the bundle to Anah. 'Nonetheless, here's the Nevermoor Council's best attempt at recording the unrecordable. Take one and pass them on.'

Hawthorne handed Morrigan the last map and she opened it up, peering closely at the curling, miniscule streets. There were dozens of little pink, red and black flags dotted all over the city, each indicating the location of a known Tricksy Lane.

Mildmay clapped his hands once. 'Now, follow me,' he said, heading straight for the Map Room door. 'We're going on an adventure!'

<hr />

It was a perfect summer day in Old Town, sunny and warm, and Unit 919 buzzed with excitement. First-year scholars weren't normally allowed outside Wunsoc during the school day, but Mildmay had obtained special permission from the Scholar Mistress to take his class out for their first ever practical lesson, with the understanding that if any of them – including Mildmay – embarrassed the Society, they would be tied to the train tracks at Proudfoot Station during rush hour.

Their destination turned out to be Temple Close, a tiny little side street not far from Wunsoc – the sort of dim, dirty lane most people would walk by without really noticing.

Mildmay pointed to a grubby little sign on the wall that read:

TEMPLE CLOSE

BEWARE!

BY ORDER OF THE GEOGRAPHICAL
ODDITIES SQUADRON
AND THE NEVERMOOR COUNCIL,
THIS STREET HAS BEEN DECLARED A
PINK ALERT TRICKSY LANE

(NUISANCE-LEVEL TRICKERY PRESENTING SIGNIFICANT
INCONVENIENCE ON ENTRY)

ENTER AT OWN RISK

'Of course,' said Mildmay, 'the safest thing would be to never find yourself in a Tricksy Lane at all. That said, it's best to have a plan of action in case you get caught unawares. So, your clear, easy, three-step plan goes like this. Step one: STAY CALM. Believe me, when you suddenly find yourself floating up into the sky, it's easy to panic. And when we panic, we lose our ability to think clearly.

'I want you all to remember these two simple things: breathe in –' he breathed in for several counts, '– and breathe out.' He let it all go in a slow, steady *whoosh*. 'Do it with me, now. Ready? Breathe in.' As one, the unit inhaled deeply. 'And breathe out.' *Whoosh.* 'Good. You'd be surprised how much it can help in a frightening situation if you just remember to *keep breathing*.'

Cadence turned to Morrigan and rolled her eyes.

'Brilliant,' she muttered. 'I would have forgotten this basic involuntary bodily function if he hadn't mentioned it. I'll write that down.' She made a stupid face and pretended to write it in the air with an imaginary pen.

'Shush,' said Morrigan, trying not to smile.

'Step two: RETREAT,' said Mildmay. 'You don't always know what you're going to get with a Tricksy Lane. You might be lucky and just get an anti-gravity trick, or closing walls . . . those two are common. But there are other, much more dangerous tricks out there. There was a Tricksy Lane over in Southey-upon-Juro a few years ago that took all the air from a man's lungs, suffocating him to death. And I read a story about one right here in Old Town many years ago that literally flipped people inside out, so that all their muscles and organs were on the outside of their bodies.'

The scholars winced and made noises of disgust – except Hawthorne, who whispered, 'Cool,' and Anah, who looked up with interest.

'Never fear,' Mildmay continued, holding up his hands to quiet them. 'That lane's gone. They bricked it up.'

Morrigan smirked and shook her head at Hawthorne, who looked almost disappointed.

'My point is, you won't always know what you're fighting when you walk into a Tricksy Lane. So, the solution is, don't fight. Retreat. *Always* retreat. *Never* think you can outwit the trick, *never* think you can overpower it, *never* think you can fight through it. Your lives are worth more than a shortcut.' He looked at each of them in turn, his young, round face as solemn as Morrigan had seen it.

'Finally, step three: TELL SOMEONE. Why is that important?'

Anah's hand shot straight into the air. 'To stop other people from getting caught in it?'

'Very good. Why else?'

'In case it isn't on the map yet,' called out Mahir.

'Correct. Why else?'

The unit fell silent.

Mildmay rolled out his council map again. 'Because it might have changed. Tricksy Lanes are mercurial – they can shift and evolve over time. Look at your maps. See Perrins Court, over in Highwall? That used to be your basic, everyday ankle-dangler. Last week, one of our more careless fourth-year scholars took a wrong turn onto Perrins Court and found himself swimming through raw sewage.'

A chorus of 'ughh' and 'ewww' rang out.

'Indeed,' continued Mildmay. 'But this young man did exactly the right thing. He stayed calm, he retreated, and he told his conductor. Well, first he took a shower, *then* he told his conductor, who told the Geographical Oddities Squadron, and we told the council, who have now updated this map. Because of the health risks, they upgraded the threat level of Perrins Court from a Pink Alert (Nuisance-Level Trickery Presenting Significant Inconvenience on Entry) to a Red Alert (High-Danger Trickery and Likelihood of Damage to Person on Entry) and installed a warning sign.'

'But sir, why don't they just brick it up, like the guts-on-the-outside one?' said Hawthorne.

'Because there's still hope for Perrins Court. It changed from an ankle-dangler to a sewage stream . . . there's always the possibility it might change back into an ordinary street one day. We only brick up the hopeless cases. The Black Alerts.'

'What does a Black Alert mean?' asked Morrigan.

'Death on Entry.'

Morrigan swallowed. How many of those lanes were out there in Nevermoor, so far undetected?

'Don't worry,' said Mildmay with a smile. 'Black Alerts are extremely rare and this street, Temple Close, is just a Pink Alert. I've brought you here for practice. Each of you is going to enter Temple Close and – following the first two steps of our three-step plan – safely retreat. Who's first?'

Predictably, Thaddea and Hawthorne were the first volunteers. They practically knocked each other out trying to get to the front of the group. But Mildmay had other ideas.

He beckoned a reluctant Francis to the front and held on to his shoulders as they stared down the narrow, cobbled laneway of Temple Close. The rest of the unit crowded in behind them, observing. Though she couldn't see his face, Morrigan could tell Francis was terrified – he was visibly shaking.

'Remember, Mr Fitzwilliam,' Mildmay said, 'BREATHE, and then RETREAT. Just remember those two things and you'll be fine.'

'Can't someone else go first?' Francis whimpered.

'Ooh – me!' Hawthorne stuck his hand in the air. Mildmay reached out and put it down for him.

Thaddea gave an impatient huff. 'Don't be such a baby, Francis. It's only a Pink Alert, for goodness' sake.'

'Thaddea, don't be mean,' said Mildmay, and then, 'Although she's right, Francis. This one's just an ankle-dangler. Worst it'll give you is a rush of blood to the head. When that happens, just take a few steps backwards – even though you'll be dangling in the air, just go through the motions as if you're walking on the ground. As the lane senses your intent to go back the way you came, it'll put you right way up again, quick as you like.' He gave Francis a gentle nudge. 'Go on now. You can do this.'

Francis took a step forward, then another.

Hawthorne began to chant, quietly and encouragingly. 'Francis, Francis, Francis.' Morrigan and the rest of the unit joined in, their whispers swelling to fill the narrow space. 'Francis, Francis, Francis.'

Another step, then a few more, until at last, when Francis was halfway down the alley, he was pulled up into the air and flipped upside down as if he weighed nothing. He dangled there a moment, one leg sticking straight up to the sky while all his other limbs thrashed about.

'Breathe, Francis!' said Mildmay. 'Stay calm.'

Francis took great, heaving breaths, and stopped flailing.

'You know what to do next, come on. One step back . . . and then another . . .'

'Francis, Francis, Francis . . .'

Though he was upside down, Francis lifted his foot to take a big, comically overacted step backwards. Another fake step, and then another, and then—

'YES!' Mildmay gave a jubilant shout, jumping up to punch the air as Francis flipped right-way-up, stumbling a little as he landed on the cobblestones. He turned back around to face them, breathless and shell-shocked, but grinning.

Each of the scholars took their turn going down Temple Close, flipping and un-flipping to cheers from Mildmay and the rest of the unit. Morrigan shrieked with laughter when her turn came to be upended, and Hawthorne loved it so much he begged to go again.

'You can have a second go, Mr Swift,' said Mildmay. 'You all can. Everyone got your maps? I want you to get into groups of three and choose a Tricksy Lane here in Old Town where you can practise retreating safely. Stay in the North Quarter. Pink Alerts only. And remember: STAY CALM and RETREAT. We'll all meet back at the gates to Wunsoc when the Courage Square clock strikes three.'

'Francis, would you like to be in our group?' Morrigan offered. Francis scowled and turned away. It was the fourth time that day she'd tried unsuccessfully to talk to him. She'd thought Thaddea's sulking had been bad, but Francis's was *much* worse. He'd spent the day alternating between shooting scornful looks at Morrigan and pretending he'd gone deaf every time she tried to speak to him.

'Seems to have forgotten which way he voted, doesn't he?' muttered Hawthorne. 'I'd give it up if I were you, Morrigan.'

Francis followed Thaddea and Anah, while Mahir led Arch and Lambeth in another direction. Cadence was left on her own, looking awkward and resentful. None of the others had even glanced in her direction. She'd been forgotten again.

'Come with us, Cadence,' said Morrigan, beckoning to her. Cadence strolled over, trying to look as if she couldn't care less.

The three of them studied Morrigan's map together. There were eleven Pink Alerts in the North Quarter to choose from. It took Hawthorne and Cadence ten minutes just to agree on a lane, and by the time they got there, Mahir's group had already claimed it so they had to start over.

'Devilish Court!' said Hawthorne, pointing at the map over Morrigan's shoulder. 'That sounds cool.'

'It's in the *West* Quarter, dummy,' muttered Cadence.

'So?'

'So he said to stay in the North Quarter.'

'It's *barely* in the West Quarter – only by one block.'

'It's still in the—'

'Oh, let's just *go*,' said Morrigan, rolling up the map, 'or the lesson will be over.'

Devilish Court was narrow and dark, so dark they couldn't see what was at the end of it. It was like gazing into a tunnel. There was a small sign at the entrance, identical to the one at Temple Close, declaring it a Pink Alert Tricksy Lane.

'I'll go first,' said Hawthorne. He made as if to break into a run, and Morrigan grabbed the back of his shirt.

'Wait! You can't just *run in*. We don't even know what sort of trick it is. Be *sensible*. Go slowly.'

With an eye-roll and a mumbled, 'Yes, Dad,' Hawthorne reluctantly slowed to a walk. Morrigan and Cadence watched in anticipation, expecting him to be suddenly flipped upside down any moment. Halfway down the alley, however, Hawthorne stopped, swaying slightly where he stood.

'Hawthorne?' Morrigan called. 'What's wrong, are you okay?'

'I don't . . . I don't feel very good.'

'Are you sick?'

He took another step forward, then paused again. 'Ugh. I think I'm gonna puke.'

Cadence made a noise of disgust.

Morrigan frowned. 'Do you think that's the trick, or is it just something you ate?' Either one was plausible, she thought, since for lunch that day he'd bolted down three roast beef and gravy sandwiches, four bowls of whelk soup and a pint of strawberry milk.

'I think it's – ugghhhh.' He leaned over, resting his hands on his knees, and his body convulsed as if about to purge itself.

'Retreat!' called Morrigan. 'Hawthorne, try taking a step backwards.'

'I can't – I can't, I'm gonna be—' He covered his mouth with his hands, swaying again.

'Come BACK, you idiot!' shouted Cadence.

Hawthorne forced his feet to take one shaky step backwards, then another, and Morrigan saw the tension instantly leave his body. He stood up straight, took another step back, then turned and ran the rest of the way.

'That was *horrible*,' he said, brushing his hair back from his pale, clammy face. He still looked a little green around the gills. 'Who's next?'

'Think I'll pass, thanks,' said Cadence, looking deeply underwhelmed.

Hawthorne glared at her. 'No way. If I did it, you two are doing it.'

She scoffed. 'No chance.'

'I bet you can't get farther than I did.'

'I bet I don't care.'

'I bet you're too chicken.' Hawthorne made clucking noises and pretended to flap his wings.

Morrigan rolled her eyes. 'Oh, for goodness' sake. *I'll* go. Here, Cadence – hold the map.' She marched down the cobbled alley until a ripple of nausea stopped her in her tracks. She waited, unsure whether she was going to fall over, or faint, or vomit all over her shoes. Or all three.

But something drew her onwards, through the sickening haze – some instinct or impulse she couldn't explain. She'd been thinking all lesson about that night in Bohemia, and the rotten-smelling alley that had led her and Jupiter to the Old Delphian. More than anything, she felt a burning curiosity to know how far the lane would let her go, what was at the end of it, and what might happen if she just . . . pushed through . . .

She took another couple of steps, then had to lean forward, hands on knees, and wait for the second awful, unbalancing wave of nausea to pass.

'You can come back now,' called Hawthorne from behind her. 'You've already gone farther than I did.'

But despite the overwhelming revulsion she felt at the thought of going any farther, Morrigan took another tentative step. This lane was hiding something. She felt a tingle in her fingertips. And there was something else – voices somewhere up ahead. Indistinct at first, and then—

'. . . and now we've got the bleedin' Stealth on our tails. Never stay on schedule at this rate . . .'

The *Stealth*. Had she heard that right?

Morrigan paused, straining to hear the rest, trying to control her urge to vomit. She had to see what – who – was hiding down this lane. She pushed ahead even as her body shook, even as behind her Hawthorne and Cadence shouted, 'Come *back*! What are you *doing*?' – and finally, just as Morrigan was certain she was about to bring up her lunch all over the cobblestones, she launched forward, pushing through an invisible wall of resistance . . . and felt her nausea disappear. Just like that.

She looked back. Hawthorne and Cadence were gone. The light at the end of Devilish Court was gone; it was like the lane had reversed itself, and instead of looking ahead into a black tunnel, the blackness was behind her.

Morrigan was standing at the mouth of the alley, on the edge of a large square she'd never seen before. The ground was rough and uneven, and thick tufty grass grew in great swollen patches where the paving stones had long ago broken and never been fixed. The square was set up like a makeshift market, dirty and sprawling, with old canvas tents and tables for stalls. They were empty, as if an event had just ended, or hadn't yet begun. The place had an air of quiet desolation. The back of Morrigan's neck prickled.

'It'll go for a lot more than that,' came a woman's gruff voice from inside a nearby tent. 'Just hold it for a few more days, until the big—'

'I need a buyer *now*,' a man's voice interrupted in an urgent whisper. 'This thing's a proper rarity, but I can't hold on to it forever, it's a menace. Look what it did to me – I'll be lucky if that's not infected.'

Morrigan felt exposed, standing in the near-deserted square, and she drew back into the shadow of the alley. She had a strange feeling in the pit of her stomach that had little to do with the nauseating Tricksy Lane.

'I told you,' the woman said. 'Be patient. If it's as good a specimen as you say—'

'It is.'

'—then it'll fetch a good price at the next auction, and your reputation will be made. Provided you can deliver again in the autumn lots.'

Morrigan felt something drip onto her forehead, and automatically wiped it off. Her fingers came away black as ink. She looked up and saw she was standing beneath the shadow of a large wooden arch. A man was perched at the top of a tall ladder, holding a paintbrush in one hand and a tin of black paint in the other, painting a sign on the arch that read:

THE GHASTLY MARK

The painter looked down at that moment, his eyes widening as he spotted Morrigan.

'Oi!' he shouted, and the tin he was holding plummeted to the ground with a clatter, spraying black paint across the cobbles. Morrigan jumped as it splashed her trousers. 'Who are you? How'd you get in here?'

She didn't hang around to answer him. The painter hurried down the ladder, nearly tumbling off in his haste to get to her, but Morrigan was faster. She turned and pelted down the tunnel-like alley, back the way she'd come, breaking through the invisible barrier halfway down, plunging headfirst into a physical sensation so sickening she felt it might be the end of her. She pushed on, running through the revulsion without slowing down. A light emerged up ahead and, seeing Hawthorne and Cadence's shocked faces, Morrigan ran even faster, shouting at them as she reached the mouth of Devilish Court.

'RUN!'

CHAPTER THIRTEEN

Fire and Ice

Morrigan raced ahead, listening for footfalls behind her. She led Hawthorne and Cadence from the darkness of the alley into the bright sunlight of Old Town, weaving through street traffic and pedestrians and never slowing, never stopping until they reached the gates of Wunsoc, breathless and exhausted, but safe. If the man *had* followed Morrigan out of Devilish Court, they'd lost him somewhere along the way.

'What was that about?' demanded Hawthorne, bent double and clutching his sides. 'What are we running from?'

Morrigan didn't know how to answer. *A man with a paintbrush?* She couldn't say exactly what it was about the hidden square that had been so deeply unsettling, but that chill on the back of her neck hadn't gone away, even though she was hot from running. She told Hawthorne and Cadence everything she'd seen and heard, and they looked just as puzzled as she felt.

'The Ghastly Mark?' said Cadence. 'Do you mean the Ghastly Market?'

'That could be it,' said Morrigan. 'Maybe he wasn't finished painting the sign.'

Cadence's eyes widened. 'That's not good.'

Hawthorne made a face. 'Oh, come on, Cadence. You don't seriously believe in the Ghastly Market?'

'You *don't*?'

'What's the Ghastly Market?' asked Morrigan.

'What's all this?' said Mildmay, arriving just as the Courage Square clock struck three in the distance.

'Oh, um . . .' Morrigan faltered. She wanted to ask Mildmay about what she'd seen, but two things immediately came to mind: firstly, that they'd strayed into the West Quarter, which was supposed to have been out of bounds. And secondly, that she'd completely ignored his three-step plan for dealing with Tricksy Lanes. How could she explain that she'd replaced STEP TWO: RETREAT with her own STEP TWO: KEEP PUSHING THROUGH AND STICK YOUR NOSE IN WHERE IT'S NOT WELCOME EVEN THOUGH THIS IS DEFINITELY AGAINST THE RULES? 'Nothing,' she finished lamely.

Mildmay looked from her to Hawthorne and Cadence, looking suspicious. 'I thought I heard someone mention the Ghastly Market?'

Morrigan blanched. 'No – well, yes. It's a funny story, actually—'

'Er, yeah, my brother Homer's been teasing me all year,' said Hawthorne quickly, cutting Morrigan off before she could say anything else. He flashed her a look. 'He says, now I'm in the Society, the Ghastly Market will be after me. But he's just jealous because he doesn't have a knack.'

The young teacher's expression softened into something like amusement. 'The old traditions continue, I see! Passing down the urban legend through the generations.' He looked past Hawthorne. 'Ah – there you are!' he called out to the rest of the unit, who were trudging up the hill. Mildmay signalled the guard stationed at the Wunsoc entrance, the gates groaned open, and he ushered everyone up the long drive towards Proudfoot House.

'What's an urban legend?' asked Morrigan.

She, Hawthorne and Cadence had all hung towards the back of the group and surrounded Mildmay, while the others swarmed ahead, chatting happily and re-enacting their successful Tricksy Lane navigations. 'Oh, it's just a story that people tell each other, repeated so often that it becomes an accepted truth. In this case, it's a silly myth told to frighten young Wunsoc scholars.' He waved a hand dismissively. 'I wouldn't pay it any heed.'

'Told you,' Hawthorne said to Cadence. 'It's not real.'

'It's *real*,' Cadence insisted. 'My mum knows a lady whose great-aunt was taken for the Ghastly Market. They never saw her again.'

Mildmay gave a deep, reluctant sigh and shoved his hands in his trouser pockets. 'Well, I suppose the Ghastly Market itself *might* have been real enough many years ago. It was supposedly a black market – a secret, illegal trading place where you could buy almost anything you can think of – weapons, exotic unnimal parts, human organs, outlawed sorcery ingredients . . .'

'Even Wunimals,' said Cadence.

'You could *buy* Wunimals?' Morrigan repeated, horrified. 'That's awful.'

'Disgusting, isn't it?' said Cadence. 'And not just Wunimals – centaurs, unicorns, dragon eggs, all sorts. Until the author-ities shut it down, of cour—'

'Magnificats?' Morrigan interrupted. 'What about Magnificats?'

Mildmay looked at her oddly. 'Why?'

'Just wondering.'

She was thinking about Dr Bramble's missing cub, of course, but Fenestra also came to mind. The idea of stubborn, grouchy, loyal, overprotective Fen being put up for sale – of some foolish person actually trying to *own* Fenestra the Magnificat – made Morrigan want to kick something.

When she'd first come to Nevermoor, meeting Fen with her shaggy grey fur and attitude problem had been a shock, because Morrigan *had* seen Magnificats before – in the news – but those were very different. Back in the Republic, President Wintersea famously had six Magnificats pulling a carriage . . . silent, obedient creatures with sleek black fur and studded collars.

In light of this new information, Morrigan couldn't help but wonder where those Magnificats had come from in the first place. Might they have been purchased on the black market? Somehow turned from intelligent, independent creatures like Fen, into little more than well-trained *transport?*

'I've heard people say,' said Cadence, talking more quietly now, 'you could even buy a knack; that the Bonesmen would come and kidnap Wundrous Society members and steal their knacks to sell at the Ghastly Market.'

'The Bonesmen?' Morrigan asked. 'What are they?'

Mildmay chuckled. 'The "Skeletal Legion" they're also called.' He rolled his eyes. 'Proper bogeyman stuff. *Supposedly* they used to emerge from dark, lonely places where carcasses were plentiful – graveyards, battlefields, riverbeds, you know – spontaneously assembling themselves from the jumbled leftovers of the dead.'

'That's what Homer always says too,' said Hawthorne, his lip curling into a bitter half-smile. 'To be careful if I smell saltwater or rotting meat, or—'

'Or if you hear the *click-clacking* of bones?' Mildmay laughed again. 'Yes, when I was in school kids used to terrorise each other with stories about gangs of Bonesmen coming to snatch them in their sleep, leaving nothing behind but a trail of bones. I told you: it's bogeyman stuff. Monsters under the bed. It's not *real*, and it's nothing to be afraid of.'

But Morrigan wasn't laughing. She had a sudden, swooping feeling like she'd missed a step going downstairs.

As Mildmay jogged ahead to talk to the others about their Tricksy Lane practice, she slowed down, holding Hawthorne and Cadence back.

'I don't think the Bonesmen are just a legend,' she said quietly. There were goosebumps up and down her arms. 'I . . . I think I saw one.'

'You think you *what*?' said Cadence.

'Where?' asked Hawthorne. '*When*?'

'A while ago, down at the docks. I didn't know what it was at the time, but it was *just* like Mildmay described.' She shivered a little, remembering the strange assembly of bones and debris, the grotesque *wrongness* of the thing.

'So if the Bonesmen are real . . .' began Hawthorne, a frown creasing the spot between his eyes.

'Then the Ghastly Market must be real, too,' finished Morrigan.

She thought about Cassiel, Paximus Luck and Dr Bramble's cub. If there was a chance of finding any of them, maybe the Ghastly Market was it.

And if her hunch was right, then she needed to return to Devilish Court and find out.

He didn't need to, but Mildmay walked Unit 919 all the way to Proudfoot Station, where Miss Cheery was waiting to take them home. She was sitting in the doorway of their Hometrain, holding a cup of tea with both hands, eyes closed as she soaked up the afternoon sunshine filtering through the canopy above.

'Oh! Hello, Marina,' called Mildmay. There was a note of surprised nonchalance in his voice that Morrigan could tell he was faking. He pushed his fringe back out of his eyes, then bounced on his toes and swung his arms slightly awkwardly. Morrigan thought she could see a faint blush in his cheeks, and she nudged Hawthorne, smirking.

'He's dreaming,' Hawthorne whispered in reply.

Miss Cheery cracked one eye open. 'Hello, Henry. All right, you lot? How was Old Town?' She stood up, pouring what was left of her tea out onto the train tracks. 'Everyone ready—'

The conductor was interrupted by a horrendous sound that was half-scream, half-sob. Morrigan turned towards the noise and was instantly knocked to the ground by what looked – and felt – like a human cannonball. A maelstrom of thrashing limbs and long, mossy-green hair.

'What'd you do to him? What'd you do? ANSWER ME!'

Morrigan recoiled as Heloise tried to claw at her face. Mildmay and Miss Cheery each grasped one of the older girl's flailing arms and hauled her away, but Heloise fought them, still trying to lunge at Morrigan. Hawthorne and Cadence rushed to help a shell-shocked Morrigan up from the ground.

'STOP!' shouted Miss Cheery, struggling to keep her grip.

'She knows something,' spat Heloise. 'She did something to him! Where is he? Where's Alfie?'

'Heloise, calm yourself,' said Mildmay. 'What are you talking about, what's happened to Alfie?'

Heloise sobbed, gulping air down into her lungs. 'Look – LOOK!'

She pulled away and thrust a note under Mildmay's nose. Mildmay read it aloud, looking increasingly confused. '"*I can't stay any longer. I don't deserve to be in the Society. Please find my W pin enclosed. I hereby withdraw from my unit. Regards, Alfie Swann.*" But Heloise . . . what can this possibly have to do with Morrigan? If Alfie wanted to leave, then—'

Heloise choked out a sob. 'Alfie didn't want to *leave*! He would never leave without telling me. He loves me! He didn't write this stupid note.'

Mildmay looked sympathetic. 'I'm sure it might seem like—'

'He didn't write it,' Heloise insisted. 'Alfie doesn't know what "hereby" means. He can barely spell his own name. He didn't write this, he *didn't*!'

Miss Cheery took the note from Mildmay and looked it over. 'That still doesn't explain what this has to do with Morrigan.'

'There's something wrong with her, everybody knows it!' Heloise screeched, her face streaked with tears. Morrigan flinched away. Everyone on the platform was staring at them now. 'She's done something to him, I know she has. She's some sort of . . . I don't know what she is, but she can control people. I've seen her do it. She made him leave! What if she's hurt him, what if she made him hurt *himself*?! She's got it in for us because of what we – because of . . . oh, ALFIE!' She trailed off into sobs.

'Heloise,' said Miss Cheery. 'I know how upset you must feel, but—'

'What's her knack?' Heloise demanded. 'Nobody knows. Know why the Elders won't tell anyone? Cos it's something dangerous. How come all these disappearances only started happening when SHE joined the Society?'

A sea of faces turned Morrigan's way. A familiar creeping sensation climbed the back of her neck, and in that instant, she realised she'd been waiting for this. Since her first day at Wunsoc, since the disappearance of Paximus Luck, the cursed girl who still lived somewhere inside Morrigan had been waiting for *this*. The accusation.

Miss Cheery took Heloise's arm again, just as the whispers began.

'Be careful,' Lambeth said quietly, but Miss Cheery didn't hear.

'Why don't you come with me, Heloise?' she said in a deliberately calm, patient voice. 'Come on. Let's get you up to Proudfoot House and we'll sort this all out. I think you need a nice cup of tea.'

Lambeth winced. 'Be *careful*,' she said again, this time looking right at Morrigan.

Morrigan frowned. 'What are you—'

But Heloise was yowling like an angry cat, and wrenched her arm out of Miss Cheery's grip. 'Shut UP! Don't you TOUCH ME!'

Heloise drew her arm back and Morrigan barely had time to register the flash of silver in her hand before the girl had lashed out. Miss Cheery cried out in pain as Heloise sliced her right across the face with one of her throwing stars, drawing a thin, shallow line of blood.

There were gasps and shouts of dismay all around them on the platform.

Morrigan opened her mouth, a strangled noise of shock and fury rising up in her, but no sound came out. Instead, she felt a wave of anger such as she'd never felt before. It crashed over her not like water but *lava*, molten fire burning her from the inside. The taste of ash sprang to the back of her throat, just like it had when the first blackmail note had appeared. Her sudden rage was a monster, clawing its way up from deep within her chest, from her lungs, searing the flesh of her throat and bursting out of her mouth, igniting the very air around her.

She felt the wrath of a hundred dragons.

She would set the whole world aflame.

A fireball sprang from Morrigan's lips.

It burned through the air, uncontrolled and without a target, singeing Heloise's skin as it whooshed past her and shot straight into the domed canopy of trees overhead, setting the station roof ablaze.

Heloise screamed.

Everyone screamed.

Morrigan heaved in deep, gasping breaths, watching the horror unfold while her fury burned itself out.

'ENOUGH!' came a cry from somewhere behind them, and along with it a vast swirling column of water flew through the air, dousing the flames, and turning them to ice in the branches overhead. The platform fell silent, except for Heloise's shaking sobs, as they all turned to see who had saved them.

Murgatroyd was standing on the footbridge. Her milky eyes blazed a brighter, colder white than Morrigan remembered them. She was breathing like she'd just run a marathon, and jets of frozen mist streamed from her nostrils. Tiny crystals of ice had formed on her cheeks. Her gnarled and knotted hands were curled into claws.

The crowd on the platform held its breath as the Arcane Scholar Mistress swept down from the footbridge towards the platform. As she stalked towards them, her hunched form began to stretch and straighten. Her stark white hair smoothed and softened to silver-blonde, her eyes brightened to an angry ice-blue, and with a sickening *crack-crack-crack-crunch* of her neck, the Arcane Scholar Mistress was gone, and only the Mundane remained.

'You,' said Dearborn, pointing to Miss Cheery even as she stared at Morrigan. Her voice was tightly controlled. Emotionless.

But she looked *frightened*.

'Escort Miss Crow to the Elders' Hall.'

CHAPTER FOURTEEN

The Elders' Hall

Morrigan stood in the shadow of a towering amethyst statue. A sinister-looking puppet master, his clawed hands poised high above Morrigan, pulled the strings of a dead-eyed dancing puppet. It hung down limply by her head.

Miss Cheery was stood to her other side, next to two fifteen-foot women carved from white marble – sweet-faced conjoined twins, their eyes covered with decorative masks. They split into two somewhere around the heart, separating like branches of a tree.

Morrigan had wanted to see inside the Elders' Hall since last year, when Cadence had stolen her place at the Elders' secret dinner. Hardly anyone was permitted to enter the inner sanctum of Elder Quinn, Elder Wong and Elder Saga – even among Society members, it was considered a rare and lucky honour.

Morrigan did not feel lucky, or honoured. She didn't want to see the Elders' Hall like this. Not for this reason.

Morrigan counted the statues, because she needed a distraction. There were nine in all – their poses dignified, their faces by turns heroic, stern, kindly or indifferent. A blindfolded man made of turquoise, a rose-quartz woman with eight pairs of arms fanning out around her. A man carved from amber whose hands were candles, dripping wax rivulets down his arms.

If she hadn't been so terrified, so utterly convinced this was the last she'd ever see of Wunsoc at all, Morrigan might have been fascinated by these mysterious, majestic figures. As it was, she was just trying – for the second time that day – not to vomit.

She and Miss Cheery had left behind the shocked crowd at the platform and walked all the way to Proudfoot House in a tense, fretful silence. Even now, Morrigan could almost feel her conductor buzzing, crackling, with a worry too awful to name.

'You're still bleeding,' Morrigan said to her, when at last she found the courage to look Miss Cheery in the face. She pulled the sleeve of her jumper over her hand and reached out to wipe away a trickle of blood, but Miss Cheery flinched away . . . then gave a weak, apologetic half-smile.

Morrigan felt tears prickle and drew in a sharp breath.

The wooden doors at the end of the hall flew open, and Ms Dearborn marched inside, the clicking of her court shoes echoing loudly in the vast space.

'You,' barked the Scholar Mistress, pointing a finger at Miss Cheery. 'Teaching hospital. Get that cut looked at.'

'But Ms Dearborn, shouldn't I stay—'

'*Now.*'

Miss Cheery hesitated, glancing reluctantly at Morrigan, but she had no choice. She left, squeezing Morrigan's arm gently as she passed.

The Elders filed into the hall after Dearborn, followed by the odious Baz Charlton, self-righteous and smug. Morrigan's heart sank. *Of course*, she thought. *Heloise's patron.*

Baz was followed by the diminutive Professor Onstald, his flat tortoise feet shuffling along at an unbearably slow pace, the enormous domed shell on his back making him look at if he might fall over at any moment. What was *he* doing here, Morrigan wondered.

Just when it seemed the room was filling with all the people in the world who hated her most, a shock of ginger hurried into the hall, pushing past Onstald and straight over to where Morrigan stood.

'Jupiter!' she cried out, unable to contain her joy at seeing him.

'Morrigan!' he said urgently, putting his hands on her shoulders. 'Are you all right?'

Morrigan stared up at her patron. He was here. Jupiter was actually here. How had he got here so fast? She didn't care. She felt a rush of relief, just knowing that she wasn't alone. His bright blue eyes burned into hers, wide with worry.

'Mog?' he prompted. The lump in her throat made it impossible to speak. She nodded, and a silent understanding passed between them.

'Is *she* all right?' said Baz, practically spitting the words in his haste to get them out. 'The nasty little troublemaker who – who done all this trouble? You're having a laugh, North.'

Jupiter ignored him.

'This is a failed experiment,' said Dearborn, pacing agitatedly up and down the hall. She cracked her neck to the side, closing her eyes briefly. 'Elders, I begged you after last year's Show Trial to take my advice, but you ignored it and here we—'

Dearborn cracked her neck again, hunched her shoulders and drew in a deep rasp of a breath. Morrigan felt a familiar creeping horror, and even the adults in the room seemed to cringe away from the Mundane Scholar Mistress as she began to warp into her Arcane counterpart. It was like watching the wilting of a flower on fast-forward. The gnarled, milky-eyed Murgatroyd emerged, brown teeth bared, and fixed her hollow gaze on Morrigan.

'I told you,' rasped Murgatroyd. 'She ought to have been in *my* school. Dearest Dulcie is correct. This *is* a failed experiment. But it is not the beastly girl who has failed. It is all of you who have failed the beastly girl. I *told* you, Dulcie—'

A wash of cool blue light was cast over Murgatroyd's face, and with a strange, gurgling yelp and a crunching of bones, Dearborn was instantly back in the room. Morrigan shuddered. 'This doesn't concern you, Maris,' Dearborn hissed. 'Stay out of it!'

The transformation reversed itself again, and Murgatroyd returned. 'But it does concern me.' She spoke in a low, chilling growl. 'I *told* you someone must teach the little beast her Wretched Arts, or the Wretched Arts will manifest without proper—'

Snap. Crunch. Dearborn returned with a sound like bones breaking. Everyone in the room winced, except for Morrigan, who was distracted by what Murgatroyd had just said. *The Wretched Arts.* Where had she heard those words before?

'This is *not* your place, you raving lunatic!' Dearborn shouted. 'The girl is a Mundane Scholar, whether you agree or not.' And without missing a beat, she turned back to address the Elders. 'Forgive me, Elder Quinn, but I did warn you this would go horribly wrong.'

Elder Quinn gave a sigh and said in a quiet voice, 'Yes, this is all very dramatic, Dulcinea, but none of it helps us decide on a course of action.' She turned to Morrigan, looking deeply weary. 'Miss Crow, you may or may not be relieved to know that Heloise Redchurch is recovering in the hospital, and will have no permanent injuries.'

Morrigan closed her eyes, exhaling a long, shuddering breath. 'I-I am. Of course I'm relieved. I didn't mean to hurt her, Elder Quinn. I swear. I don't know how it happened. I just—'

'And what about Alfie?' Baz interrupted, looking to the Elders. 'My boy Alfie Swann, he's disappeared. Heloise seems to think she –' he pointed at Morrigan, '– had something to do with it.'

Something occurred to Morrigan then. She was sure Baz had told the Charlton Five about her being from the Republic, and goaded them to attack her. Was he also behind Alfie's disappearance? Was this just an attempt to pin something on Morrigan and get her kicked out of the Wundrous Society?

Could he also be responsible for blackmailing Unit 919, then? She still couldn't figure out exactly what he stood to gain. Why would he take such a risk?

Elder Quinn clicked her tongue impatiently. 'Oh, the Swann boy. Breathes underwater, yes? Charlton, don't be ridiculous. Alfie's been struggling with his marks all year. He's obviously beginning to realise that a set of gills will only get you so far in life, and the rest requires hard work.' She waved an impatient hand as if she'd quite like to bat Baz away.

'Perhaps when he's had time to realise how privileged his life at Wunsoc is, he'll have the common sense to return to school and pull his socks up. And incidentally, we shall determine a punishment for Heloise's violent outburst. The Elders and I have worked all year to contain this . . . this *missing persons* situation, to avoid panic and rumours spreading, and now look where we find ourselves – all thanks to one dramatic schoolgirl with a big mouth.'

Baz went to reply, but was interrupted by Elder Saga stamping his hoof.

'None of this is relevant,' grumbled the bullwun. 'The question remains: what shall we do with the Wundersmith?'

'Activate her safeguard!' demanded Baz.

There was a sharp intake of breath from every adult in the room. Even Dearborn looked alarmed. Morrigan's eyes flitted from face to face. What did Baz mean by that, and why had it inspired looks of such outrage and disbelief? Her gaze landed on her patron last, and she swallowed.

Jupiter walked towards Baz with a sort of furious contained energy, his hands clenched into fists at his side, the muscles in his jaw twitching. Baz flinched back, cowering against the rose-quartz statue of the many-armed woman. The Elders all stepped forward as if worried Jupiter was about to hit the other man. Morrigan knew he was reining himself in, could see the way he forced his breaths to even out and his hands to unclench. Even so, she felt a chill on the back of her neck as Jupiter brought his face close to Baz's, and spoke in his lowest, most dangerous voice.

'Think of what you are saying. For once in your mediocre life, Charlton, just *think* about the words that drop from your cretinous mouth before you utter them.'

Several seconds of ringing silence followed these words. Baz tried to look defiant, but he seemed to have shrunk several sizes. He looked to the Elders. 'W-well I didn't *mean* . . . I just meant . . .'

His eyes still locked on Baz, Jupiter said, 'Morrigan. Go and wait outside.'

She wanted to argue. She wanted to stay and find out her fate, to know what was going to happen to her the second it was decided, but the tension in the room – and in Jupiter's voice – forced her feet to move.

Hawthorne was waiting for her in the hallway. He stepped out from his hiding spot behind an imposing marble bust. His face was pale and serious, his eyes at least twice their normal size.

'You okay?' he asked in an urgent whisper.

'Yes,' she whispered back. 'I think so.'

'Did you . . .' he broke off. 'Morrigan, did you *know* you could do that? Did you know you could . . . *breathe fire?*'

Even through her haze of worry and confusion, Morrigan dimly registered how ridiculous the question was, and it annoyed her, and she was oddly grateful that this, at least, was normal. That Hawthorne could still ask silly questions, and she could still be annoyed by them. 'Don't you think I might have mentioned a small detail like that?'

They were silent for a moment.

'What are they going to do?' Hawthorne asked.

'Shhh. I don't know.' Morrigan pressed her ear to the heavy oak door, and Hawthorne did the same. For several minutes, all they could hear was mumbling, until Jupiter raised his voice again, sounding furious.

'She's just. A little. Girl.' He said each word as if he was grinding it between his teeth. 'Stop *speaking* about her as if she's a *monster*. Murgatroyd's right, you should have—'

'—the girl is . . .' Professor Onstald's voice trailed off into mumbles again, and Morrigan pushed away from the door, feeling a tightness in her chest. She began to pace, pulling at the hem of her grey shirt, twisting it around and around her fingers.

Stop speaking about her as if she's a monster.

'They won't try to kick you out, will they?' Hawthorne asked in an anxious whisper.

'I don't know.'

'They can't!' he said loudly, then dropped his voice once again to a whisper. 'It wasn't your fault. You were protecting Miss Cheery. If anyone should get kicked out, it's Heloise. I'll tell them.'

Morrigan said nothing. Would they kick her out for this? *Could* they? If she wasn't a member of the Society she would have to leave Nevermoor, and . . .

No. She shook her head fiercely. *It was an accident,* she told herself. *They can't kick you out because of an accident.*

Baz Charlton's words echoed in her head: 'Activate her safeguard.' Whatever that meant, it clearly wasn't a good thing. Morrigan stopped pacing, and stared straight ahead. Her hands grew still. She'd suddenly realised . . . she had absolutely no idea what the safeguard was for. She had never asked.

Why had she never asked?

Moments later, the Scholar Mistress appeared at the door.

'SWIFT!' Dearborn hissed. 'Get to class!' Hawthorne mumbled an apology and left, glancing anxiously back over his shoulder. The Scholar Mistress turned to Morrigan, her face an icy mask once again, inscrutable as ever. 'Come.'

Morrigan followed her into the hall, taking two footsteps for every one of Dearborn's. Jupiter, Baz, Professor Onstald and the Elders stood in the centre of the room, dwarfed by the nine enormous stone statues, but towering over Morrigan nonetheless.

She squeezed her hands into fists, trying to stop them from shaking. Looking around at the adults, it was hard to tell whether it was good news or bad news. Baz Charlton was sporting a sulky, put-upon scowl, but Jupiter didn't seem particularly happy either.

'Miss Crow,' said Elder Quinn, beckoning her forward. The frown lines between her eyes were so deep they might have been embroidered there. 'Elder Saga, Elder Wong and I have come to a decision. It is our opinion that the pressures of Wundrous Society life have taken their toll on you, and as such—'

'You can't kick me out!' Morrigan interrupted in a panic. 'It was an accident, I never meant to hurt anybody. *Please*, Elder Quinn, you *have to believe*—'

'I do believe you,' said Elder Quinn, raising her voice over Morrigan's. 'Please be quiet, Miss Crow.' She paused, and Morrigan bit the side of her mouth, fighting the urge to defend herself. 'It is not my opinion that your actions were malicious. However. The High Council of Elders has a responsibility to *all* of those entrusted to our care. We must put measures in place to ensure the safety of your fellow unit members, and the rest of the Society. We don't know what those measures will look like in the long term, but as of this moment, you may consider your workload under review.'

Jupiter frowned. 'What exactly does that mean, Elder Quinn?'

The woman exhaled heavily. 'In an enduring sense, I'm not entirely certain what it means. But in the short term, Miss Crow will no longer attend classes with the other students, or enter Wunsoc.'

Morrigan's heart sank all the way down to her feet. She felt tears sting her eyes. Banished from Wunsoc? The thought was intolerable.

'For now, Miss Crow,' Elder Quinn continued, 'you shall continue your individual studies with Professor Onstald, who will travel to your home at the Hotel Deucalion and conduct your lessons there. Your direct access to Station 919 will be temporarily revoked. I must ask you to leave the campus at once.'

⌐■━━━

'I'm sorry I haven't been around much lately.'

Jupiter had hailed a carriage to take them home. Which was lucky, as it began to rain almost the moment they stepped inside it. (Or – was it more than luck? Could he see the weather before it arrived? Morrigan wanted to ask, but the lump in her throat was back and wouldn't let her speak just yet.)

'My work at the League has been . . . Well, no excuses. I'm sorry. That's all.' He really did seem sorry. More than that, he seemed sad.

'It's all right,' said Morrigan finally, in a croaky voice. She meant it. Although she really *had* been annoyed with him, his apology was heartfelt, and he looked so desolate and tired that she couldn't hold on to her frustration any longer. It had been getting too heavy to carry around, anyway. She was glad to be rid of it.

They sat in silence until it, too, grew heavy.

'I breathed fire.'

'Mm.'

'I didn't know I could do that.'

'No,' said Jupiter thoughtfully. 'Nor did I.'

They were silent for another block, listening to the patter of rain and the clip-clop of hooves, and then—

'But *how* did I breathe fire?'

'I'm afraid I don't know, Mog.'

'Am I – ' she paused to swallow, and choked out a half-laugh, '– am I turning into a dragon or something?'

Jupiter snorted. 'Well, let's see. Do you feel scaly?'

'No.'

'Got talons?'

She checked her fingernails. 'No.'

'Sudden urge to hoard treasure?'

Morrigan considered for a moment. 'I don't think so.'

'Then no, I doubt it.'

'Will they ever let me go back?' she asked, turning to look at him.

'The Elders will come around,' he said. 'We'll find a way to *make* them come around. I promise. And look – the summer holidays are about to start, anyway. Six whole weeks to cool off and chill out. By the time school starts back again, they'll have had a change of heart.'

'You think so?'

Jupiter thought for a moment. 'I know Elder Quinn pretty well,' he said finally. 'She's . . . not unfair. Sometimes she just needs time to see what *is* the fair thing to do.'

They settled into silence. Morrigan watched the busy streets go by through a filter of fat raindrops spattering the glass. When they were just a few blocks from the Deucalion, Jupiter cleared his throat.

'I know you might not be inclined to share confidences right now,' he said in a quiet, careful tone, 'but is there anything you want to tell me, Mog?'

She hesitated.

'Have . . . have you ever heard of the Ghastly Market?'

Jupiter took a moment to answer.

'Yes,' he said finally. 'Why?'

And he listened intently while she told him all that had happened that afternoon in her *Decoding Nevermoor* class. He didn't get cross that she'd broken Mildmay's Tricksy Lane rule, and he didn't make her promise never to do it again, and he didn't express the tiniest sliver of doubt about what she'd seen and heard.

'Devilish Court, you said?' He wrote the name in a tiny notebook he'd pulled from his pocket. 'I'll look into it.'

I'll look into it. More than anything else, it was these four words that eased Morrigan's jangled nerves that afternoon, that undid some of the residual tension from what had been her worst day since arriving in Nevermoor. Because even if the rest of the world was suspicious of her, Jupiter never would be. He believed her. He trusted her.

'Anything else?' he asked.

Of course, there were other things she wanted to tell him. There were things she was *dying* to tell him, things she'd been dying to tell him for weeks. Like how frightened she'd felt when the Charlton Five had pinned her to a tree and thrown sharp things at her head, and about the blackmail note and the ridiculous demands, and how her unit had only *just* managed to vote not to expose her secret to the whole Society . . . and the million other things she'd been storing up in her mind, bursting to tell him when she saw him next.

But now that Jupiter was here, and she had his full attention, those things didn't seem so important. She was happy just to finally have him back, and there was a whole list of other things she wanted to tell him instead.

'My conductor's the best person in the whole Society,' she began.

'Really?' His eyebrows shot up. 'The BEST?'

'Yes. Much better than you.'

Jupiter burst out laughing – the big, joyous laugh she'd been missing – and Morrigan grinned at him. She told him all about wonderful, sunshiny Miss Cheery and her seemingly limitless positivity and her polar-bear biscuit jar, and how she had the best smile and wore the coolest clothes. 'Oh – and she decorated our Hometrain herself, and it's *really* comfy. We've got beanbags!'

And she told him how she was the only one in her unit – maybe in the whole Society – who was immune to Cadence Blackburn's mesmerism (he, of course, needed several reminders of who Cadence Blackburn was). And how she was the best in her *Decoding Nevermoor* class.

Jupiter listened closely to every word, and reacted exactly the right way in exactly the right places. And it was all so familiar and so comfortable, so reassuringly *normal,* that the question Morrigan really wanted to ask – the question that had been burning at the back of her throat, threatening to burst out of her mouth like dragon fire, since she'd watched him stare down Baz Charlton in the Elders' Hall – burned itself down to ashes before she could find a way to ask it. She swept it into a quiet corner of her mind and let it sit there, ignored and unanswered.

And if she ignored it for long enough, maybe it wouldn't be important any more. Maybe it would never be important again. Maybe the question, '*What's a safeguard for?*' could sit under that pile of ashes in her mind, safe and quiet and unimportant, forever.

CHAPTER FIFTEEN

You've Never Seen Anything More Bizarre

'We want to be at the East Gate entrance.'

'Catriona, darling, that's the busiest gate. We went through this last year.'

'Dave. Trust me. East Gate is the business.'

'Yes, I *know* it's the business. That's why it will be packed with a million other Nevermoorians by now. We should have left an hour earlier if you wanted to start at East Gate. I *told* you.'

'It'll be fine, love. We'll just barge through.'

'*Barge through?* It's not a mosh pit, Cat. We're civilised adults.'

'Sweetheart, it'll be *fine*. You're talking to a champion barger. Why do you think they call me Queen Barge?'

'Nobody calls you that, darling.'

Hawthorne's mother, Cat, struck Morrigan as a grown-up female version of Hawthorne. Her hair was a bit longer, falling past her shoulders in thick chocolate-coloured curls just like his, but otherwise they were basically the same. Same blue eyes, same splotchy freckles, same gangly limbs that brought to mind a mother and baby giraffe.

The Swifts had invited her to go with them to the Nevermoor Bazaar, on the first Friday night of the summer holidays. Although Jupiter had promised to take Morrigan himself, he'd been needed elsewhere at the last minute – and knowing how gloomy she'd been since term ended a week ago, he had encouraged her to take the opportunity and go with her friend instead. Morrigan was relieved; last summer he'd promised every single week that he would take her, and every single week something else had come up. She was determined not to miss out this year.

'Lots of people call me that, my love. Ask Homer, he'll tell you. Tell him, Homer.'

Hawthorne's elder brother made a face at their parents. Homer looked more like their dad. Same fair hair, same thick eyeglasses, same sturdy, towering build like a Viking wrestler – all he was missing was Dave's scruffy beard.

At fifteen, Homer was currently in his fourth year of study at the Conservatory of Thought. Hawthorne had explained to Morrigan that students of the Conservatory took a vow of silence for their years of study and were only allowed to speak one day a year, so when Homer was with his family he carried a blackboard and chalk around his neck to communicate. Hawthorne said he mostly used it for sarcasm.

'Speak up, darling son. He's gone all shy.'

'That's not very nice, dear,' said Dave, trying not to laugh.

Homer didn't bother with the blackboard; he just rolled his eyes.

Their elder sister Helena couldn't come to the Bazaar. She was a fifth-year student at the Gorgonhowl College of Radical Meteorology, far away off the coast of the Sixth Pocket on a tiny island that sat in the eye of a perpetual cyclone. Helena only ever came home at Christmas and the summer holidays, because it was difficult and expensive to travel in and out of a cyclone. This summer, however, the storm had turned so bad that all travel was suspended until further notice – which, according to Hawthorne, suited Helena perfectly. She loved it when storms turned bad, he said. She wanted to stay in school and see the damage for herself.

The youngest member of the family Swift was two-year-old Davina, who also looked just like her dad. Baby Dave, as the family called her, was enormously fat, blonde and cheerful. The Swifts all agreed she was brilliant, maybe better than the rest of them put together. Morrigan was undecided – she'd only ever seen Baby Dave spit up milk, throw food on the floor and squeal at passing dogs.

Morrigan and the five Swifts took the Wunderground downtown for the Bazaar, and Dave made them all hold hands as a group so nobody would get lost in the swarming crowds. Cat did them the favour of singing loudly and out of tune for the whole train ride, however, which she said would make the public hand-holding less embarrassing by comparison. (*I'm not with these people*, read Homer's blackboard.)

When at last they arrived at Temple Station and battled the crowds to reach the East Gate, the sun was just about to set. There were thousands of people waiting at the gate to be granted entry to Old Town, and the anticipation was palpable. Dave hoisted Baby Dave onto his shoulders for a better view. Hawthorne grabbed Morrigan's arm and squeezed it, bouncing up and down on his tiptoes and looking like he might burst with excitement. Even Homer was gazing up at the East Gate, lost in silent awe.

'See?' said Cat, smiling at her husband. 'Told you. The business.'

The space inside the East Gate was obscured by a sort of shimmering silvery haze that looked a bit like a gigantic pane of rippled glass, except for the fact that it moved in the breeze. Across the top of the great stone arch, enormous, brightly burning letters of fire read:

WELCOME TO THE NEVERMOOR BAZAAR

And underneath, an ambitious promise wrote and rewrote itself in the air with smoke siphoned from the fiery letters:

You've Never Seen Anything More Bizarre

'Magic!' cried Cat, grinning as she nudged Homer in the ribs.

Homer rolled his eyes, picked up his chalk and wrote: *Cheap parlour trick.*

Cat laughed. Morrigan found she agreed with her: it *was* magic. It had to be. It was *wonderful*.

Dave leaned down, beckoning Hawthorne and Morrigan in. 'It's an illusion,' he said. 'Built by magicians, see?' He pointed up to where a small team of tuxedoed men and women perched on a corner of the arch. They were deep in concentration, using a combination of convoluted hand gestures and machinery to direct the smoke message, over and over. It looked like tedious, complex work. 'You can always identify a magician's illusion, even if you can't see the magician herself, by spotting the seam. Wait for it . . . THERE! Did you see it?'

'Oh!' Morrigan did see it now. There was a moment when the illusion sort of . . . flinched. If she watched carefully, she could feel a slight jarring sensation each time the message got to the end of the word *bizarre* and restarted – an almost imperceptible stuttering seam of imperfection in the loop.

'That's not a cheap parlour trick, Homer,' said Dave, straightening up and ruffling his eldest son's hair. 'That's *craftsmanship.*'

Morrigan agreed with that too – but impressive as the illusion was, she couldn't help giving the words themselves a bit of side-eye. She *had,* in fact, seen quite a few bizarre things. Most of them at the Deucalion.

'Right, you three,' said Dave, addressing Hawthorne, Morrigan and Homer. 'Got your money? Good. Keep it close – lots of pickpockets at the Bazaar. I want you to meet Mum and Baby Dave and me back here at midnight on the dot. Not a *second* later, you understand? If you're not back at the East Gate by midnight, I'm gonna let Mum come after you and do a street performance of her one-woman play about the lady who loses her children and goes mad and ends up thinking she's a squirrel. All right?'

Morrigan laughed, but Homer and Hawthorne were wide-eyed. 'Please don't do the song, Mum,' said Hawthorne.

'No promises, boy-o,' said Cat, pointing a finger at him. 'You'd just better be back at midnight, you hear?'

The two boys nodded.

'All right then,' she said. 'Have fun—'

'But be safe,' added Dave.

'Eat lots of treats—'

'But *please* not too much sugar—'

'And let's see who can find the most ridiculous souvenir this year!' Cat finished with two thumbs up and a mad grin.

'But nothing sharp, nothing alive, nothing explosive, nothing bigger than the front door and no *weapons*,' said Dave, with a meaningful look at Hawthorne.

Just then there came a noise like a thousand tinkling bells, and the shimmering, glassy veil over the East Gate melted away, disappearing into the Gossamer and revealing an Old Town utterly transformed.

There was a moment of pleasurable, stunned silence as the crowd took in the sights and sounds of the Bazaar, before they all began pushing their way to the front, eager to be the first inside. Morrigan and Hawthorne grinned at each other, happily buffeted along amidst the river of people flooding through the gates.

As soon as they'd lost sight of Cat and Dave, Homer wrote something on his blackboard and held it up for Hawthorne to see.

11:45. Temple doors.

Hawthorne gave him the thumbs-up, and Homer wiped his message and wrote something else.

I know it's hard for you, but try not to do anything stupid.

Hawthorne made a face at him and the two boys parted, Homer flicking his little brother's earlobe before disappearing into the crowd.

'I thought we were meant to stick together?' asked Morrigan. 'Your dad said—'

'Oh, never mind Dad, he's a worry-wart,' Hawthorne said airily. He took two maps from a woman passing by on stilts, folded one into his pocket without looking at it and handed the other to Morrigan. A title across the top read, *Precincts of the Nevermoor Bazaar.* 'Trust me, we don't want to stay with boring old Homer. He's gone to find his boring old friends so they can be boring and old together. I think we should go clockwise, all right? South Quarter first, then west, north, and back here to the East Gate to meet Homer.'

As they wandered past the Temple of the Divine Thing and made their way down Grand Boulevard, Morrigan examined her map. The Bazaar sprawled across all four quarters of Old Town and was divided into dozens and dozens of little precincts, each with its own purpose. A tannery, an antiques market, a witches' market, a perfumery . . .

'There's a cheese market in the West Quarter that goes for a whole block!' said Morrigan, squinting at the map's tiny writing. 'No, hang on – it says it's a fire-twirling show. Or . . . wait. No, sorry, it's a dog show. It keeps changing!'

'It'll be all three.' Hawthorne was walking very fast, holding on to Morrigan's sleeve and steering her left and right to dodge other people as she concentrated on the map.

'Oh. On different nights?'

'Same night.'

Morrigan stopped in her tracks, checking the map again.

'Hurry *up*,' pleaded Hawthorne, 'We've only got a few hours, so we need to get to South Quarter quickly. Come on, I know a shortcut.'

He led her down Callahan Street, off the side of Grand Boulevard.

'Dreadfully disorganised, isn't it?' Morrigan said, still frowning at her map. Some of the precincts seemed to be labelled with three, four, even *five* different purposes or events, most of which seemed completely at odds with each other. She held up the map for Hawthorne to see. 'Look – we're about to come to Ambrosia Square, right? This map says Ambrosia Square is hosting a tango lesson *and* a tea party. But that's ridiculous, Ambrosia Square is so small, how can it be—'

Morrigan looked up just as they reached what she knew should have been the entry to the little square, and found herself face to face with a curtain of flowing, many-coloured silks.

'This is how,' said Hawthorne, and he led her through the silk curtain into the middle of a tango lesson. Ambrosia Square – normally a quiet courtyard lined with tiny terraced houses – was alive with dramatic music and swirling dresses, tempestuous men and women crossing back and forth in each other's arms. Morrigan jumped as a bottle smashed, spraying red wine across the makeshift dancefloor. A fight broke out just as Hawthorne grabbed Morrigan's arm and pulled her back through the silk curtain the way they'd come.

Through the curtain *again*, and Ambrosia Square had transformed into a bustling – but very civilised – tea party. A pianist played tranquilly on an upright piano in the corner while a brigade of hostesses went around refilling people's cups and piling little cakes onto three-tiered trays.

'What— *how*?' asked Morrigan.

Hawthorne shrugged. 'Who cares? Come on – we're not stopping here.'

At the other end of Ambrosia Square, they stepped through a curtain of feathers into the Avian Market, where hundreds of hanging cages held birds of every description – some exotic and brightly coloured, some tiny and jewel-like, some huge, terrifying birds of prey that reminded Morrigan of her grandmother. There were birds that spoke in multiple languages, birds that were trained to hunt, and some that flew in formation.

Morrigan wanted to stop and look at them, but Hawthorne hurried her along, through another curtain made of creeping vines into a flower market overflowing with colour, and then a lantern market with a thousand coloured lights casting psychedelic patterns all around them, then a loud and smelly fish auction, a prayer meeting, a vigorous debate on Wunimal rights, a farmer's market full of fresh fruit and vegetables, then a carnival with a carousel, a ghost train, a jumping castle and sideshow alley . . .

'Hawthorne, stop – don't you want to go on the ghost train? Slow *down*, I'm getting a stitch!'

But he wouldn't slow down. He knew exactly where he was going, and though he refused to tell Morrigan ('It's a surprise!'), she had an idea what it might be about. She knew her friend too well.

Morrigan had expected the Bazaar to be crowded, and she'd known there would be lots of stalls selling peculiar things. All last summer she'd witnessed the Saturday morning post-Bazaar ritual over the breakfast table as Hotel Deucalion guests and staff alike compared endlessly fascinating stories and souvenir hauls.

But seeing it for herself really was something else. It was like walking through the scenery from a hundred different plays. Morrigan's head was spinning, she could hardly take in one strange thing before they'd moved on to the next.

It was confusing and thrilling, and tricky to tell how much was real and how much was illusion. Everywhere they went, Morrigan made a game out of trying to spot the seam, just as Dave had told them. Now that she knew what she was looking for, it was also easy to see the people working hard in the background, trying to keep the illusion going. They were usually up high – perched on a balcony or a rooftop, overlooking the scene and concentrating hard.

'There!' she shouted, grabbing Hawthorne's arm. She pointed up at a fourth-floor window above Cooper Court (which according to the map was doubling as an outdoor nail salon and an arena for unicorn-based equestrian events). A man and woman were stationed there, muttering to themselves in a constant stream and never taking their eyes off the courtyard below.

'Do you have to do that?' Hawthorne grumbled. 'Can't we just enjoy the magic *without* poking our noses behind the curtain?'

'But it's *fascinating*!'

When they passed through a veil of steam into a noisy open-air restaurant bursting with food stalls, Morrigan felt certain they'd be stopping at last. This, surely, was what Hawthorne had been looking for.

One woman was cooking on three enormous silver saucer-like pans simultaneously, flames and jets of steam shooting up into the air around her. Her flagrant abuse of spices made Morrigan's eyes water, but there was also the smell of something unidentifiably meaty and delicious. Other stalls offered stews, flatbreads, hot chips, fried dumplings and crabs boiled in barrels . . . and, Morrigan noticed with disgust, buttery sautéed snails, deep-fried pig intestines, crunchy fried grasshoppers, and rats roasted on skewers like strange, fleshy popsicles.

'Rat skewer?' she suggested to Hawthorne, making a face. 'Or pig intestine? What'll it be?'

But *again,* he hurried her to the other end of the precinct, where they hit a wall of fairy floss – a flat, cloudy curtain of pink spun sugar. Hawthorne turned to her and grinned, tearing off an enormous strip of floss and letting it melt on his tongue before leading her on through the sweet, sticky, paper-thin curtain and into their surprise destination.

'Sweet Street!' announced Hawthorne, throwing his arms wide as if he'd just welcomed Morrigan into his spiritual home. Sweet Street encompassed three whole blocks and was packed with chocolatiers and toffee-makers, people stirring huge metal pots full of popping caramel corn, cake stands and creperies, tables piled high with rock candy and bonbons, and an ice-cream parlour that specialised in two-foot-high sundaes.

Hawthorne was in his element. She could tell this was a place her friend returned to every year, because he had very firm ideas about which stalls promised the best use of their time, money and stomach space.

'Sugarplum donuts are a MUST,' he told her, pointing out a stand that sold hot fried donuts injected with oozing purple sugarplum jam and rolled in cinnamon sugar. 'And sherbet roses. But forget the crepes. Overrated.' He also steered straight past a chocolatier offering every kind of truffle imaginable (coconut truffles, peach truffles, peppermint, champagne, praline, grasshopper . . . what *was* it with all the grasshoppers?) and straight to one where thick straps of chewy caramel were hand-stretched and sold by the metre.

When Morrigan couldn't possibly eat another bite, she momentarily left Hawthorne chewing and wandered through a mist of grey fog into an alley of fortune tellers offering readings by crystal ball, tarot cards, palms, tea leaves and bird entrails. There was even one who invited her to spit in his hand so he could read her future from it. Morrigan politely declined, backing away from him as he became more insistent, and accidentally stepping through another curtain into . . .

Nothing. Morrigan could see nothing. She could hear nothing.

It wasn't that it was dark. She wasn't peering into blackness. She wasn't looking at anything at all. She'd gone blind.

She cried out – *Hawthorne!* – but her voice was gone. Or could she just not hear it? Maybe he had heard her. She touched a hand to her throat and felt the vibrations as she yelled again for her friend, but no sound reached her ears. She'd gone blind and deaf.

Stay calm, Morrigan told herself. *Stay calm.*

She felt someone brush against her, and caught the scent of strong perfume on the air. Another person bumped into her and large hands grabbed her shoulders roughly. She smelled stale, smoky breath as the hands patted all over her head and face, as if trying to figure out who she was, and then pushed her aside.

Stay calm stay calm stay calm. What was step two? Oh – *retreat.* Morrigan forced herself to take a careful step backwards, and another, but then another hand grabbed hers, a much smaller hand than the last – a child's hand, like hers.

Is that you, Hawthorne? she cried, but of course no sound met her ears. Her hand grasped on to a shoulder, and it was the same height as her own, perhaps a little taller – it might be him.

The hand pulled her onwards. Together they made their way through the bumbling, blinded crowd, buffeted this way and that, clutching tight to each other until finally they burst through the darkness on the other side.

Morrigan felt like a free-diver coming up for air. The world was colour and light and sound again. She gasped as if to catch her breath, though she hadn't been holding it. She blinked into the newfound brightness as her eyes adjusted, turning to Hawthorne. 'What was *that?*'

But it wasn't Hawthorne who'd pulled her through.

Cadence Blackburn stood beside her, breathing heavily.

'Cadence!' said Morrigan, unable to hide her surprise. 'What are you—'

'It's real.' Cadence's eyes blazed with fear and excitement. 'The Ghastly Market! Morrigan, it's real – and it's happening *now.*'

CHAPTER SIXTEEN

The Ghastly Market

'I saw a man turn down Devilish Court.' Cadence was steering Morrigan through the crowded Bazaar at breakneck speed, past noisy stalls and through curtains. 'I yelled at him to stop him but he didn't hear me, and then he was gone.'

'You— what? Ow, Cadence, you're hurting my arm.' Cadence loosened her grip but didn't let go, and didn't slow down. 'What are you saying, you were just *walking* past Devilish Court and you *happened* to see someone—'

'No, dummy, I was standing across the street watching it. I was thinking about all the disappearances, and about what you told us, about the Ghastly Market, and what you saw. And this afternoon I realised – if it is real, if what you saw *was* the Ghastly Market being set up, and if it *is* them that's behind the disappearances, then it's bound to happen tonight, right? Opening night of the Bazaar! The timing is too perfect.'

'I guess,' said Morrigan, 'but Cadence, wait—'

'So I waited to see who would show up at Devilish Court. And get this: it's not even a Pink Alert any more. It's changed. It was upgraded to a *Red* Alert. But this guy just went straight in, didn't even look twice. Then I saw another man go in five minutes later, and this one was wearing a mask. And then a woman went in, and she had a scarf wrapped around most of her face – in the middle of summer! So then I went to find you. Hawthorne told me you were coming to the Bazaar together. I've been looking for you *everywhere,* and I finally spotted you just before you slipped into the Courtyard of Nothing. Come on, this way.'

'But I should at least tell Haw—'

'He'll be *fine*,' Cadence insisted. 'Come *on*, we have to hurry.'

Minutes later they arrived at the familiar mouth of Devilish Court, which was so narrow Morrigan thought it barely qualified as an alley. The plaque on the wall had indeed been altered.

DEVILISH COURT

BEWARE!

BY ORDER OF THE GEOGRAPHICAL
ODDITIES SQUADRON
AND THE NEVERMOOR COUNCIL,

THIS STREET HAS BEEN DECLARED A
RED ALERT TRICKSY LANE

(HIGH-DANGER TRICKERY AND LIKELIHOOD OF DAMAGE TO
PERSON ON ENTRY)

ENTER AT OWN RISK

Morrigan read it through twice. '. . . *likelihood of damage to person on entry.* Does that mean the trick has changed?'

'It must have, if they've reclassified it. But I've been thinking: you got through that spew-feeling trick before, right? And those people I saw, they've obviously gone through to the other side too. I think whatever Devilish Court has changed into, it *must* be possible to push our way through it.'

'A Red Alert, though . . .'

Morrigan looked from the sign to Cadence and back again, pulse quickening as she felt her resolve strengthen. She'd wanted to investigate the Ghastly Market, to look for Cassiel and Paximus Luck and the others. This was her chance! Both to help Jupiter in his hunt for the missing people, but also to prove that it wasn't *her* – that Heloise was wrong. Maybe if she could find the missing people, the Elders would let her back into Wunsoc?

She nodded vehemently. 'You're right. Let's do it.'

Cadence smiled, and together, they marched down Devilish Court. Nothing happened at first, and Morrigan had a moment of hope that perhaps there was no trick any more, that the sign had it wrong . . . until suddenly, she felt as if all the air was being sucked out of her lungs.

'Keep going,' Cadence said in a tight, breathless voice, tugging her onward.

As Morrigan became increasingly desperate for air, her survival instinct kicked in and thrashed wildly within her, trying to pull her back the way they'd come, back to light and oxygen and safety.

'Trust me,' said Cadence, squeezing her hand. 'All right?'

And Morrigan realised . . . she *did* trust Cadence. (When had that happened, she wondered.)

She fought back against her instinct, stubbornly putting one foot in front of the other. Her lungs were empty, her head felt as if it would burst, and she was frantic for air but there was none to be had, just a burning in her chest and—

They burst through some invisible barrier, gasping for breath and finding it at last. Morrigan thought she might collapse from the pain in her lungs and the dizziness in her head, but they'd made it. Wordlessly, Cadence pointed upwards.

Like a mockery of the spectacular Nevermoor Bazaar welcome sign above East Gate, a shabby white wooden arch curved over their heads and on it – newly painted in black letters – were three words:

THE GHASTLY MARKET

'It *is* real,' panted Morrigan.

'I knew it,' said Cadence fiercely.

They gaped at the square, which was no longer empty but heaving with buyers and sellers, none of whom looked particularly friendly. This place had none of the charm of the Nevermoor Bazaar. The Bazaar was shiny and magical and welcoming; the Ghastly Market felt like it had been spat on, walked over and rubbed in the dirt.

'I can't wait to tell Mildmay how wrong he was,' muttered Cadence, then nudged Morrigan in the side. 'Oi – don't stare so much, you'll draw attention. Just be cool.'

But as they made their way through the market, Morrigan couldn't help staring, and she definitely couldn't be cool. The wares on offer here were unlike any she'd seen in the other precincts. To her left, a table of assorted unnimal organs, fresh and bloody. To her right, an array of jars holding pickled unnimal heads and limbs, and even, she noticed with revulsion—

'Is that a *human head*?' she shrieked, pointing at a shrunken, strangely peaceful face floating in a jar of yellowish preserving liquid.

Cadence steered her away, muttering from the corner of her mouth, 'Be. Cool.'

They passed a black canvas tent with a sign outside that simply read: SECRETS BOUGHT AND SOLD, and further along, a woman offering to smuggle anyone in or out of the Wintersea Republic 'for a fair price'.

'Teeeeeeth!' shouted a man as they walked by his stall, making both girls jump. 'Teeth and fangs, get yer teeth and fangs here. Unnimal, Wunimal, human toothy pegs alike, get 'em while I've got 'em. Molars, canines, wisdoms, tusks. Use 'em for hexes, use 'em for jewellery, I don't care what you use 'em for, long as you pay me. TEEEEEEEEEETH, get yer teeth here!'

The farther into the Ghastly Market they went, the darker and uglier it became, until Morrigan wanted to close her eyes and run back. She longed for the bright lights and joyful music of the Bazaar. The jostling crowds at the Ghastly Market were easy to get lost in, and the clientele here didn't seem inclined to make eye contact with anyone, but nonetheless, Morrigan was beginning to feel . . . visible. Two children alone, their golden *W* pins gleaming at their necks. They were utterly out of place.

She hastily unpinned the evidence of her Wun status and shoved it in a pocket. 'Take your pin off,' she whispered to Cadence.

There was one tent, right in the centre of the market, that seemed to have drawn a bigger crowd than any of the others. A huge cluster of people queued before one very large, surly-looking man who was standing guard at the tent door and holding the leashes of four formidable-looking dogs. He ushered people inside in pairs, counting them as they went, and then suddenly held up a hand to stop the next people in line.

'Right folks, we've reached capacity. The auction is full. Better luck next time.'

'You're joking, aren't you, son?' complained a bearded man at the front of the queue. 'Come on, be fair. I've been waitin' months for this.'

'Then you should have arrived earlier,' said the doorman. 'Strictly limited numbers. First come, best dressed. You know how this works, I saw you at the spring auction.'

The customer leaned in to whisper conspiratorially. 'Listen, I've uh . . . I've come for that big item. You know the one I mean. And I'm planning to bid high. My money's as good as anyone else's.'

Morrigan and Cadence exchanged a look. *Big item.* Could it be one of the missing people?

'I'm sure it is, but your punctuality's dreadful,' said the doorman. 'You'll have to wait for the autumn lots. Good day.'

The man pulled desperately at his beard. 'Come on, mate – that beast'll be long gone by—'

'I said GOOD DAY,' snapped the doorman. 'Now get out before I have my friends chase you out.' He tilted his head towards the four chained dogs, who started growling on cue. The bearded man sloped away. As he went to pass by Cadence on his way out, she held out a hand to stop him.

'You're not going to take that, are you?' she asked.

The man sneered and tried to push past her, but Cadence simply said, 'Stop,' and he stopped. She peered up into his face and spoke in a voice like a swarm of bees. 'Go back there and show him what happens to people who disrespect you.'

Morrigan saw something shift in the man's eyes, as if his will had suddenly been galvanised. He stormed back up to the front of the queue and began shouting and pressing his stubby finger to the doorman's chest. The dogs snarled and barked, straining at their leashes, and the dispersing queue of people reformed again, drawn like magnets to the promise of a brawl.

'Come on,' murmured Cadence. Using the disturbance as a cover, they slipped through the opening of the tiny canvas tent . . . and emerged inside what looked like a dark and sumptuous ballroom, lit by candelabra.

Morrigan let the canvas drop behind her, and instantly the noise from outside was doused like a flame, replaced with a quiet, civilised chatter and the clinking of wine glasses. It was strangely disorienting. She spotted an unattended table which held an assortment of masks, hoods and veils and a sign that read *For Your Discretion and Convenience.* Grabbing a pair of rubber unnimal masks, Morrigan pulled the hairy gorilla face down over her head and thrust the fox at Cadence, who made a face at it.

'Nobody's going to notice me,' she protested.

'Look around,' said Morrigan. The rubber gorilla mask muffled her voice. 'Do you see anyone here showing their face? Do you want to be the odd one out? *Put it on.*'

Cadence's description of the people she'd seen going down Devilish Court suddenly made sense; everyone here was trying to disguise themselves in some way. Nobody wanted to be recognised in a place like this.

And then Morrigan saw it. At the opposite end of the room, sitting in a cage atop a high, red-curtained platform like some kind of trophy . . .

'Dr Bramble's Magnificub!' Morrigan said with a gasp.

The cub had a ruff of thick, matted, dirty white fur, and big blue eyes like crystal orbs. Hissing and yowling, clawing madly through the metal bars, he fought like a lion, though he was clearly terrified and desperate for escape. Morrigan cringed. She wanted to run right over and set him free, but that would have been idiotic in the extreme.

The atmosphere at this end of the tent was less civilised. The crowd jeered and roared with laughter as they threw things at the poor cub – food, stones, empty bottles – trying to aggravate him even more. It worked; instead of cowering against the back of the cage, he fought ever wilder, ever louder, his bright blue eyes shining with terror. Morrigan watched, feeling queasy and helpless. Beside her, Cadence's breaths came in short, sharp bursts.

'Our first big drawcard today, ladies and gentlemen!' shouted a man standing next to the Magnificub behind a wooden podium. He wore a brown tweed suit and a mask that covered the top half of his face, and he held a cane that he occasionally hit against the metal bars of the cage with a ringing *thwack*. 'I present to you the grand – and extremely rare – Magnificub. Little beastie doesn't look like much now of course, but we all know how enormous – and enormously useful! – a fully grown Magnificat can be. Fiercely independent creatures of an extremely Wundrous nature, Magnificats will nonetheless make capable and docile beasts of burden – especially if you choose to cut out their tongues from infancy! It's all the rage in the Republic. Don't be afraid, ladies and gentlemen, of the notoriously fierce Magnificat intelligence – oh no! Contrary to popular belief, they *can* be subjugated if you go about it the right way.'

Morrigan felt bile rise in her throat. She swallowed hard, trying to control herself. They were going to *cut out his tongue*? That poor little cub? Morrigan had a sudden, sickening realisation – was *that* what President Wintersea had done to the six Magnificats who pulled her carriage? Is that why they never spoke?

She thought of funny, mean Fenestra, of how the enormous grey Magnificat bossed Jupiter around and teased Morrigan and did exactly as she liked and said exactly what she pleased. Then she imagined Fen silent and docile, chained to a line of other Magnificats, kept in a cage and forced to pull a carriage her whole life, and the sick feeling in Morrigan's stomach intensified. It was so *wrong*.

'So who here will be brave enough to tame this handsome Magnificub? Who can master the beast? Or if you can't be bothered with all that, you can always skin it and wear it as a coat.'

A small, involuntary sound escaped Morrigan, and Cadence elbowed her sharply in the side, muttering, 'Shush.'

The auctioneer cleared his throat. 'Without further ado, ladies and gentlemen, we will open the bidding at an extremely reasonable five thousand kred. Do I hear five thousand kred? Five thousand over there to the tattooed gentleman; do I hear five-five?'

Morrigan felt a *thud* in the pit of her stomach. They were going to auction off the poor terrified cub to the highest bidders.

'Five-five from the lady in the green cloak; do I hear six? Thank you, sir, six thousand from the tattooed gentleman. Now, do I hear six-five? Who will bid six-five? Six-five to the gentleman in the dog mask; do I hear seven?'

The bidding went for some time and rose to such a feverish pitch with so many bidders that Morrigan couldn't keep track of the auctioneer's words any more, they all bled into one. The Magnificub was tiring now, swaying and cowering, exhausted by the barrage of shouting and the loud, ringing *thwack* of the auctioneer's cane every time it smacked against the metal bars of the cage.

Morrigan's heart pounded. She felt close to tears. For one heart-breaking second, she locked eyes with the Magnificub, and perhaps it was her imagination, but she felt instantly that he was pleading for her help.

Morrigan and Cadence turned to each other at that moment and, as if tuned to the same wireless station, they said in unison: 'We have to do something.'

'Any ideas?' asked Cadence. Her voice was shaking.

Morrigan didn't answer, but instead raised her trembling hand.

'Twelve thousand to the dwarf in the gorilla mask,' said the auctioneer, pointing directly at Morrigan. 'Do I hear twelve-five, ladies and gentlemen – thank you sir, twelve-five to the tattooed gentleman; do I hear thirteen? Thirteen thousand kred to the lady in the red scarf. Do I hear – yes, thirteen-five to our tattooed friend, very good, sir. How about fourteen, ladies and gentlemen, do I—'

'Fifteen!' called Morrigan in the deepest, meanest, most grown-up voice she could muster. Cadence choked out a tiny cough, and this time it was Morrigan's turn to elbow her in the ribs.

'Fifteen to the gorilla! Do I hear—'

'Sixteen,' came a deeper, meaner, much more authentically gravelly voice from the tattooed man.

'Eighteen,' countered Morrigan. There were noises of surprise from the crowd, underneath which Cadence muttered to Morrigan, 'Where exactly are we getting this money from?'

'Nowhere,' Morrigan whispered behind her mask. 'Shush.'

'Twenty,' said the tattooed man. He sounded angry.

'Twenty-five,' Morrigan shouted, and the crowd went silent.

'Twenty-five thousand kred,' repeated the auctioneer in disbelief. 'Twenty-five thousand kred going once . . . twenty-five thousand kred going twice . . .' He paused, raising an eyebrow in the direction of the tattooed man. 'No counter-offer, my friend? All right then, twenty-five thousand kred to the small gorilla.' He sounded bemused, but slammed his auction hammer down, sealing the deal. 'See my clerk for payment and collection. Moving on to our last lot, ladies and gentlemen . . .'

Morrigan had stopped listening. Her blood was rushing in her ears, and the obvious question beat like a drum in her heart: What now? What now? *What now?*

But Cadence had spotted the clerk, who was standing by the Magnificub and waving Morrigan over. 'Don't worry, I've got this.'

⌫◄▬▬

The clerk was deeply unimpressed.

'What's this supposed to be?'

'It's your money,' said Cadence. She had pulled off her fox mask and handed it to the young man, who looked insulted, and then confused. 'Twenty-five thousand kred. I counted it. Twice.'

'This isn't . . . this is some kind of . . .' The clerk shook his head like a dog trying to shake off a bath. 'What do you think you're playing at?'

Morrigan looked over her shoulder to the other side of the tent, where the auction was continuing. She wanted desperately to just get out of there, to run away and not look back. But there was no way she was leaving without the Magnificub, who had finally exhausted himself and was now slumped, sad and helpless, on the floor of his cage.

She could hear only snatches of what the auctioneer was saying, but the crowd seemed excited about whatever he was concealing behind the large red velvet curtain.

'Imagine the uses . . .' The auctioneer's voice floated across the room at intervals. '. . . sea merchants and pirates . . . such a talent. Not to mention hunting beneath . . . or assassins . . .'

'I'm not playing. You're confused,' said Cadence, her voice as smooth as a bow pulled across a cello. 'I'm *paying* for this cub with twenty-five thousand kred. Which is in your hand. I just gave it to you.' She nodded at the mask in the clerk's right hand, and then at the key to the Magnificub cage clutched tightly in his left. 'And now you give me the Magnificub.'

'And now I give you . . .'

'That's it . . .'

'But . . .'

'That's it.' Cadence's voice was soporific. The young man blinked slowly and turned to unlock the cage. 'Very good.'

C.·◼▬·

Minutes later, they reached the door of the tent, leaving the dazed clerk locking Cadence's fox mask into a heavy metal box, earnest in his belief that it was twenty-five thousand kred in cash. Morrigan was struggling to keep hold of the terrified cub. She held the end of his chain in one hand just in case, but was trying to carry the poor thing – which was a bit like carrying a fully-grown Saint Bernard. She'd had to abandon the gorilla mask because the cub seemed frightened.

They skirted the edge of the buzzing crowd, still gathered around the last item. The auctioneer's gunfire patter cut through the noise. 'Eighteen-five to the swarthy gentleman with the peg leg. Eighteen-five, do we have nineteen? Small price to pay for such a rare gift, folks . . .'

Morrigan tried to keep her grip, whispering a soothing stream of nonsense into the Magnificub's ear. 'Shhh. You're all right. My, aren't you a fine cub. Fen's been out looking for you. Hush now. Don't you want to come with us and meet grumpy old Fenestra? Course you do. She's a Magnificat, just like you.'

Cadence was standing on tiptoes, trying to see what had everyone so excited. 'It's something in a tank,' she whispered to Morrigan, who grunted back at her. 'Like, a really big fish tank.'

'Let's just get out of here,' Morrigan hissed. 'Can you *please* help me?'

But Cadence had stopped several paces behind and was staring through the crowd at whatever was inside the tank. Her eyes bulged. 'Morrigan . . . look.'

'We have to *go*. I can't hold on to him much—'

'Morrigan,' Cadence said more urgently, pointing at the tank. '*Look.*'

Reluctantly – and with difficulty – she returned to where Cadence stood. Perhaps believing she was taking him back to his tormenters, the cub yowled and hissed, digging his claws painfully into her arms. But in the shock of what she saw inside the tank, Morrigan instantly forgot her pain.

Behind the glass, beneath the water, chained to a rock . . . was a teenage boy.

He was alive. He was utterly dejected and hopeless-looking, blue-lipped with chill, but he was alive.

Well, of course he was. He could breathe underwater.

'Alfie!' cried Morrigan. She couldn't help herself; the name tumbled from her mouth before she could stop it. Her voice rang out over the noise of the crowd and the auctioneer, and a deafening silence fell as every pair of eyes turned to look at Morrigan, Cadence and the Magnificub – who was now screeching and yowling, struggling desperately to get away.

'Who are those children?' shouted the auctioneer. 'Who allowed children in here? Somebody grab them!'

Half-a-dozen burly, mean-looking security personnel seemed to materialise from nowhere. Cadence grabbed Morrigan's wrist, trying to tug her away, but Morrigan was rooted to the spot.

It was happening again. She could feel it.

Her fear and revulsion and rage swelled inside her like a symphony, until they were somehow bigger than her body. It was a different feeling this time: not burning, but *building*. She felt the bold, ballooning reach of her power as it tried to grasp something solid, as it swallowed everything in its path, amplified everything around her in its search for . . . for *something*. For a tool. An instrument.

And in a glorious, golden moment, Morrigan felt it settle on the thing that was closest to her: the desperate Magnificub, fighting to get out of her grip . . .

. . . and succeeding at last.

He leapt from her arms a yowling cub. But by the time he had landed on the ground he was a towering, terrifying beast, grown strong on Morrigan's own uncontainable Wundrous power. He roared with a sound like a whole pride of lions, baring his teeth at the auctioneer, who promptly fainted.

The tent descended into screaming chaos as the cat took swipes at the crowd, pouncing here and there among them, joyful in his well-earned vengeance. Using his antics and the terror of the crowd as their cover, Morrigan and Cadence ran to Alfie's tank, only to find their way blocked by their rival bidder, the tattooed man. Intricate black ink crept over every uncovered inch of his body.

'You did that,' he said, staring straight at Morrigan. 'How? How did you do that? What are you?'

Morrigan made to push past him towards Alfie's tank, hoping to somehow get to him, to get him out and take him with them. The man made to lunge for her, but Cadence kicked him hard in the shins and he yelped, clutching his leg in pain.

'Oi!' he shouted, and three of his friends – each one covered in muscle – started towards them.

'Run!' shouted Cadence, grabbing Morrigan's wrist.

They ran to the mouth of the tent, weaving through the panicked auction-goers now streaming back into the busy, noisy chaos of the Ghastly Market outside.

With a pang of mingled hope and regret, Morrigan saw the ferocious Magnificat shrink slowly back to his former size as he disappeared into the crowd, leaving a trail of destruction behind him – stalls trampled, tables upended, and vendors bellowing at each other in the confusion, not realising the real culprit was getting away on four fast paws.

Run, little cub, she thought fiercely, hoping against all odds that he would somehow get to safety, but knowing she and Cadence could do no more to help him. They had to help themselves now.

'There she is!' came a rough voice from behind them. 'Grab her!'

They dodged their pursuers, deliberately knocking over even more tables behind them as they went. Cadence sent flying a barrel that turned out to be filled to the brim with brightly coloured snakes, and the chorus of screams that rose up in their wake spurred Morrigan and Cadence to run even faster.

They sprinted all the way back to Devilish Court, past the suffocating trick, through the seemingly endless precincts of the Nevermoor Bazaar, and at last arrived – sweating, lungs heaving – outside the gates of the Temple of the Divine Thing, just before midnight.

Pacing between two bracketed torches bearing bright pink flames was Hawthorne, ashen-faced and speechless, apparently unable to channel his worry into adequate words. Homer more than made up for his younger brother's silence, however, with a series of shouty blackboard messages featuring lots of exclamation marks and capital letters, hastily erased and written over while Morrigan and Cadence stood, silently absorbing the fury as they fought to catch their breath.

Most of the boys' anxiety was, of course, over the fact that Hawthorne had lost Morrigan somewhere in the Bazaar and been looking for her everywhere. She didn't mind, really. Homer's blackboard made her remember something.

Reaching into a concealed inner pocket of her jacket, she retrieved a small piece of soft, silvery-black paper.

Without pausing to explain, Morrigan snatched Homer's chalk from out of his hand mid-sentence, pressed the paper against a wall and wrote:

> *Found Alfie Swann and the Magnificub.*
> *Devilish Court. Ghastly Market.*
> *Tell Jupiter.*
> *Bring Stealth.*

Then she whispered Jack's name three times – 'John Arjuna Korrapati, John Arjuna Korrapati, John Arjuna Korrapati,' – held the paper to the mouth of a flaming pink torch, and watched the ashes fly away.

CHAPTER SEVENTEEN

The Hotel Deucalion Academy for One

'Please, Mog. Don't go down any more Tricksy Lanes.'

Jupiter's face was drawn and lined with worry. On Cadence and Morrigan's information, he'd stormed Devilish Court the night before, taking with him the Stealth, the Stink, the Geographical Oddities Squadron, and even Fenestra (who was worth ten Stealth and at least fifty Stink, in Morrigan's opinion).

But they were too late. The cub's dramatic exit had raised too many alarms and by the time they'd arrived, the market had been dismantled, the perpetrators scattered, and all that was left was a graveyard of dirty, anonymous market stalls, a hand-painted sign that read *THE GHASTLY MARKET,* an empty glass tank . . . and one miserable teenage boy, sitting alone on the cobbled ground in his wet clothes, shivering from cold.

At least they'd got Alfie back.

But there was no hint of joy in Jupiter's face that morning, nor even of satisfaction in a job well done. Nothing but grave determination to extract a promise from Morrigan never again to enter a Tricksy Lane.

'I mean it,' he said, his blue eyes flashing. 'They're far too dangerous. It isn't worth the risk.'

Morrigan made a face. How could Jupiter *say* that? If she and Cadence hadn't gone down Devilish Court, they would never have found the Ghastly Market. They would never have set the Magnificub free. Jupiter and the Stealth would never have known where to find Alfie Swann. She opened her mouth to say all of this, but Jupiter held up his hand to stop her.

'Alfie's knack is gone.' He spoke in a hushed, almost reverent voice, as if breaking the news of a terminal illness.

'Gone?' echoed Morrigan. Jupiter nodded. 'Gone . . . how?'

'We don't know.' He sighed deeply, rubbing a hand over his tired eyes. 'It's not clear yet whether it was *taken*, exactly, or . . . sometimes a severe trauma might . . .' He trailed off, and Morrigan could hear the bewilderment in his voice. He had no idea. The Stealth had no idea.

'What about Cassiel and Paximus Luck?' Morrigan asked quietly. 'And the cub – has anyone found it yet?'

'No sign of Cassiel. We know Paximus was there, because we found a list of auction items, but he's gone now. We think perhaps . . .' He trailed off, unable or unwilling to finish that thought. 'Anyway, we're not giving up. Fen's people are out looking for the cub. Now they know he's out on the streets, not locked away in a cage somewhere, they stand a much better chance of finding the poor thing.'

Morrigan frowned. 'Who *are* Fen's people?'

'Friends of hers. Other Magnificats, mostly – they keep to themselves, but there are a few of them around. They look out for each other.'

'But . . . isn't the Wundrous Society helping? What about the Stealth? Shouldn't *we* be investigating—'

'There's no "we" here, Mog,' said Jupiter, his voice slightly raised. 'You are not part of the investigation. Understand?'

'That's not fair.' Morrigan could hear the whine in her voice, but couldn't help it. 'I found the market – well, Cadence and I found it. *We* set the cub free. *We're* the ones who—'

'You're the ones who showed your talents to a room full of people who would pay a lot of money to take them from you,' Jupiter snapped. Morrigan recoiled slightly.

'I didn't show them anything deliberately,' she muttered, thinking of the Magnificub's strange transformation. 'I told you already. I don't know how it happened, it just . . .'

'Happened,' Jupiter finished for her with a sigh. 'I know. I'm afraid I can't explain that one either.'

He'd lost his thin veneer of patience, but she could sense there was something more behind his frustration. He looked her dead in the eye, and she saw that he was afraid. 'Morrigan, trust that everyone is doing all they can to find those still missing. And, *please*. No more Tricksy Lanes.'

The rest of Morrigan's summer holidays went by like a strange, slightly stifling dream. Jupiter's absences were still frequent, but during those in-between times when he was home, he seemed determined to make up for them – and also, Morrigan strongly suspected, to keep her so busy and entertained that she had no reason, temptation or opportunity to go hunting for any more clues about the Ghastly Market.

It quickly became clear that he'd roped in the staff to help make this summer at the Deucalion as distractingly spectacular as it could possibly be. There were rock concerts and midnight picnics on the rooftop. A croquet tournament on the south-facing lawn and near-nightly fireworks displays. And although Morrigan kept pestering Jupiter for details of the Ghastly Market investigation every chance she got, it was hard not to be *somewhat* diverted by the parade of relentless festivities.

Frank threw a pool party almost every weekend, complete with epic make-your-own sundae bars and water-balloon wars. Jupiter had a waterslide installed, and brought in realistic inflatable polar bears that tossed people high in the air, caught them in their soft rubber arms and dunked them underwater, to endless screams of delight from Morrigan, Hawthorne and Jack.

One weekend, Morrigan had the brilliant idea to invite all of Unit 919 over. Excited and nervous for the opportunity to prove to them she wasn't dangerous, that the Elders had it all wrong, she even went so far as to write out individual invitations on fancy parchment.

She thought carefully about what she wanted to say – that she was sorry about what had happened at the station, that it was an accident and she would never hurt anyone on purpose, and please would they come over for swimming and snow-cones this Saturday. She closed the invites up carefully with a wax-sealing kit that Jupiter lent her, and had Hawthorne hand-deliver them on her behalf. But when the day arrived, only he and Cadence showed up.

Morrigan tried not to be dispirited, and made the most of the day by giving Cadence a tour of the hotel, which turned out to be an interesting test of their fragile new friendship. Unlike Hawthorne (who, to Morrigan's satisfaction, had boundless enthusiasm for everything the Deucalion had to offer, no matter how weird), Cadence's reaction was mixed.

She was politely perplexed by the rain room ('What, so it just . . . rains? Inside? All the time? *Why?*'), and she hated the theatre, with its dressing room full of costumes that each came with their own accent and mannerisms (Morrigan did *warn* her not to try on the Puss-in-Boots costume; Cadence was still meowing and scratching behind her ears an hour after she'd taken it off). But she loved lounging on the sandy island in the middle of the lagoon pool, complete with swaying palm trees and gentle, tinkling ukulele music that drifted on a warm breeze.

Hawthorne still had to train over the holidays with the Junior Dragonriding League, but he made his way to the Deucalion most afternoons, exhausted and sooty. He, Morrigan and Cadence would usually play cards in the Smoking Parlour, inhaling the latest summery scent rolling out from the walls. The parlour was trialling a new seasonal range, with mixed results. Coconut smoke, ocean breeze smoke and strawberries-and-cream smoke were big hits. Insect repellent smoke, Wunderground commuter sweat smoke and potato-salad-at-a-picnic smoke were dramatically less successful.

Since she wasn't allowed to get involved with Jupiter's investigation, Morrigan tried to concentrate more on figuring out who was blackmailing Unit 919. Though as she wasn't allowed to leave the Deucalion and most of her unit weren't speaking to her, she had to admit there wasn't an awful lot to be getting on with.

The one good thing, Morrigan thought, was that their blackmailers must be on summer holiday also. So at least

Unit 919 would have a respite from any more demands until classes began again.

But no such luck.

'Look at this,' said Cadence one morning, passing a note to Morrigan as they settled into a pair of sun loungers. She popped on her sunglasses and lay back while Morrigan read.

Cadence Lenore Blackburn.

Your patron has an important public appearance tomorrow morning.
You will find a creative way to make him humiliate himself.
If you fail, we will reveal the secret of Unit 919.

Remember:
Tell no one.
Or we will tell everyone.

Morrigan blanched. She didn't like Baz Charlton, but if somebody had told *her* to choose between protecting her unit and publicly humiliating her own patron, she honestly didn't know what she would do.

This did at least eliminate a suspect – surely Baz wouldn't demand his own humiliation! But even so, it didn't bring Morrigan any closer to knowing who *was* behind it.

She glanced sideways at Cadence, who had propped her hands behind her head and was basking in the bright warmth.

'I wasn't sure whether you'd get one of these,' Morrigan admitted.

'Me neither,' said Cadence, frowning. 'I didn't think they'd even notice me.'

'So, um,' Morrigan went on, trying to sound casual, 'what's this public appearance tomorrow morning?'

'It was this morning – the note came yesterday. He was attending parliament to petition for stricter border laws. Big, important speech.'

'Oh.' Morrigan waited, but Cadence said nothing more. 'So . . . what happened?'

'Well, I had to really think about it, you know.'

'Right.'

'I was up all night, trying to decide what to do. I couldn't sleep.'

'Of . . . of course.' Morrigan held her breath.

'But in the end, I just couldn't choose between making him drool through the whole thing, speak in a baby voice, or drop his trousers at the end and shout "BAZZY WANT POTTY".' Cadence grinned. 'So, I went with all three.'

Fireworks and waterslides and rock concerts were fine, Morrigan thought. But this, truly, was her favourite moment of the summer so far.

Towards the end of the holidays, Jupiter announced his return from one of his longer expeditions by waking a reluctant Morrigan and Jack at dawn and bringing them to the rooftop, where he'd tethered a gigantic hot-air balloon. It was a dreamy, magical thing to float high above Nevermoor's rooftops watching the sun illuminate the city in pink and gold, with no sound but the occasional blast of heat from the burner. Morrigan never wanted her feet to touch the ground again. And she never wanted this summer to end either.

But she wasn't stupid. She knew this was all part of a grand combined effort to keep her distracted and happy and safe at the Deucalion, to steer her away from the Ghastly Market investigation and to soften the blow of her Wunsoc ban.

And Morrigan appreciated their efforts, she really did. However, the fact remained that when the new term began, Hawthorne and the rest of 919 would be heading back to their classes at Wunsoc, and she would be left behind. The Elders still hadn't decided whether it was safe for Morrigan to return to campus, and were insisting that for now, the ban must remain in place. Jupiter had pleaded and cajoled and threatened and stormed and pleaded again, all to no avail.

'Gregoria Quinn is the most implacable person I've ever known,' he fumed one day after returning from another fruitless mission to the Elders' Hall. (Later, Morrigan looked up the word 'implacable' and decided that she agreed with him entirely.) 'I mean for goodness' sake, if it wasn't for you, the Stealth might never have saved— might never have . . . brought Alfie home.'

There was a moment of unease that came with those words. Because, after all, the Stealth had not really *saved* Alfie, had they? At least, not in the eyes of the Elders, or of Baz Charlton . . . or of most people at Wunsoc, in fact. According to Jupiter, they were all acting as if Alfie had died, when really he'd just become a bit more . . . normal.

'At least he's *alive*,' Morrigan kept saying any time Alfie's missing knack was brought up in conversation. Jupiter always agreed with her, but she knew that deep down, he was thinking about how it would feel to no longer be a Witness.

Morrigan wondered how *she* would feel if somebody told her she wasn't a Wundersmith any more. Given that the whole situation had caused her nothing but grief, she suspected she might throw a party. But even so, she could imagine how it would feel for *Jupiter* to have his talent taken away without his consent. The thing that made him unique and important. It would be like a little death.

'Do you think . . . could he maybe get it back?' she asked. 'If they ever find the person who took it, I mean.'

'We can't be certain someone *did* take it,' said Jupiter. 'I'm not totally convinced that's even possible. Alfie can't tell us much; he's still in shock and barely remembers a thing. Maybe – *hopefully* – it's just the trauma of it all, and he'll regain his talent in time.'

'And if he doesn't,' said Morrigan, 'will he be allowed to stay in the Society?'

Jupiter was quiet for a moment, and she wondered if he was about to tell her a comforting lie. But he simply gave a blunt, bewildered shrug.

'I'm honestly not sure, Mog,' he said. 'That's up to the Elders.'

Inevitably summer ended, and Professor Onstald arrived at the Deucalion to continue his boring lectures on the evils of being a Wundersmith.

The staff knew how Morrigan felt about Professor Onstald's lessons. (They ought to; she'd done *quite* a lot of complaining about them.) Even so, they strove to make her teacher feel welcome at the hotel.

Or at least, that's what Morrigan thought.

In the beginning.

'I'm afraid this is the only space where we can accommodate you today,' said Kedgeree on the first morning, as he showed Onstald and Morrigan into the Deucalion's second biggest ballroom, on the fifth floor. 'Everywhere else is occupied. Very busy time of year for the hotel industry, you understand.'

Moving at Onstald's glacial pace, it had taken them almost half an hour just to get down the hall from the elevator, but Kedgeree didn't seem to mind. He kept up a stream of cheerful chatter the whole way, apparently oblivious to Onstald's impatient little snorts and huffs of reply. Now, heaving his usual rattling breaths as he gazed upon the ballroom, the tortoisewun looked deeply appalled.

'Are you . . . telling me . . . I must teach . . . in this . . . this . . .'

'—very elegant space that's currently being prepared for our Annual Autumnal Ball, yes,' interrupted Kedgeree, with an apologetic shrug. 'But don't worry, Frank's promised he won't disrupt your lesson at all. Right, Frank?' he called out to the vampire dwarf, who was across the room setting up a sound check for his favourite swing band, Iguanarama.

'You won't even know I'm here,' Frank boomed into the microphone. There was a squeal of feedback. Onstald flinched. 'Oops, sorry.'

The hardest thing for Morrigan was trying to concentrate on Onstald's litany of Wundrous misdeeds while Frank paraded an increasingly ridiculous variety of distractions through the ballroom, accompanied by his constant refrain of, 'Ignore me, ignore me – I'm not here!' She kept a straight face through three consecutive rehearsals of Iguanarama's chart-topping dance hit, *Swing, Swing Your Scaly Tail*. She even managed to read an entire chapter on the tyrannical

Wundersmith Tyr Magnusson while tranquilly ignoring the giant, floating champagne bubbles that were slowly filling the room.

But the final straw – for Morrigan's poker face and Onstald's patience – was when Frank brought in a flock of squawking geese dressed in black jackets and bowties.

'What . . . is the . . . MEANING . . . of THIS?' demanded the tortoisewun, while Morrigan dissolved into giggles.

Frank turned to them, his face a picture of innocence, and said, 'Well I'm sorry, Professor, but *someone* has to train the extra catering staff!'

The next day, Kedgeree moved them to an art studio in the east wing. It reeked of oil paint and turpentine, but Kedge opened the windows wide and took care to point out that it was, at least, free of tuxedoed waterfowl.

However, it was also close to the Music Salon, and Dame Chanda took to wandering the hall outside, practising her arias. Each time her angelic voice floated past the studio, crowds of squirrels, bluebirds, badgers, foxes and field mice swarmed through the open windows, drawn irresistibly to the sound. Onstald made Morrigan close the windows, but the paint fumes became unbearable and the creatures kept coming, only now they were scratching at the glass and whimpering to be let in.

Martha prepared lunch for them every day and after several mumbled complaints from Professor Onstald, Morrigan realised that the maid was deliberately sabotaging his meals. Giving him soup that was just a touch too cold, bread a touch too stale, tea a touch too weak. Meanwhile, she always slipped Morrigan a foil-wrapped chocolate or a tiny iced honeycake with her lunch, and never gave Onstald a single sweet treat. It was a small act of pettiness, but by gentle, tender-hearted Martha's standards, it was a declaration of all-out war, and Morrigan adored her for it.

Each day that week brought a move to a new room with its own fresh variety of nuisance, and it didn't take long for Morrigan to figure out exactly what the staff were doing. It lifted her spirits in a way that even pool parties and hot-air balloon rides could never have done. Every morning she jumped out of bed, excited to see what they would come up with that day to make Onstald's head explode.

But the pièce de résistance of Hotel Deucalion resistance, came – of course – from Fenestra. On Friday morning, when Morrigan and Onstald had settled into their latest improvised classroom (a disused badminton court on the seventh floor) and begun their lesson, Fen sauntered in. She didn't say a word, but sat behind Morrigan, glowering over her head at Professor Onstald and purring so aggressively that it made the floor vibrate.

Morrigan knew that if anyone else had interrupted their lesson, Onstald would have demanded they *leave at once*. But Fenestra wasn't the sort of cat who inspired demands.

That evening, a messenger arrived with an ivory envelope addressed to Morrigan.

Miss Crow,

I write to inform you that my fellow Elders and I have reconsidered your exile from the Wundrous Society campus. After careful review – and a strong recommendation from Professor Onstald, who assures us that the behaviour he has seen from you this week has been satisfactorily non-threatening – we are pleased to invite you to return to Wunsoc, and to your Decoding Nevermoor class with Mr Mildmay, on Monday.

Needless to say, we will continue to closely monitor your conduct.

Please do not disappoint us.

Kind regards,
Elder Gregoria Quinn

CHAPTER EIGHTEEN

Riddles and Bones

Autumn of Two

The tiny encircled *W* on Morrigan's station door lit up. She stood there for a full minute, matching her breaths to its gentle, pulsating glow, before finally steeling herself to press her imprint against the light.

The door swung open to reveal a huddle of faces that looked pretty much as she'd expected. Cadence and Hawthorne, at least, seemed pleased to see her. The others were at best warily awkward, and at worst openly hostile.

Given the week they'd just had, Morrigan could hardly blame them.

Cadence and Hawthorne had filled her in over the weekend. In the five days she'd missed, there had been *four* new demands, one after the other.

First, Mahir had been ordered to paint rude words in thirty-seven different languages all over the Hall of Tongues. Then Hawthorne had to set a section of the dragon stables on fire – though from the way he told the story, he seemed to have quite enjoyed it.

'And nobody suspects a thing!' he said. 'Because *Burns with the Fire of a Thousand Wood-Burning Stoves* sleeps in that section, so I just blamed it on him. He's got terrible gas, *Burns with.*'

Anah was deeply shaken by her own criminal exploits – she'd had to steal medical supplies from the teaching hospital (just a few pairs of rubber gloves and a bedpan, according to Cadence, but Anah had spent the rest of the week wailing about what the nuns who raised her would say).

The worst demand had come for Arch, who'd had to steal a lock of hair from Ms Dearborn. Morrigan imagined that was about as safe as stealing a scale from a dragon.

'I thought he might die of fright, but he got it,' Cadence had told her, grim-faced. 'Only he felt so bad afterwards that he left it with an anonymous apology note for her to find on the steps of Proudfoot House. The idiot.'

'And she's been on the war path ever since,' muttered Hawthorne.

Morrigan now approached her stony-faced unit.

'Hi,' she said, giving a nervous wave. 'Er, how's it going?'

'Oh, *terrific*,' said Thaddea, glowering at her. 'We've all just been here taking massive risks to keep protecting your secret. How 'bout you? Nice week at home in your fancy hotel, was it?'

'Shut up, Thaddea,' said Hawthorne, but he was drowned out by the *chug-chug-chug* of Hometrain arriving. Morrigan sighed as she watched Thaddea and the others march into the carriage without sparing her a second glance.

It was, perhaps, the hair-stealing event that had led Dearborn to announce a surprise exam period, starting that very day.

Morrigan had it easy, compared to the others. That was one benefit, at least, of having only two classes on her timetable. Onstald's examination paper was tediously predictable; a monstrous many-paged booklet full of long-winded questions like, 'Name the three worst Wundersmiths in history, ranking their top five most dreadful acts of evil and/or stupidity', and 'Why was the Great War of the Age of Poisoners entirely the fault of Wundersmiths? List twenty-seven reasons'. It took Morrigan three days to complete it.

The test for *Decoding Nevermoor* later in the week was much trickier, but also *much* more interesting.

⊱───

'All right, Nine-One-Niners, listen up!' Mildmay's voice cut through the echoing chatter that bounced around Proudfoot

Station. He held a finger up to his lips, and the scholars fell silent. 'I know we're all up WAY past our bedtimes for a Thursday and probably starting to feel a bit tired and silly at this time of the morning, but let's try to stay cool, all right? One last time, let's go through the rules—'

Cadence groaned. 'We've been through them already.'

'Humour me, friends,' said Mildmay. 'Altogether now, rule number one is . . . ?'

'No Brolly Rail, no Wunderground, no hansom cabs, no buses,' droned the unit as one.

He held up two fingers. 'Rule number two?'

'No asking for directions or talking to strangers.'

'Three?'

'No maps, no guidebooks.'

'Four?'

'Back before dawn, safe and sound and whole.'

He held up his hand, fingers splayed. 'And the fifth and final rule?'

'A failure for one is a failure for all.'

'That's right,' he said, nodding. 'To pass this exam, you and your team must all be back by sunrise – that's three hours from now.' He looked around at each of them in turn. 'You and your ENTIRE team. If you want to succeed, you'll need to work together on this one. And remember: if one team out of the three fails, the whole unit fails. Understood?'

The only answer was a vague sort of mumbling.

Mildmay grinned, apparently choosing to ignore the lacklustre response. 'Terrific! Now, each group is going to hop inside a brass railpod which will take you to your starting point, a Wunderground station somewhere in this wild and wonderful city of ours. You'll notice they don't have windows, so you'll really have no idea where you're going. When you arrive, you'll find your first clue, which will lead you to the next, which will lead you to the next, and so on . . . three clues per team, and you'll need to bring all of them back with you within the time limit if you want to pass. Remember, we're testing your ability to navigate Nevermoor AND your ability to work together. No scholar left behind. Understood? Right – in you hop.'

Cadence, Arch and Lambeth filed into the first spherical brass railpod; Thaddea, Anah and Hawthorne took the second. Mildmay waved at them all and called out, 'Good luck!' as the doors closed.

Morrigan had hoped Mildmay would put her in a team with the only two people in the unit who liked her, but no such luck. She, Francis and Mahir stepped into the third pod and travelled in a stony, awkward silence for close to three-quarters of an hour.

At some point she felt, as the other two must have, the nerve-racking realisation that they really were travelling *quite* far – perhaps to the outer edges of Nevermoor – and that the three-hour time limit they had to make their way back was now dwindling closer to two hours.

When the train finally stopped, it was at an above-ground Wunderground station; little more than a concrete platform next to a set of tracks. The three scholars emerged from the train into the cool night air. It was dark. The station was, officially, closed – only private Wunsoc trains and railpods ran at this time of night (another perk of Society membership). The sky above was cloudless, and the stars shone brightly in a way that you didn't often see in central Nevermoor, because there was so much light pollution. Morrigan breathed in deeply; the air felt cleaner and sweeter. She read the station sign: Polaris Hill. That confirmed her suspicions; they'd come all the way down to Betelgeuse, one of the outer boroughs. She frowned. How were they going to get from Betelgeuse back to Old Town before dawn?

'There's the first clue!' said Mahir, pointing to a clock on the station wall. A small envelope with the number 919 was stuck to it. Francis got there first and tore it open to read the contents aloud.

'A garden of night,' he began. 'A killer's delight. A weapon for cowards. Death by flowers.'

'What's that mean?' asked Mahir.

The gears in Morrigan's brain were slowly grinding. *A garden of night . . . Death by flowers.* 'What sort of flower can kill someone?'

'A . . . poisonous one?' said Francis uncertainly.

'No,' said Mahir, his eyes wide with excitement. 'One of those giant killer flytraps with teeth! The ones in the southern rainforests that eat people whole.'

'But where—' began Morrigan. 'Oh! No, Francis is right. *A weapon for cowards.* It *is* talking about poison! We're meant to go somewhere poisonous flowers grow. *A garden of night.* Which garden though?' Morrigan ran through a list of Nevermoor's green spaces, counting on her fingers. 'There's the Garden Belt in Old Town. St Gertrude's Green. Um . . . Oxborrow Fields, that's not really much of a garden though . . .'

'Eldritch Murdergarden!' Francis said, clicking his fingers. 'It's got almost any poisonous plant you could think of. I've bought death caps from there before. They have a little shop.'

Morrigan wrinkled her nose. 'What are "death caps"?'

'Poisonous mushrooms. They're actually rather tasty . . . in very, very small doses.'

'You bought poisonous mushrooms,' Mahir said, blinking at him, 'from somewhere called a *murdergarden?*'

Francis shrugged, and said again, 'They have a little shop.'

Morrigan made two mental notes: firstly, to never again eat anything Francis offered her; and secondly, to ask Jupiter why in the *world* he'd never told her there was a poisonous garden in Nevermoor. For goodness' sake, he *knew* that sort of thing was right up her alley.

'Garden of night – killer's delight. That must be the place. We're in Betelgeuse, which means Eldritch is east of here, so . . .' Morrigan paused, picturing the Living Map inside her mind. 'Francis, what's the closest Wunderground station to the Murdergarden?'

'Old Marlow Road.'

'If I can get us there, can you get us to the garden?'

He frowned for a moment, then nodded. 'Yes, I think so.'

'Mahir, how long before dawn?'

Mahir checked his watch. 'Hour and a half. We'll never make it.'

'Don't say that.' Francis twisted the front of his coat nervously. 'Hester will kill me if I fail an exam.'

Morrigan didn't want to admit it, but really, Mahir was right. She couldn't see how they'd make it all the way back to Wunsoc by dawn, when the use of public transport was forbidden and they still had to pick up two more clues from two mystery destinations.

Still. There was no way Morrigan was going to admit defeat in one of her *only* two exams. Dearborn would think she'd been proven right – that the wretched Morrigan Crow was a *failed experiment,* unworthy of a proper education.

'We ARE going to make it,' she said, rolling up the sleeves of her cloak. 'But I hope you're both wearing comfortable shoes.'

They ran all the way to the gates of the Eldritch Murdergarden. It took twenty of their precious remaining minutes, and the only living things they passed on the way were a pair of noisy urban foxes, several rough sleepers huddled in shop doorways, and a dustman who got the fright of his life as the three of them clattered past at breakneck speed.

The black gates to the garden were locked at this hour, but clenched in the teeth of a silver skull-and-crossbones mounted on the gates was another little envelope labelled '919'. Mahir snatched it and read the note inside aloud.

'Not bronze or gold, but Houses old. Abundant wealth; dubious moral health.'

'Another riddle,' said Morrigan. '*Not bronze or gold.* Well, that's got to be silver, doesn't it?'

'*Houses old.* That's not very specific,' said Francis. 'There are lots of old houses in—'

'Oh!' Mahir shouted. 'The Grand Old Houses!'

'Grand Old Houses?' asked Morrigan.

'The old families in the Silver District,' said Mahir. 'That's what they call them – the Grand Old House of St James, the Grand Old House of Fairchild . . . all rich, nasty aristocrats. *Abundant wealth; dubious moral health.* Makes sense, doesn't it? But I wouldn't have a clue how to get there.'

'Me neither,' said Francis. 'Not without the Wunderground.'

Morrigan closed her eyes, trying to picture the Living Map again. She'd seen the Silver District somewhere before. In her mind, she was picturing water . . . canals. Little boats sailing through foggy, swirling mists . . .

'The Silver District is in Ogden-on-Juro!' she declared triumphantly. 'It's that borough that's sinking into the River Juro – I saw it on the Living Map.'

'That's *ages* away.' Francis slumped against the Murdergarden gates and they made a clanging noise. 'It'll take us an hour to run there, at least. I can't run for an hour!'

'Told you.' Mahir too leaned against the gates and slid all the way down to the ground, landing with a soft *oof.* 'There's no way we're making it back to Wunsoc by dawn. We might as well give up now.'

'Snap out of it,' Morrigan barked at them. She'd remembered something else she'd seen on the Living Map. 'How did you two ever pass your trials last year with this sort of attitude? Get up and follow me. I have an excellent idea!'

'This is a horrible idea,' shouted Francis over the wind.

'Yes,' agreed Morrigan.

'But you said—'

'I lied.'

Mahir groaned. 'We've been waiting for ten minutes. It's not going to show! I'm freezing up here, let's just—'

'It *will*,' said Morrigan. 'It'll show. They run every hour. Just one more minute. Trust me.'

She was trying her very best to channel the indomitable life force of a certain ginger-bearded madman she knew. But it was hard to quell the nausea swelling up inside her as she stared down from where she, Francis and Mahir stood – precariously balanced – on the rails of the Centenary Bridge, into the fathomless black waters of the River Juro below. She began racking her brain for an alternate plan, but then, from underneath the bridge, the bow of a rubbish barge came into view, cutting swiftly through the water for a vessel of its size. Morrigan felt relief wash over her.

'On three,' she shouted over the noise of the flowing river. 'Ready?'

'No,' yelled Mahir.

'No,' echoed Francis.

'That's the spirit. One – two – JUMP!'

Francis and Mahir jumped, but only – Morrigan was certain – because she had such a ferociously tight grip on each of their arms that they had very little choice in the matter.

The three scholars screamed all the way down until they landed on a soft pile of putrid-smelling rubbish.

'Urrggghh. Morrigan, I will NEVER –' Francis tried to stand, but fell over instead, sliding all the way down to the end of the rubbish pile, and causing a small landslide that brought Morrigan and Mahir sliding right along behind him,

'– EVER FORGIVE YOU FOR THIS,' Francis finished, glaring at her.

'You'll forgive me when you pass your exam,' Morrigan muttered as she struggled to her feet. Truthfully, she was feeling a bit annoyed with herself. Why didn't her excellent ideas ever involve something easy or pleasant?

But the barge got them to Ogden-on-Juro faster than even a trip on the Wunderground would have done. And although they had to jump in the water at one point and swim to the shore, at least the chilly waters of the River Juro washed *most* of the disgusting rubbish smell from their clothes . . . even if it meant they were now wet and freezing.

'A t-t-tunnel of g-green,' read Francis, lips blue and body shaking as he read the note they'd found stuck to the ostentatious silver gates enclosing the sinking Silver District. 'F-fit for a . . . q-queen. A m-m-monarch . . .'

'Oh h-here, let m-me read—' said Morrigan through chattering teeth. She tried to snatch the note from him with her frozen, clumsy fingers. 'A tunnel of green, fit for a queen. A monarch alone. A g-graveyard of bones.'

'Av-avenue of t-trees,' said Mahir immediately. 'Queen's Heath. There's a path through the h-heath that's planted with trees that have all g-grown over.'

'Queen's Heath,' echoed Morrigan. She stamped her feet up and down and rubbed her hands together, trying to force some warmth back into them. 'That was

Queen Septemberine's h-hunting ground, wasn't it? Six or seven m-monarchs ago. I read about her in *A History of Nevermoorian B-barbarism*.'

'*A graveyard of bones!*' said Mahir. 'You're right. And they say nobody else was ever allowed inside the heath during Septemberine's lifetime: *a monarch alone*. It fits!'

'But Queen's Heath is in Highwall,' said Francis, his face falling. 'Two boroughs north. We don't have anywhere near enough time.'

'I think I know a way,' said Morrigan urgently. 'Spitznogle Street. We just passed it on the way here – it's only two blocks back. It's marked on the Living Map as a Swindleroad, I'm *sure* it is.'

Mahir looked surprised. 'How do you know that?'

'I memorised the geographical oddities.'

Mahir's eyes widened at that, and Morrigan shrugged. 'Well, not all of them. Not yet. But most of the Tricksy Lanes and some of the Swindleroads . . . and remember what Mildmay told us about Swindleroads? They swallow you up and spit you out somewhere else, sometimes miles away. It *can't* be a coincidence that there's one this close to our third clue. I bet you anything you like that we're meant to go down Spitznogle. I bet it takes us to Queen's Heath . . . or closer to it anyway.'

'But Mildmay said we're not supposed to go down Tricksy Lanes,' Francis protested. 'And we haven't even studied

Swindleroads properly yet. They wouldn't put something in the exam that could be dangerous.'

Morrigan groaned. 'Oh, for goodness' *sake*, Francis, haven't you figured out the Society by now? They don't *care* if it's dangerous. They don't *care* if we've studied it or not. They're not colouring inside the lines, and they don't expect us to either.'

'Colouring inside— what are you *talking* about?' asked Mahir.

'Sometimes you just have to know which rules to obey, and which ones to break,' said Morrigan, remembering something Jupiter had once told her. 'When to follow the plan, and when to improvise.'

'But we don't *have* a plan,' said Francis weakly.

'Exactly,' said Morrigan. 'It's time to improvise.'

Spitznogle Street was long, narrow and dark. It was impossible to see what was at the end of it. Morrigan stood at the entrance, flanked by Francis and Mahir. Her hands shook, and she was beginning to regret her brainwave, just a little.

'Right,' she said. 'So we should just . . .'

'You're going first,' said Francis, in a terrified squeak.

'Right,' Morrigan repeated. 'Of course.'

She took a tentative step into the darkness, then another. Then, with a shake of her head, she decided it was all or nothing. Taking a long, deep breath, Morrigan broke into a run, clattering down the black alleyway until she saw a light – small but growing – up ahead. *Yes,* she thought, picking up speed, until finally she emerged . . .

Not on the other side of Spitznogle Street in the Silver District.

Not on the Queen's Heath in Highwall.

Not anywhere, really.

She stopped herself just in time, before her nose met the brick wall at the end of the alley, rising in front of her, blocking the way out. It grew right before her eyes – twelve feet high, then fourteen, then twenty . . .

She sighed, staring at the bricks, deeply reluctant to turn around and tell Mahir and Francis that she'd been wrong, when from behind her came a long, deep creaking sound. She heard a familiar *click-clack, click-clack,* and the unsettling *scccrrrrape* of something being dragged along the cobbles.

Morrigan's throat burned. Her nostrils filled with the hideous smell of dirty riverwater and decaying flesh. A creeping, oppressive cold spread through her chest. She turned slowly, and was faced with something she'd hoped never to see again.

The Skeletal Legion. The Bonesmen.

There were more of them this time. A horde had gathered – two dozen at least, maybe more – and were crowding into the alley mouth behind her. They pressed in shoulder to shoulder, wall to wall, four men deep. *Click-clack, click-clack, scccrrrape. Click-clack, click-clack, scccrrrrape.*

Just as she remembered – and as Mildmay had described – they had clearly been assembled rather haphazardly from the leftover bones of the people and unnimals that had died and been cast down to the bed of the River Juro over centuries, along with – it seemed – whatever else happened to be nearby. One of them had a rusted old umbrella frame instead of an arm, and another rolled along on a long-corroded, seaweed-strewn shopping trolley instead of legs. One of them was a human skeleton topped with the tiny skull of what looked like a cat. It could almost have been comical, but Morrigan had never felt less inclined to laugh.

The salty chill burned her chest, her breath coming in great rattling heaves. She squeezed her eyes shut, feeling an impotent fury at her own feebleness. She was supposed to be a *Wundersmith*, wasn't she? Why couldn't she do what a Wundersmith was meant to do? Why couldn't she do the things she'd seen Ezra Squall do? Why couldn't anyone *teach her how?*

It was a dangerous thought, one she would never have voiced aloud. But in that moment, for the first time ever, Morrigan wanted very much to be a real Wundersmith.

As if bidden by the thought, there came a loud whinnying bray from somewhere behind the Bonesmen. A great clattering gallop thundered down the alley towards Morrigan, a rider of black smoke cleaving straight through the horde of Bonesmen as if they weren't there at all.

Morrigan's breath caught in her throat. She realised what it was immediately – the Hunt of Smoke and Shadow had returned. She shivered, remembering Ezra Squall's last words to her – *Lesson two will take place as soon as you request it.*

The huntsman stopped directly in front of Morrigan and seemed to grow even larger, billowing up as if . . . as if to *protect her*, as if to form a shield between her and the grotesque skeleton monsters.

The black shadow-horse reared back on its hind legs, fiery steam shooting from its nostrils, its fierce red eyes blazing. As its hooves thundered back down onto the cobblestones, the enormous black smoke hunter on its back leaned down and held out a hand to Morrigan.

Morrigan's lungs burned and, realising she had stopped breathing, she gulped in a mouthful of cold air. Her pulse thumped in her neck.

The huntsman waited, perfectly still, hand outstretched.

Not a threat. Not a command.

An invitation.

Morrigan stepped backwards into the stone wall, shaking her head. 'I-I'm not going anywhere with you.'

The huntsman said nothing. His eyes, like the eyes of his horse, swirled red and pitch like glowing liquid embers. Like lava. The horse stamped impatiently.

'I'm not going with you!' Morrigan shouted again.

The huntsman again said nothing (she wasn't sure he even had a mouth with which to speak), but turned very slightly back towards the click-clacking horde of Bonesmen, and again to Morrigan with what looked like a mocking tilt of his smoky black head.

You've got a point, Morrigan thought miserably.

She didn't have a choice. Heart pounding, she reached out to grasp the smoky hand, feeling the strangest sensation as they connected, as if she was touching air made solid. With hardly any effort at all, the huntsman pulled her up into the saddle, and the horse instantly took off, scattering the horde of Bonesmen as it galloped through.

CHAPTER NINETEEN

Stolen Moments

It was different this time. The Hunt of Smoke and Shadow had stolen Morrigan once before – last winter, after her final Wundrous Society trial. It had felt like being tossed on the waves of a black-smoke ocean, or swept away by a hurricane of shadows, or tumbled over and over in an endless, dizzying tunnel, until finally the Hunt had dropped her on the Gossamer Line platform. Laid her at the Wundersmith's feet, like a dog brings a dead rat to its master.

But now, saddled in front of the towering ember-eyed huntsman, Morrigan felt more like an arrow that had been shot from a bow. The shadow-horse carrying them moved at such impossible speed they might have been flying through the Gossamer. City lights streamed past in their wake, and the wind roared in Morrigan's ears, deafening her.

And then it stopped.

There was silence but for the sound of Morrigan's own rapid breathing. She blinked, trying to clear her vision. The huntsman had disappeared, and she was standing alone inside a cavernous hall. Pockets of light reflected in the marble floor, flickering from lanterns bracketed on the walls.

Morrigan walked the length of the room, her heart thumping, each footstep echoing. It was lined with snow globes. Not the tiny little ones you can shake in your hands. Looming, life-sized snow globes. Each one carried inside it a tableau of life – sculptures of men, women, children, Wunimals and unnimals, beautifully crafted in their own fascinating little scenes and poses. Encased in glass and shrouded in swirling, snowy mists that never slowed and never settled.

A woman swimming in the ocean.

A wolfhound curled up by a fireplace.

Two young men embracing beneath a gaslight.

Morrigan pressed her nose against the glass cradling the woman and the ocean. She was beautiful, her face a perfect oval emerging from dark blue waves, eyes to the sky. The scene was so lifelike Morrigan felt she could almost dive into the ocean and swim alongside her. She held both hands to the glass dome, feeling a strange sort of loneliness, right in her chest.

'You're not supposed to touch the exhibits,' said a soft voice from behind her.

Morrigan spun round, inhaling sharply.

A familiar face, inches from her own. Pale and ordinary but for the small white scar splitting one eyebrow down the middle.

Ezra Squall. The Wundersmith.

(*The* other *Wundersmith*, Morrigan amended in her head.)

She stumbled backwards into the glass of the snow globe, looking left and right for an escape route. Every inch of her was tensed, ready to flee, but her brain hadn't yet caught up to her body. She felt slow and stupid, and all she could think about was the face in front of her. The face of the evillest man who'd ever lived.

But . . . was Squall really *here*? Had he found a way back into Nevermoor after all these years in exile? Or was this the same trick he'd pulled last year, when his ghostly form had visited Nevermoor on the Gossamer Line, pretending to be his own assistant, the kind and mild-mannered Mr Jones?

There was, most unfortunately, only one way to find out.

With the deep reluctance of someone trying to pet a rabid dog, Morrigan reached out one tentative, trembling hand. She steeled herself, half expecting to hit the warmth and solidity of a human body, and preparing to run if it happened . . . but her hand fell straight through Squall's shoulder as if he was made of air.

Gossamer Line, she thought, closing her eyes in relief. Squall's real body was still safely back in the Wintersea

315

Republic, far away, locked outside of Morrigan's city where he could do no harm to her, or to anyone else in Nevermoor. She realised she'd been holding her breath, and she heard Mildmay's voice in the back of her head. *Step one: STAY CALM. Breathe in. Breathe out.*

Squall gave a rueful smile. 'Hello again, Miss Crow.'

'Where am I?' Morrigan demanded. She was surprised and relieved to hear that her voice wasn't shaking, even if her hands were.

'I do hope the huntsman minded his manners.' He spoke in a pleasant, conversational tone. They could have been strangers discussing the weather.

'*Where am I?*' she repeated, and this time her voice gave the *tiniest* tremor. She clenched her jaw.

Squall held out his arms, gesturing around the hall. 'The Museum of Stolen Moments. Heard of it?'

'No.'

'No. Of course you haven't. This is a Spectacle.' He paused, and gave a careless little shrug. 'I hear you've been receiving a rather substandard education. Thought I'd do you a favour. Expand your horizons a little.'

Morrigan said nothing. She forced her face to remain expressionless, but how did he know *anything* about her education at Wunsoc? Had he been travelling here on the Gossamer, watching her in secret? Or did he have spies to do that for him?

'Personally,' continued Squall, casually running his ghost-like hand through the ocean inside the globe, 'I always thought the Committee for the Classification of Wundrous Acts got it wrong on this occasion. A Spectacle is something that inspires awe and delight, something that baffles the brain. The Museum of Stolen Moments is *much* more than that. It ought to have been declared a Phenomenon, or at least a Singularity.'

Spectacle, Phenomenon, Singularity . . . Morrigan had no idea what he was talking about. She opened her mouth to ask, then snapped it shut. She would not be drawn. She would not be lured into any kind of discussion with this monster. Her eyes darted around the room, looking for the best means of escape. Should she run? Or would he just call back the Hunt?

Squall was silent for a moment, lost in his thoughts. 'She had such a talent,' he murmured, almost to himself.

It was the curious wistful note in his voice that made Morrigan give in. Inwardly cursing herself, she asked the obvious question. 'Who?'

'Mathilde Lachance. The Wundersmith who created all of this. It's a masterpiece, don't you think? It must have required the use of at least five of the Wretched Arts. Nocturne, of course, and Weaving. Tempus, probably Veil, maybe even . . .' He cut himself off, catching sight of Morrigan's face. Her expression must have betrayed the hunger she felt at hearing those words, the sudden *click* in her mind as she recalled what

Murgatroyd had said in the Elders' Hall – *someone must teach the little beast her Wretched Arts* – and she remembered at last where she'd heard those words before. From Squall himself, last year at Crow Manor. He had called them 'the Wretched Arts of the Accomplished Wundersmith'. He had offered to teach them to Morrigan, and she had declined.

Squall smiled. 'Ah. But I mustn't give too much away. They wouldn't like that, would they? Your *Wundrous Society.*' He said the last two words with palpable disdain. Morrigan tried to hide her disappointment, while memorising those four precious words he'd let slip – *Nocturne, Weaving, Tempus, Veil. Nocturne, Weaving, Tempus, Veil.* What did they *mean?*

'How are you enjoying life at Wunsoc?' His voice was casual. He began to pace back and forth, his hands clasped behind his back. 'Is it everything you dreamed of and more? I hear your fellow scholars are acquiring knowledge and skills the likes of which they'd never imagined. Before you know it, they'll all be experts in their fields, famous the realm over. The greatest living dragonrider. Nevermoor's foremost linguist. A mesmerist of unparalleled talent.' He turned to Morrigan with sad eyes and an exaggerated pout. 'And you, a child forbidden to use her strength or develop her gifts. Curbed and controlled by the very people who fear her the most.'

Morrigan shook her head. 'That's not – they don't *fear* me, they just . . . it's for my own . . .'

Morrigan trailed off as she saw the Wundersmith's eyes light up with some mixture of amusement and outrage. 'Your own *what*? Your own safety? Your own good, your own protection? Oh dear. I see you've learned to lie a little better. At least to yourself.'

She didn't respond. He was right, and she couldn't bring herself to deny it. The Elders *were* afraid of her.

Squall was watching her carefully. He knew he'd touched a nerve. 'And what has your hunchback professor taught you, hmm? Tell me what you've learned about those wicked, wily Wundersmiths of old.'

'I'm not telling you anything, and he's not a *hunchback*, he's a *tortoisewun*,' Morrigan snapped, then cursed herself again for letting him goad her into conversation. She squeezed her hands into fists. *Stay calm.* 'Why did you bring me here?'

'To do just what a Wundersmith does.' One corner of Squall's mouth twisted into a quarter-smile. He'd stopped pacing and was standing in front of a snow globe that held four gleeful young men hanging out the sides of a careening motorcar, the wind blowing back their hair. 'To grant your fondest wish. To give you the thing you want more than anything else.'

'And what's that?' Morrigan asked through gritted teeth.

'An education.' He resumed his pacing. 'That's what you were wishing for just now, down the bottom of that dark, dead-end alley, was it not? So. Welcome to your second lesson. Would you like to learn how to summon Wunder?'

She wanted to say no. She wanted to spit right through his incorporeal face, to flee the museum and go straight back to Wunsoc. The rest of her unit would surely have made it back by now, and they'd fail the exam unless everyone was present. Yet another reason for them to be angry at her. Morrigan wondered what had happened to Francis and Mahir, if they'd waited, if they'd also entered the alley . . . *No*, she thought. *Probably not.*

But Hawthorne, at least, would be worried about her. Possibly even Cadence. She needed to get back and let them know she was all right.

But the temptation to stay was overwhelming. The High Council of Elders was committed to keeping Morrigan's power locked up and leashed. Onstald refused to give her even the smallest bit of useful information. Even Jupiter, who'd sworn he would prove to her that Wundersmiths weren't all terrible, had come up with nothing.

And here was Ezra Squall, Nevermoor's greatest enemy, offering Morrigan the key.

Would you like to learn how to summon Wunder?

Something deep inside her stirred.

'Yes or no, Miss Crow?' Squall prompted. His complacent expression told Morrigan that he already knew the answer, but wanted to hear it from her.

She sighed, and then said in a low, reluctant voice, 'Yes.'

'The first of the Wretched Arts, then, and perhaps the most important.' He clapped his hands together and went to stand in the very centre of the hall, as if it were a stage. He raised his voice, letting it fill the cavernous museum. 'The Wretched Art of Nocturne. The summoning of Wunder. Singing to make it so.'

Singing? It sounded like a joke. Singing was for people like Dame Chanda. For the angel, Israfel. Surely it was *not* one of the Wretched Arts of the Accomplished Wundersmith.

Squall held up a hand for silence. '*Little crowling, little crowling,*' he sang softly, '*with button-black eyes.*'

A chill crept along the back of Morrigan's neck. She'd heard him sing this song before. Last winter, on the Gossamer Line platform. Moments before he'd swept her away on the blinding Gossamer train, back to the Republic. Back to Crow Manor, where Squall had threatened her family. Morrigan took a deep breath and rooted her feet to the ground, trying to fight the sudden urge to flee.

'*Swoops down into the meadow where the rabbits all hide.*' Squall moved his fingers slightly in midair. His eyes were closed. '*Little rabbit, little rabbit . . .*' He trailed off, opening his eyes to look down at his hand with interest. 'It's like training a dog, you see. Except the dog isn't a dog. It's a monster. And the monster has ideas of its own. Can you see it?'

'Wunder is invisible,' said Morrigan warily.

'Invisible when dormant, yes,' he conceded. 'But *summoned Wunder shows itself to summoner and smith*, the old saying goes. Meaning when Wunder answers the call of a Wundersmith, it creates . . . a sort of agreement with the summoner.'

'An agreement . . . to show itself?'

'Precisely.' He nodded, closely watching the movements of his own hand. 'And although Wunder is intelligent, it doesn't discriminate. Once it's been summoned, any old Wundersmith can see it. *Summoner and smith,* you see? But only if you're paying attention. Only if you know what to look for.'

Morrigan gasped. She *could* see it – a tiny, shimmering thread of golden-white light that Squall weaved in his hand. It swam between his fingers like an eel. She watched, mesmerised, as he lifted his hand and blew away the little strand like a puff of dandelion seeds. It scattered to the wind and disappeared.

She already knew what Wunder looked like, of course. Jupiter had shown her last year, after she'd safely returned from Crow Manor. He'd pressed his forehead to hers, and for one blazing moment, she had seen the world – and herself – as her patron did. The Wunder that had gathered around her was blinding. This tiny little thread on its own was different, but no less astonishing. No less beautiful.

'Your turn.' Squall gestured to the centre of the room and backed away, surrendering the stage. 'Sing.'

Morrigan shook her head, horrified. 'I can't *sing*.'

'Wunder doesn't care. You can't offend it.' He snorted. 'You can't be worse than old Owain Binks. Every time he summoned Wunder people came running because they thought someone was being murdered. Come now, sing something. Hurry up.'

She hesitated, and then began shakily, '*Little crowling—*'

'NO!' He held up both hands to stop her, rushing forward. Morrigan shrank away, and he stopped abruptly. 'No. Not that. Each Wundersmith must have their own, individual way of calling Wunder. Choose another song.'

'I don't know any other songs,' she protested.

'Nonsense,' Squall said impatiently. 'Everyone knows at least one. Didn't your worthless family ever sing you a lullaby? Think back to your days as a mewling, red-faced infant.'

Morrigan was about to roll her eyes at the thought of her father or grandmother ever doing anything so foolish as singing her a lullaby, when she was struck by a sudden, vivid memory.

She was young – maybe six or seven. Her tutor at the time was Mrs Duffy, the latest in a never-ending string of hapless men and women her father had brought to Crow Manor to teach Morrigan reading, writing and arithmetic . . . or, more truthfully, to keep her out of his way so that he could carry on pretending she didn't exist. Most of Morrigan's tutors had been content to avoid direct contact with Morrigan and never meet her eyes during their lessons. Some had gone further to protect themselves from the curse – Miss Linford had insisted on keeping a door between herself and Morrigan, just to be safe.

But this one was different. Rather than avoiding Morrigan, Mrs Duffy seemed to feel it was her duty to constantly remind her of the drain she was on society and on her family. What a dreadful burden she was, what a danger she presented to everyone around her – to everyone in the Unnamed Realm – just by having been born.

Mrs Duffy had taught Morrigan a song, and whenever Morrigan failed a quiz, or misbehaved, or spoke out of turn, she would make her sing it. Over and over again, until the tutor told her to stop.

It had been an awful, frightening song to Morrigan when she was very young. But it was the only song she knew all the words to. They were burned indelibly into her brain.

She began to sing in a quiet, hesitant voice.

'*Morningtide's child is merry and mild.*' Her voice cracked. She cleared her throat. '*Eventide's child is wicked and wild.*'

Squall cocked his head to one side, a deep frown etched into his forehead.

'*Morningtide's child arrives with the dawn,*' Morrigan continued. Her singing was dreadful, but her voice projected into the vast space and became stronger with every note. '*Eventide's child brings gale and storm.*'

Squall took a step towards her. He looked like he was remembering something.

'*Where are you going, o son of the morning?*' he sang softly. When he sang, Squall's voice was unsettlingly gentle and sweet. Much lovelier than Morrigan's. It shouldn't sound like that, she thought. It should sound ugly and jagged. Like his heart.

She took a shaky breath.

'*Up with the sun where the winds are warming.*' Morrigan paused, wanting to stop, but then . . . there was a sudden feeling like static electricity in her fingertips. A slight hum of resistance, like pressing into a strong wind. She looked up at Squall.

He nodded his encouragement, eyes gleaming, and sang, '*Where are you going, o daughter of night?*'

Morrigan waved her hands back and forth a little, testing the sensation. It felt like beams of moonlight were dancing through her fingers. '*Deep down below where the pale things bite.*'

Wunder had been waiting for her. That's what Jupiter had said.

Waiting for me to do what?

I guess we'll see.

This was what it had been waiting for. She'd thought it would be difficult to summon Wunder, but it was like . . . it *wanted* to be summoned. It gathered fast – a hundred tiny threads made of a million tiny specks of light, surrounding her head and body . . . swimming, skimming lightly over her. It was quick and curious. It felt *alive*.

'Concentrate on your hands,' said Squall.

Wunder was eager to please. As soon as he said the words, as soon as the idea entered Morrigan's mind, the floating golden threads seemed to gravitate towards her outstretched, upturned hands, pooling in her palms like sunbeams made liquid.

That's just what Wunder felt like. Like being warmed by the sun, like holding pure energy. Like *being* pure energy. Morrigan's hands vibrated. She couldn't even see them any more, she could only see the Wunder engulfing them like strange, amorphous gloves. Two clouds of light. It made her feel strange. Powerful, and yet somehow under siege at the same time.

And now she'd summoned it, she didn't know what to do with it.

'How do I make it stop?'

Squall gave her a look of mixed incredulity and pity. 'Why would you ever want to do that?'

Morrigan felt panic creep in. It had all felt so right, just a moment ago. She was holding Wunder in the palms of her hands, as if she was born to do exactly that. But a different sensation was stealing upon her, a sense that she was no longer holding Wunder. That it was, in fact, holding her.

'Make it go away,' she said, her voice rising. 'Make it stop.'

But Squall did nothing. He stood staring at her, and as she watched him through the golden haze of gathering Wunder, her dread grew. He had tricked her. He wanted her dead. He was going to let Wunder destroy her.

'Do something!' she demanded. 'Make it stop!'

But still, Squall did nothing.

Acting on instinct, Morrigan shook her hands as if she was flinging mud from them. 'No,' she shouted. 'NO!' She didn't know who she was talking to – herself, Squall, or Wunder itself.

But it was the Wunder that listened. She felt it flee – no, *charge* away from her like she'd sent it on a mission. In one cataclysmic instant, the globe nearest Morrigan shattered, pouring out its snow-flecked water in a great wave. The sculpture inside was torn from its peaceful glass home and spilled across the marble floor in a tangle of wet limbs and hair.

Morrigan stared at it, breathing hard, her brain still trying to catch up to what had just happened.

A tangle of wet limbs and hair. It was the sculpture of the swimming woman, her body no longer floating with unblinking eyes to the sky but curled in on itself, dressed in a soaking-wet blue bathing suit and . . . and *breathing*. Or trying to. Heaving a long, rattling, watery breath that sounded like her lungs had already filled with half the sea. And then stopping.

She wasn't a sculpture at all.

Morrigan ran to the woman's side and shook her, turned her over, thumped her back. 'Breathe!' she shouted, and she knew there was something she ought to do, that if Jupiter was here he would know just what it was, but she couldn't do anything except panic, her mind at once racing ahead and miles behind. 'BREATHE!'

'You're much too late.' Squall's voice was barely audible over the sound of Morrigan's own beating heart. Tears burned her eyes and blurred her vision. She didn't understand. The woman was limp and heavy in her arms and she . . . she didn't *understand*. 'Years and years and years too late.'

'What is this place?' Morrigan stared in horror at the globes lining the walls, filled not with sculptures, she now knew, but with people. Real, living people.

'Here stands a Spectacle,' Squall announced, as if reciting from memory. 'The Museum of Stolen Moments. Crafted by the Wundersmith Mathilde Lachance. Sponsored by the Honourable E.M. Saunders. A gift to the people of Nevermoor. Winter of One, Age of Thieves.'

'A gift to the people of Nevermoor?' Morrigan whispered, looking down at the vacant, lifeless eyes of the drowned woman.

'They thought it was, yes,' said Squall indifferently. 'I suppose that's why it was classified a Spectacle, rather than a Phenomenon. The good people of Nevermoor thought they'd been gifted an art exhibition. Lifelike works of Mathilde Lachance's artistic genius. But dear Mathilde's genius wasn't creating falsehoods . . . it was capturing reality. Preserving it.' He crossed the wet floor in slow, deliberate steps and stood above Morrigan, gazing down at the woman's empty face, his own its eerie, living twin – blank and unfeeling. 'Mathilde wasn't cruel. If anything, she was merciful. She only took her subjects as they reached the very cusp of death. I don't know if it was death itself that fascinated her, or the idea of immortality. Either way, these lucky souls will never die.' He looked around the room, then shrugged. 'Or they'll die forever, every moment of every day. Whichever way you want to look at it.'

Morrigan clenched her teeth, trying to make herself stop shivering. They both had it wrong, she thought – Squall, and the Committee for the Classification of Wundrous Acts. She had no idea what a Spectacle was, but this wasn't one. It was a Monstrosity.

She laid the woman down gently on the floor, and struggled to stand on shaking legs.

'Ready to try again?' Squall looked at her expectantly.

Morrigan looked at each of the snow globes in turn, finally seeing what she'd missed. The young men in the motorcar weren't leaning out of it; they were being *thrown from it* by the force of some unseen collision, their faces frozen not in glee, but in wide-eyed terror. Between the two men embracing beneath the gaslight, a glint of silver showed that one had a knife pressed to the other's stomach. Now Morrigan could see the thin red stream bleeding out from beneath the second man's coat.

Even the shaggy wolfhound by the fire was near death, a closer look at his milky eyes and patchy, ragged fur betraying his advanced age. Morrigan wondered how many breaths the old dog had had left, before he'd been entombed in this glass prison.

The illusion had shattered. Morrigan was suddenly overwhelmed by the dread and revulsion she should have been feeling all along.

What was she *doing* here? She was all alone with a monster. Again. Standing in a museum of horrors, surrounded by living exhibits – real people, forever preserved in the moments of their death. Like vegetables pickled in jars.

Not a museum at all. A mausoleum.

Morrigan stumbled past Squall, disgust rising like bile at the back of her throat. She felt sick. She had to get out. She had to get back to Wunsoc, back to safety and normalcy.

'Where do you think you're going?' he called calmly after her. She ignored him, focusing on putting one foot after the other. *Get out. Get out of here.* 'So that's that, is it? You're just giving up?'

Get out get out get out don't listen don't answer just GET OUT.

'What are you so afraid of? That you might one day be as powerful as they suspect? Are you frightened of your own potential for greatness, little Crowling? Are you *really* such a coward?'

'I'm NOT a coward!' Morrigan shouted, whirling back around to face him. 'And I'm not like you either. Or Mathilde Lachance. I'm not a *monster*.'

'You are both.' He spoke in his usual soft, tightly controlled voice, but something simmered beneath the surface. 'You are the most cowardly, monstrous, beastly, *wrong* child I have ever had the pleasure and misfortune to know. And I do *know* you, Miss Crow, make no mistake.' His dark eyes glittered in the lamplight as he walked towards her. 'I know that you are vindictive and wilful, and just a *touch* too clever. I know you can't be bound by the same rules as those other children, because you are *not* those other children. You are a Wundersmith, Miss Crow. We are different. We are better and worse than all of them put together. Don't you understand your place in the Society yet? Don't you realise you could bring them all to their knees if only you would *try*?'

Morrigan shook her head. She didn't want to hear it. She didn't want to hear that she was *different*. She'd been hearing it all her life, and she knew exactly what it meant. Different was dangerous. Different was a burden. 'Stop. You don't know anything about me.'

'How about having a little *motivation*?' Squall roared. He looked desperate now, enraged even. 'You have been given a *gift*, a gift people would kill for, a gift people *have died for*, and you are SQUANDERING IT.' His words bounced off the ceiling, echoing in an endless, angry chorus.

Morrigan flinched. She gathered all her courage, and spat back at him, 'If people have died for it, it's because YOU murdered them.'

'Perhaps I should have murdered you too, you wretched disappointment,' he snarled, and for an instant his face was the foul mask of a man possessed, the black-eyed, black-mouthed Wundersmith of legend emerging in a moment of uncontrolled fury.

Then it was gone. And the mild, perfectly contained man was back.

Just like that.

Morrigan felt chilled to her core, as if she'd swallowed a pint of icy water.

Trembling and terrified, she ran from the Museum of Stolen Moments without looking back . . . through the doors, down the steps, into the cold embrace of a capricious and unknowable city.

CHAPTER TWENTY

Nocturne

A week later, Morrigan Crow no longer existed. As far as Francis and Mahir and the rest of her unit was concerned, she was a complete non-entity. They had stopped talking to her, stopped looking at her, stopped acknowledging she had ever been a member of Unit 919.

Well . . . not all of them, obviously. Hawthorne was still Morrigan's staunchest friend. And – bizzarely – Cadence seemed to like her even *more* since she'd caused the entire unit to fail their exam.

Hawthorne had in fact been as disappointed as the rest of them when Morrigan's inexplicable detour had cost them a pass. Exams at Wunsoc weren't graded – they were strictly pass/fail. A pass meant that you had met the expectations of the course. A fail, on the other hand, meant very serious meetings for each of the scholars with their patron, teacher and conductor. (Morrigan's very serious meeting had been delayed indefinitely, as Jupiter was still away.) It meant the shame of every other unit in the school knowing they'd failed their exam and mocking them for it. Worst of all, it meant a long, looooong lecture from Ms Dearborn about Unit 919's shocking lack of commitment to their studies and how they'd all have to pull their socks up before she decided their socks would be taken from them altogether.

Like the rest of Unit 919, Hawthorne was perfectly entitled to be annoyed with her. But as soon as Morrigan told him about Squall and the Bonesmen, his frustration had faded to grey-faced fright.

'So . . . Squall *saved you* from the Bonesmen?'

Morrigan grimaced at that thought. 'I suppose so. Yeah.'

'The Wundersmith saved you . . . from the Ghastly Market.'

'Yeah.'

'That's . . . weird.'

In the face of opposition from the rest of 919, Hawthorne was more aggressively loyal to his best friend than ever. He'd taken to flicking rolled-up bits of paper in the face of anyone who skipped over Morrigan when they were handing the polar-bear biscuit jar around, or who made sniffy, passive-aggressive comments in her presence about *people who don't deserve to be in the Society.*

When she'd left the Museum of Stolen Moments that night it had been just before dawn, but by the time she'd figured out where in Nevermoor she was (back in Eldritch, as it turned out – way, way south of Old Town), she'd realised that getting back to Wunsoc before the sun rose was going to be an impossibility.

Still, she had *tried*. She hadn't given up. She'd run and run until her lungs and the muscles in her legs burned. All the way to the borough of Wick, when she finally realised there was no point in running any more. The sun was in the sky. The streets were already bustling with morning commuters and newspaper sellers. With the burden of failure weighing heavy in her heart, Morrigan had finally accepted her defeat, jumped a Rush Line train and dejectedly made her way back to the campus, where Mildmay and the rest of Unit 919 were waiting, their expressions ranging from disappointed to livid to definitely-plotting-murder.

They'd all failed, because of her. Well, *not* because of her, obviously – because of the Bonesmen and Ezra Squall. But she couldn't exactly tell them that. 'Sorry I'm late – I've been hanging out with Ezra Squall, you know, the evil Wundersmith.'

Morrigan decided to tell them part of the truth – that she'd been cornered by the Bonesmen – but was unable to describe exactly how she'd managed to get away from the Skeletal Legion, when hulking Alfie Swann and the legendary

Paximus Luck had both been captured. The general conclusion among her unit, therefore, was that Morrigan was fibbing about the Bonesmen to get herself out of trouble.

It wasn't fair that a fail for one meant a fail for all, but really . . . *nothing* in the Wundrous Society was fair.

She'd apologised profusely, of course, for days on end – but no apology could change the fact there were eight *very* disappointed patrons, one anxious conductor and two incensed Scholar Mistresses to deal with. She couldn't really blame the other scholars for despising her.

Morrigan should have cared about all that, she knew she should, but in truth she just felt a little . . . flat. She was tired of so desperately wanting the friendship and approval of her so-called brothers and sisters. (*How* that phrase made her cringe now. When she thought back to the person she was a year ago, that *idiot* who believed she'd have eight readymade siblings if only she could pass the trials . . . as *if* anything was ever that simple.)

No. None of that really mattered any more.

Morrigan had bigger fish to fry.

She had summoned Wunder.

'*Morningtide's child is merry and mild*,' she sang softly to herself one morning, treading a twisted path through the Whinging Woods – the only place she could be sure of total privacy (there were the trees themselves, of course, but she could ignore their cranky mutterings for the most part, and they didn't seem to have the slightest interest in what she was doing. Too busy moaning about wood-rot and the maddening overconfidence of squirrels). *'Eventide's child is wicked and wild.'*

Morrigan hummed a little, wiggled her fingers gently at her side.

Come on, she urged, while some other part of her said, *No, don't do it.*

That second, sensible voice inside Morrigan's head used to be much louder. It was growing more distant by the day.

It had taken a few days to work up the courage to try calling Wunder again, and when she'd finally attempted it, it hadn't come easy. Not at first, not like in the museum.

Morrigan wondered if that was because she'd felt so guilty even *trying*. Perhaps Wunder could sense her feelings about it, and was staying away.

But in the week since her exam had been hijacked by Squall, since she'd first sung those words and summoned Wunder, Morrigan's feelings about what she'd learned that evening had . . . changed.

She'd left the Museum of Stolen Moments in a state of mingled fury and fear, freshly horror-struck by the reminder that she was a member of the Free State's most exclusive and most hated club. They were their own little two-person society, she and Squall. The Wretched Society.

But in a way, Morrigan's unit had done her a favour by shunning her. It turned out there was something slightly contrary in her nature. They were so convinced of her guilt that she'd stopped feeling guilty at all, at least about failing the exam. Let them be angry at her, if that's what they wanted. Let them retreat from her. She could retreat even farther, even faster.

She had a refuge now. She had something that belonged to her. A secret.

'Morningtide's child arrives with the dawn.'

There it was. The now-familiar tingle in her fingertips. The swarming, abundant feeling of contentment. And the edge of disquiet, like pressing gently on a shallow wound.

Morrigan smiled to herself.

Hello, you.

It responded every time now. So easily, so *quickly* – she understood now what Jupiter had meant last year. Wunder really was *waiting for her* – gathering to her constantly, waiting patiently for her to learn how to command it. Squall might be evil, and he might be her enemy, but even so . . . he had taught her something priceless, something she'd never have learned without him. No one in Wunsoc wanted her to learn – not the Elders, or the Scholar Mistresses, or Professor Onstald. They wanted to control not just her power, but Morrigan herself.

She was being careful, of course. She was only calling tiny bits of Wunder, and letting them disperse without building up. That was the trick, she'd figured out this past week. If she took care with it, she could hold on to that feeling of power without losing control. Morrigan knew now to pause between lines, and let it drift away. To never sing a second verse.

'Eventide's child brings gale and storm.'

It was *wonderful*. This small, secret act of defiance. After months of feeling like she was in limbo, that she was in the Society but somehow still not a part of it, this was something that finally felt *right*. Morrigan knew now how it must feel to be Hawthorne, riding on the back of a dragon. Doing the thing he was born for. Or Cadence – the rush of power she must feel with every seamless act of persuasion she committed.

And yet . . . there was that voice in the back of her head. Distant, but still there. She heard it every time she crept away to practise her new trick, every time she let the song tumble from her mouth and felt Wunder respond to it.

This is dangerous. You shouldn't be doing this. It's wrong.

But how – *how* could it be wrong? She was born a Wundersmith, that wasn't something she could help. Jupiter had said last year that it was her gift. Her calling.

And you get to decide what that means, he'd told her. *Nobody else.*

'Where are you going, o son of the morning?'

Just because some Wundersmiths of old had used their talents for evil, it didn't mean Morrigan would. *You're not*

Mathilde Lachance, she told herself repeatedly. *You're not Ezra Squall.*

'*Up with the sun where the winds are warming.*'

Morrigan was a Wundersmith too. And *she* would decide what that meant. Nobody else.

'*Where are you going, o daughter of night?*'

A thread of light danced through her fingers. She smiled.

'*Deep down below where the pale things bite.*'

Morrigan left the Whinging Woods for Proudfoot House at a pace that made Professor Onstald look like a cheetahwun. She was deeply reluctant to leave the solitude of her Nocturne practice, and especially to spend another *Decoding Nevermoor* lesson in the company of people who mostly resented her.

She'd never actually skipped a class before. But in that moment, standing on the steps of Proudfoot House, all she wanted to do was turn and run again. Down the dead fireblossom-lined drive, out the gates and all the way home to the Deucalion.

In this imaginary scenario, nobody would question her early arrival home. Martha would be waiting with a tray of Morrigan's favourite teatime treats. The Smoking Parlour would pour out her new favourite seasonal scent from its walls (clean cosy jumper: for maximum autumnal comfort and well-being). And most importantly, Jupiter would be there, back from his latest expedition after two weeks away. He would listen patiently to the news of Squall and the museum and Morrigan's mastery of Nocturne and her exam failure, and he wouldn't be cross or worried or disappointed at all, and everything would be fine.

But all of that was imaginary.

Her lesson in the Map Room was real, and she was running late for it. Heaving a sigh and straightening her shoulders, Morrigan cast one last longing look back down the drive towards the campus gates, towards escape . . .

. . . and she saw him.

Jupiter North, running up the drive as if she'd conjured him there by magic. Ginger hair flying behind him, a smile lighting up his whole face. He stopped and bent forward to catch his breath, clutching his brolly and waving it at her. She beamed and waved back.

'Mog!' he bellowed from a distance. 'I've come to bust you out!'

Morrigan watched his broad grin fade to confusion as his eyes dropped to her other hand, where she was absent-mindedly – and expertly – lacing a golden thread of Wunder through her fingertips.

CHAPTER TWENTY-ONE

Something Wonderful

Jupiter didn't ask a single question. He didn't have to. The whole story came tumbling out of Morrigan's mouth in rushed, fragmented pieces before he could even say a word. She told him all about the gang of Bonesmen and the hunter on horseback, the Museum of Stolen Moments and Squall's surprise visit. About her secret new skill and the drowned woman and the snow globes of death. (She even managed to slip in – very briefly – the part where they all failed their *Decoding Nevermoor* exam, but unsurprisingly, it wasn't the thing that caught Jupiter's attention.)

'Squall?' Jupiter said in a choked voice. 'You— he . . . he was *here*, in Nevermoor? *Again*? Why didn't you tell—'

'You weren't here to tell!' Morrigan jumped in, and it was difficult to keep the accusation out of her voice. Jupiter flinched.

'But you should have told *somebody*.' He led her down the tree-lined drive towards the gates. 'You've been calling Wunder for a whole week because *Ezra Squall* taught you how? You can't keep something like that to yourself, Mog, it's dangerous.'

'Shhh,' she hissed, looking around to make sure nobody could overhear them. 'Who else *could* I have told? I can't tell the Elders, or Miss Cheery, or anybody here. If they knew Squall came to see me, that he spoke to me . . . just imagine what—'

'Fenestra!' Jupiter interrupted her. 'You could have told Fen. Or Jack!'

Morrigan opened her mouth to retort, then closed it. 'I . . . er, yeah. Well, I didn't think of that.'

'And where *was* this – this museum of – what was it?'

'Stolen Moments,' said Morrigan. 'Somewhere near Eldritch, I think. I ran for ages before I knew where I was. But anyway, aren't you pleased? I can *call Wunder*.' She smiled, her eyes wide in joyful disbelief. 'I can really do it! And Jupiter, I'm *good at it*.'

'I have absolutely no doubt of that.' A smile crept into the corner of his mouth, as if against his better judgement. He glanced at her sideways. 'I told you, didn't I? Wundersmiths *can* be a force for good. And I know you're going to be a very good Wundersmith. Onstald has it all wrong.'

Morrigan's happiness faltered a little. 'No. Onstald is right,' she said, as they walked through the gates and towards the Brolly Rail stop. Jupiter waved cheerfully at the security guard, who was glowering at Morrigan. Junior scholars weren't supposed to leave campus during school hours, but there wasn't much anyone could say about it with Jupiter by her side. 'Weren't you listening about Mathilde Lachance? The Museum of Stolen Moments—'

'—is just one Wundrous Act.' He lifted his umbrella, poised to leap when the rail came whizzing by, and indicated that Morrigan should do the same. 'And Mathilde Lachance was just one Wundersmith.'

'What about Squall?' she said, pulling out her own black oilskin brolly. She gave its silver filigree handle a quick polish with her cloak. 'And all the others in Onstald's book? What about Tyr Magnusson and Odbuoy Jemmity and—'

'Ah!' shouted Jupiter triumphantly as the rail approached. 'Glad you mentioned him. That's why I've come. Now, ready – JUMP!'

It was virtually impossible to hold a conversation while whizzing through the air at high speed. When Morrigan reached for the lever to release her brolly from the steel loop at their usual stop, Jupiter shooed her hand away before she could pull it.

'Wait for my signal,' he yelled over the sound of the wind streaming past Morrigan's ears. It seemed they weren't going home just yet.

They rode on for quite some time and Morrigan's arms were beginning to ache from clutching so tightly to her umbrella. When her muscles felt like they were on fire and she thought she might just have to let go and hope for the best, Jupiter nudged her and pointed at a soft bit of ground at the corner of a park.

'There!'

Leaping from the rail as it looped past the green space, Morrigan landed a bit clumsily, but at least upright. Jupiter stumbled and skidded along the grass on his knees.

'Nice landing,' came an amused voice from behind them. 'Ten out of ten.'

Morrigan turned around in surprise. 'What are *you* doing here?'

'Oh, hello, Jack,' said Jack, emerging from the shadow of a tree. 'Haven't seen you since the summer hols, how's life? Excellent, thanks for asking, Morrigan, so kind of you. I do hope you're also well.'

'Hello, Jack,' she said, rolling her eyes. 'How's life?'

'Oh, stop fussing, you'll embarrass me.' He smirked and tilted back on his heels, hands in pockets. It was a very Jupiterian gesture, Morrigan thought.

'What *are* you doing here?' she asked.

'I wanted him to meet us,' said Jupiter. 'He's been helping me, the clever chap. We've got something to show you.' He dusted his knees off, striding into the park. Morrigan and Jack followed.

'What sort of something?'

'Something very important,' Jupiter called back to her. As was usual when Jupiter had a bee in his bonnet, she had to jog to keep up with his long legs. 'Something I promised you months ago. Something *wonderful*.'

Morrigan turned to Jack, who raised his eyebrows. He was positively brimming with self-satisfaction.

The park was . . . well, you couldn't really call it a park. It was dense and jungle-like, and the grass looked like it hadn't been cut in at least a year, but she saw the top of a bench peeking out from the undergrowth. Probably it had *once* been a proper park, Morrigan thought, but then nobody was looking after it so nature decided to take back over and run the place.

Jupiter pushed his way into a thick copse of trees, pulling aside tangles of creepers and branches and trying to make a path for Morrigan and Jack behind him. 'Jack and I have been talking about what you told us, Mog. About Onstald's book, and the things he wrote about Wundersmiths. I promised you I'd find proof, didn't I? Well, we've been looking for months, and we've found it. Right here.' He turned back to smile at her. 'In Jemmity Park.'

The trees cleared, and they came to a high stone wall covered in thick vines of climbing ivy. Jupiter pointed up.

Towering high above them, Morrigan spied the mast of a pirate ship, the top of a Ferris wheel and a huge, looping rollercoaster track.

'Oh! Wait, no – *this* is Jemmity Park? Seriously?' She peered along the seemingly impenetrable stone wall and felt a swooping disappointment. 'So it's . . . it's really locked?'

'Yes,' said Jupiter. 'Brilliant, isn't it?'

Morrigan looked at him blankly. 'Not really.'

'No, it *is* brilliant,' Jack enthused. 'We figured it out.' For someone who was standing outside a fantastical secret playground he'd never be able to get into, he certainly looked like all his Christmases had come at once. 'Tell us again what the book said about this place. Can you remember?'

Morrigan sighed. Of course she could remember. Onstald had made her write a three-thousand-word essay on the topic, *and then* build a diorama of it – including tiny little diorama children with devastated faces, standing outside the locked gates. That thing had taken *three days,* and now that Morrigan was standing outside the closed walls of Jemmity Park herself, she could keenly understand their disappointment.

'Odbuoy Jemmity was asked by a local businessman to build a magical adventure park with a carousel and a rollercoaster and waterslides and everything. So he did. On the opening day, people came from all over Nevermoor to see it, but Jemmity himself never showed up. When the man who'd commissioned the park tried to open it, he couldn't. The park wouldn't let anyone in – nobody could get over, under or through the gates. So all the sad children and their sad parents went home, and Jemmity Park remains untouched to this day. But they planted all these trees and hedges around it so people wouldn't have to look at it and get annoyed and— Jupiter, what are you doing? I don't think you should be doing that.'

Jupiter was battling against the hedgerow and the climbing vines, ripping out handfuls of leaves and tossing them over his shoulders, trying to clear away the foliage to show her something – which was difficult, as the foliage kept regrowing, almost as fast as he could strip it back.

'You're probably right,' he said.

'You're still doing it.'

'Right again! Okay, quick,' puffed Jupiter, holding off a particularly eager creeper that kept trying to spiral up his arm. 'Look.'

It was a small stone podium, with a purple diamond-shaped plaque on top that read:

Here stands a Spectacle
Crafted by the Wundersmith Odbuoy Jemmity
Sponsored by Hadrian Canter, CEO of Canter Finance
A gift to the children of Gresham
Winter of Seven, Age of the East Winds

'A gift to the children of—'

'Gresham, yeah,' said Jack excitedly, swatting away a vine that was tickling his face. 'That's the name of this borough. Weird place for an adventure park, isn't it?'

'Why?'

'Look around! It's the poorest borough in Nevermoor, it always has been. I mean, there's virtually nothing here. The Wunderground doesn't even come here. And yet for some reason there's an enormous, locked, secret playground hidden in the middle of the neighbourhood's *only* green space?'

'I suppose,' Morrigan conceded. 'But—'

'Shh. *Listen*,' said Jupiter, holding a finger to his lips. Morrigan and Jack fell silent. At first all Morrigan could hear was birdsong, and the faint rustle of wind through the trees, but then . . .

'Someone's in there!' There were voices. Children's voices. A scream, followed by peals of laughter. And . . . 'Is that music?'

'Carousel music, I think,' said Jupiter.

Morrigan was confused. 'So . . . it's *not* locked, then?'

'Not exactly,' said Jack. 'Not to everyone.'

'How did you find it?'

'My friend Sam from the Graysmark School told me about it. He grew up in Gresham, and he said there was this amazing park that he used to play in as a kid, but now he's too old so he's not allowed inside it any more – the park just won't let him in. None of the other boys believed him. But I remembered what Jupiter said – what you told him about Jemmity Park – and I made Sam bring me here. It's all true. The park only lets you in if you're twelve or younger—'

Morrigan gasped, standing up ramrod straight. 'That means I could—'

'—and only if you're a resident of Gresham.'

'Oh.' She slumped again. How disappointing. 'So, what are we doing here?'

'Don't you get it?' Jack said, exasperated. 'Tell her, Uncle Jove.'

Jupiter slapped his hand emphatically against the purple plaque. 'Onstald was *wrong*, Morrigan. He was wrong about Jemmity Park. Odbuoy wasn't some cruel trickster, building a land of wonders and then never allowing anyone inside. He didn't create a *Fiasco*. He created something *wonderful* – for a small, deserving group of people. For the children of Gresham, who'd never had anything like this before. Right here in the middle of Nevermoor's poorest neighbourhood. He gave them something that was *just theirs and nobody else's*.'

'And I've been digging into the Gresham council records. This land we're standing on? Originally, it was a block of flats. Until Hadrian Canter – an extremely wealthy man – bought the land, back in the Age of the East Winds. He kicked hundreds of people out of their homes, and demolished the whole lot so that he could build an adventure park, which he planned to charge people an arm and a leg to visit. It would have meant nobody who lived around here could even afford to enjoy it. I guess Odbuoy Jemmity didn't think that was very fair. So, he built the park just as requested, but he . . . added a couple of extra rules.' Jupiter laughed. 'Which I'm sure made Hadrian Canter really happy.'

'I'm sure,' Morrigan agreed, grinning.

They all fell quiet, listening to the faint sounds of music and laughter. It was the happiest Morrigan had ever felt to be excluded.

The afternoon turned to chilly, grey twilight, and a cold wind bit at Morrigan's face, but she didn't care a bit. Black hair flying, eyes streaming, and with a lightness inside that she hadn't felt since the night of her inauguration, she sailed with Jupiter and Jack on the Brolly Rail through Nevermoor's SBD (Serious Business District), waiting for the signal to jump.

'Onstald was wrong,' she shouted over the wind. Just saying those words made her feel euphoric. 'And if he was wrong about Odbuoy Jemmity, then maybe . . .'

She wasn't quite sure how to finish that sentence. If he was wrong about Odbuoy Jemmity, then maybe what? Maybe he was wrong about Wundersmiths? Or at least about *some* Wundersmiths?

Morrigan tightened her grip on her umbrella.

Maybe he's wrong about me.

'We're not done yet, Mog,' Jupiter shouted back. He pointed to an empty patch of sidewalk. 'There! By the solicitors' office.'

They landed triumphantly in front of an office building signposted MAHONEY, MORTON & MCCULLOUGH FAMILY SOLICITORS. Jupiter led them down a little farther to an unnamed side street, at the end of which was a gate to a dark, narrow underpass, after which they emerged in a small cobbled courtyard, then another little underpass, another gate, two more courtyards, a dirty alley that smelled of wet dog, and then a teensy-tiny cobbled walkway with a sign on the wall that read:

WAVERLEY WALK

BEWARE!

BY ORDER OF THE GEOGRAPHICAL
ODDITIES SQUADRON
AND THE NEVERMOOR COUNCIL,
THIS STREET HAS BEEN DECLARED A
RED ALERT TRICKSY LANE

(HIGH-DANGER TRICKERY AND LIKELIHOOD OF DAMAGE TO
PERSON ON ENTRY)

ENTER AT OWN RISK

Morrigan was surprised. 'Jupiter, you said no more Tricksy Lanes.'

'Rules were made to be broken, Mog.' He raised one eyebrow. 'But *just* this once, understand? Only because you're with me, and *only* because I know exactly what this Tricksy Lane is hiding.'

'Something wonderful?' asked Morrigan, grinning.

'Something *unbelievable*,' said Jack.

Waverley Walk's trick was an unpleasant one. It got skinnier and skinnier the further down it they went, until Morrigan found she was being compressed between two brick walls ('Keep going, you two!' Jupiter had squeaked from up ahead, looking so uncomfortable she thought his head might pop like a water balloon), and then quite abruptly—

'Cascade Towers!' Jupiter shouted over the roaring, rushing sound of a waterfall as they lunged out from between the alley walls, gasping for breath.

Not just *a* waterfall, though – a dozen waterfalls, maybe more. Some were vast, impenetrable white-water curtains that crashed spectacularly to the ground; others delicate and crystalline with a sound like tinkling glass chimes. It was a symphony of water, falling from nowhere and disappearing into nothing, arranged in the three-dimensional form of a glorious, glittering skyscraper.

Morrigan's shoulders dropped and she swayed a little on the spot. Decima Kokoro's creation was not at all what she'd expected. She felt utterly thunderstruck. A street back, she'd never have known any of this was here. There'd been no sound of water, no change in the air to hint that behind these gloomy buildings there might be a structure of such deafening, magnificent beauty.

And it really was *beautiful*.

She shook her head, disbelieving. 'He called it a *Fiasco*,' she yelled over the rushing water. Suddenly she was past shock, moving swiftly to anger. 'Onstald, he said it was a *Fiasco* bordering on a *Monstrosity*. But it's . . . it's . . .'

'Yeah,' shouted Jupiter. 'It's . . . yeah. Exactly.' He and Jack were gazing up at Cascade Towers with expressions of dazed, idiotic awe that Morrigan felt mirrored in her own face. 'Shall we go inside?'

He opened his umbrella, and Jack and Morrigan followed suit, and together they stepped through the gentlest section of waterfall they could see. It was as simple as that. Onstald's book had described the great difficulty of trying to get inside Decima Kokoro's building without being soaked to the skin or washed away or *drowned*. But the three of them emerged on the other side of the water-wall, shook the water from their brollies, and were perfectly dry. The deafening noise disappeared.

Morrigan had expected it to be dark, damp and cave-like inside Cascade Towers, but instead she found a bright and pleasant space. Cool green light filtered through the sheets of water and cast rippling patterns across the floor. The building was huge and empty. Silent. Like a cathedral made of sea glass.

'Why doesn't anybody use it? Don't they know it's here?' she asked in a hushed voice. It felt as if they'd entered a sacred, magical place, and she didn't want to break the spell.

'I don't know. Not sure who owns it. I'm still trying to find out.' He trailed his fingertips along a wall of calm, glassy water.

'How did you find it?'

'Well, it took me a while,' he said. 'But luckily I know lots of people who know lots of things. And I'm nosy by nature, aren't I?'

They crossed the vast floor to where Jack stood in front of another podium, with another purple diamond plaque.

Here stands a Singularity
Crafted by the Wundersmith Decima Kokoro
Sponsored by Senator Helmut R. Jameson
A gift to the people of Nevermoor
Spring of Seven, Age of the East Winds

'A Singularity,' Morrigan repeated. That word brought the memory of her encounter with Ezra Squall rushing back into focus. 'That's what Squall called the Museum of Stolen Moments. He said the Committee for the Classification of Wundrous Acts declared it a Spectacle. But Squall thought they were wrong, because they didn't understand what it really was.'

Jack looked from Morrigan to Jupiter and back again, his one visible eye narrowed. 'The museum of what? When did you see Squall?'

'I don't get it, though,' Morrigan continued, ignoring him. 'According to Onstald's book, the Wundrous Act Spectrum only has five classifications – Missteps, Blunders, Fiascos, Monstrosities and Devastations. It doesn't say anything about Spectacles or Singularities. But they obviously exist, because . . . well, because we're standing in one.' She threw her arms up. 'So why doesn't Onstald know about them? He wrote a whole book about Wundrous Acts, for goodness' sake! Why does he think this place was classified a Fiasco?'

'What's this about Squall?' Jack repeated, in a slightly higher-pitched voice. He lifted his eye patch as if to get a better read on the situation.

'Good question, Mog. I'm afraid I don't know.' Jupiter scratched at his beard. 'But I suggest you start by asking Professor Onstald himself.'

'Oh, I will ask him,' Morrigan said. She was suddenly filled with a fresh, fierce determination. How could Onstald have written an entire book about Wundersmiths and Wundrous Acts when he was obviously so misinformed? Had he ever bothered *looking* for Cascade Towers or Jemmity Park, or any of the other Wundrous Acts in his book? 'I'll ask him first thing tomorrow.'

'Go in easy, though, won't you?' said Jupiter. 'Nobody likes to be told they got something wrong. Especially something they wrote a whole book about.'

'No promises,' she said grimly.

A few moments went by in silence while Morrigan brooded and Jupiter gazed up in silent appreciation of Cascade Towers, until Jack finally burst:

'*Is anybody going to tell me about Squall?!*'

CHAPTER TWENTY-TWO

The Treacherous Timekeeper

'Have you sorted your costume yet?'

'Costume?'

'For Hallowmas,' said Hawthorne. 'It's tomorrow.'

'Erm.' Morrigan blinked, struggling to engage with the conversation. She'd barely slept the night before and her mind was well and truly elsewhere as they marched up the path through the Whinging Woods to Proudfoot House. 'No. I hadn't really thought about it.'

'You know what I think you should come as?' Hawthorne looked carefully around, then whispered, 'A *Wundersmith*!'

Morrigan made a face. 'That's the most ridiculous idea you've ever had.'

'Nah, listen – nobody knows you're *really* a Wundersmith except—'

'Except,' interrupted Morrigan, counting on her fingers, 'you, Jupiter, Jack, Fenestra, Miss Cheery, Professor Onstald, the Elders, the Scholar Mistresses, everyone in our unit and all of their patrons.'

'Yeah, but nobody else.'

'Oh! Let's not forget our mystery blackmailers, whoever they are. And Ezra Squall, and—'

'*Anyway,*' he pushed on determinedly, 'that's what makes it such a good idea! It's, um – what's the word? Homer used it the other day. It's . . . *ironic.*'

'What does that mean?'

'It means . . . I dunno, who cares. Just imagine everyone's faces when you show up at the party dressed as a Wundersmith! Black mouth, talons, big old cape . . . scariest costume in the room. BOOM. Instant street cred.'

'BOOM. Instant expulsion.' Morrigan rolled her eyes. That wasn't even what Squall really looked like. 'What *party,* anyway?'

'Whichever one we want!' Hawthorne jumped up to touch an overhanging branch, getting excited. 'Unit 918 are having a party at Freddie Roach's house. Freddie's in my *Reptilian Care* class, he's nice. Or Homer's friends are having a party. I bet he'd take us with him if we promise to keep at least three metres away from him at all times and wear masks that fully cover our faces.'

'But we're marching in the Black Parade, remember?' Morrigan said, shivering. 'We don't have to wear costumes for that, just formal black uniforms.'

She pulled her coat tighter around her and buttoned it all the way up to her chin. Autumn had really kicked in. Outside the walls of Wunsoc that meant crisp air and piles of satisfyingly crunchy leaves to stomp through. Inside Wunsoc, the wind was bitingly cool, there was an ever-present smell of wood smoke and sweet rotting apples, and the Whinging Woods had become a vibrant canopy of woven reds, golds and oranges (something none of the muttering trees seemed particularly happy about, but when were they ever?).

'That's not until midnight! Hey, I bet Jack knows someone who's having a party, maybe he could—'

'Jack will be at the Deucalion,' said Morrigan. 'And really, I suppose I ought to be there too, for whatever Hallowmas nonsense Frank has cooked up.'

'Ooh, can I come?'

'Of course.'

'Cool. I'm going to be a pirate, I think. Or a ghoul. Or a dinosaur. I'm not really sure yet. Or a vampire, maybe . . .'

Hawthorne kept up a constant stream of costume ideas for the entire walk to Proudfoot House. He didn't seem to require any real input from Morrigan, which suited her perfectly as it meant she didn't have to listen.

She'd been awake half the night, brooding over how she should tackle her conversation with Onstald. Jupiter was correct, of course. Nobody liked to be told they were wrong. But did that mean nobody *ought* to be told they were wrong?

After all, Onstald had spent the whole year teaching Morrigan things that were heinously false. He'd declared himself an expert on a topic he obviously knew nothing about and he'd made Morrigan believe she was doomed to repeat the failures of every evil, idiotic or just plain useless Wundersmith that came before her.

The more she thought about it, the angrier it made her. She'd worked herself up into a fury all morning, thinking about Cascade Towers and Jemmity Park and the count- less other Wundrous Acts that could still be out there in Nevermoor, ready to be discovered if only someone would bother to look for them.

When Morrigan stormed into Professor Onstald's classroom, shoulders back and head high, she was ready to have a very serious conversation with her tortoisewun teacher.

'What . . . is all . . . this . . . racket?' asked Professor Onstald, as Morrigan threw open the door and marched into the room, throwing her book bag down onto a desk.

'You're wrong,' said Morrigan, surprising herself a little. Fury or no, she hadn't intended to put it quite so baldly.

'I beg . . . your . . .'

'Pardon, yeah,' Morrigan interjected, too impatient to let him finish. Onstald's beady eyes grew a little wider, his mouth opening slightly in surprise at her rudeness. She didn't care. She wouldn't be put off. 'You're wrong about the Wundrous Act Spectrum. Your book says there are only bad Wundrous Acts, only Missteps and Blunders and . . . and Monstrosities, and all that.'

Professor Onstald stared at her. 'There *are* only . . .'

'But that's not true,' Morrigan barrelled on. 'What about Singularities? And Spectacles?'

She paused, waiting for Onstald's response. His wrinkled, leathery face was blank.

'Cascade Towers isn't a Fiasco at all,' she continued. 'I know, because I've seen it.'

His mouth dropped open. 'You've . . . seen . . .'

'Yes, and it's *wonderful*. There's a plaque there, a purple diamond plaque, and it says, "*Here stands a Singularity*". Not a Fiasco – a *Singularity*. A gift to the people of Nevermoor. And Jemmity Park *isn't* locked to everyone – it lets in poor children who deserve to have it all to themselves. The Committee for the Classification of Wundrous Acts declared it a *Spectacle*, and a gift to the children of Gresham. There's a purple plaque that says so.'

Morrigan saw that Professor Onstald was becoming more and more agitated, but she couldn't stop. She could barely pause for breath, so desperate was she to make him understand.

'Don't you see what that *means*? You got it wrong, Professor. Your book says every single Wundersmith throughout history has been stupid or wicked or cruel or wasteful. But Decima Kokoro wasn't useless – she was a genius. Odbuoy Jemmity wasn't cruel – he was generous and kind.'

'Keep . . . your . . . voice down.' Professor Onstald looked nervously towards the open door. A few people walking past in the hall peeked curiously inside, wondering what the noise was all about. 'Somebody . . . will . . .'

'I don't *care* if somebody hears me,' snapped Morrigan. She felt the pricking of angry tears, and cursed her treacherous eyeballs into infinity. Why must getting angry make her feel like crying? It wasn't *at all* the message she wanted to send. She curled her hands into tight fists. 'I won't be quiet until you listen to me. Don't you see – if you were wrong about Kokoro and Jemmity, maybe you were wrong about other Wundersmiths too. Isn't it worth trying to find out the truth? If there are more Wundrous Acts out there that are *good*, don't you want to . . .'

Morrigan trailed off, suddenly aware that Professor Onstald had not expressed even the smallest amount of surprise. He hadn't called her a liar, or asked how she knew these things, or even looked confused at the mention of 'Spectacles' and 'Singularities'. He was only worried about whether someone else might hear the things she was saying. He kept glancing fitfully towards the door.

A long and weighty silence fell between them.

Morrigan looked down at the huge book on the professor's desk, placing a hand on its faded cover. *Missteps, Blunders, Fiascos, Monstrosities and Devastations: An Abridged History of the Wundrous Act Spectrum.* When she spoke this time, her voice was barely audible above the ticking of the clock on the wall.

'An *Abridged* History. Edited. Abbreviated. Shortened.' She looked up at Onstald, recalling his words from their first lesson. 'You already knew all this, didn't you? You left things out deliberately. You *lied*.'

With a long, wheezing breath, Onstald opened his mouth to respond, a trail of spittle stretching between his wrinkled lips. 'I . . . revised.'

'You LIED!' Morrigan was shouting now. She couldn't help it. 'You've been lying this whole time. You tried to make me believe that all Wundersmiths are evil. But you knew that wasn't true, didn't you?'

'All Wundersmiths . . . are . . . ev—'

Unable to hear these words again, unable to bear it, Morrigan opened the book and flipped aggressively through the pages until she came to the chapter about Odbuoy Jemmity.

And then she ripped it out. The whole chapter. She gritted her teeth and tore the pages into tiny pieces and let them fall to the floor like confetti.

'STOP. LYING.'

Professor Onstald had just opened his mouth to respond to this shocking act of vandalism when Henry Mildmay burst into the room, looking worried and a bit flustered. He carried an awkward armful of books and maps, and his fringe flopped down into his eyes.

'Oh! I'm sorry Professor Onstald, I was passing by and I thought I heard shouting.' He looked from Morrigan to the aged tortoisewun to the pile of torn-up paper on the floor, a deep line of confusion creasing his brow. 'Is everything all right?' He looked at Morrigan when he asked this, but it was Professor Onstald who answered.

'Everything . . . is fine . . . young man.' Morrigan noticed the way he addressed Mildmay as if he were a schoolboy, rather than his colleague. For some reason, it only irritated her more. How *dare* he be so rude to Mildmay, especially when the younger teacher was so good and kind, and Professor Onstald was such an awful old liar? It wasn't right. 'Go . . . about . . . your business.'

But Mildmay was still staring at Morrigan with a look of curious concern. 'Miss Crow, are you—'

'She . . . is *fine*,' asserted Onstald. 'Your . . . continued . . . presence here . . . is most inappropriate, boy.'

A touch of colour rose in Mildmay's cheeks. 'Of course, Professor Onstald,' he said. 'My apologies.' With one last enquiring glance at Morrigan, he ducked his head and turned to leave, but instead hit his knee on the edge of Onstald's desk. He cried out in pain and dropped his books and maps all over the desk, scrambling to pick them up, even more red-faced, and in his embarrassment, he tripped, casting an armful of belongings into the air yet again.

In the moment of noise and confusion, something very strange happened.

Morrigan felt suddenly as if the world and everything in it was grinding to a halt. The air around her felt as thick as molasses. It was like time had slowed down to an unbearable speed – or as if time had become solid and was somehow holding her in place. Her mind worked as fast as ever, but even her *eyeballs* were moving at a snail's pace, refusing to look where she desperately wanted them to look. In her peripheral vision she saw that across the room, Mildmay too appeared almost immobile, his belongings floating in the air – floating in *time* – around him.

It felt like an eternity passed. Just as Morrigan was wondering if she had somehow made this happen, if her ill-formed talents as a Wundersmith were betraying her yet again, she realised who was really responsible.

Moving across her line of sight at his usual tortoise pace (which was now, of course, many, *many* times faster than her own near-frozen speed), Professor Onstald crossed the room in small, shuffling steps, heaved *An Abridged History* up into his arms, and left the classroom.

It was Onstald. He'd made it happen. He'd *slowed time.*

Moments later, the world stuttered back to life. Mildmay's books and maps clattered to the floor and he hit his knee on the corner of the desk again, crying out in pain.

Morrigan gasped for breath and ran to the door. Too late. The professor was gone. 'How did he do that?!'

Mildmay was breathing as if he'd just run a marathon, pressing one hand to his chest. 'Good grief. I had no idea . . . I always assumed Professor Onstald was Mundane. I didn't know he was a *Timekeeper.* I didn't know there were any Timekeepers *left* in the Unnamed Realm.'

'What's a Timekeeper?'

'A very rare knack,' said Mildmay. He was still gazing at the door Onstald had disappeared through, shaking his head, eyes wide. 'There are different strands of Timekeeping, different ways to use and manipulate time – preservation, shrinking, looping, stretching. Seems like old Onstald is a *stretcher of time.* I can hardly believe it.'

Morrigan gave an angry, derisive snort. 'Sounds about right. He's a stretcher of truths too. And he took the book!'

She slammed her fist on the desk. She'd wanted to take the book from Onstald, the proof of his fraudulence. To take it home and pore over its pages with Jupiter, to see what other Blunders and Monstrosities might turn out to have been *gifts to the people of Nevermoor.*

'Oh dear. What, er – what book was it?' asked Mildmay distractedly, gathering his things from the floor. Morrigan bent down to help.

'*An Abridged History of the*—' She stopped herself just in time, pressing her lips together as she handed him a rolled-up map. It would be impossible to tell Mildmay the title of the book without potentially giving herself away as a Wundersmith. 'I forget. Some stupid history textbook.'

'Oh, well . . . I'm sure he'll bring it back.' Mildmay headed to the door, still looking flustered and slightly in shock, as if he hadn't quite recovered yet from the effects of Onstald's bizarre knack. Morrigan could understand. Her head still felt a little fuzzy. 'I should go. Lessons to plan. I'll see you, Miss Crow.'

'A *Timekeeper?* Crikey. Are you sure?'

'Well, that's what Mildmay said. And he *did* stretch time . . . or least, that's what it felt like.'

Morrigan breathed deeply, inhaling clouds of chamomile smoke as they rolled out from the walls. She had come home in a terrible state, shouting for Jupiter as she ran down the hall to his study, ready to lay out the whole terrible episode. Her patron had, wisely, suggested they have the conversation in the empty Smoking Parlour, and asked Kedgeree to put on a calming scent. Morrigan had recounted the whole thing in furious detail, and was most gratified when she got to the bit where she realised Onstald knew the truth all along, and Jupiter had literally jumped up out of his seat. It had taken quite a bit of chamomile before he'd finally stopped pacing and sat down again.

'But *why* has he been lying?' said Morrigan. It was the umpteenth time she'd asked the question that afternoon, and Jupiter couldn't answer it any more than she could.

'I'll have to go to the Elders,' he said, finally. 'They need to know the truth more than anyone.'

'Tomorrow?' Morrigan asked hopefully.

'Tomorrow,' he agreed. 'I'll talk to them when I see them before the Black Parade. After Frank's party. I promise.'

CHAPTER TWENTY-THREE

Hallowmas

The Deucalion glowed a wicked golden-orange on Hallowmas night. Every light in the hotel had been extinguished so that the building was as dark as a witch's cauldron except for several well-chosen rooms in which hundreds of candles were brightly burning. From the street, the candlelit windows made the precise formation of a gaping, toothy mouth and a pair of devilish eyes, so that the Deucalion's façade resembled a gigantic jack-o-lantern. The effect was chilling.

'I know I say it every year,' said Jupiter, gazing up at his hotel from the forecourt with undisguised pride, 'but you've outdone yourself, Frank.'

'Very spooky,' said Morrigan. Jack murmured his agreement beside her, and Martha squealed, applauding enthusiastically.

Charlie clapped Frank on the back and said, 'Think we've got Hallowmas in the bag this year, Frank. Them lot at the Hotel Aurianna won't know what hit 'em.'

Jack glanced sideways at Morrigan, and they both held their breath. The last thing any of them needed was for Frank to go off on another rant about his chief rivals.

But Frank's pallid face split into a confident grin, his eyes and his canines glinting in the Deucalion's firelight. 'Hallowmas belongs to me, my friends. Nobody walks the fine line of whimsical horror and ghoulish delight better than Frank. Nobody.'

Morrigan cast an amused look at the others. Martha smiled and bit her lip, while Jupiter tried to cover up his snort of laughter with a fake coughing fit.

'What's on the agenda tonight, Frank?' asked Jack, as they all made their way back inside to the candlelit lobby, where costumed guests were already gathering in anticipation of the night of terrors ahead. Serving staff handed around glasses of midnight black punch and trays of tiny canapes that closely resembled real hairy spiders and human fingers. Jack had only arrived home from school that afternoon, so unlike Morrigan, Jupiter and the staff, he hadn't been subjected to the last week of Frank's obsessive fine-tuning of the Hallowmas programme. 'Glad you asked, young Jack.' Frank cleared his throat importantly. 'Six o'clock onwards:

junior members of the Deucalion staff welcome hordes of beastly little trick-or-treaters.'

'What are the treats?' asked Jupiter.

'Oh, the usual,' said Frank. 'Jelly skeletons. Maggot munchies. Chocolate eyeballs.'

'And the tricks?'

'I thought we'd hold them down and shave their eyebrows.'

Jupiter sighed. 'No, Frank.'

'Tar and feather them?'

'Definitely not.'

'Tattoo their foreheads?'

Jupiter exhaled heavily, puffing out his cheeks. 'Can we try to think of something that won't result in a class action lawsuit?'

Frank's face soured a little and he gave a sulky shrug. 'Seven o'clock: the Nevermoor Chamber Orchestra will perform funeral dirges in the Music Salon. Eight o'clock: a beautifully gory performance of *Death at First Bite* by the notorious all-vampire theatre company, the Thirsty Thespians – I had to call in a dozen different favours to wrangle that one. They're very secretive you know, and they *never* usually perform for normals,' he said, looking quite deservedly smug. 'Nine o'clock: spooky disco and costume competition in the second ballroom – always good to cater for the *youth*, I think.'

'Hawthorne will be pleased, he loves dancing,' said Morrigan – who, despite her *youth*, had absolutely no intention of attending a disco. She glanced at the clock behind the concierge desk, wondering where Hawthorne *was*. He was supposed to have arrived before sunset, but it was already dark. They had planned to go trick-or-treating together. Jupiter had initially said no, but relented after much pleading, and only then because Jack had reluctantly promised to accompany them. Martha had put together a last-minute, unidentifiable monster costume for Morrigan that involved a lot of purple pipe cleaners and green tulle, and was already itching like crazy.

'Around eleven,' continued Frank, 'most of our guests will head downtown to get a spot at the Black Parade before midnight. Meanwhile, back here at the Deucalion, I will be eschewing this year's parade to host my own, *highly exclusive, top-secret, invitation-only* midnight event.' Frank paused dramatically. Morrigan raised an eyebrow at Jack, who smirked. 'I have procured the services of The Marvellous Malau.'

'Ooh,' said Martha, her eyes lighting up. 'I've seen him in the newspaper!'

Morrigan had never heard of The Marvellous Malau. 'Who is he?'

'Only the Free State's *greatest living clairvoyant*,' declared Frank.

'According to his own adverts,' muttered Jack.

Frank ignored him. 'Malau will be conducting a séance right here on the roof of the Deucalion. He says being outside under the full moon will bring us closer in tune with the spirits.'

'A spooky old séance, hey,' said Jupiter, looking impressed. 'Bang on trend, Frank. Communion with the dead is quite fashionable right now. All nonsense, of course, since no self-respecting ghost would show up for a clairvoyant who advertises in the *Looking Glass* and calls himself "marvellous". But still, *very* fashionable.'

'You just wait, Jove,' called the vampire dwarf as he wandered away to greet his guests. 'Malau is the real thing. The society pages will be screaming about this for days.'

Just then, a sudden screech of wheels drifted up from the forecourt outside, followed by a clattering of footfall up the front steps, and a troop of half a dozen black-coated, heavy-booted Stealth officers hurrying into the Deucalion. They were led by a stern-looking woman with close-cropped, wiry grey hair and golden epaulets on her shoulders.

'Good evening, Inspector Rivers,' said Jupiter. He had a welcoming but weary expression. It occurred to Morrigan that if the woman was bringing bad news, both Jupiter and Jack – who'd cautiously lifted his eye patch as the Stealth filed in – already had an inkling of it.

'Captain North,' said the Inspector, gesturing to her officers to stand by. Some of the costumed guests looked disturbed by the sudden intrusion, but a few were delighted, as if they were certain this was part of the Hallowmas fun.

She pulled Jupiter to one side and spoke quietly, but of course Morrigan, Jack, Charlie and Martha merely sidled closer to hear. 'I'm sorry to interrupt. HQ wanted to send a messenger, but I thought I should speak with you in person. It's bad news. We've had three more. All taken today.'

Morrigan felt her chest constrict a little. *Taken.* Who'd been taken?

Jupiter's eyes narrowed. He rubbed a hand over his ginger beard. 'Three more *disappearances?*'

Inspector Rivers nodded. 'We've had an anonymous tip-off.' She lowered her voice. Morrigan, Jack, Charlie and Martha all leaned in to listen. 'It's back, Captain, and it's *tonight.*'

Morrigan glanced up at Jupiter; the colour had drained from his face. They were talking about the Ghastly Market. She was sure of it.

'I see,' he said slowly. 'And did this . . . anonymous tip-off give a location for the event, or is that too optimistic of me?'

Inspector Rivers shook her head, looking grim. 'We've sent out all the officers we can spare to search the likely locations, but as you know, our numbers are small.'

'And it's unlikely to be in the likely locations,' added Jupiter.

'Quite. So we're working with the Stink –' she caught herself, and gave a little cough, '– excuse me, with the Nevermoor City Police Force, and we've even recruited some members of the Wunsoc teaching staff to assist in the search.'

'The *teaching staff*?' sputtered Jupiter. 'Is that a good idea?'

'They insisted, Captain,' she said. 'And I quite understand why. One of their own is among the missing. Stolen from inside the walls of Wunsoc itself, if you can believe that – right out of his own living quarters. Signs of a struggle. Water all over the place . . . and bones.'

'Bones,' Jupiter repeated.

'A femur,' said Rivers, with a significant look. 'A few fingers.'

A muscle in Jupiter's jaw clenched, and Morrigan knew why. The Skeletal Legion. The *Bonesmen*. That confirmed it; the Bonesmen had taken another three people for the Ghastly Market. Morrigan pictured the little trail of leftover bones in her mind, and she shuddered.

There was something else too, she thought, a little snag in the story—

'Did you say . . . there was *water*?' Morrigan asked the inspector, unable to help herself.

Rivers gave her a sidelong look, then glanced back to Jupiter, and said, 'From the pond in his room. We think they must have dragged him right out of it.'

Morrigan frowned as she connected the dots. 'You're talking about Professor Onstald, aren't you? The tortoisewun?'

Inspector Rivers pressed her lips together, refusing to look at Morrigan. Morrigan took that as silent confirmation.

She couldn't help thinking that perhaps Onstald hadn't really been kidnapped at all. Perhaps, in fact, he had made *himself* disappear because he was afraid of being exposed by Morrigan as a fraud. The thrill of angry satisfaction she felt at that thought was immediately chased by shame.

And something else.

Some other fear was tickling the back of Morrigan's brain, so subtle she couldn't yet name it.

'Who are the other two?' she asked Rivers.

The woman made an exasperated face at Jupiter.

'Hush, Mog,' he said. 'Inspector, I'm at your service. I'll grab my coat.'

'Actually,' said Rivers, holding up a hand to stop him, 'what I'd like is for you to be on standby. It's better if you're here, ready to move as soon as we've narrowed down the possibilities. Right now, we're looking for a needle in a haystack. I'll send a runner for you the minute we have a decent lead.' Jupiter nodded his agreement.

'In the meantime, we're urging all Wundrous Society members to remain in their homes,' the Inspector continued. 'A strict curfew is in place. There is a very real threat to all Wuns in Nevermoor tonight.'

'But what about the Black Parade?' asked Morrigan, suddenly stricken. It was going to be her and Hawthorne's first time marching! They'd been looking forward to it since last year's parade, when they'd watched the rows of solemn, black-cloaked, candle-bearing Wunsoc units marching in silent procession through the streets of Nevermoor. (Where *was* Hawthorne? The tiny, tickling fear grew more insistent.)

'The Black Parade has been cancelled,' said Inspector Rivers.

Morrigan felt the bad news hit her like a slug to the chest. Cancelled. Her first ever Black Parade. *Cancelled.* Whoever was behind these disappearances – whoever was targeting Wuns – was now controlling everyone, making people fear even leaving their homes. Morrigan felt anger surge through her, accompanied by the now strangely familiar taste of ash at the back of her throat.

'And, Captain North,' continued Rivers, 'we're calling on all Wundrous Society members to cancel any gatherings or festivities they may have planned. This is not a night for our people to be out in the streets. We're hoping, since everyone looks up to you, that you'll set a good example.'

Jupiter looked as if he wanted to argue with this idea, but thought better of it. 'Of course,' he said. 'I'll let my staff know immediately. We'll put the word out. And I'll be here all night, Inspector, awaiting your summons.'

Inspector Rivers gave him a brief nod, turned on her heels and departed, her troops following her obediently out the door.

Jupiter looked across the lobby, to where Frank was entertaining a knot of delighted guests by making his fangs extend and retract on command. 'Suppose I'd better give him the bad news.'

Morrigan's heart sank.

No Black Parade. No trick-or-treating. More disappearances.

And another, much more insistent worry she couldn't ignore. *Where was Hawthorne?*

'Sorry I'm late!' came a boisterous voice from the entry, and in strode the strangest looking creature Morrigan had ever seen.

Its decaying, bloodied grey skin was lashed with blood. It had bright green scaly claws with green talons and a matching spiky tail. Its legs were rectangles of silver covered with buttons, bolts and bottle caps. And completing the strange ensemble was a pirate's hat, red brocade coat, frilly white cravat and black eye patch.

Morrigan exhaled. She blinked repeatedly, feeling sharp relief at the arrival of her best friend, but also the fresh shock of . . . *whatever she was looking at.*

'I couldn't decide what to come as, so Mum made me a pirate-zombie-robot-dinosaur costume and—' Hawthorne stopped abruptly when he saw Morrigan's face. He looked down at his ensemble. 'What, too much?'

⌐••━━-

Morrigan had never seen the Deucalion in such a sombre state. After the Stealth left and she'd filled Hawthorne in, the first thing the two friends did was run to the station door in her bedroom, hoping to check on the rest of Unit 919 and make sure they all knew to stay indoors tonight. But the *W* symbol was unlit, and the door wouldn't budge no matter how hard they pushed it. Frustrated and worried, all they could do was return to the lobby and wait. Morrigan was, at least, relieved to change out of her itchy costume. (Hawthorne had also shed his talons, tail and silver robot legs, though rather more reluctantly.)

Jupiter was pacing the black-and-white chequered floor – coat on, boots laced, umbrella in hand, ready to bolt when the Stealth called on him. Morrigan knew he hated staying put and waiting for news just as much as she did but that he was trying to stay calm and cheerful for everyone else's sake.

Frank, meanwhile, was *furious*. It had taken an hour just to convince him the whole thing wasn't the Hotel Aurianna trying to sabotage him. Once he accepted it really was the Wundrous Society, that was almost as bad.

'Another BLATANT example of Wun privilege at its worst,' he roared, adding as an aside to Jupiter and Morrigan, 'No offence.' He paced irritably up and down the now emptied lobby. The costumed crowd had already been sent home, disappointed, and the guests who were staying at the Deucalion had all been up to the Golden Lantern cocktail bar for a happy hour that was to last all night, to make up for the cancelled festivities.

'None taken,' said Jupiter. 'I quite agree, Frank.' He shot a tiny wink in Morrigan's direction.

'The Thirsty Thespians have left,' said Frank glumly. 'Probably laughing at me. Yesterday they said I could have a role in their winter production of *Creatures of the Night*, but that's not gonna happen now, is it? And The Marvellous Malau is distraught. Inconsolable! He said he could feel the disappointment of the spirits through the Gossamer, so now I've got a bunch of dead people angry at me too. He's gone up to the Golden Lantern to drown his sorrows.'

The vampire dwarf broke into a sobbing wail and Martha led him over to the loveseat, putting a consoling arm around him. He wept into her side so loudly, so heartrendingly, and for such a tedious length of time, that finally Jupiter told him he could still have the midnight séance on the rooftop with the remaining hotel guests, as long as he pulled himself together and stopped crying.

'The Stealth are out in force, doing everything they can,' Jupiter said. 'There's nothing we can do now except wait to hear from them. We might as well enjoy what's left of Hallowmas, then get a good night's sleep and hopefully by this time tomorrow everything will be right as rain.'

Frank immediately set off to fetch Malau, and Martha and Charlie went to the rooftop to check that everything was set up and ready to go.

'I'll be here at the desk, sir,' said Kedgeree. 'I'll send for you the second we get word from the Stealth.'

'Good man.' Jupiter turned to Morrigan, Hawthorne and Jack. 'Come on, you three. It's All Hallows' Eve. Let's get chatty with ghosts.'

After spending the bulk of his evening enjoying the hospitality of the talented Golden Lantern bartenders, The Marvellous Malau was a little sozzled by the time he started the séance.

'The spirits are – *hic* – with us, dear friends,' said the clairvoyant. He sat on a cushion on the rooftop, at the centre of a large circle of guests. 'They are all around us, on this night of All Hallows' Eve, when the walls between the living and the dead are th-thing . . . *thingest.*' He paused to rummage around in his head for another word. 'Skinniest?'

Frank had set the scene for the séance *wonderfully*. The rooftop was lit by hundreds of long, tapered black candles which flickered atmospherically but never seemed to blow out, despite the cool breeze. Everyone sat on elegant black velvet cushions and an artificial – but beautifully eerie – white fog hovered on the edges of the circle.

It was a shame the effect was wasted on a group of guests who were mostly eager to return to their endless free cocktails on the sixth floor.

'I'm getting a message from an older gentleman . . . for somebody over . . . here.' He waved vaguely to half the people in the circle. 'A gentleman with a D-name. Somebody's father or uncle? A grand – *hic* – grandfather perhaps? Darren? David? Dominic? Doo . . . Doody? Drogley? Er . . . Derek?' Malau continued, heroically sticking to his story. 'Digby? Dwayne?'

'Ooh!' shrieked a young woman wearing a plastic tiara and a bright pink 'Bride-To-Be' sash. She was at the Deucalion with a group of raucous young women who didn't have a lot of interest in celebrating Hallowmas. Frank invited them to the séance to make up the numbers, and they'd already been told twice to stop yelling out rude words while The Marvellous Malau was communing with the dead. 'Could it be Wayne? My father-in-law's name is Wayne. Is it him?'

Malau appeared to consider this for a moment. 'Yes, that's the one. He has a message for you. He says . . . please take good care of his son. Love each other.'

The group of girlfriends all 'awwwed' as one, and the Bride-To-Be looked a little bit teary. 'I didn't think he wanted me to marry Benji!'

'Oh, he does,' continued Malau. 'He says nothing would make him happier, and he'll be watching over the two of you from the Better Place.'

The bride's face fell. 'The Better Place? What do you mean? Wayne's not dead.'

It was all too much for Morrigan and Hawthorne, who tried valiantly to hide their silent giggles. But then Hawthorne snorted loudly, and it was all over for Morrigan, whose face was already streaming with tears of laughter.

From across the circle, Jupiter raised his eyebrows at them, and looked pointedly towards the door. Still giggling, Morrigan grabbed Hawthorne's arm. They stood up and were just about to flee the séance when The Marvellous Malau stood also, pointed directly at Morrigan, and declared in a sharp, ringing voice –

'You breathed fire.'

The laughter died in Morrigan's throat. She faltered, eager to leave but seemingly rooted to the spot.

Malau tilted his head to the side, a curious little frown creasing the spot between his eyes. 'You breathed *fire.*' His voice was suddenly commanding and clear. There were no slurred consonants, no fumbled words. 'Like a dragon. Did you enjoy it?'

Morrigan blinked. She looked sideways at Hawthorne and then at Jupiter, who both appeared equally shocked. The séance circle had turned in their direction now and were all peering at Morrigan with great interest.

Morrigan felt her face grow hot. She couldn't, of course, admit to such a thing. 'No. No, I never did that.'

'Yes,' said Malau flatly. 'You did.'

How did he *know*? Perhaps the man wasn't such a char-latan after all.

'I don't know what you're talking about,' Morrigan insisted, in a voice as steely as she could make it.

Jupiter stood up suddenly, his movements elegant and precise. He tilted his head and took a step closer, staring at her face. 'I think you know exactly what I'm talking about,' he said.

Morrigan stared at him. 'Jupiter, what are you—'

'Inferno,' said the Bride-To-Be. She rose also, and walked towards Morrigan with cat-like grace. 'The Wretched Art of Inferno.'

Morrigan swallowed, repeating the words in her mind. *The Wretched Art of Inferno.*

'What . . . what is this?' She looked from the bride, to Jupiter, to Malau and back again. 'Jupiter, what's happening?'

The rest of the people on the rooftop rose as one body and started to gather around her in a knot – even Hawthorne. They stood in a tight, unbroken ring, shoulder to shoulder, their movements too smooth, too exact, to be natural.

As one, they opened their mouths and spoke.

'The Wretched Art of Inferno,' they said, their voices pitched in perfect, eerie unison. Every word clipped, every consonant crisp. 'An unlikely first manifestation in a young Wundersmith, though not unheard of. Inferno is a formidable tool in the hands of an accomplished smith –' they leaned back ever so slightly, surveying her coolly over their noses, '– but of course, *you* are far from accomplished.'

Morrigan was reminded sharply of last Hallowmas, when the Witches of Coven Thirteen had pulled this same trick, speaking together with spooky precision. It had been part of her and Hawthorne's trials for the Wundrous Society, and the witches had been acting on the orders of the Elders.

Was this just another Wundrous Society thing? Another test? Surely not tonight, she thought . . . *surely* not with half the Society out looking for their missing people, and a lockdown in place on the rest. This wasn't the night for tricks.

'Who are you?' she asked again. 'What do you want?'

As one, they tilted their heads gently to the side. The corner of every mouth twisted into a familiar grin. The sight of it made Morrigan's breath catch in her throat. Cold, sickening fear pooled in the pit of her stomach.

'You,' she whispered.

The air had grown still. Without the slightest hint of breeze, without the smallest bit of help, every candle on the rooftop was suddenly extinguished. Swirls of smoke rose from the dead wicks. Silvery moonlight reflected in the wide eyes surrounding Morrigan, all fixed squarely on her own.

'I'm not afraid of you.' Her voice trembled.

Hawthorne stepped forward, away from the pack, and put a hand on her shoulder.

'I told you once before.' He spoke with a coolness and conviction that was not his own. 'You must learn to deceive more skilfully, Miss Crow.'

CHAPTER TWENTY-FOUR

The Wretched Art of Inferno

Morrigan's insides curled as Ezra Squall's words came from her best friend's mouth.

'Stop,' she whispered. 'Leave him alone.'

The corners of Hawthorne's mouth pulled back into a sinister grin that didn't fit his face. 'Shan't.'

He lifted his right hand and slapped himself, hard. Morrigan yelped, and as he raised his left hand to repeat the action she lunged forward, snatching it away.

'STOP! Please, stop it – what are you DOING?!'

Hawthorne's hands dropped, and he grew still, his face emotionless. He stepped calmly backwards, his head drooping to his chest. It was as if somebody had flicked a switch and turned him off.

The rest of the séance guests followed, their movements seamlessly synchronised. The group parted down the middle, giving Morrigan a clear line of sight to the far edge of the rooftop.

There, leaning casually against the balustrade in a tailored grey suit, was Ezra Squall. He smiled, and watched Morrigan for several moments. She stood perfectly still. Her primal instinct was to run away, but she couldn't leave Hawthorne and Jupiter and the others.

'What did you do to them?' she called, trying to ignore the tremor in her voice.

'Just a little parlour trick.' Squall held his hands out – palms downward, twisted into claws – and made his fingers dance like a puppeteer twitching strings. 'Shall I teach you?'

Morrigan didn't respond. Her heart was racing. If she narrowed her eyes, she could see the faint shimmery outline of the Gossamer around him. A subtle, almost invisible haze of golden light.

So, then. He still wasn't here in Nevermoor. Not physically. That was a relief, but it didn't make any sense. Morrigan crossed the rooftop, stopping metres from where he stood, careful to keep some distance between them.

'How did you do that?' she demanded. 'You can't do anything through the Gossamer, you told me that yourself.'

Squall pressed his hands together, as if in prayer, and held them to his mouth. 'Ah, but you see – this is the great cosmic marvel of the thing. I'm not doing it. *You're* doing it.'

Morrigan glanced back at the group, still and silent as sculptures. She shook her head; there was no way she'd done that. How could she? Why would she? Where would she even *begin*?

Squall seemed to understand her scepticism. 'Not directly, of course. But you *have* allowed Wunder to gather and gather and gather to you, unchecked and unused. That energy must go somewhere. Instead of building and depleting Wunder the way a Wundersmith ought to – by regular, practised use of the Wretched Arts – the energy that has been swarming to you for many years now has built to . . . well, to this,' he said, gesturing to Morrigan with a bemused smile. 'To this churning, scorching, insupportable mass. Wunder has grown tired of waiting. And while you've lacked the courage to use it, you are allowing it to use you.'

His face split into a grin and he tilted his head backwards, closing his eyes as if to savour the joy of his next words.

'And even better . . . you are allowing *me* to use Wunder *through* you.'

Morrigan's mouth had gone dry. 'No!' It felt like an accusation, and she immediately wanted to fling it away from her. Like mud. 'No, I'm not. That's impossible.'

'Yes, I know it is,' said Squall, his eyes alight. His soft, delighted chuckle tumbled into the quiet night, sending a chill down Morrigan's back. 'Isn't that *exciting*? Here you are, burning like a beacon, so bright and uncontrolled that all it takes is the tiniest little push through the so-called impenetrable Gossamer.' He closed his eyes and leaned slightly forward, pressing his outstretched hands into the air itself, and Morrigan could see the palest glimmer of golden light bleeding out from the space between his fingers. More than that, she could *feel* it. As Squall pushed against the Gossamer, a wave of pure energy, warm like the sun and gently humming, rippled through her.

'I'm sorry,' he said, smirking and holding out his hands, 'you didn't *really* believe you had the skill to make the little star-thrower and her friends turn their weapons on themselves, did you? Or to turn the wee Magnificub into a raging beast?' He laughed.

'And when I . . . when I breathed fire,' Morrigan said, swallowing hard as the taste of smoke and ash stirred in her memory, 'that was you, too? You did that?'

A shadow of uncertainty crossed Squall's face. 'No,' he said. 'That spark of fury was all yours. But it was Wunder that unleashed it.'

He paused, considering for a moment. 'Wunder is both intelligent and impulsive. Wunder wishes to be used and directed by the only people born with the ability to use and direct it, but if we're not careful – if we allow it to express itself too freely – *it* will use *us*, instead of the other way around.'

Morrigan shook her head. 'I don't understand. What are you saying?'

'I am saying you breathed fire because Wunder *wanted* you to breathe fire.' Squall had an unsettling, fanatical look in his eye. A strange thrill ran down the back of Morrigan's neck. She found his zeal for Wunder contagious, and that realisation made her feel a bit sick.

'I am saying that for one shining, triumphant moment you became a dragon,' Squall continued, 'because Wunder grew tired of you being a mouse.'

Morrigan breathed sharply through her nose. She didn't like the idea that her free will could be taken from her by some invisible, unknowable force that she felt she would never fully understand.

'You must never forget, Miss Crow – Wunder is a parasite,' Squall continued. His soft voice carried across the rooftop. 'Wunder is your enemy. A villain that never sleeps, and never rests. Never forgets or gives up. It exists in a perpetually watchful state. It is waiting, always, for you to let your guard down. Because the Wundersmith is its only lifeline to the real world. We are the conduits through which Wunder can experience itself as *real,* as *living.*'

He'd worked himself into a state and was pacing now – excited, agitated, and a little mad, Morrigan thought.

'Imagine you're a ghost!' he cried. His raised voice echoed, bouncing around in the dark. The words spilled out across the surrounding rooftops like pebbles skimming over water. 'Wandering the world you once lived in, unable to speak to anyone, unable to touch anything. People look straight past you, walk right through you. How would that make you feel?'

Morrigan felt a sting in her heart. She didn't need to imagine any of this. She had already experienced it for herself last Christmas, when she'd travelled to her old home at Crow Manor on the Gossamer Line. A house full of people, and nobody but her grandmother could see or hear her. Her own father really *had* walked right through her.

'Lonely,' she said quietly. 'Like . . . like nothing.'

'Precisely. Like you're watching the world from behind a pane of glass. And then – one day, out of nowhere – you are *something*. You are something, because somebody can hear you. Someone can *see you*. A friend, at last! A kindred spirit! Someone to communicate with. *True love.* That is the story of Wunder and the Wundersmith.'

'You just said Wunder is the enemy,' said Morrigan, confused.

'It amounts to the same thing,' he said, a hint of icy impatience cutting through his calm veneer. 'Wunder is . . . obsessively, dangerously in love with the Wundersmith. That energy has to go somewhere. Do you realise, Miss Crow, how close you have come to self-combustion this year? Do you realise that the things I've done have *saved your life*?' He laughed. 'Not to mention the other favours I've granted you.'

'Favours?' Morrigan could hardly believe what she was hearing.

'Yes, *favours*,' he snapped. 'Who taught the star-thrower and her bullying beau a lesson they won't forget? Who got the useless, lying tortoise out of your way? You're welcome, incidentally.'

It felt as if something weighty and terrible had dropped onto Morrigan's chest. 'The Ghastly Market,' she said in a hushed voice. 'That was you.'

He inclined his head, taking a tiny little bow. 'Ta-da.'

'Alfie, and Professor Onstald . . . *You* took them. To be sold like unnimals.'

His eyes rolled skywards. 'Goodness, no. That sounds too much like hard work. All I did was pull a few strings.' He wiggled his fingers again. 'You'd be shocked at how easy people can be to manipulate. Even inside the impenetrable walls of your precious Society, I was able to find a pair of willing hands. But then, I've always had a knack for finding the weakest link in the chain.'

Morrigan frowned. 'Somebody in the Society has been *helping* you? Who?' she demanded. But Squall stayed silent, miming the pull of a zipper across his lips.

It was a sickening thought. Not even Baz Charlton would stoop so low. *Surely*.

She shook her head. She *refused* to believe it.

'Oh, don't look so appalled,' Squall said, leaning back against the balustrade again, a frown creasing his brow. 'And don't act as if you weren't pleased. I have done this for *you*, after all. I confess, I did think you'd be a little more grateful.'

'Grateful for what?' Morrigan spat. 'Hurting people doesn't *help* me.'

A corner of Squall's mouth tugged upwards. 'The Society has been far too comfortable for far too long. I wanted them to feel their foundations quake a little. Admit it, Miss Crow – didn't it feel good to see them *tremble*?' He leaned forward, lowering his voice. 'When you breathed fire, wasn't there some tiny, dark part of you that saw the fear in their eyes, and liked it?'

Morrigan said nothing. She was remembering that day at Proudfoot Station. Remembering the monster that had swelled up inside her. The righteous fury that had coursed through her veins like electricity and transformed her – just for one moment – into the most powerful person in Wunsoc.

She could still see the frightened faces on the platform. Had Morrigan *enjoyed* that, she wondered. Had some small part of her *liked* the thought of striking fear in someone's heart . . . instead of being the one who was always afraid?

She looked away, refusing to answer Squall's question.

'Yes. I thought so.' His smile was a jackal's smile, hungry and dangerous. 'And I'm glad to have given you that glimpse of your *true* self. Although I must admit I'm surprised to find you here just talking to me,' he continued, gazing out across the moonlit Nevermoor skyline. 'I rather thought you'd be off doing something heroic. Thought you considered yourself the "no friend left behind" sort. Awfully glad to find I was wrong.'

Morrigan raised an eyebrow. 'Professor Onstald's not exactly a *friend*,' she said. 'And anyway, the Stealth is out looking for him. They don't need my help.'

'I didn't mean the thing with the shell.' The wind carried his soft, amused voice straight to Morrigan's ears. 'I was referring to the other abductees. The mesmerist and the oracle.'

'Cadence and Lambeth,' she whispered.

Morrigan felt something clench in her stomach.

'You've taken Cadence and Lambeth,' she said, a little louder. 'They're my friends. How is that supposed to *help* me?'

Squall gave a humourless laugh. 'I've done no such thing. I'm afraid my little Society puppet – my *pair of willing hands* – may have got a bit greedy. There are powerful people – inside the Free State and out – who would pay almost any price to get their hands on some of the knacks going to waste in the Society. Those are two very useful gifts. And if the rumours are true,' he continued, rocking on his heels, 'there's a fourth item up for auction tonight. Highly covetable.' There was a hint of a laugh in his voice. 'Perhaps I'll put in a bid myself. I've always wanted an angel for the top of my Christmas tree.'

'Cassiel,' she said quietly, but Squall didn't seem to hear.

Morrigan's hands curled uselessly into fists. She knew she couldn't fight him. She couldn't do anything to him. He wasn't even *here*.

'You know where the market is,' she said, fighting to keep her voice steady. 'You know where my friends are. *Tell me.*'

Squall tilted his head to the side. 'Well, yes. That's precisely why I've come. But nothing comes for free. We shall make an exchange.'

'What do you want?' she asked through gritted teeth.

He shrugged. 'The same thing I've always wanted. To educate.'

'I've told you already. I am *never* going to join you. You're a monster and a murderer.'

'There are far greater monsters – ' his eyes flashed, '– and far greater dangers. Miss Crow, we have a shared enemy you could never imagine. If the Wundrous Society doesn't take you off the leash, if you aren't given the freedom to grow, to become the Wundersmith *I need you to be* . . . then terrible things are coming down the line. For both of us.'

Morrigan stared at him, dumbstruck. *Shared enemy?* He was her only enemy.

'So now it's time for your third lesson,' he went on. 'The Wretched Art of Inferno.'

She shook her head, exasperated. She felt a familiar, frantic fury building inside of her. 'My friends need help *now*. I don't have time to learn tricks!'

She needed to get off this rooftop. She needed to find Cadence and Lambeth, before something terrible happened.

'No.' Squall spoke in a low, fierce voice, pushing away from the balustrade and taking two deliberate steps forward. Morrigan heard the séance circle stir, but she didn't turn around. She didn't want to take her eyes off him for a second. 'I quite agree. You're running out of time. The Wunder that's gathering to you is growing desperate. It has reached a critical mass, and unless you can channel it, give it a purpose, it will *burn you from the inside out.*' He glared at Morrigan, his black eyes a reflection of her own. 'But if the threat to your own life isn't enough, I'm happy to provide some extra motivation.'

He made a subtle gesture, and on his command the group gathered behind her walked forward as one – moving past Morrigan, past Squall himself, and stopping at the balustrade, shoulder to shoulder, peering out into the darkness.

Morrigan was reminded of the first time she'd come to the Hotel Deucalion, on Morningtide, the first day of the new Age. That had been a joyous occasion, and had ended – to her amazement – with all the guests climbing up on the balustrade, umbrellas held aloft, and taking a leap of faith off the rooftop. Stepping boldly! Every one of them had floated down, down, down, thirteen storeys to land on the ground, safe and unharmed.

As if he could see the picture in her mind, Squall raised both hands in a swift, flicking motion. Morrigan gasped as in one jerky movement, the entire group jumped up with both feet and landed neatly on the rail.

Squall turned to smile at her. 'Do you think they brought their brollies?'

'Stop – no! Hawthorne, get down. *Get down.* Jupiter!' She ran forward and tugged at Hawthorne's hand, then Jupiter's, trying to pull them back onto the rooftop, but they wouldn't budge. She spun round to face Squall in fury and frustration. 'Why are you doing this?!'

'I told you already.' He spoke so quietly she had to move forward to hear him over the sound of blood rushing in her ears. '*You're* doing this. If you were half the Wundersmith you ought to be by now, it wouldn't be possible for me to tap into your power like this. You must understand: your lack of control this year has been a very useful window into Nevermoor for me, and by *teaching* you control – by teaching you anything at all – I am likely shutting that window for good. But the fun is over. My long-term plans are much more important, and I *need you alive.*'

'Let them go,' Morrigan repeated. She ground the words between her teeth, trying to make her panic sound like wrath, and pressing her hands into fists.

'Gladly,' said Squall in a low, calm voice. 'And I'll also show you where your friends are, as promised. But first, you must channel some of that surplus Wunder into learning the Wretched Art of Inferno, otherwise you, and they –' he gestured to the line of unwitting sleepwalkers on the rail, '– and the oracle, and the mesmerist, and the angel, and the professor may all meet a spectacularly unpleasant end tonight. It's up to you, Miss Crow.'

Morrigan said nothing. She couldn't speak. Something inside her felt heavy and hot. She pressed a hand to her chest, her breaths coming in jagged bursts.

'THERE!' Squall shouted, pointing at her. His eyes were suddenly wild. 'There. That feeling. That fire in your heart, that spark of anger and fear. Focus on it. Feel it. The flickering, burning anger inside – THAT is Inferno.

'Now close your eyes and imagine reaching into your chest. Imagine closing your fist around that flame and holding it in your fingers like a cage. Close your eyes. DO IT.'

Reluctantly, Morrigan squeezed her eyes shut. She could see it in her mind's eye: it was more than a spark, it was a bonfire. Searing her from the inside out, creeping into her lungs and burning at the back of her throat. The taste of ashes. She shook her head, balling her hands into fists.

'I can't.'

'You can,' Squall insisted. 'You are a Wundersmith. You are in control of that fire. It shrinks and grows on *your* command. You must decide if it will light a candle, or burn down a city.'

In her mind's eye, Morrigan could see it. A beacon of bright golden flames burning behind her ribcage. She imagined closing her fingers around it, just as he said – controlling it, dousing it gently. The fire hissed, and Morrigan imagined sparks of shimmer-bright Wunder shooting out from between her fingers, like tiny fireworks. She flinched.

'If you are afraid of it, then you are not in *control* of it,' Squall shouted. 'You are not a *mouse,* Morrigan Crow. You are a *dragon*. Now open your eyes. Focus. And *breathe.*'

Morrigan did so. Blazing up from her lungs came a breath like a wind in the desert. This was not the wild, uncontainable fireball that nearly consumed Heloise that day at Wunsoc. This, at last, was something Morrigan could control.

In that instant, she knew what to do. She knew that Wunder would obey her.

Her gaze settling on a single tapered black candle, Morrigan exhaled a thin stream of fire, purposeful and precise. It found its target. The wick blazed into life – and then, as if they had been waiting for a sign, waiting for Morrigan's permission, the hundreds of unlit candles covering the rooftop lit up once more, in perfect unison. The rooftop was filled with a warm, flickering glow.

A surprised laugh spilled from Morrigan's mouth.

She had done this. Not him.

She turned to Squall. The firelight reflected in his dark eyes, and though he didn't smile, the look of grim satisfaction was unmistakeable.

He began to hum. Just a few sweet notes, barely recognisable as a song, but enough to make the back of Morrigan's neck prickle. The sound was answered by a long and haunting howl, somewhere out in the darkness.

'I did what you wanted.' Morrigan eyed him warily. 'We made a deal. You said you'd tell me where my friends are.'

'Actually, no,' said Squall. 'I said I'd *show* you where your friends are, and I intend to keep that promise.' With another careful flicker of movement from Squall, the people on the balustrade jumped off backwards onto the rooftop. They returned, expressionless, to their original positions in the séance circle. Another howl pierced the air. Morrigan thought it sounded like it came from somewhere far below them, down in the street. 'Shall we go?' He cocked his head towards the edge of the roof, as if he intended for the two of them to leap off and fly all the way to the Ghastly Market.

Morrigan barked an incredulous half-laugh. 'Are you mad? I'm not going *anywhere* with you. You're going to tell me where Cadence and Lambeth are.'

He gave a little shake of his head. 'I think not.'

Another howl from below – closer this time. It sounded like it was coming from the hotel forecourt. And there was something else. The braying of a horse, and the clattering of hooves on stone.

'I'm *not* going with you,' she said again. 'Do you think I'm an idiot?'

'Yes. I think you're precisely the kind of idiot who would do something stupid to save her friends.' Squall's smile was pitying. 'And I'll prove it.'

He made a small, casual gesture with his left hand, and then . . .

It all happened too quickly for Morrigan to even think.

Hawthorne was suddenly running from his place in the frozen circle, heading straight for the rooftop's edge at full pelt.

'Hawthorne, *no!*' she shrieked. Gripped by instinct and terror, Morrigan ran after him without even making the decision to do so. She reached out to grasp at Hawthorne just as he leapt joltingly up the balustrade and, seizing the back of his coat, was yanked forward by his momentum. Together they tumbled from the roof and plummeted down, down, down, Morrigan's screams muffled by pillows of cold autumnal air.

CHAPTER TWENTY-FIVE

Traitor

It felt as if the ground was rising to meet them.

Morrigan closed her eyes as they sped downwards and, still gripping Hawthorne's coat as if that might somehow save them both, she waited for the moment of impact. Waited to shatter every bone in her body when it hit the hotel forecourt.

But the moment didn't come.

A chorus of howls erupted from the darkness below. A piercing bray of horses, a clash of hooves. Morrigan's eyes flew open just in time to see a hundred fiery eyes staring up at her, and the shadowy figures of horses, hounds and huntsmen emerging from a roiling cloud of smoke.

Morrigan and Hawthorne didn't crash. They didn't land, didn't lose even a second of momentum. They fell into the amorphous black cloud that was the Hunt of Smoke and

Shadow, and never met the ground. Morrigan was once again astride a shadow horse, galloping through the near-deserted streets of Nevermoor at a pace so fast, it was impossible to register where they were headed. She glanced across and saw Hawthorne on the horse next to hers. Morrigan wondered if any part of him understood what was happening, if he in his puppet state could feel the terror she felt.

When they stopped at last, shaken but whole, they slid from their mounts, finally feeling solid ground beneath their feet. The black fog that cradled and surrounded them cleared to reveal an imposing stone building. Etched into the stone, above the grand arching entry, were five words that made her heart sink.

THE MUSEUM OF STOLEN MOMENTS

She stooped to catch Hawthorne as he collapsed to the ground, trying to prop him upright. 'Are you okay?'

'I . . . think so. Yeah.' He was dazed, but seemed to at least be himself again. 'What—what happened? Where are we?'

The Hunt of Smoke and Shadow withdrew, but didn't leave. Their glowing red eyes peered out of the darkness as they skulked nearby, half-hidden and watchful. Morrigan looked around for a sign of Squall, but they seemed to be alone.

She gazed up at the museum. The doorway was open, and noise drifted out from inside. Laughter and chatter. The clinking of champagne glasses. 'This is where Ezra Squall brought me before. I think we've found where the Ghastly Market is being held tonight.'

Hawthorne made a strange choking sound. '*How*?'

'Squall,' she whispered. 'He was on the rooftop – during the séance – do you remember any of it?'

He shook his head. 'I don't know. I remember we stood up to leave. We were laughing. And then . . . it's like I was suddenly dreaming. There was something in my head, like a strange voice, but I felt calm. I just wanted to go to sleep.'

'That was him. The voice in your head, that was Squall.' Hawthorne turned a ghostly shade of white at this news, but Morrigan went on. 'He made you jump off the rooftop, and I tried to stop you but we both fell, and the Hunt of Smoke and Shadow caught us and brought us here. Hawthorne, the Ghastly Market is happening *inside this building,* and they have Cadence and Lambeth and Professor Onstald . . . it's all Squall's doing and—'

'Get out of here!' came a hoarse whisper that made them both jump. 'Shoo!'

A lone figure had emerged from the museum and was scuttling down the steps towards them. Morrigan tensed to run, grabbing Hawthorne's arm, but he stopped her.

'I think it's Mildmay,' he whispered, and then a little louder, 'Mildmay! Is the Stealth already here, have they found—'

'You have to run,' Mildmay said in a hushed voice as he approached. He took their arms and began steering them away, glancing over his shoulder at the open museum door. Morrigan felt a rush of relief even in her confusion. They wouldn't have to deal with this alone. If someone from the Society was there, help must already be on the way. Mildmay stopped when they reached the shadows. 'Get away from here, *now*.'

'Are the Stealth in there?' Morrigan pressed, trying to see over his shoulder. 'Are they shutting it down? They said they'd send a runner to fetch Jupiter when—'

'Please, Miss Crow, you have to leave here *now*. You have no idea how much danger you're in. If anyone sees you – if he knows you're here . . .'

'If who knows?'

'The Wundersmith,' hissed Mildmay. 'Don't you realise? He's trying to lure you here, he wanted me to bring you myself but I . . . I couldn't. I wouldn't do it any more.'

Morrigan's head was spinning. 'Squall wanted *you* to bring me here? Why would he— what do you mean, you wouldn't do it any—'

Oh.

Morrigan's mouth dropped open and stayed there.

My little Society puppet. That's what Squall had said. *My pair of willing hands.*

'You! You're the one who's been helping Squall all this time.'

There was a soft intake of breath from Hawthorne. Mildmay looked as if he might be sick. Sweaty and faintly greenish, he trembled. But he didn't deny it.

'Miss Crow . . . please.' He bit back a whimpering sound. 'You have to believe me, I'm so very sorry for what I've— for my part in . . .' He was wringing his hands, his forehead wrinkled like a puppy. Morrigan thought he looked genuinely upset. But was he upset at what he'd done, she wondered, or just that he'd been discovered? 'I never . . . none of this was my idea! Squall, he forced me.'

He ran a hand through his hair, his chin quivering and eyes watering in a way that made Morrigan feel revulsion instead of pity.

'I was weak,' he continued. 'I admit it. I was bitter and jealous. Everyone knows I'm the weakest in my unit. The boring one. *Map boy,* that's what they always called me.' His face twisted into something ugly. 'I wanted to be important, so when the Wundersmith came to me, when he asked for my help – *me,* of all people! – I thought I'd found a way to get back at them. Squall's the most powerful man in the Wintersea Republic! He promised me a place in his empire, a seat at his right side – how could I turn that down?' He paused. 'At first all I had to do was pass on bits of information. I didn't know anyone was going to get hurt. You have to believe me.'

'What sort of information?'

'Rare knacks. Who had them. Where they lived, their daily routine, that sort of thing. When they were –' his next words were barely audible, '– when they were likely to be alone.'

'Who to kidnap and how to kidnap them, in other words,' said Morrigan, and her voice shook with anger.

Mildmay rubbed the back of his neck, still unable to look at her.

Hawthorne made a strange sort of stifled noise. His jaw was working overtime, clenching and unclenching, and Morrigan could tell he was trying to bite back his own fury. Hawthorne was just about the most loyal person she knew.

'You arranged for them to be snatched by the Bonesmen and put up for sale,' he hissed at Mildmay. 'You make me sick.'

Mildmay looked distraught. '*Please* – don't you see I'm trying to help you? Morrigan, the Wundersmith wanted me to set you up too. But I refused. I couldn't do that to you, not to my best student. I refused to work for him any more. That's why I'm here! I knew he would try to lure you to the Ghastly Market tonight, so I've been waiting outside, hoping to stop you. I couldn't let them sell you too, I just—'

'But you'd let them sell Cadence! And Lambeth!' Morrigan shouted, then dropped her voice to a harsh whisper. 'How *could* you, Mildmay?'

The young teacher sobbed, and his eyes were beseeching. 'I'm sorry. I can't explain it. I was just . . . I was sick of being on the outside, Miss Crow. You know what that feels like, don't you? To be different. We're the same, you and I, we—'

'Morrigan's nothing like you!' Hawthorne spat back at Mildmay, and Mildmay flinched. 'She would never betray her friends.'

The teacher dropped to his knees, shaking, and covered his face with his hands. Several moments passed in near silence, his quiet heaving sobs the only sound other than a distant hum of civilised chatter from inside the museum.

And then . . . the sound of someone clapping.

'Bravo, Henry,' came a soft voice from the darkness. 'What a performance.'

Mildmay jumped frantically to his feet, whirling on the spot to see who'd spoken. His eyes grew wide as Ezra Squall stepped into the light, a sinister smile curving one corner of his mouth. His solo round of applause rang out in the street. Morrigan felt Hawthorne draw nearer and dig his fingernails into her arm, heard his breathing speed up. Since he didn't remember anything from the rooftop, this was, she realised, the first time her friend had ever really come face to face with the Wundersmith.

'He came here on the Gossamer,' she whispered to Hawthorne, squinting to see the tell-tale shimmer of light that was surrounding Squall and trying to sound braver than she felt. 'He can't touch us.'

'Yeah, but his Hunt can,' Hawthorne pointed out, barely moving his mouth. As if on cue, a low growl emanated from the shadows surrounding them. Morrigan shivered.

Squall whistled soft and low, and the wolves appeared. They circled Mildmay, fur black as pitch and eyes like glowing embers, and the teacher cowered away from them, a shrunken man.

Squall sneered down at him. 'Henry would love for you to believe he was trying to save you from the auction, Miss Crow, but he knows I didn't bring you here to be sold. He knows I set up this entire affair so that *you* could be the hero who shut it down. So that you can finally become the Wundersmith they all fear you will. You need to be allowed to start using the powers you have been gifted,' said Squall, raising his voice even louder, 'before the Wunder you've been gathering becomes as bored as I am and CHOKES THE LIFE RIGHT OUT OF YOU.'

Morrigan jumped at those shrill words. Her heart pounded somewhere in the region of her throat.

'Please, Morrigan,' implored Mildmay. His eyes were red and swollen. 'Don't listen to him. Run. Just *run away.*'

'Oh, well done, Mr Mildmay, very well done.' Squall let out a high-pitched giggle like a madman. '*Henry* here has decided it's against his interests to allow you to shut down the Ghastly Market, Miss Crow. It's become quite the little earner for you, hasn't it, dear boy? You're getting yourself a reputation among Nevermoor's wealthiest and most nefarious. Wouldn't want to let them down, would you?' Squall paused, turned to look directly at Morrigan, and spoke slowly. 'Do you understand what I'm saying, Miss Crow? He. Is. Trying. To. Stall. You. He means to keep you out here until the auction is over and the sale of your friends has earned him a decent fee. He's been taking a cut of every sale.'

Morrigan watched Mildmay closely. As Squall spoke, a strange transformation was taking place. Her teacher's boyish, tear-stained face – screwed up in distress and red from sobbing – began to relax. He wiped his eyes with the sleeves of his shirt. With a big dramatic sniff, his face split into a familiar, slightly sheepish grin.

It was all so Mildmayish, Morrigan thought, a chill creeping down her neck. Yet somehow not like Mildmay at all. Somehow, it was like looking at a total stranger.

He chuckled. He checked his wristwatch. He *shrugged*.

'Well, that ought to have done the trick.' All the usual heartiness had returned to his voice. 'They should be just about sold by now, I think. Thank you for your time,

Miss Crow. You always were my most attentive student.' He took a deep bow, still laughing.

Morrigan felt hot, angry tears spring to her eyes. She couldn't speak; she could barely think. She bared her teeth and, with a snarl like a raging unnimal, launched herself at Mildmay, knocking him to the ground.

'Traitor!' she screamed and lunged at him again, no longer caring who heard. She could almost feel the rage boiling inside her veins. Hawthorne stepped between them, trying to pull her away.

'I should remind you that this isn't one of the Society's silly little tests, Miss Crow,' said Squall. He stood apart from them, skirting the edge of the shadows. 'This is real life. If you fail, there will be real consequences. Tick tock.'

Taking great heaving breaths, Morrigan looked from Mildmay sprawled on the ground, to Hawthorne, his eyes wide, to the Museum of Stolen Moments. The sound of murmuring chatter from inside the building had quietened a little. Were they already too late? 'Hawthorne. Let's go.'

'Mildmay will get away,' he said. 'We have to get the Stealth and—'

'We have to get Cadence and Lambeth and the others.' She glanced down at Mildmay, who seemed suddenly panicked. A deep, reverberating growl filled the air. The Hunt of Smoke and Shadow was emerging from the dark.

The two friends ran. Only when they'd reached the museum steps did Morrigan look back, turning at the sound of a sudden unearthly howl. Through the darkness, she saw a hundred red eyes, burning like fire.

'I'll take care of our dear friend Henry,' Squall's cold voice rang out from the shadows. 'Never fear.'

CHAPTER TWENTY-SIX

The Auction

They ran up the steps and into the museum entrance hall. It was empty and bare, except for a table of masks, like at the last market. Morrigan grabbed the first one she saw – a screaming ghoul – and hastily pulled it over her head.

'Here,' she whispered, handing a glittery court-jester mask to Hawthorne. 'Put this on, quick.'

'What do you think will happen to him?' The grinning rubber face couldn't disguise the tension in his voice.

'Who, Mildmay?' said Morrigan, trying her best to sound unconcerned about the fate of her once-favourite teacher. Her eyes flicked back to the open door. 'Nothing good.'

They followed the sound of voices into an antechamber that led to the main hall. Morrigan was desperate to run straight through this room and into the next, where she thought the auction must be taking place, but she knew better than to draw attention. There were masked guests dotted all around, drinking and laughing and occasionally pausing to admire a globe as if it were art.

It was surprisingly easy to blend in, even though Morrigan was at least a head shorter than everyone there. Hawthorne had fortunately shot up like a weed this past summer, and his shoulders were broader than she remembered, probably from his many hours of dragonriding training. It put him almost on a height with some of the adults, much to Morrigan's relief.

'This is *bonkers*,' Hawthorne whispered from behind his mask as they made their way across the room as slowly and calmly as they could bear. 'I mean, these globes – once you know what they are – are just . . .'

Morrigan felt too queasy to respond. How had she not seen the truth about this place immediately, she wondered. Some of the scenes inside the glass were quiet and subtle, easy to misinterpret. But there were also scenes of unmistakable death and destruction. A stampede of elephants, kicking up dust as they barrelled towards a waterhole crowded with wildlife. A cresting tidal wave, about to decimate an entire village. A muddy, blood-spattered battlefield with cannonballs in flight. Morrigan shook her head.

'Marvellous,' mused one portly man in a tuxedo, examining a nearby globe. He wore a white, featureless mask that made him look like death itself. 'All real, you know. Real people in there.'

He tapped on the glass, peering inside as if it were a zoo enclosure. 'Caught in the moments just before their deaths. The auctioneer told me. Extraordinary thing.'

'Oh. Intriguing.' The woman with him sounded only mildly interested. 'Can they hear us, do you think?'

'Good question.' He tapped on the glass again. A group had gathered round him now, watching. 'I say, you in there, dead chap – can you hear me? Blink once for yes, twice for no.' The group guffawed as if he had said something tremendously funny.

'Dying chap, you mean.' The woman gave a foul little giggle. 'Not quite dead yet, surely. That's the point!'

Morrigan felt sick to her stomach. At Hawthorne's insistent tug of her elbow, she kept walking, staring resolutely ahead, determined not to look at the scene inside the globe. But as they reached the door to the main hall, she couldn't help herself, and glanced back.

It was a teenage boy, maybe sixteen or seventeen, in a brocade jacket and tall black boots. He was riding on horseback down a cobbled street, and perhaps his horse had got a fright or something, because it was rearing back, the whites of its eyes showing. The boy looked equally terrified. He'd been thrown from his saddle and was about to land on the cobblestones at such an angle, and with such force, that anyone could see . . .

Morrigan swallowed, blinking back tears.

She couldn't bear it. The disgust, the unfairness of it all – of the Museum of Stolen Moments, of Mildmay's betrayal, of the Ghastly Market itself. Morrigan felt like there was a wild creature living inside her, clawing to get out. Squall's words rang in her ears.

You are not a mouse, Morrigan Crow. You are a dragon.

She wanted to do something to help these people, trapped in death. And she wanted Mildmay brought to justice. She wanted to unleash, wanted to sweep away the horror of this place, wanted to make those masked idiots *stop laughing* – but she had to bite it down, to clamp a lid tight on her anger.

'Cadence and Lambeth,' she whispered to herself. 'You're here for your friends. Don't get distracted.'

Morrigan closed her eyes and imagined reaching into her chest and caging the fire that lived there, gently dousing its heat. Just a little.

The lost souls of the museum would have to wait.

Hawthorne gasped loudly as they entered a second, much larger hall. He tried to cover it up with a cough, while subtly pointing to the ceiling. Morrigan looked up, filled with dread.

The hall was arranged to highlight the lots up for sale, raised high on platforms so they could be seen by the entire crowd – and so they couldn't escape. The only way Morrigan could see to bring the platforms down was by a system of heavy chains and pulleys, each of them attended by a pair of brutish security guards in skull masks.

Just like Alfie in his giant fish tank, they had each been made the centrepiece of a grotesque display, a mockery of their unique knacks. Professor Onstald, at the farthest end, was chained to the minute hand of a giant clock, currently positioned at five minutes to the hour so that he was, at least, nearly upright. Morrigan wondered how many hours he'd been there, and how many revolutions of the clock face he'd already made, the blood rushing unpleasantly to his head and back all the time. How long could he bear it?

Cadence, on a platform against the wall to their right, had been dressed in flowing silks of radiant purple and lots of heavy gold jewellery. Beside her stood an enormous golden lamp, and Morrigan blinked at the thing, trying to make sense of what she was seeing.

'Ugh. They've dressed her as a *genie*,' said Hawthorne, disgusted. 'Is that what they think a mesmerist is? Someone who goes around granting wishes, obeying orders? They've obviously never met Cadence before.'

Morrigan suddenly realised that at some point Hawthorne had begun to remember Cadence. She wondered what had changed. Was it the *Recognising Mesmerism* lessons kicking in at last? Or was it because he and Cadence had finally – sort of – become friends?

Hawthorne craned his neck to look around the room. 'Oh! Look – up there. Is that him? The one Jupiter's been looking for?'

He was looking almost directly above them, where an angel (*celestial being*, Morrigan silently corrected herself) seemed to be hovering in midair. A closer look, however, revealed that he'd been bound with heavy rope at the joint where his wings met. He was dangling from the ceiling, his wingspan forcibly displayed at its most impressive, hands tied behind his back. Spinning idly from fishing wire all around him were fake clouds made of cut-out plywood covered in cotton balls, like the scenery from a bad play.

Morrigan blinked. It wasn't Cassiel. Morrigan had no idea what Cassiel looked like, but she knew this wasn't him.

Because it was Israfel.

She shook her head. There was no time to ponder this now.

'They've tied Cadence's hands,' Hawthorne observed, scowling. 'And taped her mouth shut. Are they trying to stop her mesmerising them?'

Morrigan saw that he was right – and that Israfel's mouth was also taped, to stop him singing his way out.

At the other end of the hall, the crowd was migrating from beneath Onstald's platform to Lambeth's. She was perched on a throne in the centre of her platform, wearing an elaborate golden crown that was far too big for her head. Her eyes were wide as she looked down at the bidders, and she gripped the arms of her throne as if it were the only thing keeping her afloat in an ocean full of sharks. She was whispering something, over and over.

Morrigan narrowed her eyes, trying to make out what she was saying. Was it a prayer? A plea for help? Something in her heart squeezed. *Poor, tiny, terrified Lambeth.*

'Gather round, ladies and gentlemen, gather round,' yelled the auctioneer. He had a jolly, grandfatherly voice that carried across the room – but, fittingly, he wore the mask of a wolf.

Lambeth's voice became louder and more panicky as she repeated her line of gibberish. Morrigan could *just* make out the words now.

'Calling. Dying. Freezing. Burning. Flying,' she was saying, over and over, shaking on her throne. 'Calling. Dying. Freezing. Burning. Flying.'

Hawthorne frowned. 'What does that mean?'

'Before I open the bidding on our final item I must, once again, thank you for coming to our humble little auction. You are the very worst and the very richest people we could think to invite, and for those two reasons it's been wonderful to have you here.' There were peals of laughter and a long round of applause for this terrible joke. Morrigan felt Hawthorne grip her arm, and she wondered if he was telling her not to react, or trying not to react himself.

'Final item,' she whispered to him, feeling something tighten in her chest. 'So they've already sold the others.' And sure enough, the guards by Cadence's platform began to lower it, heaving on the enormous metal chain.

Panic gripped Morrigan like a great, icy hand. What should they do? What *could* they do? If they ran to help Cadence, they would give themselves away and leave Lambeth to her fate. If they went to help Lambeth – well, even if they could somehow reach her up high, then Cadence would be gone before they could get to *her*. And what about Onstald? And Israfel?

She had never felt more helpless. Squall had set this whole thing up, had put her in this terrible position, because he hoped she would put her knowledge of the Wretched Arts to use. But what good were her measly talents here? She could call Wunder. She could *light some candles*, for goodness' sake. But it had been Squall who'd fought off the Charlton Five's attack; Squall who'd transformed the Magnificub. What could Morrigan do?

You can call Wunder, she told herself. *You can do that. Start with that.*

'*Morningtide's child is merry and mild*,' she sang quietly. Her voice wobbled. Hawthorne turned to look at her in alarm. '*Eventide's child is wicked and wild—*'

'Morrigan—?'

'*Shhh.*' Morrigan closed her eyes. It wasn't answering. She couldn't feel it. Why wasn't it *working*? '*Morningtide's child arrives with the dawn.*'

The auctioneer in the wolf mask was working the crowd. 'You have waited patiently for this one, I know, and your considerable, sickening wealth is no doubt burning a hole in your collective pockets—'

'*Eventide's child brings gale and storm . . .*'

'—and so, let us begin. May I present our most anticipated lot in the history of the Ghastly Market: Her Royal Highness, Princess Lamya Bethari Amati Ra.'

Morrigan stopped singing. Hawthorne grew completely still. *Princess who?*

'A member of the Royal House of Ra in Far East Sang, Princess Lamya is fourth in line to inherit the throne from her grandmother, the Queen. When the Royal House of Ra learned that their spare was a short-range oracle, they sent her off to be educated by our fancy friends at the Wundrous Society.' There were jeers from the crowd. 'In doing so, they committed high treason against the ruling Wintersea Party – who, according to my Republic sources, seem to be under the impression that little Princess Lamya is bedridden due to frail health. The enterprising Queen Ama has paid off some poor village waif to laze about in the palace for a few years, pretending to be her granddaughter!'

Morrigan couldn't believe what she was hearing. Lambeth wasn't from the Free State. She was from one of the four states of the Wintersea Republic, just like her. She wasn't meant to be here! And she was a *princess*!

'I did think she seemed a bit posh,' whispered Hawthorne. 'Shhh.'

Morrigan's father worked for the Wintersea Party, so she had some idea of what they were like. If it was true – if Lambeth really *was* a member of the royal family in Far East Sang, and if they really had smuggled her out of the Republic, against Wintersea Party law – she was in even greater danger than they'd realised. People in the Republic weren't even allowed to know the Free State existed.

'*Where are you going, o son of the morning?*' Morrigan sang. She could barely get the words out, she was shaking so badly.

The auctioneer confirmed her suspicions. 'It's bad news for the entire House of Ra if the Wintersea Party finds out.' He mimed getting his head chopped off, and the audience burst into appreciative laughter. 'Treason is of course punishable by execution in the Wintersea Republic. That makes this prize all the more valuable – the possibilities are endless, folks.'

'We have to do something,' Hawthorne hissed. 'We've got to cause a distraction, or . . . or something! Morrigan, *help*.'

But Morrigan wasn't listening. '*Up with the sun where the winds are warming.*' Eyes squeezed shut, she tried to block out the auctioneer, and Hawthorne, and the obnoxious crowd, and pay attention to how the air felt around her. '*Where are you going, o daughter of—*'

She stopped. It was working. It was here.

Subtle at first – just a ripple in the atmosphere. A tingle in her fingertips.

And then she opened her eyes, and the world had turned so golden-bright it was like standing on the sun.

'Once you've acquired Princess Lamya's extremely rare and useful knack,' continued the auctioneer, grinning maliciously, 'you may wish to ransom her back to her family, or hold on to her for blackmail purposes, or sell her to the Wintersea Party and watch the House of Ra topple! Do what you will, ladies and gents, but we're setting the price high. We'll start with fifteen thousand kred. Do I hear fifteen thousand?'

It was a different feeling to before. When Morrigan had first called Wunder in this room, the sensation of holding raw power in her hands had swiftly given way to a total lack of control. She hadn't known what to do with the Wunder once she'd called it, and it *knew that*. Somehow it knew, and it had mutinied.

This was not that. This was seamless.

The Wunder that gathered to her now was perfectly aligned with her intention. Her righteous anger at everything that had happened tonight – everything that had happened this *year* – had at last given it the purpose it craved. Morrigan thought of Mildmay's greed and betrayal. She thought of the cruelty of Mathilde Lachance, imprisoning people within their own deaths. She thought of Ezra Squall, who'd been pulling her strings like a puppet all this time, who'd arranged this nightmare just so Morrigan could be the one to end it. And she thought of the casual malice – the *evil* – of anyone who thought they had the right to buy and sell a knack, to buy and sell a *life*.

The nearest globe shattered and its contents burst spectacularly into the room.

It was the young men in the motorcar, spinning out of control as they screamed in terror, and smashing into another globe.

The auctioneer and the bidders barely had a moment to register what had happened before the second globe spilled its tragedy out across the floor – a boat on a storm-tossed, lightning-struck sea, its crew overwhelmed. The vessel came to a grinding crash and took another globe out with it – a woman engulfed by a swarm of bees. And then another – an avalanche of rocks tumbling down onto the roof of a cabin. Then another, and another.

Morrigan had set off a domino effect. She quickly realised these scenes of destruction were bigger than the globes that contained them. They grew as they gained their freedom, merging together to create a chaos that was now rapidly filling the hall. The stampeding elephants split the crowd in two.

A Great White Shark lurched from its shattered glass prison amidst a cacophony of screams.

The auction guests scrambled to find safety, but the tumult was relentless. Globes smashed one after the other – an angry mob, a duel to the death, a frenzied battlefield.

Morrigan stared as this horror unfolded in a matter of moments.

What had she *done*?

She'd only wanted to cause a distraction. She thought she could save her friends *and* free the people inside the globes, to finally let them rest in peace. But this wasn't just a distraction – it was *madness*. How could she help Lambeth and Cadence now? She couldn't get anywhere near them. She wouldn't even be able to save *herself* from this.

'MORRIGAN!'

Hawthorne lurched towards her, grabbing hold just as a nearby globe broke open and unleashed an ocean wave bigger and more terrifying than anything Morrigan had seen in her life. The two friends clung to each other, unable to do anything but stare at the wall of water that crested above them, waiting for it to crash. They couldn't possibly survive this.

And then everything just . . . stopped.

The deafening noise of screams, and bellowing unnimals, and rushing water, all went suddenly, deathly quiet. The tsunami above their heads slowed to an imperceptible speed, almost quivering with tension. All Morrigan could hear was the sound of her own heartbeat and Hawthorne's rapid breathing.

The silence was broken by a weak, wheezing voice from across the hall.

'Hurry! I can't . . . hold it . . . much . . . longer.'

CHAPTER TWENTY-SEVEN

None Sing So Wildly Well

Professor Onstald looked directly at Morrigan from where he was tied to the clock face, and gave one slow, deliberate blink of his shiny eyes.

He'd done it again. Slowed the world to a crawl. It was as if a great cosmic giant had pressed a finger to the planet, holding it back from its normal speed of orbit.

It was the second time in as many days that Morrigan had witnessed Onstald's extraordinary talent. But this time . . . this time was *so* much stranger.

Then, there had been books and papers and a clock ticking on the wall, and Mildmay, and Morrigan herself, almost frozen in time.

Now, Morrigan somehow remained untouched by the phenomenon – as did Hawthorne, still clinging to her – while the pandemonium around them stood perfectly still. The tidal wave curled above their heads. There was a lightning strike, white-hot and blinding, stuck in the moment of splitting a giant fir tree right down its centre. There were people in masks and fancy clothes everywhere she looked, unable to move, caught up in scenes of destruction they couldn't escape. There was an *iceberg* – nearly as tall as the ceiling – threatening to crush everything in its path. All those stolen moments had become one enormous frozen tableau, one giant mess of a snow globe.

'What is HAPPENING?' shouted Hawthorne, his voice echoing in the vast, silent hall. His breathing was so sharp and fierce Morrigan thought he might hyperventilate. 'Did you do that? Did you make it stop?'

'No.' She suddenly realised that in the hurried mess of Hallowmas, she'd somehow forgotten to tell Hawthorne the details of yesterday's episode with the tortoisewun. 'It's Professor Onstald. This is his knack.'

Hawthorne seemed to take this revelation in his stride.

'How are we going to free them?' he asked, jumping into action. He led Morrigan out from underneath the wave, weaving a path through a clutch of masked guests who'd frozen in their attempt to make a run for it. 'I could try to climb that chain up to Lambeth, and you go help Cadence, and then—'

'No.' Morrigan stopped. 'No – wait a second.'

Lambeth's words were repeating in her head.

Calling. Dying. Freezing. Burning. Flying.

Those weren't just nonsense words that she'd been jabbering out of fear. Morrigan should have known better. The radar in Lambeth's mind had tuned into something. She was describing the strangeness she saw on the horizon, in the only way she could understand it.

Calling. Morrigan had called Wunder.

Dying. Everyone here was dying, a hundred times over in a hundred different ways.

Freezing. Onstald had frozen time.

That left—

'Burning,' she whispered. 'Flying.'

And in speaking those two words aloud, Morrigan was struck by a moment of pure clarity. She knew exactly what to do, because her next steps had been laid out before her by Lambeth, the oracle.

'Hawthorne,' she said. 'Go. Help Cadence. Her platform's nearly at the ground – climb up and untie her, and then you'll need to carry her out of here. Go back the way we came, right out of the museum. Get as far away as you can.'

Hawthorne shook his head. 'But – you're coming too, aren't you?'

'I have to help Israfel first. No time to explain.' She saw the obstinate look on his face and said more forcefully, 'Hawthorne, go! Help Cadence. Onstald can't hold on forever.'

'But what about Lambeth, and Onstald?'

'I'll take care of them, just *go*.'

Despite his obvious doubts, Hawthorne turned and ran as fast as he could through the mire of catastrophes, heading for Cadence.

Morrigan looked to where Israfel was held up high by the rope tied around the joint of his wings, right between his shoulderblades.

Step four. *Burning*.

She could do this. Before Squall's visit to the rooftop that night, Morrigan would never have believed it. But now she knew – Wunder was with her. It *wanted* to help her.

She closed her eyes, picturing that spark of energy inside, the caged flame in her chest. There was no time to think too hard about it, no time to worry if it would work. She didn't have the luxury of worry. The flickering grew brighter with Morrigan's certainty and, opening her eyes, she exhaled fire.

The *precision* of it was exhilarating – that feeling of perfect alignment with the source of her power. The rope around Israfel's wings burned through in the exact spot she'd intended it to, but he didn't drop. Israfel stayed aloft only because Professor Onstald's knack was keeping him there. Her first success singing through her bloodstream, giddy with self-belief, Morrigan tried again with the rope binding his wrists, and somehow – miraculously – it worked exactly as she'd hoped. She didn't even sear his skin.

They didn't have long. Morrigan could feel a tremor in the air, as if time itself was quaking. Onstald couldn't control it much longer.

'Israfel,' she called up to the angel in a clear, strong voice. She knew he could hear and see what was happening around him, because she'd experienced it herself in Onstald's classroom. The world had stopped, her body had frozen, but her mind had been unaffected. 'Listen to me. You're going to unfreeze in just a few moments. I need you to fly to Lambeth – to Princess Lamya. Take her and get out of here.' She pointed to Lambeth's platform. Israfel said nothing, of course, but Morrigan felt certain he'd understood. His deep brown eyes were fixed on hers.

She heard a wheezing, grunting sound behind her. Hawthorne had returned, half-dragging, half-carrying the statue-like Cadence with him.

'I thought I told you to go straight—'

But she was drowned out by the horrendous, creaking groan of the iceberg shifting, a sound like the world itself was about to end. Time was speeding up again. Grindingly slow at first, but picking up speed.

'GO!' Morrigan shouted at Hawthorne.

'No!' he insisted. 'We're not leaving without you, idiot.'

Cadence was slowly coming back to herself. She swayed on the spot, almost knocking Hawthorne over, but he caught her just in time and propped her up.

There was a sound of beating wings from above; Israfel, too, had unfrozen and launched magnificently into the air, heading directly for Lambeth's platform, just as instructed.

'Hawthorne, *go*,' Morrigan insisted. 'Cadence, get him out of here. I know what I'm doing. I'll be right behind you, I promise.'

He stared at her a moment, tight-lipped and white-faced, then nodded reluctantly, and ran with Cadence into the antechamber.

It was a lie, of course. Morrigan did *not* know what she was doing.

But she had to try. Because ancient Professor Onstald, as much as he *despised* Morrigan, had used his last remaining strength and *stopped actual time* to save her and her friends. How could she leave him there alone?

'I'm coming to help you,' she called out to him, trying to see a path through the madness that was once again gaining momentum. If she could reach the chain that controlled Onstald's platform . . . well, what then? She didn't know.

Morrigan screamed as the lightning-struck tree crashed to the ground right in front of her, nearly landing on her head and effectively blocking off Onstald's side of the room.

The tortoisewun could barely lift his head. He looked up at her and his wrinkled, leathery mouth formed a single word.

'RUN.'

Morrigan shook her head, her mind whirring – there must be a way to save him, there *must*!

Onstald gave a weak nod, his energy draining by the second.

'Go!' he ordered her. 'Run!'

Morrigan's heart sank, tears of frustration burning in her eyes. There was no way to get to him. This was it for Onstald, and he knew it, and he wasn't going to drag her down with him. He was saving her life.

A look of understanding passed between them, and then Morrigan turned and ran. Through the epic turmoil of the main hall, ducking low and scurrying like a mouse through a den of monsters. Through the antechamber, out of the entrance hall and into the cool, black night. She didn't stop running until she'd reached Hawthorne and Cadence, huddled a block away, trying to catch their breath. A handful of auction guests had also managed to escape and were melting into the darkness of the surrounding streets.

Morrigan looked back at the museum. Despite every danger and disaster she knew that building contained, strangely none of them spilled out. She wondered how long it would be until the chaos burned itself out, and the people she'd freed from the globes would finally be at rest.

The stunned silence was broken by the beating of wings as Israfel descended. He landed lightly beside her, Lambeth in his arms, shaken but safe.

'Thank you,' said Morrigan, still breathless. 'We need to . . . get the Stealth. Can you help?'

'You need to get away from here,' said Israfel. Hawthorne and Cadence jumped a little in surprise. His speaking voice was as Morrigan remembered it: like a memory of something lost. The golden veins in his black wings caught flashes of light from the museum, so that he seemed to glow. He looked exhausted. Morrigan remembered what Jupiter had told her about Israfel, that night at the Old Delphian. *People like Israfel absorb other people's emotions.* 'Stay together. Make your way back to the Hotel Deucalion. And – listen to me, this is important – you *must* cover your ears while you run. Press your hands against them as tight as you can, and don't let go until you're at least three blocks away. Understand?'

The others looked confused, but nodded in agreement.

They turned to run. As Morrigan watched the other three pace ahead of her, something made her pause.

Could they really just leave? The Museum of Stolen Moments was imploding, a hundred different death scenes toppling like dominos, all contained within the magic of its walls. The auction guests inside . . . they were the *very* worst kind of people, she knew, but still . . . did they really deserve to meet their end this way? Caught up in the churning chaos of other people's disasters? Shouldn't she *do* something?

And what about Professor Onstald? The tortoisewun had spent the last few months berating her, telling her how evil

Wundersmiths were . . . and yet he had sacrificed himself for her and her friends. He chose to save the life of a Wundersmith instead of his own.

'Morrigan Crow.' She turned back to see Israfel hovering behind her, suspended above the ground by the slow, rhythmic beating of his wings. His gaze was hard, but there was kindness in his eyes as he looked down at her . . . and something else. A raw bewilderment that Morrigan – who felt baffled by the world on a near daily basis – found deeply relatable. 'You saved my life tonight. I find myself in your debt.' He watched her for a moment, pressing his mouth into a line. Morrigan could tell he wanted to say something more, but wasn't sure if he should . . . or perhaps he couldn't quite find the right words. Israfel breathed a deep sigh. 'You'd do well not to mention that to the folks at Wunsoc. I shouldn't be in your debt.'

Morrigan didn't know what to say to that.

'It complicates things, you see?' he pressed, giving her a significant look. 'For both of us.'

She did not see, but Israfel was already rising into the air, turning back towards the museum where flashes of light illuminated the windows. There was a sound of shattering glass – another globe had broken – then a bright orange fireball, quickly doused by a crashing wave. Plumes of smoke curled from the windows like demons. A faint cry in the distance made the hair on Morrigan's neck stand up.

'What are you doing?' Morrigan called up to him. Tears pricked behind her eyes and her voice felt thick in her throat. Was he going to try to go back inside the building? Would he, too, get trapped in the maelstrom? 'Are you going to try to save them?'

'No,' he said. 'They're beyond saving.' His low, mournful voice carried to her on the wind, and pierced a little bit of her heart she didn't know existed.

'Then what are you—'

'Go home,' he commanded.

Morrigan heard Hawthorne, Cadence and Lambeth at the end of the street, calling her name. She covered her ears and turned to run, but again, something stopped her.

She looked back to see the Angel Israfel alight on the steps of the museum, a dark, distant figure silhouetted against the lightning-lit doorway. He stood there, unmoving, for several moments. Morrigan wondered what he could possibly be doing, and then . . . she remembered.

None sing so wildly well.

She remembered what Jupiter had told her, that night at the Old Delphian Music Hall.

A perfect and unbroken peace, he had said. *Loneliness and sadness will be a distant memory. Your heart will fill up, and you'll feel the world could never disappoint you again.*

Israfel couldn't save them.

He could only sing to them.

438

Jupiter had warned her about listening to Israfel. She knew she shouldn't.

But when would she ever have this chance again?

Morrigan let her hands fall away from her head. Above the sound of her friends calling her name, above the roaring of waves and the booming of cannons, above even the new sound of distant sirens coming closer . . . she heard the sweet, celestial voice of Israfel for the first time.

Just for a second. Just one note.

When Morrigan tried to recall – days and weeks and years later – the sound of that single note, the *feeling* of it, she would remember being warmed by the sun in winter, and held by a mother she'd never known. She'd remember a joyful, bone-deep certainty that she had never hurt another living being. That nobody had ever truly hurt her, and nobody ever could. She'd remember the smell of earth after rain.

She'd also remember what came next. The clatter of foot-steps on cobblestones, and the feel of strong hands closing fast over her ears, blocking out all sound. Looking up to see a pair of wide, wild blue eyes in a forest of ginger hair. The bittersweet feeling of crashing back to earth, knowing she would land somewhere safe.

CHAPTER TWENTY-EIGHT

Closing a Window

'Five arrests. A few bored rich people and a dodgy politician.' Jupiter sighed. 'More escaped, and unfortunately they were able to slip through the cracks among the chaos. Like the cockroaches they are. The ones who've been questioned are all claiming they were only there for the thrill of the thing, of course. None of them will confess to having bid on anything.'

Jupiter threw himself down onto one of the day beds in the Smoking Parlour. The walls were pouring out a gentle, almost buttery lemon smoke ('to increase mental sharpness and zest for life', according to the schedule on the door), which was slowly helping to cure Morrigan's brain fog. In the wake of last night's relentless havoc, her zest for life could probably do with a little tweaking. Currently the only zest she had was for staring at walls and eating bowls of chicken dumpling soup.

Jupiter took a deep whiff of lemon smoke, rubbing his eyes tiredly. After personally seeing Lambeth, Cadence and Hawthorne to their homes, and taking Morrigan back to the Deucalion, he'd gone straight back out to help the Stealth's investigation. It was past lunchtime already, and he hadn't slept at all.

When he'd emerged from his trance-like state on the Deucalion rooftop, dazed and befuddled, to find that Morrigan and Hawthorne had disappeared, he was instantly certain it had something to do with the Ghastly Market. He'd rallied everyone he could think of – his colleagues in the League of Explorers, members of his own unit, plus Fenestra, Frank, Kedgeree, Dame Chanda, Martha, Charlie and Jack – to help the Stink and the Stealth scour the darkest, most secret and most dangerous places they could think of. But to no avail . . . until the Stealth received another mysterious anonymous tip with the location of the Museum of Stolen Moments, which they found hidden behind a tangle of backstreets in a rundown, deserted part of the city.

Nobody knew who'd tipped them off, and Morrigan wasn't about to tell them it was probably Squall.

She got up to pour Jupiter some tea. 'But the ones who were arrested will go to prison, won't they?' she asked.

Jupiter gratefully accepted the cup Morrigan handed to him. She curled up in the armchair opposite, hugging a cushion to her chest. 'There's nothing to charge them with, Mog. No evidence of any wrongdoing. No record of money changing hands. Black market trading is illegal, but there's no evidence of any *actual* trading – not now that the museum is destroyed. They're all claiming they thought it was a party.' Jupiter made an angry growling noise in the back of his throat. 'Scum.'

'And Mildmay?'

'Mmm, speaking of scum.' He grimaced. 'Gone. Disappeared into thin air, as far as anyone can tell.'

'The Hunt of Smoke and Shadow,' Morrigan said simply. She'd already recounted her version of the night's events, though she wasn't sure how much of it Jupiter had chosen to share with the Stealth. 'Do you think they . . .' She couldn't bring herself to end that sentence. She wasn't even sure how she *meant* to end it. Finished him off? Chased him out of Nevermoor?

'Perhaps,' said Jupiter, ignoring the ambiguity. 'Though we didn't find any evidence of . . .' He trailed off also, and covered it by taking a sip of tea. 'So, who knows. Maybe he got away. If he's smart – and I think we can agree he must be reasonably cunning, to have fooled so many people – then he'll have run very far away by now, and he won't stop running. But not to worry, Mog. The Stealth haven't given up. They'll find him eventually, and he'll be brought to justice.'

442

Morrigan was silent for a while. 'I liked him. Before . . . you know.'

'I know.'

'He was my favourite teacher.'

'From a choice of two,' Jupiter pointed out. 'But yes. I know.'

He drank his tea, almost finishing the whole cup, while Morrigan tried to wrestle her thoughts into some sort of order.

'He was nice to me,' she said finally. 'Mildmay. He was funny, and his classes were fun, and I felt like I was good at something. And Professor Onstald . . . he hated me. He was horrible, all year long, and I felt like *I* was something horrible.' She swallowed hard against the lump forming in her throat. 'But Mildmay set up the Ghastly Market. He betrayed all of us. And Onstald saved my life.'

Jupiter stayed quiet.

'I can't . . . I can't match those things up.' Morrigan looked at him, frowning. She didn't know quite how to say what she meant, but he nodded, encouraging her to try. 'The second thing doesn't change the first thing. Not for Mildmay, and not for Onstald.'

'I don't know what to tell you, Mog.' Jupiter sighed. 'Some people are brave bullies. Some people are friendly cowards.'

'Not so friendly in the end, though, was he?' said Morrigan, thinking of the way Mildmay had shrugged when he was found out. That sheepish little grin. *You always were my most attentive student.* 'Scum.'

Jupiter stood up and began pacing. He pinched the bridge of his nose. 'What I don't understand is how Squall was able to orchestrate all of this when he can't even get inside Nevermoor. You *are* sure he was travelling on the Gossamer?'

'Yes,' said Morrigan. 'I told you – Mildmay was helping him.'

'With the Ghastly Market, yes, but . . . Mildmay couldn't do the things you described. All that puppeteering business on the rooftop. You said he wasn't even there.'

'He wasn't.' Morrigan felt something squeeze inside her chest as she remembered what Squall had told her. She swallowed. 'Jupiter, it was me. Squall said that I'd . . . given him a window.'

Jupiter stopped pacing. 'A window?'

'A window into Nevermoor,' she clarified. 'He said because I didn't know how to use the Wretched Arts, all the Wunder that was gathering around me had nowhere to go. It was burning so bright it only took a little push through the Gossamer. That's how he could use Wunder through me. That explains the thing with the Magnificub at the first Ghastly Market. It was me. Well . . . it was him *through* me. And the puppeteering on the rooftop, and . . .' Morrigan paused. She'd never told Jupiter about Heloise and her throwing stars. But before she could finish, he gave a miserable groan.

'Stupid.' Jupiter sank back down onto the day bed. His voice was muffled as he rubbed his whole face in his hands. 'Stupid, stupid idiot.'

'Who, Squall?'

'No, *me*. I could see it.' Turning a deep shade of purplish-red, he gestured vaguely to Morrigan. 'You. Wunder. Critical mass. I saw it growing and growing around you – it got so bright sometimes I had to filter it out, or I'd have been nearly blinded just looking at you.'

Morrigan's eyes doubled in size. 'You can *do* that?' The depth and breadth of Jupiter's talent as a Witness was still a mystery to her.

'Yes, I can. And I ignored it instead of doing something about it.' He sighed, looking right at her, his forehead creased. 'I thought it must be normal for a young Wundersmith! Mog, please believe me – I had no idea this would happen. I didn't know Squall could—'

'I know you didn't!' Morrigan cut in. 'Don't be ridiculous. It's not your fault.'

'It *is* – partly, at least. I should have realised the danger you were in. I should have known Squall would take advantage if he could. I've been preoccupied for months – so focused on Cassiel and Paximus Luck and Alfie Swann, when I should have been focused on what was happening right in front of me.'

'Cassiel!' Morrigan said, sitting up straight. 'I forgot all about him! So, what happened to him? And Paximus Luck?'

'The Stealth has a lead on Paximus, which they're following across the border into the Republic – that's *strictly* confidential. But as for Cassiel,' Jupiter shrugged, looking baffled, 'I honestly have no idea. I've chewed through more resources at the League of Explorers than I can possibly justify, looking for him on-realm and off. We've handed it over to the Celestial Observation Group for now. They don't quite have our reach, but they can watch the skies. They'll keep me informed.'

'So you don't think it was anything to do with Squall or the Ghastly Market?'

He didn't answer immediately. Staring at the floor, he sat and breathed in the lemon smoke.

'No,' he said finally. 'No, I think that one's unconnected.'

'Is Israfel upset?' Morrigan asked. 'Were they good friends?'

'Cassiel isn't really anyone's friend.' Jupiter inhaled sharply and seemed to come to himself, sitting up and returning to their previous thread of conversation. 'I don't understand. Why has Squall shown such *restraint*? If you really gave him a window into Nevermoor – a way to use his own powers through you – then surely he could have made you do almost anything! Commit terrible crimes, or – or *leave Nevermoor*!' His eyes bulged at that realisation. 'And where is he *now*? Why did he just let you go?'

Morrigan had been thinking about this all morning. 'He said something funny.'

'Funny ha-ha, or—'

'Funny peculiar. He said that he and I have a shared enemy.' She frowned, trying to recall Squall's exact words. 'He said I had to be given the freedom to become the

Wundersmith he needs me to be. Because . . . terrible things are coming. And though by teaching me to use my powers, he was shutting the window, his long-term plans were more important. He said he needed me alive.'

'Mog,' Jupiter said in a tight voice, 'he's playing mind games with you. Trying to make you believe there's some terrible enemy lurking out there, and that he can help you defeat it. He wants to frighten you, so that he can use your fear to control you.'

'I know,' said Morrigan, sounding much more certain than she felt. She swung around in the armchair, dangling her feet over one side. 'But is he right about the window through the Gossamer? Maybe I should learn to use the Wretched Arts properly, so he can't use them through me anymore.'

Jupiter was silent, but Morrigan could see he was suddenly energised, eyes bright with some new impulse.

'Jupiter?' she prompted him.

He leapt to his feet. 'Grab your brolly.'

By the time they made it to Proudfoot House and Jupiter had let her in on the plan, Morrigan was filled with the kind of queasy dread she associated with last year's Show Trial, or waiting to die on Eventide, or sticking one's hand into a bucket full of venomous snakes.

447

Jupiter knocked sharply on the Scholar Mistresses' office door. He didn't even wait for an answer, but marched straight to where Ms Dearborn stood, behind the room's only desk. Morrigan followed a few cautious steps behind, desperately trying to avoid eye contact with the Scholar Mistress.

'I'd like to speak to Mrs Murgatroyd, please.'

Dearborn stared at him, blinking. 'Excuse me?'

'Murgatroyd. I need to speak to her. Now.' Morrigan could see the muscles in his jaw working. Cracks appeared in his thin veneer of politeness. 'It's a matter of urgency.'

'Well. As you can undoubtedly see,' Dearborn said coolly, 'she isn't here.'

'MURGATROYD,' Jupiter repeated, looking her right in the eye. He clapped his hands. 'Oi! Murgatroyd. I know you're in there somewhere. Come out. I need to speak to you.'

Morrigan winced. What was he *doing*? Trying to get himself killed?

'Captain North, how dare you,' snapped Dearborn, recoiling. 'If you think that either she or I will to respond to—'

'I'll tell you exactly what I think.' Jupiter's raised voice was drawing curious glances from a few Society members as they passed the office door. 'You've been playing power games with my scholar's education all year long. Your baseless fears have done Morrigan more harm – put her, and the rest of the Wundrous Society, in more danger – than you could possibly understand, and you've broken the trust that should exist between patron and Scholar Mistress. From now on I'll be taking a much closer interest in Morrigan's schooling. Murgatroyd, GET OUT HERE.'

'Stop that – Maris, *no—*'

Dearborn's face twisted into something awful. She rolled her neck uncomfortably, her fingers curling and muscles juddering. Morrigan heard that strange, now-familiar sound of bones popping and crunching, and the dreaded Murgatroyd was suddenly before them. Her cracked, purpling lips split into what might equally have been a smile or a threat. She narrowed her sunken grey eyes at Jupiter.

'Rude.' The Arcane Scholar Mistress spoke in a guttural growl. 'What do you want?'

Jupiter didn't hesitate. 'You said Morrigan ought to have been in your school. In the Elders' Hall that day, you said we'd all failed her.'

Murgatroyd stuck out her lower lip, looking doubtful. 'Did I?'

'*Yes,*' said Jupiter. 'You said someone had to teach her the Wretched Arts. And you were right. Somebody here, in the Wundrous Society, needs to teach Morrigan the Wretched Arts before she learns them from a *more dangerous source.*' Jupiter gave her a meaningful look. 'Do you understand what I'm—'

'He's back, then,' Murgatroyd interrupted. She directed her question at Morrigan. 'Squall. Been visiting, has he?'

Morrigan blinked, instinctively turning away from the intensity of Murgatroyd's flat, murky grey gaze. She looked at Jupiter instead, who nodded at her.

'Er – yes.'

'Taught you some tricks, has he?'

'Y-yes.'

Murgatroyd looked neither surprised nor frightened by this news. She sucked air through her sharp brown teeth. 'Thought so. Heard about you shutting down the Ghastly Market. Thought you must have learned something nasty along the way.' Morrigan bristled at what felt like an accusation, but the Scholar Mistress gave her an appreciative little nod. 'Good for you.'

'Oh. Um . . . thanks.'

Murgatroyd sighed, sneering at the doors to Proudfoot House. 'Warned 'em, didn't I? Trio of old fools. Said it from the beginning; it's asking for trouble, trying to squash down a thing like that. Like sticking a lid on a pot full of fireworks. Dangerous.'

'You'll take her, then?' Jupiter pressed. 'You know she doesn't belong in Dearborn's school. She belongs with us, in the School of Arcane Arts.'

Morrigan felt a lurch of dread. She knew Jupiter wanted the best for her, but did he *really* think this was a good idea?

It was bad enough having Dearborn as her Scholar Mistress; it was universally agreed that Murgatroyd was *much* worse.

However, her dread was keeping company with some other, much more subtle feeling. A tiny background hum of vindication. What *was* so mundane, after all, about being a Wundersmith?

The Scholar Mistress appeared to be thinking about it. 'Well . . . she's not *exactly* Arcane, is she?'

'She's not Mundane either,' said Jupiter flatly.

'No.' Murgatroyd sniffed, watching Morrigan with an appraising eye. She leaned in close – closer than Morrigan would have liked – and spoke in an unsettling rasp. 'Gregoria Quinn thought she could tuck you away inside these hallowed halls, where you wouldn't become a problem for the rest of the Free State. Wouldn't become another mess for the Wundrous Society to clean up. I told her, the fool – safest place for a firecracker is out in the open.'

Another mess for the Wundrous Society to clean up. Again, Morrigan resented the implication. She said nothing, but stared the Scholar Mistress right in the face, unblinking.

'Mmm.' Murgatroyd gave a single, decisive nod. 'Go on, then. I'll take the little beastie.'

Morrigan wasn't sure how she felt about that, but Jupiter's whole body relaxed as he heaved a great sigh of relief.

'Thank you, Scholar Mistress,' he said.

She dismissed them with a careless flick of her wizened hand, and as they made their way down the hall, Morrigan could hear Murgatroyd cackling to herself like a witch.

'Oh-ho, Dulcie's going to *spit*.'

CHAPTER TWENTY-NINE

The Final Demand

The next morning, everyone at Wunsoc was summoned to the manicured gardens at the back of Proudfoot House. Elder Quinn, Elder Wong and Elder Saga were gathered on the balcony, looking grave.

'By now you have all heard about the tragic demise of Professor Hemingway Q. Onstald, the eldest of our teaching staff and an honoured member of the Society.' Elder Quinn spoke into a microphone, her voice ringing clearly across the grounds. 'We all owe a great debt of gratitude to Professor Onstald, who perished while performing a tremendous feat of bravery and sacrifice. At this point I'm confident there isn't a soul among you who remains unaware of the existence of the Ghastly Market, the story of its destruction, and the heinous fact that the abduction of Society members for the market was perpetrated by one of our own.'

The garden filled with low, angry muttering.

It was safe to say nobody here would ever forgive Mildmay for his crimes. Least of all Morrigan and her friends. He would probably be safer around the Hunt of Smoke and Shadow.

The scholars of Unit 919 had come straight here from Hometrain and were gathered in a tight knot. Morrigan and Hawthorne had been asked by the others to tell their stories of Hallowmas night at least a dozen times now, and were still occasionally getting requests to hear certain parts again. Naturally, Morrigan had neglected to mention the part about Ezra Squall, instead letting them assume that Mildmay had arranged everything on his own.

Miss Cheery was keeping very close. She hadn't stopped fussing over Cadence and Lambeth for two days, and Morrigan and Hawthorne too. Cadence pretended to be annoyed by it, but Morrigan could tell she was secretly pleased. The conductor was standing behind them even now, arms folded, guarding her unit like a mother bear.

Lambeth, meanwhile, hadn't yet said a single word to anyone, and seemed even more distant than usual. Morrigan wondered what was going through her head. She hoped 'Princess Lamya' knew her secret was safe with them – with her, Hawthorne and Cadence – and she made mental note to tell her so, as soon as they were alone.

Elder Quinn went on. 'What I will say is this: It has been many, many years since one of our own has so deeply shamed the Wundrous Society. I pledge to you that the traitor, whose worthless name shall never again pass my lips, will be found and will be brought to justice. You have my word.

'Tomorrow afternoon we will bid farewell to our brave friend and colleague, Professor Onstald, at a memorial service in the Elders' Hall. All who wish to pay their respects are encouraged to attend. Meanwhile, it must also be mentioned that two of our junior scholars . . .'

Morrigan's attention was snatched away just then, as she felt someone slip a note into her hand. She turned to see who'd done it, but the crowd was thick and close, and all she managed to spot was a swish of robes disappearing somewhere far behind her.

It was a folded-over piece of paper, with her name written on the side.

'. . . showing the precise bravery and resourcefulness that won them their place among us, and—'

'That's us,' Hawthorne whispered in her ear. 'Brave and resourceful. She forgot hilarious and good-looking.'

But Morrigan had stopped paying attention to Elder Quinn. She unfolded the note, hands trembling, and read it through twice.

Morrigan Odelle Crow

We have kept the secret of Unit 919.
But you have a dangerous secret of your own.

Reveal yourself as a Wundersmith to everyone present,
before the clock has struck the hour
or we will reveal the truth about Republic deserter
Princess Lamya Bethari Amati Ra
to the Wundrous Society
and to the world.

Her heart jolted, her mind taking a moment to catch up.

The blackmail hadn't been about her at all! The secret they'd been threatening to reveal wasn't her secret. It was Lambeth's.

A heavy, sick feeling crept into Morrigan's stomach. Unit 919 had protected her against the blackmailers, each faithfully carrying out their own task, even when they *really* didn't want to.

And now it was her turn. She closed her eyes, swallowing her anger and dread, more determined than ever to find who was behind this. They wouldn't get away with it.

'Go on, Morrigan.' She felt Miss Cheery give her shoulder an encouraging squeeze and a gentle little shove forward.

'Wh-what?'

'Elder Quinn just called your name. You and Hawthorne.' Morrigan looked up at the big, warm smile from her conductor, but couldn't bring herself to smile in return. 'Go on, daydreamer, up you go.'

She felt something twist and blacken inside her as she followed Hawthorne through the crowd, all the way up the white marble steps to where the Elders stood, beaming down at them. It felt like a death march. Blood rushed to her face and thrummed in her ears.

As they reached the Elders, the bell in the clock tower on Proudfoot House began to strike the hour. Nine o'clock. Nine chimes. Morrigan's mind raced.

One.

The black-cloaked crowd below applauded, long and loud, lifting their hands up. Hawthorne turned to grin at Morrigan as he waved at them, his cheeks turning a deep shade of pink. He nudged her forward a little, mistaking her reluctance for shyness.

'Go on,' he said. 'You earned it.'

Two.

How quickly the sombre mood had turned to celebration. And it was *her* they were celebrating – her and Hawthorne. She spotted Jupiter's proud, almost tearful face in the crowd, and her mouth felt dry. How could she go and ruin this?

And not just ruin the mood, Morrigan thought – ruin *everything*. Ruin any chance of a good life at Wunsoc. For herself, and her whole unit.

Three.

Elder Quinn's words from the beginning of the year were still etched in her memory:

If anyone is found to have broken our trust . . . all nine of you will face expulsion from Wunsoc. For life.

She was about to ruin her own life, plus eight others.

Four.

Her unit would never forgive her, and when everyone else in the Society found out what she really was, they would hate her. She'd be lucky if they didn't chase her off campus with torches and pitchforks.

Five.

But . . . Lambeth. An image sprung into Morrigan's head of tiny, frightened Princess Lamya, perched on her throne at the auction. Of the terror in her face when the auctioneer spoke of her family's treason, and of what the Wintersea Party would do to them – to her *whole family* – if they found out the truth.

Six.

She could see the auctioneer in the wolf mask in her mind, could hear his jolly, avuncular voice. *'Treason is of course punishable by execution in the Wintersea Republic.'* Her stomach churned.

Seven.

Everyone here was supposed to be family. Loyal for life; that was the promise of the Wundrous Society. But Mildmay had broken that promise. The comfortable illusion of Wunsoc – the idea that this was some safe haven where everyone protected each other and nothing bad ever happened – had long since been shattered for Morrigan. Lambeth was not safe here. Not if her secret got out. She thought of Professor Onstald, who had used his last ounce of strength to save them.

How could Morrigan live with herself if she protected her own secret, instead of protecting her friend?

There was nothing for it.

She clutched the note tight in her shaking hand.

Eight.

Elder Quinn stepped up to the microphone again as the applause died down. 'These two children,' she began. 'Have done something extraordinary, something that utterly embodies the values we hold—'

'I'm a Wundersmith,' Morrigan said over the top of her.

Nine.

The clock struck the hour.

She heard a soft, strangled noise of surprise from Hawthorne. Then, so everyone present could hear, so her blackmailers could have no doubt, she shouted: 'I'm a Wundersmith!'

The morning seemed to hold its breath.

There was a sudden, uncertain chuckle somewhere in the crowd. Then another. Then, as if they'd all been given permission to find her proclamation funny but still didn't quite know why, a gentle rumble of laughter skittered across the garden. Pockets of muttering erupted here and there before swiftly dying out.

Then silence fell again, as they realised the truth of it.

There was no 'gotcha!' from Morrigan. Nothing from the Elders.

'Impossible!' came a shout from somewhere near the back, and it was joined by others as the understanding grew that this was not a joke, that the Elders really had invited this dangerous entity into their midst. Nobody wanted to believe it. 'She's lying!'

Morrigan looked at her own unit, their faces by turns blank with shock or red with anger. In the near total stillness, she saw a lone figure making his way towards the balcony, pushing people out of his way. Jupiter looked frightened but fierce, as if he was one step ahead and knew something bad was about to happen, and that made Morrigan even more afraid.

But Elder Quinn held up a hand to stop him. Jupiter halted at the bottom of the steps. He watched the Elders warily for a moment, and then seemed to understand something. The fear in his eyes cleared away, and was replaced with something Morrigan couldn't quite decipher.

'Well.' Elder Quinn's voice crackled over the public-address system. 'Ladies and gentlemen. It seems we have another cause to celebrate this morning.'

Morrigan felt her brain trip over those words. She opened her mouth, then closed it again, blinking at the frail wisp of a woman. *Another cause to celebrate?* Had Elder Quinn even heard what she'd said?

'Unit 919 has just passed their fifth and final trial,' she announced with a small, satisfied smile. 'You all remember quite keenly, I am sure, what it was like to undertake your own Loyalty Trial, when you were first-year scholars. The nature of the trial is different for each unit, of course, but the object remains the same: a test of your commitment to your oaths.'

Understanding dawned on a few of the faces below. Morrigan watched as the members of 919 took in what Elder Quinn was telling them. She turned to Hawthorne beside her, whose mouth was hanging open.

'This marks the completion of Unit 919's final test, and so we welcome them – for the second time, and with even greater pride – to the Wundrous Society proper. Unit 919, the loyalty you have shown each other this year in the face of various dangers and difficulties will serve you for the rest of your days. You are sisters and brothers for life. Not because you took an oath, but because you proved it.'

The crowd seemed baffled, still not quite able to figure out if Morrigan's bizarre announcement had been a joke, or part of the test, or if they really *were* looking at the first Wundersmith to join the Wundrous Society in more than a hundred years. The first since Ezra Squall. Morrigan watched their confusion turn variously to alarm, to scepticism, to laughter, to anger. It was clear nobody knew quite what to think.

'Elder Saga, Elder Wong and I wish to remind you that although the Society has a rich history of nurturing diverse and sometimes dangerous talents, we would never knowingly invite a corrupting force into our ranks. Indeed, by destroying the Ghastly Market and saving two Wundrous Society lives, Miss Crow has shown herself to be a force for good – a useful, interesting, good person, whom we are delighted to call one of our own. She may be a Wundersmith, but truly from today onwards, she is *our* Wundersmith.'

Elder Quinn's reassurances were met with stony, worrying silence.

'I would remind you all,' she went on, and her voice had an edge to it, 'that your oath extends not just to your own unit members, but to every Wundrous person that makes up our Society, from the eldest to the youngest. The truth about Morrigan Crow will remain within Wunsoc, and I expect every single one of you to uphold your oath and protect this secret from outsiders. Remember: sisters and brothers, loyal for life.'

The crowd responded as one. '*Tethered for always, true as a knife.*'

Elder Quinn nodded, looking satisfied.

'Well then.' She beckoned the rest of Unit 919 up to the balcony. 'If our youngest scholars will come forward – that's the way, quickly now – I invite the rest of you to join me in congratulating Unit 919 on this most important milestone.'

The mood in the garden didn't seem particularly celebratory, although on the Elder's command – and under her stern gaze – they managed to give a half-hearted round of scattered applause before being dismissed.

As the crowd dispersed in all directions, every eye was on Morrigan.

Morrigan felt numbed by what had just happened. Hawthorne didn't seem to have digested it either, and kept making strange little sputtering noises somewhere between outrage and amusement.

Everyone had left, except the scholars of Unit 919. When the ceremony was over, Miss Cheery had run up the stairs and hugged every single one of them before dashing back to Hometrain. Those whose patrons were present received hearty handshakes and congratulations. Jupiter had tried to look pleased for Morrigan, but she hadn't missed the blazing look he'd cast the Elders as he departed.

Now the scholars huddled awkwardly on the balcony, nobody quite ready to go off to class yet, and nobody quite sure what to say.

'I don't understand,' said Thaddea finally. 'Why did they blackmail us to keep Morrigan's secret, when they were just going to make her tell everyone anyway? What a dirty trick.'

'That was the *test*, Thaddea,' said Mahir.

'I know that was the *test*, Mahir,' Thaddea said, mimicking his voice. 'I just mean . . . it's so . . .'

'Mean?' said Cadence.

'Yes!' cried Thaddea. 'It's so *mean*. To all of us, but especially to Morrigan.'

Everyone looked up in surprise at that, not least of all Morrigan herself, who just about choked on her own tongue. Hawthorne *did* choke, but he managed to cover it up with a cough.

'What did it say, Morrigan?' Arch nodded at the note in Morrigan's hand with a curious little frown. 'To make you give yourself away like that?'

She closed the piece of paper protectively in her fist. 'I . . . I can't tell you.'

Mahir laughed. 'What? What do you mean, you—'

'I just can't.'

'Don't be ridic—'

'It's about me, isn't it?' Lambeth's quiet voice came from the back of the group, and she stepped forward, looking miserable but determined. Everyone fell silent. 'Elder Quinn said that our whole unit passed the Loyalty Trial, but she was wrong. I didn't pass.

'You all made a choice to put your sisters and brothers before yourselves. But I chose to be dishonest. I let you believe it could only be Morrigan's secret you were protecting. I told myself that was true, but . . . deep down, I wondered . . . if it was really *my* secret.'

'What secret, Lambeth?' asked Arch kindly.

She took a deep, steadying breath. 'My name isn't Lambeth Amara. It's . . . Princess Lamya Bethari Amati Ra. I'm a member of the Royal House of Ra, from the Silklands in Far East Sang.' She paused, looking around at their stunned faces. 'Lam. Just call me Lam.'

It was strange, Morrigan thought, as she watched the poised, graceful confession. Lam was the smallest of all of them, but in that moment, she seemed ten feet tall. She really was *regal*.

'Far East Sang.' Thaddea's face turned patchily red. 'You're from the *Republic?*'

'Yes.'

'Are you a spy?' Francis demanded.

Hawthorne scoffed and rolled his eyes. 'Francis, she's not a spy, she's a *princess*.'

'She might be both! My aunt says there are lots of Wintersea Republic spies in Nevermoor. Why else is she even *here*?'

'Oh, get a grip!'

'I'm not a spy,' said Lam. 'My family sent me here to learn how to use my knack. It used to give me terrible headaches that made me sick. Since I've been at Wunsoc, I've learned how to cope with my visions better.

'But . . . they should never have sent me at all.' Lam's eyes turned red, and her voice wobbled a little. 'It's illegal for people from the Republic to cross the border into the Free State. We're not even supposed to know there *is* a Free State. If the Wintersea Party found out, they'd throw my whole family in prison, or . . . or worse. Much worse.' She was trembling. 'My grandmother told me I had to keep it a secret or I'd be putting us all in terrible danger. But I'm a dreadful liar, so I decided it was better to hardly speak to you at all. I'm sorry.'

'We can't tell anyone.' Morrigan looked around at all the members of her unit in turn. 'This stays between us. Agreed? Sisters and brothers, yes?'

'Loyal for life,' they responded firmly as one.

Lam sniffed, looking relieved and slightly overwhelmed. She opened her mouth to say something, when—

'EXCUSE ME,' boomed a cold voice from the garden below. Dearborn glared up at them. 'But I believe you bothersome malingerers all have classes to attend, do you not?'

The nine scholars scurried inside Proudfoot House, down the hall to the bank of spherical brass railpods waiting to whisk them away to their lessons.

Morrigan dawdled for a moment, smoothing and straightening her uniform quite unnecessarily.

Hawthorne raised his eyebrows. 'Right. Good luck, then.'

'Thanks.' She adjusted the cuffs of her new white shirt and felt a little tingle of nerves and excitement. 'See you at lunch?'

'Yep,' he replied, boarding a pod bound for the Extremities department. 'Remember – take *lots* of notes. I want to know exactly how weird it is. And see if you can get Murgatroyd to do that ice thing again! That was cool.' He grinned as the doors slid closed, shoving his face up to yell through the crack: 'Get it? It was *cool*.'

Morrigan snorted, and turned back to where Lam and Cadence stood waiting for her, holding the door of their pod.

'You coming, or what?' asked Cadence, and Morrigan leapt aboard just as she pulled a lever labelled SUB-SIX: THE SCHOOL OF ARCANE ARTS.

Acknowledgements

Thank you, thank you, thank you to the best publishers in the business – Hachette Children's Group, Hachette Australia and NZ, and Little, Brown Books for Young Readers – for the creativity, hard work, thoughtfulness and joy you've brought to this whole caper. I couldn't have hoped for a better publishing family.

I'm especially thankful for the talent and guidance of my editors Helen Thomas, Alvina Ling, Suzanne O'Sullivan, Samantha Swinnerton and Kheryn Callender.

Thank you to the best international PR dream team an author could wish for: Ashleigh Barton, Dom Kingston, Tania Mackenzie-Cooke, Katharine McAnarney and Amy Dobson. You've made all this extroverting nonsense an unexpected delight.

Many thanks to Louise Sherwin-Stark, Hilary Murray Hill, Megan Tingley, Mel Winder, Ruth Alltimes, Fiona

Hazard, Katy Cattell, Lucy Upton, Nicola Goode, Fiona Evans, Alison Padley, Helen Hughes, Katherine Fox, Rachel Graves, Andrew Sinclair, Andrew Cattanach, Caitlin Murphy, Chris Sims, Daniel Pilkington, Hayley New, Isabel Staas, Jeanmarie Morosin, Justin Ractliffe, Kate Flood, Keira Lykourentzos, Penny Evershed, Sarah Holmes, Sean Cotcher, Sophie Mayfield, Emilie Polster, Jennifer McClelland-Smith, Valerie Wong, Victoria Stapleton, Michelle Campbell, Jen Graham, Virginia Lawther, Sasha Illingworth, Ruqayyah Daud, Alison Shucksmith, Ashleigh Richards, Sacha Beguely, Suzy Maddox-Kane and all the account managers who have helped share Nevermoor with booksellers and readers.

Thank you to Beatriz Castro and Jim Madsen for the incredible cover art.

Huge thanks to Molly Ker Hawn, Jenny Bent, Victoria Cappello, Amelia Hodgson and everyone at the Bent Agency. Thanks also to the splendid folks of Team Cooper – the mutual support, cheerleading and admiration within this crew makes me happier than I can say.

A million thanks to all the readers, booksellers, librarians, teachers and bloggers who have loved and supported Nevermoor. If you have taken Morrigan into your heart and passed her on to someone else, thank you so much. Your kindness and enthusiasm have been overwhelming and I'm so grateful for every recommendation, review, letter, tag and tweet.

Thank you to my goddaughter Ella for letting me use the name Paximus Luck. (She came up with it spontaneously when she was only three years old, so I guess the rest of us should just quit now.) Thanks also to Aurianna, a very funny girl I met in Naperville whose name I went and nicked for this book. She made me laugh; I made her a hotel.

Aspiring authors! Get you an agent with the heart, humour, hustle and chutzpah of Gemma Cooper. A grade-A premium Pollyanna who's always on your side, reliable as heck, and ready to fish you out of the ankle-deep water you imagine yourself to be drowning in, without even breaking a sweat. Bonus points if they will text you inspiring photographs of elderly Japanese cheerleaders for encouragement at two a.m. Thanks GC.

And finally, endless thanks and love to my family and friends, especially Dean and Julie, the best hype team around. Sal, thanks as always for being my early reader and sounding board, and for the totes-lols motivational quotes and weirdly specific essential oils.

And, Mum, thanks for literally everything else. Most Wundrous mum ever, eleven out of ten.

Reading Notes

Morrigan Crow has been inducted into Unit 919 of the Wundrous Society along with new members Archan, Anah, Cadence, Francis, Hawthorne, Lambeth, Mahir and Thaddea. But her new friends (apart from Hawthorne) aren't entirely happy to have been grouped with a Wundersmith.

Morrigan may have defeated her deadly curse, passed the dangerous trials and joined the mystical Wundrous Society, but her journey into Nevermoor and all its secrets has only just begun. And she is fast learning that not all magic is used for good.

This is an action-packed and riveting fantasy series. It is also about a search for love, friendship, family and identity. For, despite being based on a fantastical premise, *Nevermoor* and *Wundersmith* are fundamentally about what it is to be human and what it means to be part of a community.

Below are discussion points about the different ideas presented in the book.

Family, Friendships and Love

A family emblem. Those words tugged gently at Morrigan's heart. She prized her golden W pin above all her other possessions (except, perhaps, her brolly), but it was still just that . . . a possession. An object that could easily be broken or lost. The imprint felt different; it was a part of her. And it proved that she was a part of something important, something bigger than just herself. A family. (**p 46**)

Morrigan's story is of a search for family. Her own family showed no affection for her. Jupiter and his staff at the Hotel Deucalion have become a protective second family. And now becoming part of Wunsoc is equally special to her – to become part of a group of her peers. By the end of the novel has she found a third family?

She was tired of so desperately wanting the friendship and approval of her so-called brothers and sisters. (How that phrase made her cringe now. When she thought back to the person she was a year ago, that idiot who believed she'd have eight readymade siblings if only she could pass the trials . . . as if anything was ever that simple.) (**p 336**)

Discuss Morrigan's feelings as they are reflected here and compare them to your own experiences of having tried to make friends with someone and failed.

Forces of Good and Evil

She could still see the frightened faces on the platform. Had Morrigan enjoyed *that, she wondered. Had some small part of her* liked *the thought of striking fear in someone's heart . . . instead of being the one who was always afraid?* (**p 395**)

Ezra Squall constantly taunts Morrigan with her capacity to be both good and evil. Is this battle with oneself one of the major themes in this novel?

Individual Talents

Each member of the Unit has an extraordinary power. How challenging is it to use such talents for good rather than evil?

Coming of Age & Rite of Passage Trials and Tests

Morrigan's trials didn't end in *Nevermoor: The Trials of Morrigan Crow*, for in this sequel she faces personal challenges which involve both taking risks and learning when to exercise caution. What else does she learn about herself?

Stay alert for a message from the Wundrous Society
with news of Morrigan's next adventure.

hachette
CHILDREN'S BOOKS

If you would like to find out more about
Hachette Children's Books, our authors, upcoming events
and new releases you can visit our website,
Facebook or follow us on Twitter:

hachettechildrens.com.au
twitter.com/HCBoz
facebook.com/hcboz

Teachers notes are available from the
Hachette Australia website:
www.hachette.com.au/teachers-and-librarians/